JOIN THE FUN FROM THE BEGINNING WITH *PINK JINX*

"4 Stars! A hoot and a half! Snappy dialogue and outrageous characters keep the tempo lively and the humor infectious in this crazy adventure story. Hill is a master at taking outlandish situations and making them laugh-out-loud funny."

—*Romantic Times BOOKclub Magazine*

"Hill has yet again given us an adventure that is unbelievably funny! I am eagerly looking forward to another treasure hunting book from the incomparable Sandra Hill."

—TheBestReviews.com

"A hilarious story filled with adventure, romance, danger, and mystery."

—BookLoons.com

"With this comic contemporary romance's great plot, witty dialogue, humorous asides, and quirky characters, readers will be impatient for book two."

—*Booklist*

✦

"Loaded with snappy dialogue, heartwarming moments that will pull at the most hardened heartstrings, engaging characters, and incredible sexual tension! It is always a great time to pick up a book by Sandra Hill."

—ChicklitRomanceWriters.com

✦

more . . .

THE CAJUN COWBOY

TALL, DARK, AND CAJUN

Also by Sandra Hill

The Cajun Cowboy

The Red-Hot Cajun

Tall, Dark, and Cajun

Pink Jinx

Pearl Jinx

Sandra Hill

WARNER BOOKS

NEW YORK   BOSTON

Copyright © 2007 by Sandra Hill
Excerpt from *Wild Jinx* copyright © 2007 by Sandra Hill
All rights reserved. Except as permitted under the U.S. Copyright Act of 1976, no part of this publication may be reproduced, distributed, or transmitted in any form or by any means, or stored in a database or retrieval system, without the prior written permission of the publisher.

Warner Books and the "W" logo are trademarks of Time Warner Inc. or an affiliated company. Used under license by Hachette Book Group USA, which is not affiliated with Time Warner Inc.

Cover design by Diane Luger
Cover art by Tom Hallman

Warner Books
Hachette Book Group USA
237 Park Aveune
New York, NY 10017
Visit our Web site at www.HachetteBookGroupUSA.com

Printed in the United States of America

First Printing: July 2007

10 9 8 7 6 5 4 3 2 1

There is an Amish thread in this book, and it is with much respect and many prayers that I dedicate this book to the Plain people of Nickel Mines, Pennsylvania, who suffered such a serious tragedy this past year. It is also dedicated to all those, Amish and otherwise, who manage to practice a simple lifestyle in the midst of all of our modern world's turmoil.

And, of course, I dedicate this book, like all my others, to you, the readers, who support my books. You are a priceless gift. Over and over, you tell me how important humor is in your lives. Perhaps, like the Amish, we all need to find joy in simple things, like laughter, love, and family.

To show my appreciation, I once again have something free for you on my Web site. Last time it was an original novella, not available anywhere else. This time . . . well, come visit and see what I have to offer. You are always welcome.

Fondly,
Sandra Hill
www.sandrahill.net

Dear Reader:

I hope you like my second Jinx treasure-hunting book.

Caleb holds a special place in my heart, being ex-Amish and an ex–Navy SEAL. His seventeen-year estrangement from his twin brother was particularly poignant to me. And funny. Especially with Tante Lulu along for the ride.

Spruce Creek also has a special place in my heart. My husband and I have a cottage there, and yes, there are caverns and snakes and premier fly fishing. One of the many Warrior Paths that crisscrossed Pennsylvania at one time traversed the very mountainside that is visible from our front deck. I often imagine I see Indian braves standing on the high cliff that overlooks our property, which is appropriately named Indian Lookout. For sure, they used the ice caves that are situated directly across our stream.

And "Robber" Davie Lewis really did exist, calling himself an equalizer as he stole from the rich and gave to the poor; however, the cave he hid in was not the imaginary Spruce Creek Cavern, but probably Indian Cavern in nearby Franklinville.

This book in no way reflects the real Amish people of Sinking Valley or the inhabitants of Spruce Creek, Pennsylvania. As a side note, the Amish of Lancaster County are well known, but here in central Pennsylvania, you haven't lived till you've gone to the Wednesday-morning farmers' and flea markets in Belleville. They start at six a.m. and end at noon. They auction everything from butter to fresh produce to cows. I kid you not!

Please continue to follow the madcap adventures of my Jinx treasure-hunting team. Next up will be that rascal Tee-John LeDeux in *Wild Jinx*. Of course, you will want to know how Lizzie, the Amish J-Lo, does on *American Idol*. Laughter and sighs guaranteed!

And please visit my Web site for a free gift to show my appreciation for all your support, past, present, and future.

Wishing you smiles in your reading,

Sandra Hill
www.sandrahill.net

Pearl Jinx

Chapter
1

Crazy is as crazy does . . .

Caleb Peachey jogged along the road, his eyes on the log cabin up ahead. It sat nestled in the thick woods on the banks of the Little Juniata River, almost hidden from view. He hoped to find the crazy woman at home this early in the morning.

Crazy Claire, that's what she was called by some of the locals. Dr. Claire Cassidy, historical archaeologist, by her colleagues. PhDiva, by him. Actually, he was beginning to feel like the crazy one as he attempted to make contact with the elusive woman. In fact, he was beginning to wonder if she even existed. *Crazy Claire is gonna be Crazy-Friggin'-Dead Claire if she doesn't stop hiding from me.*

Five miles back and a half-hour ago, at dawn, he'd left the Butterfly Bed & Breakfast in Spruce Creek, where he and his team from Jinx, Inc., a treasure-hunting firm, would be staying. He'd arrived here in central Pennsylvania yesterday morning. The rest of the team would be here this afternoon, but the project itself couldn't start until Dr. Cassidy was on board, per orders of the National Park Service, which made sure no historical artifacts were disturbed. Now, he could understand the government being worried about metal detecting on a battlefield, trafficking in relics, defacing previously undiscovered prehistoric rock wall art, that kind of thing, but dammit, they were just going to take some pearls out of this cavern . . . a privately owned cavern, to boot. They weren't exploring King Tut's tomb here.

Stopping in the clearing before the house, he bent over, hands on thighs, and breathed deeply in and out to cool down, not that he had broken a sweat or anything. Hell, he'd been a Navy SEAL for ten years, up till two and a half years ago, and they ran five times as far before breakfast, wearing heavy boondockers, not the two-hundred-dollar ergonomically designed Adidas he had on now.

He knocked on the door. Once. Twice. No response except for some cats mewling inside. Same as yesterday, except there was a battered station wagon here now, which he took as a good sign. The woman hadn't responded to the messages he'd left on her answering machine, either. *Hi! This is Claire. Your message is important to me. Blah, blah, blah!* Caleb mimicked in his head. Apparently not *that* important.

A fat calico cat—probably pregnant—sidled up to him and gave him the evil eye, as only a cat could do. Then she sashayed past, deeming him unworthy of her regard.

With his side vision, he noticed another cat approaching, but, no, it wasn't a cat; it was a rat. Okay, it was a teeny-tiny dog that resembled a rat, and it started yip-yip-yipping at him as if it was a German shepherd, not a rat terrier.

Caleb couldn't fathom people who wanted such itty-bitty things for pets. But then, some people even took slimy creatures into their homes. Like snakes. Having a fierce aversion to snakes, he shivered.

The dog stopped yipping and gave him the same you-are-so-boring look as the cat through its beady eyes and sauntered off, around the side of a modern addition to the old cabin.

He decided to follow.

The back of the cabin was a surprise. While the front was traditional log-and-chink design, the back was all windows facing the river, down below some fifty feet. Cushioned Adirondack chairs had been arranged on a wide deck. An open laptop sat on a low wooden table.

You-know-who must be home. Ignoring my calls. Son of a bitch! Oooh, someone is in big trouble.

He turned toward the river. And inhaled sharply at the view. Not just the spectacular Little Juniata with the morning sun bouncing off the surface, creating diamond-like sparkles, fish actually jumping out of the water to feed on the seasonal hatch of newborn insects hovering above. He was familiar with this river, having grown up in an Amish community about ten miles down the road in Sinking Valley. What caused him to gasp was the woman standing waist-deep in the middle of the river. She wore suspendered waders over a long-sleeved white T-shirt. Her long dark-red hair was pulled up into a high ponytail that escaped through the back of a Penn State baseball cap. Auburn, he thought her hair color was called.

Could this possibly be the slippery Dr. Claire Cassidy? Crazy Claire? For some reason, he'd expected someone older, more witchy-looking. It was hard to tell from this distance, but she couldn't be much older than thirty, although who knew? Women today were able to fool guys all the time. Makeup to look as if they were not wearing makeup. Nips and tucks. Collagen. Boob lifts, ferchrissake!

The woman was fly fishing, which was an art in itself. Caleb was the furthest thing from a poet, but the way she executed the moves was pure art in motion. Like a ballet. Following a clock pattern, she raised her long bamboo rod upward with her right hand, stopping abruptly at noon to apply tension to her line. Then she allowed the rod to drift back slowly in the forward cast, stopping abruptly at eleven o'clock, like the crack of a whip. The follow-through was a dance of delicacy, because the fly should land on top of the water only for a few seconds, to fool the trout below water level that it was real live food. Over and over she performed this operation. It didn't matter that she didn't catch anything. The joy was in the casting.

And in the watching.

Dropping down to the edge of the deck, elbows resting on raised knees, Caleb breathed in deeply. The scents of honeysuckle and pine filled the early-morning air. Silence surrounded him, although it was not really silence if one listened carefully. The rush of the water's current. Bees buzzing. Birds chirping. In the distance, a train whistle. He even saw a hawk swoop gloriously out of the mountains, searching for food. He felt as if he'd been sucker punched, jolted back to a time and place he'd spent seventeen years trying to forget.

The Plain people, as the Amish called themselves, were practical to a fault. Fishing was for catching fish. No Lands End angler duds or fancy Orvis rods or custom-made flies. Just worms. But his *Dat* had been different.

As stern as he was in many regards, he had given Caleb and his four brothers an appreciation for God's beauty in nature and the heavenly joy of fly fishing. Much like that minister in the movie *A River Runs Through It*, Caleb's old man had made fly fishing an exercise in philosophy, albeit the Old Order Amish way of life. Caleb smiled to himself, knowing his father would not be pleased with comparison to an *Englisher*, anyone not Amish, even a man of God.

And, for sure and for certain, as the Amish would say, they didn't believe in that wasteful "catch and release" business, which the fisherwoman in front of him was doing now with a twenty-inch rainbow. How many times had Caleb heard: "To waste is to destroy God's gift"? No, if an Amishman caught a fish, he ate it. With homemade chowchow, spaetzle oozing with butter, sliced tomatoes still warm from the garden, corn fritters, and shoofly pie.

Stomach rumbling with sudden hunger, Caleb shook his head to clear it of unwanted memories, stood, and walked down the railroad tie steps to the edge of the river.

The woman glanced his way, then did a double take. After a brief hesitation, she waved.

Yep, she must be crazy.

He was a big man, six-four, and still carried the musculature that defined a Navy SEAL. The tattoo of a barbed-wire chain around his upper arm usually gave women pause. Plus, he was a stranger. But did she appear frightened? Nah. She just waved at him. He could be an ax murderer, for all she knew. She was brave or stupid or crazy, he figured. Maybe all three.

Enough!

He waded into the cold water. It soon covered his shoes, his bare legs, his running shorts, and then the bottom of his T-shirt. Once he reached the woman, whose mouth was now gaping open, he gritted his teeth, then snarled, "Your phone broken, lady?"

She blinked. Tall for a woman—maybe five-nine—she was still a head shorter than him and had to crane her neck to stare up at him. "Ah, the persistent Caleb." Then she smiled and shook her head as if he were not worthy of her attention. Just like her damn fat cat and her damn rat dog.

Taken aback by her attitude, he failed to register the fact that she had, unbelievably, resumed fishing. *She's ignoring me. I don't fuckin' believe this. Three days of chasing my tail, and she thinks she can ignore me. I. Don't. Think. So.*

Without warning, he picked her up and tossed her over his shoulder in a fireman's carry, just barely catching the bamboo rod in his other hand as it started to float downstream. With her kicking and screaming, he stomped through the water, probably scaring off every fish within a one-mile radius.

"Put me down, you goon."

"Stop squirming. I'll put you down when I'm good and ready. We're on my clock now, baby."

"Clock? Clock? I'd like to clock *you.*"

"I'd like to see you try."

"I mean it. Put me down. Aaarrgh! Take your hand off my ass."

"Stop putting your ass in my face."

"You are in such trouble. Wait till I call the police. Hope you know a good lawyer," she threatened to his back.

"Yeah, yeah, yeah. I'm shakin' in my boots . . . rather, Adidas."

"Ha, ha, ha! You're not going to be making jokes once you're in the clink."

The clink? Haven't heard that expression in, oh, let's say, seventeen years. Once on the bank, he propped the rod against a tree and stood her on her feet, being careful to hold on to one hand lest she take flight or wallop him a good one.

"What the hell do you think you're doing?" she demanded, yanking her hand out of his grasp, then placing both hands on her hips.

Ogling your hips. "Getting your attention."

"You got my attention when you failed to complete the Park Service forms for the project . . . *a month ago.*"

Oh, so that's what has her panties in a twist. "They were fifty-three friggin' pages long," he protested. The dumbass red-tape forms asked him as Pearl Jinx project manager to spell out every bleepin' thing about the venture and its participants. There were questions and subquestions and sub-subquestions. He'd used a red Sharpie to write "Bullshit!" across the empty forms and mailed them back to her. "Okay, my returning them that way probably wasn't the most diplomatic thing to do, but, my God, the Navy doesn't do as much background checking for its high-security special forces as your government agency requires."

She snorted her opinion. "It's not *my* agency. I'm just a freelance consultant, specializing in Native American culture. You must know that Spruce Creek is situated right along what were once some major Indian paths. In fact, an Indian path from the village of Assunepachla, located near present-day Frankstown, merged with the Indian path from Standing Stone in Huntingdon, and that joint path took the Native Americans over Kitchinaki, Great Spruce Pine Land, till they came to Spruce Creek, which they called Oligonunk, or 'Place of the Cave.' Spruce Creek was considered a good resting place for weary warriors."

Blah, blah, blah. "So?"

"So, Indian Caverns in Franklinville is only a mile or two away from the cavern you'll be working, and it was loaded with artifacts. We have to be sure nothing of historical value is disturbed by your project."

If I needed a history lesson, sweetie, I would flick on the History Channel. "I'm aware of all that, but you're changing the subject. I must have put a dozen messages on your answering machine in the past thirty-six hours and God only knows how many before that. Guess how many times you called me back?" He made a circle with a thumb and forefinger. She was lucky he didn't just give her the finger.

"That doesn't give you the right to manhandle me."

"That was not manhandling. If I was handling you, babe, you'd know it."

"What a chauvinist thing to say!"

"Call me pig, just as long as you call me."

She threw her hands in the air with disgust, then shrugged her waders down and off, hanging them from a knot on the same tree where the rod rested. Underneath she wore dry, faded jeans and thick wool socks, no shoes. She turned back to him. "You idiot. I've been gone for the past week. I got home late last night. That's why I didn't return your calls."

Ooops! "Oh." Caleb had been working for two years on various Jinx treasure-hunting projects, but this was the first time he was a project manager. It was important to him that it be a success. Pissing off a required team member was not a design for success. "Sorry," he said, "I misunderstood."

She nodded her acceptance of his apology and offered her own conciliatory explanation. "I like to spend time in the woods."

"How about using your cell phone to check messages?" *There I go, being abrasive again.*

"I don't believe in cell phones. Besides, what would be the point of taking modern conveniences into the forest?"

He rolled his eyes. *She doesn't believe in cell phones. What century is she living in?* He tried to sound polite when he asked, "So, you've been camping?"

"Not exactly." Without elaborating, she started to walk up toward the cabin.

He hated it when women stopped talking in the middle of a conversation, especially when the guy was being logical, not to mention bending over backward to tame his inner chauvinist. He caught up with her.

"What was so important that you had to get in touch with me right away?" she asked when they reached her deck.

"Right away was three days ago, babe."

She arched her brows at his surliness, and probably at his use of the word *babe,* too.

Tough shit! He tamped his temper down, *again,* and replied, "The Pearl Project starts tomorrow."

"And?"

"We've been told that you have to be there as a Park Service rep from the get-go."

"And?"

"And you haven't confirmed." Her attitude was really

starting to annoy him. *Behave, Peachey. Don't let her rile you. An impatient man is a dead target.*

She arched an eyebrow at him again. "Since when do I need to confirm anything with you?"

Uh-oh! Are we gonna have a pissing contest over who's in charge? I can guarantee it's not gonna be her. If we have to vet every little anal thing, we'll be here in the boonies for months instead of weeks. He put his face in his hands and counted to ten. When he glanced her way again, he said, "We have to find a way to work together. Truce?" He extended a hand.

She hesitated, but then agreed, "Truce," and placed her hand in his. Her hand was small compared to his, with short, unpolished nails. He could swear his heart revved up at just the feel of her calloused palm pressed against his calloused palm. *Am I pathetic or what?*

"Are you hungry?"

That question caught him by surprise. Was her new strategy torture by niceness? Or erotic, calloused palm handshakes? "Yeah," he answered suspiciously.

"Good. I picked some wild blueberries yesterday and have muffins cooling inside."

He didn't immediately follow her but sat down on one of the chairs to take off his wet shoes and socks. Meanwhile, the delicious aroma of baked goods wafted out to him. The rat dog trotted over and eyed his shoes. Just as it was about to take a chomp out of one of them, Caleb grabbed the shoes and set them up on the arm of the chair. When he turned, he saw the dog running off with one of his wet socks in its mouth.

"Boney!" Dr. Cassidy yelled out through the screen door at the thief. Four cats of various sizes were rubbing themselves against her ankles. The fat calico wasn't among them.

To his surprise, the dog stopped, peered back at its mistress dolefully, dropped the sock, and trotted off the porch and into the brush.

"You named your dog Boner?"

She made a clucking sound of disgust. "Not Boner. Boney. You know. Napoleon Bonaparte. Little dog. Napoleon complex."

Well, at least she has a sense of humor. "Did you know that Napoleon had a fear of cats? Ailurophobia."

"No. Seriously?"

"Yep. Learned it in a history-of-war class. An aide found the general one time in his bedroom with a cutlass in hand, trembling, because he thought there was a cat behind a drape."

"Fascinating."

Yep, that's me. Mister Fascination. Okay, I see five cats so far and one semi-dog. What next?

What next, he soon learned, was Indian tom-tom music, along with some guttural chants, coming from a tape deck inside: "Ay-yi-yi-yi! Ay-yi-yi-yi-yi . . ." Two cages in one corner, one holding what looked like a porcupine with a splint on its leg and the other holding a bird with mangled feathers. *And* the good doctor taking off her T-shirt, whose sleeves were wet, leaving her with just a sports racerback running bra kind of thing. Nothing scandalous. It was midway between a granny-type cotton undergarment and a hoochie mama Victoria's Secret scrap of sexiness, but still . . . It was pink. And there was all that skin. Bare arms. Bare midriff. Bare collarbones. Plus, she was ripped, which would explain the exercise mat and hand weights over there. Not weightlifter ripped, but female-athlete ripped. And worst of all . . . or best of all . . . she had breasts that could make a grown man weep.

Good thing I'm not looking. Nope. I. Am. Not. Looking. And I'm not getting turned on.

"It's hot in here, don't you think?" she asked, belatedly explaining her striptease, he supposed.

She began to set a tray with supersized muffins, butter, mugs of coffee, sugar, and cream, unaware of how tempting she looked. Forget muffins. He'd like a taste of—

To his surprise, she gave him a once-over, too. A once-over that paid special attention to his wet shorts. Then, with a bland expression, giving no clue to her assessment, she said, "It feels like today will be a scorcher."

Tell me about it! "It's probably your oven." *Shit! Could I sound any more dorky?*

She glanced at him again, and this time she smiled.

While she continued to set the tray with small plates and napkins, he studied her cabin. It was either that or ogle her body, which would not be smart. *Pink? What kind of serious archaeologist wears pink? Shiiit!*

The cabin was nice. Dried herbs hung from the low rafters of the kitchen, giving it a fragrant, cozy atmosphere. Colorful suncatchers at the windows caught and reflected the light like prisms. He assumed that a bedroom and bathroom were off to the left. To the right was the addition, which was completely open, making a combination kitchen/library/office/living room. A huge stone fireplace was flanked on one side by a half-dozen baskets, some woven, others coiled, and on the other by a rustic, low, armless rocking chair that looked home-made. Two log walls of the addition held floor-to-ceiling bookcases with a built-in PC desk in the corner. The shelves overflowed with books, many of them related to the Lenni Lenape tribe of the Delaware nation. Also, Indian relics: an impressive arrowhead collection, a peace pipe, several tomahawks, and framed photographs. And a small flat-screen TV.

He walked over to check out one of the pictures.

Then wished he hadn't.

It was a side view of Dr. Cassidy facing some man of obvious Native American heritage. Her long auburn hair was in braids. His black hair was, too, and adorned with a single feather. They both wore Indian ceremonial outfits. His chest was bare. On top she appeared to be nude, as well, except for the numerous bead-and-feather necklaces she wore. On bottom, he sported a loincloth with leather flaps covering his belly and ass. She wore a low-riding, knee-length, fringed leather skirt and beaded moccasins. Her arms were raised, shaking some kind of rattles. He could care less about the man. But her . . . wow! . . . Her side was bare from armpit to hip, exposing a perfect view of the side of one of her breasts.

Not the way I want to be picturing the archaeologist assigned to our project. She'll be talking Indian legends and I'll be thinking, "Wanna come over to my teepee and show me your beads?"

A thought suddenly occurred to him. "Are you married?"

"No. Why do you ask?"

He was walking back to the kitchen and waved over his shoulder at the photograph. "Geronimo back there."

She made a tsking sound at the political incorrectness of his remark. "That's Henry Hawk, a professor at the

University of Pennsylvania. He's a full-blooded Lenni Lenape Indian. Geronimo was an Apache."

Well, big whoop!

"I'm not topless in the photo, by the way." She grinned, obviously reading his mind. "Lots of people think I am, but I'm wearing a flesh-colored leotard."

That's just great! Ruin a guy's fantasy, why don't you? "Don't you believe in historical accuracy?"

"Yeah, but I was young and naive then. I let the promoter talk me into accuracy once. Turned out that people were watching my jiggling breasts as I danced, instead of learning about Indian rituals. That was the last time they tried that."

Oh, good Lord! Now I add jiggling to my fantasy.

Dr. Cassidy carried the tray out to the deck and motioned for him to move the laptop. While closing the lid, he noticed it contained notes on some Indian mating ritual. He wasn't dumb enough to ask if that's what she and Geronimo were doing in the photograph. *Not now. But I'll bet my Navy SEAL Budweiser pin that I hot damn will later.*

After three muffins and sipping his second cup of coffee, he leaned back. "That was great, Dr. Cassidy. Thanks."

"You're welcome. The wild berries are smaller, but I think they're sweeter. And please, call me Claire."

He nodded. "So, what were you doing in the woods when you were *not camping*?" he asked, repeating her words.

"I don't camp in the traditional sense . . . you know, tents and kerosene stoves. I build a wigwam up in the mountains like the Lenni Lenape Indians did and cook over an open fire."

"Alone?" He was picturing her with some guy . . . okay, him . . . bending over the fire. Maybe dancing a little, making those beads and other things jiggle. Then, they'd go into the wigwam, and—

"Usually."

"Huh?"

"I usually go alone. I like the solitude. And I'm able to explore and dig for Indian artifacts at my leisure."

He could understand the solitude part—he was a loner himself—though he liked his fantasy better. "And you planned all along to be back here for the start of the project tomorrow?"

"Of course. I always honor my commitments."

And she couldn't have told me that. Not even one little phone call or e-mail. He decided to hold his tongue. "You're not going to make me fill out those forms, are you?"

She shook her head. "Not all of them. I'll help you, if you're willing."

He liked the fact that she was willing to bend the rules and decided reciprocation was in order. "I'll help *you*."

"You're staying at the Butterfly Bed & Breakfast?"

"Uh-huh. It's convenient, with the cavern right there on the property. Abbie is giving us a nice deal on rooms."

She cocked her head to the side, probably at his use of Abigail Franklin's first name.

"I met her grandson Mark in Afghanistan, and we've kept in touch occasionally," Caleb said.

"The Navy pilot?"

He nodded.

"How's he doing?"

"As well as a young man with one arm could, I suppose. You should know, Jinx is here because Abbie contacted me."

"Abbie's a smart cookie. Don't underestimate her because of her age."

"You say that as if I should be wary."

"Let's face it, cave pearls don't have a huge value. They lack luster," Claire pointed out.

"There's some kind of chemical fusion bath that was invented recently. It supposedly gives them luster. Market value could be over five hundred thousand dollars, maybe a million."

She didn't look convinced.

"What?"

"Abbie's always been kind of secretive about the historical documents related to her home, which is on the National Register of Historic Places, and the cavern. I wonder if there might be something else, and she's just using your firm on the pretext of the pearls."

In other words, we do the grunt work, and she skips off with the real bonanza. This was something Caleb would have to investigate, but not with Ms. Indian Preservation on his tail. "All I can say is that Abbie has been very accommodating. Not just to me. The other members of my team will be staying at her B & B, too."

"And they are . . . ?"

"Adam Famosa, a professor at Rutgers, and John LeDeux, a police officer from Louisiana. This is a relatively simple job. No need for the usual six-man team."

"And you're the project manager?"

"Yep. You'll meet Veronica Jinkowsky, owner of Jinx, and her on-again, off-again husband, Jake Jensen. Ronnie is a lawyer, and Jake is a professional poker player. They won't be staying, though. They're off to another treasure hunt in Mexico."

She nodded.

Caleb wouldn't be surprised if she had already researched every one of them, as well as the cavern to be explored and the targeted treasure.

"A college professor, a police officer, a poker player, a lawyer, an ex–Navy SEAL . . . What qualifies you guys to be treasure hunters?"

"Good question. Actually, each of our fortune-hunting expeditions is unique and requires different skills. Could be anything from deep-sea treasure to buried gold to a lost heirloom. Once an elderly Southern belle hired us to dig up her back yard in hopes of finding her family's silver from the Civil War days. Some of us are climbers. Others have diving experience. Those of us on this project put in an additional fifty hours to get certified in cave diving."

"Is cave diving so different?"

"Actually, yes. There are almost forty different swimming techniques just for negotiating underground water passes. We don't take on jobs we can't handle, or if we do agree to a project requiring special expertise, we hire someone to join the team. Mostly, though, we all share a love of adventure."

"Did you find the lady's silver?"

"Yeah. That and a couple of dead Yankee soldiers."

She appeared satisfied with his explanation.

"What is it *you* hope to find on this project, Claire?"

"Well, artifacts, most likely. Arrowheads, tools, that kind of thing. Caves have long been used as dwelling places, burial sites, storage houses, places of worship. Add to that the fact that Pennsylvania has been homeland to the Lenape tribe for more than ten thousand years."

"Ten thousand years!"

She shrugged. "As you probably know, a cavern of any size is at least a million years old. We're talking ancient and near history here. Near history being the past few hundred years, of which we have more concrete evidence. The Lenape were among the first Indians to come in contact with Europeans in the 1600s."

"Uh-hum," he said. *Good God! She's giving me a lecture, like I'm one of her students.*

"It would be really great if there were pictographs, as well. Cave paintings," she blathered on, pleased, no doubt, that she had a captive audience. "Oh, and aside from the usual artifacts, I would love to discover some new fetishes. I only have a few now."

He couldn't help himself. He had to chuckle. "Yeah? I've got a few myself. I'll tell you mine if you'll tell me yours."

She stared at him for a long moment. "Oh, you! I meant Indian fetishes. Like small carvings in wood or stone. A turtle, for example. Things that hold some mystical spirit important to—" She let her words trail off as she realized he'd known what kind of fetish she'd meant all along.

"Yeah, well, back to what you hope to find. I've studied all the maps and history. I suspect the only things, other than pearls, that we're going to find are bats and bugs and"—he shivered reflexively—"snakes. I do hate snakes."

Claire tilted her head to the side. "Didn't Abbie tell you about Sparky?" Then she smiled. Smirked, actually.

The fine hairs stood out on his body. "Okay. Who's Sparky?"

"A snake."

"A snake with a name?" *Uh-oh, this does not sound good.* He must have turned a bit green, because she grinned. *Oh, great! A sadist, on top of everything else.*

"A big ol' snake."

"Define *big.*"

"Ten feet long and, well, not quite as wide around as your tattoo." She pointed to his left bicep where the barbed-wire tattoo peeked out from under the sleeve of his T-shirt.

Well, he would hope not! His biceps was sixteen inches in diameter and had been eighteen when he was an active SEAL.

"More like the size of your wrists."

Okay, that's better, but still one mother of a snake.

"Sparky's been living in Spruce Creek Cavern for at least ten years. Not that there aren't other snakes, but Sparky is the Big Daddy. Every so often, he sticks his head out, but then slithers back in before anyone can catch him."

Yeah, but has anyone ever shot him? With an AK-47?
"Are you pulling my leg?"

"I wouldn't think of touching your leg."

Okay, I recognize an insult when I hear one. He thought about taking her hand and placing it on his bare thigh, just to annoy her, but sanity persuaded him to re-strain himself. "I. Hate. Snakes."

"Afraid of them?"

"Hell, no. Just don't like 'em." Probably stemmed from all those years as a kid when he'd helped hand-plow the fields and uncovered lots of the slimy buggers . . .

usually black or garden variety, but even the occasional rattler. And he'd had to deal with plenty in SEAL survival training, too.

"You had to know coming here that an underground cavern would have snakes."

"Sure, I knew that. I just didn't expect any anacondas."

She laughed, and her whole face lit up, even her eyes, which were a pale, pale green.

Nice. But he could see how some people might consider her eyes sort of woo-woo, fitting into the crazy category.

"Don't worry, he's not poisonous . . . though he has been known to bite."

"You're really enjoying yourself at my expense, aren't you?"

"Yep!" But then she switched subjects and floored him. Women had a talent for doing that to a guy, one minute talking about the latest hot chick movie and the next asking him something personal, something he absolutely does not want to discuss, like the size of his . . . oh, let's say . . . rifle, or why he hasn't ever married, or what's that huge chip on his shoulder with the word *Family* chiseled on it.

What Claire zinged him with was: "Peachey . . . that's an Amish name, isn't it? An Amish Navy SEAL? That's an oxymoron, isn't it?"

I'm a moron, all right. Left myself wide open. Why don't I just paint a target on my chest that says "Shoot me."

Chapter 2

Tick, tick, tick, tick, tick . . .

The man was so good-looking he made her teeth hurt.

His brown hair was cut short in a military style, sort of shaved on the sides. His facial features were sharply chiseled, almost gaunt. His eyes were a warm whiskey color. And his body . . . Well, suffice it to say he gave new meaning to the word *buff*.

Not that it mattered. Claire wasn't that superficial. In fact, in Claire's experience, eye-candy men were rarely worth the sugar high. Besides, he wasn't at all her type. She'd always been more into long-haired, artistic types, not Rambos . . . even educated Rambos.

Still, as Claire drove Caleb back to the B & B, she couldn't help but be aware of him sitting next to her, throwing off heat like a testosterone furnace. Oh, he wasn't hot for her. Mostly he was annoyed that he had to have her around, a thorn in his very fine ass.

I did not think that. Good Lord, am I regressing to my

teenage years? I'm thirty-five years old, for heaven's sake. "Where are you from, Caleb?" *That's a nice safe topic.*

"Here and there."

So that's the way we're going to play it. "For example?"

She could practically hear his brain gears rev up. Should he ignore her question and risk getting on her bad side? Or give in now and avoid a hostile work atmosphere? "Until two and a half years ago I had an apartment in Coronado, California, near SEAL headquarters. Then I moved to New Jersey, where I did some commercial diving for a bridge construction company. Now I live wherever Jinx sends me." His response was delivered in a toneless manner meant to discourage further questions.

But that didn't stop her. "No roots?"

He shook his head and flashed her a glower.

Hah! As if she'd be deterred by a mere glower! "I'm not asking out of nosiness."

His snort spoke for him.

"Really. When I work as a consultant, I need to know everything about the participants as well as the project."

"Give me a break!"

She wasn't going to let him bully her into doing less than a full job. "You were raised Amish?"

He didn't answer, but after a telling instant of silence, he nodded.

"Pennsylvania Amish?" Over the years, the Amish had spread themselves across the United States, starting from Pennsylvania, as land grew scarce and too expensive for their growing families. In fact, you could find Amish in about twenty-five of the states. Many of the sects had different rules on living, some stricter than others. In Pennsylvania, the general public usually associated them with the Lancaster area, but there were many in the nearby Kishacoquillas Valley, or "Big Valley," too.

Again, the reluctant nod. "Sinking Valley."

Well, that was a surprise. And even closer. The Old Amish community of Sinking Valley was less than ten miles away. In fact, she shopped at some of their roadside stands for fresh produce. Their quilts were exquisite.

"Did you know that the Lenape Indians referred to themselves as the People, just like the Amish refer to themselves as the People? Of course, that term meant different things to the Lenape than it does to the Amish. Still, it's really fascinating, isn't it?"

He gave her a look that pretty much said, "Do you ever stop?" She tended to talk too much sometimes. It was a bad habit of hers. But really, it was interesting that Caleb had been raised Amish.

"Look!" he said, anticipating her next question. "I left seventeen years ago, when I was seventeen, and haven't been back since. I assume I'm still under the *Bann*. And no, I'm not going to tell you all the gory details. So knock it off."

Claire was shocked. And deeply touched. Not by Caleb's surly attitude, but the fact that he was being shunned, one of the most barbaric practices of any culture, in her opinion. There had to be a story there, why he'd been willing to risk coming back after all these years to the region where he was not welcome. "Just one more question. Please. Do you still have family here?"

He shrugged. "Last count, a mother, a father, grandparents on both sides, four brothers, and three sisters. Maybe some nieces and nephews. Some of my family could be dead by now, for all I know."

Caleb's response raised more questions than answers, but his rigid jaw and her promise of just one last question restrained her. *All those family members, and none kept in touch? How sad!*

"How 'bout you? What's your history?"

Well, she supposed she owed him tit for tat. And really, she had skeletons in her closet she'd rather not discuss, either. "My mother was a drug addict, and I never knew my father."

He blinked several times, probably trying to wade through her nervous rambling, though why she should be nervous around him was a puzzle. Well, not such a puzzle. He was so good-looking he gave hunk a bad name.

"Anyhow, I was raised in various foster homes till I was sixteen and went psycho. After a year of trying to kill myself with wild sex and endless booze, I was taken in by a Philadelphia shelter, which helped me get my act together." That was the short story, with all the colorful and painful details glossed over.

He pondered her words, then turned his head to gaze at her. A smile twitched at his lips. "How wild?"

She smiled back at him. "Very wild, but that's old history."

"Shucks!" Any other man would have waggled his eyebrows at her to accompany the remark. Not him. After that provocative single-word response, he resumed staring forward. She was beginning to realize that he was a man of few words and not prone to playful flirting. Finally, he asked, "Why the interest in Indians?"

"I met Henry Hawk, the guy in the picture, in college. He was from Delaware, a full-blooded Native American. He had a really fascinating family and history. Long after he was gone, I remained fascinated. Not with him, but his culture . . . the Lenni Lenape. To tell you the truth, my mother once hinted that my father was Native American and resided in Pennsylvania, though I realized later that she'd been with so many men she had no way of knowing for sure. That's probably part of the reason for my interest in Indians, searching for my roots and all that. A Pocahontas syndrome is what I call it. Yeah, yeah, I know, you're probably thinking that I look as much like an Indian as you resemble a midget. Though I once about starved myself to death trying to achieve high cheekbones."

"Hey, I didn't say anything . . . about you not looking Native American."

"You thought it."

"I'm sure there are plenty of auburn-haired, green-eyed Indians."

She made a face.

"The Lenape, huh?"

"Len-NAH-pay," she said.

"That's just great! A woman who corrects a man's pronunciation."

"Sensitive, are we?"

He made a mock growling sound. "So the guy in the picture was your college friend?"

"Yes. That photo was taken about fifteen years ago at the annual meeting of the tribes in Oklahoma." When he didn't say anything, she suddenly felt uncomfortable in the silence and made the mistake of blathering on. "I was wearing the attire of a Lenni Lenape maiden. If you'd examined the photo closer, you would have noticed it was hardly the body of an older woman like I am now. I was a college student then."

He muttered something like, "You look fine to me."

She shot him a surprised glance, but his expression betrayed nothing.

Luckily, they arrived at the B & B, forestalling any further questions from either of them. Or her continuing to babble on like a windup doll. Five vehicles were parked near the barn. The vintage Mercedes sedan she recognized as Abbie's, and a big-wheeled pickup truck belonged to her grandson Mark, though he probably couldn't drive it now if it was standard shift. Two vehicles had New Jersey plates—a dark green Jeep Grand Cherokee that she assumed was Caleb's and a Lexus. Then there was a cherry red Chevy Impala from Louisiana.

"Some of the gang is here," Caleb announced unnecessarily. "I didn't think they'd get here till this afternoon."

Claire had planned to drop Caleb off, then go in to State College, the town where the main campus of Penn State was located. One of her former colleagues was holding some research materials on cavern exploration for her. Two men were approaching her car, though, so she unhitched her seat belt and got out along with Caleb. One of them was older than she, dark-skinned, probably late thirties, long black hair tied back into a low ponytail. From the background materials she'd been given, she guessed it was Adam Famosa, from Rutgers, who was of Cuban descent. He was not unattractive . . . and he knew it. The other, early to mid-twenties, could only be the Cajun, John LeDeux, with those mischievous eyes, an overconfident stride, and a T-shirt with the logo "Bite Me Bayou Bait Company." *Girls from twelve to thirty must fall all over him. Good thing I'm thirty-five.*

Caleb introduced her to both men, who gave her unabashed surveys from head to toe, with special attention to her pink running bra. *Men!* At the same time, they appeared wary, probably having been warned that she was going to be a stumbling block. The enemy, so to speak.

"What's the plan?" Adam asked Caleb.

"Once Ronnie and Jake get here, we set up a meeting. Hopefully at seven here at the B & B. The owner, Abbie Franklin, has lent us her library to use as our control center, where we can spread out all our materials."

Adam nodded. "I picked up the diving equipment in Barnegat. Mr. Redneck USA here brought the rappelling ropes and hanging ladders. We've studied the background material you sent us. So we're all set."

"How long do y'all think we'll be here?" John asked with a heavy Southern accent. "I gotta be back in Loozee-anna by September 15th. I'm startin' my new job as a police officer. I cain't wait. There's people who're gonna pee their pants when they see me in uniform." John grinned at them all.

"That's two months away. We'll be done long before that," Caleb said.

"Will you schedule a little time for me during your meeting tonight?" Claire interjected. "I need to go over the Park Service regulations."

"More regulations!" Caleb scoffed.

"Don't be difficult," she chastised Caleb, to the

amusement of the other two men. "At the beginning of any project, I like to clear the air, to avoid any misunderstandings."

"You do realize that *you* are not running this show?" Caleb folded his arms over his chest.

"I never asked to run anything, but I won't be disregarded, either."

He stared at her pink jogging bra, then gave her a look that said she would be pretty hard to disregard.

"Listen, mister—"

"I've read some of your papers on the Lenape," Adam interrupted. "Very interesting."

Caleb continued to hold Claire's gaze.

"We have Indians in southern Looz-ee-anna, too," John said. "The Houma Indians have similar ethnographics to the Lenape. Their methods of dealing justice were remarkable for their time. And I saw a linear chart once that compared the interpersonal dynamics of all Native Americans. You're probably familiar with it—the one put together by Professor Thibadeaux at Tulane. Anyhow, it was amazing how all the tribes ran neck and neck on almost all factors."

Caleb broke his gaze with Claire. He and Adam regarded John as if he'd sprung two heads.

"You gotta understand, *chère,* these two lunkheads think ever'one below the Mason-Dixon Line has the IQ of a mudbug. They's biased agin us rednecks." John winked at her.

Adam made a hissing sound.

"I see yer not married, darlin'," the Cajun said, scanning her ring finger. "Guess it's yer lucky day. I'm not married, either."

"You've got the finesse of a bulldozer." Adam gave John a pitying shake of the head.

John was not about to be pitied. "Hey, you know what they say down on the bayou . . ."

Both Caleb and Adam groaned.

"Ya cain't catch any alligators iffen ya don't put out any bait."

Claire smiled. "And I'm the gator?"

"Oh, yeah."

"I'm flattered, John, but you're much too young for me."

"I, on the other hand, am much closer to your age," Adam pointed out.

"But, Claire, older women and younger men make the best combination. All that stamina, dontcha know. I kin give ya references."

"Sex references?" She arched her eyebrows.

"The best kind."

"You are such a loser, LeDeux," Adam said.

Adam and John were clearly open to a little side action on this project. *Not from me!* Her eyes connected with Caleb's again, and she could tell that he'd been thinking the same thing. With a subtle shake of her head, she indicated to him that she had no interest in his colleagues. Not that way.

Caleb smiled. She wasn't sure if it was because she wasn't going to hop in bed with the Mutt and Jeff of dating games. It didn't matter. When he let loose, his eyes smiled, too. She liked his smile. A lot.

After the two men left, Claire prepared to leave. "Do you want to get together sometime today and fill out those forms?"

His lips said, "Sure," but he probably thought, *Hell, no!*

"Will you come back to my place, or should I come here?"

"Here is fine."

He would no doubt find a way to put it off. Still, she nodded, got into her car, then told Caleb through the open window, "You should know something about me."

"What's that?" He leaned against the door frame, putting his face level with hers.

"I believe in being up front and honest."

"Yeaaaah?"

"Much to my surprise, I find myself attracted to you."

He grinned. "And that's a bad thing?"

"Yes and no. You should stay away from me. Far away."

"Why is that?"

"My biological clock is ticking. And your sperm bank is looking mighty attractive."

"Whaaaat? You're kidding, right? Ha, ha, ha! Why aren't you laughing?" His face couldn't have been any greener if she'd suddenly had snakes crawling out her ears.

Beware of chain-smoking, devious grandmothers . . .

"I'm sick and tired of your pity party, boy. Get up off your be-hind and help me around here."

Mark Franklin was watching *The Price Is Right*

when his grandmother barged into his bedroom, making that sudden demand in a strident, no-nonsense voice. "Stop treating me like a kid, Gram. I'm twenty-five freakin' years old."

"Then start actin' like it." She stubbed one cigarette into an ashtray on the bureau near the door and immediately lit up another. After taking a long draw and exhaling a cloud of smoke, she looked at her watch, then at his pajama bottoms, then back to her watch. "It's noon, for heaven's sake! Get the heck up and take a shower. I need your help."

He raised the stump of what used to be his left arm. "What? You want me to dig your vegetable garden? Or fix the roof? How 'bout I change the beds for all your guests? Or scrub the toilets?"

"Pfff! What I want you to do is thank God you're alive and stop wallowing. There's a whole heck of a lot you can do. Start with getting involved in this cave project." His grandmother was like a pit bull tugging on his pants leg. *Ruff, ruff, ruff, ruff!*

"Why should I?"

She sank down into an upholstered chair near the window and sighed. He could swear there were tears in the old bird's eyes. In that instant, she looked every one of her seventy-five years. "Because I'm so far in debt I might lose this place if one of us doesn't start earning some money," she revealed in a small voice.

"Maybe if you'd make this a smoke-free B & B, you'd get more business."

Her response was to blow smoke rings in the air. "Joke all you want, but the only way I see us avoiding a sheriff's sale is by making this project a success."

"Sell my truck."

"Are you kidding me? That clunker is ten years old. What do you think I would get for it? Two thousand? On a good day, maybe three thousand. Besides, you need it for a trade-in when you get a vehicle with automatic transmission."

Mark had been doing his best the past year to avoid feeling anything, but man, she made him feel like crap now. This house and this property had been in his family for two hundred and fifty years. And his grandmother was in danger of losing it? How could he not have known? "Why didn't you tell me before?"

"Because you had your own problems. Took all your energy to heal . . . in the beginning. That was before you started this wallowing business." She ground her cigarette stub into the ashtray and lit up another one.

At this rate, Mark figured he would be getting lung cancer without ever having smoked. "You don't need me, Gram. You have Caleb and the rest of the Jinx crew."

She looked him straight in the eye. "They're not family."

"Don't lay a guilt trip on me. Please."

"The way I figure it, boy, is you're already guilty enough, just for being alive."

Mark didn't have to be reminded that he was the lone survivor in his crew over in Af-friggin'-stan. He closed his eyes and pinched the bridge of his nose, willing himself not to say something foul to his grandmother.

"By the way, Lily called again last night."

"You better not have invited her for dinner again. Because I won't come down."

He'd known Lily since they were both five years old, playing in her dad's hayloft on a farm down the road a

ways. They'd been engaged before his deployment.
They were unengaged now, although he'd had to tell
Lily that at least a dozen times so far. Lily could do bet-
ter than a one-armed, unemployed ex-pilot.

"I heard she's takin' her clothes off and doin' the
hootchie cootchie over at The Red Zone—that stripper
joint over at State College."

"I know what The Red Zone is, Gram, and I don't believe for one minute that Lily is stripping. She undresses
in the dark, for Pete's sake!" His face heated up at having disclosed such an intimate thing to his grandmother.

But she didn't seem to notice. "Maybe she's drinkin'.
Booze'll turn a wallflower into a Gypsy Rose Lee every
time. I hear they do lap dances over at that place. Do
you think Lily does lap dances?"

"You're making all this up. Just to get me out of bed.
You are freakin' unbelievable!"

"Tsk-tsk! Such language!" She stood and walked out
the door, puffing on her blasted cigarette.

He was the one who was angry now. He levered his
legs off the bed and stomped to the open doorway,
yelling after his grandmother. "I'll try to help you, but
you're nuts if you think I'm going do any cave diving.
And I better not see Lily hiding around some corner,
either."

At the first landing, she craned her neck around and
smiled so big it was a wonder her jaw didn't crack.

"You think you've won, don't you, you old bag? And
you better stop smoking those coffin nails. And I am not
shoveling bat shit out of that cave for your rose garden,
like you made me do when I was a kid. Do you hear
me?"

Now at the bottom of the stairs, she glanced up at

him where he was leaning over the railing. "Cripes! The whole world heard you. The bats in the cave are probably holding their wings over their ears."

He closed his eyes on a long sigh. "Why can't you just leave me alone?"

Her direct, unsmiling gaze told him why. She loved him too damn much, that was why. Instead of speaking those words, she said, "Haul your sorry butt down to my sitting room after you shower. I have a secret to tell you about the cavern."

His grandmother knew how much he loved the cavern . . . at least he had before being wounded. The sly old witch. First she lured him with guilt, then with secrets. If he wasn't careful, she would have hookers lined up in the front parlor, just waiting to help him unwallow.

He grinned at that image.

Or Lily.

He stopped grinning.

I'm a goner.

Mano to mano, warrior to warrior . . .

Caleb was sitting on the back patio of the Butterfly Bed & Breakfast, admiring the view.

He should have been working on the unopened laptop at his side. Or making some business calls from his cell phone. Instead, he sat sipping at a mug of delicious black coffee that Abbie had prepared from some fresh-ground Cajun beans LeDeux brought from Louisiana.

It was a great setting. A two-hundred-fifty-year-old brick house in the Federal style on roughly three acres, all bordering a privately owned stretch of Spruce Creek, which had been world-famous for its fly fishing long before ESPN Outdoors had discovered it. You didn't have to be a fishing enthusiast to enjoy it here, either. The sound of the rushing stream. Flower beds bursting with color and butterflies everywhere. The heavy scent of lilacs in the air. Sunlight peeking through the massive pines and oaks. Dozens of varieties of birds and the occasional deer. Geese squawking as they cruised by. The place oozed tranquility.

Not that Caleb felt tranquil. Not after Crazy Claire's titillating comment to him earlier today. She was seeking a stud, and Caleb did not consider that a compliment. He knew sure as sailors love sex that the witch wanted his swimmers, nothing else. He could laugh it off, or tell her to fuck off, literally, if he didn't find her so damned hot.

"Hey, Peach."

Caleb jumped and almost spilled his coffee. He turned and saw Mark coming out of the kitchen doorway onto the patio. It was the first time he'd seen Mark in more than a year. Mark had declined to see Caleb since his arrival, making one excuse after another via his distraught grandmother.

The boy looked like hell. He wore a long-sleeved white T-shirt sporting the words "Top Gun," with one sleeve pitifully empty from the elbow down. The shirt and his faded jeans hung on his body, which must have dropped at least twenty pounds since he'd shipped out to Afghanistan two years before. His hair was overlong, but he'd shaved, which accentuated his sunken cheekbones. His pallor could only be described as ghostly.

Putting his mug on the patio table, Caleb stood and

met Mark halfway. Stretching out an arm, he shook Mark's right hand, then pulled him into a bear hug. "It's good to see you again, buddy," he said huskily against Mark's ear. *There but for the grace of God go I.*

Mark held himself stiff as a board.

When Caleb stepped back, he said, "Welcome back to the living."

"Hah! I don't feel like I'm living," Mark said, dropping into one of the patio chairs and indicating with a wave of his hand that Caleb should sit back down, too. Mark poured himself a mug of coffee from the carafe Abbie had left on the table. An awkward process when done one-handed, but Caleb knew enough not to offer his help. Mark leaned back, slouching, and exhaled loudly. "I'm so shit-faced screwed up."

"Aren't we all?"

Mark grinned, which Caleb took as a good sign.

"You're out of bed. That's a start."

Mark raised his eyebrows at him. "My grandmother been blabbing to you?"

"A little. She's worried about you."

"She likes worrying. It's a pastime with her. Pfff! How 'bout you? I hear you left the teams. I thought you loved being a SEAL."

"I did love it, but I was getting too good."

Mark nodded. He didn't have to be told that Caleb meant his kill totals had been going through the roof. Didn't matter that they were the vilest tangos in the world, either. After a while, a warrior could take down only so many terrorists before it started to eat away at his soul. And yeah, that's what SEALs were. Warriors. Navy pilots, like Mark, were, too.

"You still engaged?"

"No." The terseness of his reply was a neon sign blinking, "Don't ask."

He hoped the chick hadn't ditched him because of his arm. It was surprising how many women failed to support their broken heroes. But it was more likely that Mark had pushed his girlfriend away. That happened too often, as well.

"Speaking of Gram, where is she? She lured me downstairs with some big secret, then disappeared."

"She took LeDeux and Famosa over to Spruce Creek Outfitters to pick up some last-minute equipment. Dr. Cassidy will be here soon to go over some details."

"Crazy Claire?"

"Oh, yeah." It was Caleb's turn to grin. "Do you know her?"

Mark shook his head. "Just heard of her. She's notorious in these parts."

"For being crazy?"

"That, and other things."

"Hey, I heard that." Claire came strolling around the side of the house, a five-inch notebook in one arm and her yipping dog in the other. She wore the same outfit she'd had on earlier, except for an open white button-down shirt on top.

He and Mark cringed at having been caught talking about her.

"Do you have any extra coffee for this crazy lady?" She winked at Mark and made a silly face at Caleb.

The second she set her mini-dog on the ground, it barked a half dozen times at Caleb's shoe, just to show Caleb who was boss, then shot like a bullet toward the stream and the squawking geese. The geese didn't stand a chance and they knew it, taking off with wings flapping and feathers flying.

Once the chaos settled down, the rat dog went off to sniff the entrance to the cave, no doubt getting the scent of Sparky, whom Caleb had yet to see, thank God.

Claire sank into a chair on the other side of the patio table from him and Mark.

After pouring Claire a mug of coffee, he introduced her to Mark, then asked, "Did you have to bring your rat with you?"

She made another crinkly-nosed face at him. It was probably the female version of giving the bird. "Boney was lonely."

"Boner?" Mark's eyes widened incredulously.

"Jeesh! You men are all alike." She went on to give Mark the Napoleon/Boney explanation she'd given Caleb earlier.

He and Mark exchanged quick glances that pretty much said, *Yep. Crazy.*

"So, Mark, will you be working on this project?" she asked.

A rush of crimson stained Mark's pale cheeks. "My grandmother wants me to, but man, my balance isn't so great. That's all the Pearl Project would need. Me falling into a cave pit."

"There are lots of things you could do," Caleb said. "Besides, we work in pairs on this project. So if you fall, your partner does, too."

"Oh, that makes me feel better."

"I've noticed you rubbing your stump a lot," Claire remarked.

Oh, my God! First time he ventures out, and she's got

*to call attention to his handicap. And stump? Did she
really use the word* stump*?*

Mark's face flushed again, and he appeared as astonished as Caleb that a virtual stranger would call attention to his . . . stump.

"I don't mean to offend you, Mark. I just wanted to tell you that Native Americans, my specialty, were very familiar with the phantom limb syndrome. Not that they called it that, of course, but being warriors in the early days and going into battle often resulted in serious injuries. Anyhow, I make some ointments, passed down through the generations of tribes, and there's one that would relieve the distress on your limb a great deal. If you're interested. It's a mixture of goldenrod, pawpaw seeds, honey, vinegar, and red clay. I make a paste, and you could use it at night with a sock to hold it in place. Of course, there is also . . ."

A sock? Caleb swore under his breath. Bloody hell, he'd like to tell her to *put* a sock in it. Her mouth, that is.

On and on she went with her Indian crap while he and Mark just gawked at her. The nutcase was totally oblivious to the fact that neither of them was responding to her discourse.

"Crazy," he mouthed to Mark.

Mark grinned and rolled his eyes. At least he wasn't offended anymore.

"On the other hand . . ." she began.

Caleb put his face in his hands. Every time a woman said, "On the other hand," a guy had to know he was in for a marathon of female opinion.

"The phantom limb syndrome really is a mental thing. Your balance problem, as well. The Lenni Lenape did the most wonderful thing with meditation to center the soul's focus. They set up a sweat lodge and drank lots of a specially prepared tea. Once they went into a trance, the medicine man led the person into his soul path and practiced exercises to regain wholeness.

"You see, a person is what he thinks he is. Nothing more. If you think of yourself as whole, you are. I could help you."

She dropped down to the patio and sat Indian style, legs crossed and folded under herself, and began chanting, "Ooohm, ooohm, ooohm."

Caleb could barely restrain himself. "Uh, this special tea? Aren't you talking about peyote? Indians used that a lot. And, uh, correct me if I'm wrong, but peyote is now an illegal substance."

Claire smacked him on the arm. "No, silly! Peyote comes from a cactus and was used by southwestern Indians. I'm talking about natural stimulants." She turned back to Mark. "I could set up a wigwam for you, right here in your back yard, and show you how to meditate."

Mark looked at Caleb with a silent plea for help. Claire really was earning her "crazy" nickname.

"Uh, maybe we can talk about this later," Caleb said to Claire. "We need to give our attention to the project now."

"Oh. Right. Have you been in the cavern yet?" she asked Caleb as she stood and dusted off her ass.

He nodded. "Abbie has given me the tour several times. And I ran cables for extra lighting yesterday. How 'bout you, Claire?"

"No tours yet, and I can't wait. Abbie is proprietary over who she allows to go inside. It's never been a commercial enterprise like other caverns in the area—Indian

Caverns, Lincoln Caverns, Penn's Cave, Woodward Cave."

Mark pondered her words. "I haven't been inside since my first deployment four years ago, but I can't imagine that anything has changed. You want a walk-through?"

"I'd love it!"

"You'd have to hold my hand," Mark teased, waggling his eyebrows at her. "For balance."

At least, Caleb thought he was teasing.

"Gladly," she said, waggling her eyebrows back at Mark. "You know how we older women are with younger men."

"No, but I wouldn't mind finding out." More eyebrow waggling.

"Excuse me while I go hurl!" Caleb said.

Mark and Claire laughed.

Caleb didn't think it was funny.

As Caleb followed the two of them across the back yard and over an arched wooden bridge, he muttered, "Who's going to hold my hand?" Luckily, no one heard him, especially Ms. Ticking Clock.

Chapter
3

Honey, we have company . . .

"I'm so excited. How about you?"

Caleb shot her a look of alarm.

"Puhleeze! I meant I'm excited about exploring the cave. It's the same when I dig for arrowheads in a new site or find a special antique at a flea market. Goose bumps. Thrill of the hunt. That kind of excitement." She paused. "You thought I meant you."

"Did not," he lied, "though you did throw me before with that ticking time-bomb crap."

She grinned at his choice of words.

They were waiting for Mark to return with a key for the huge double doors at the entrance to the cavern. Even though it wasn't open to the public, the Franklin family had been forced to erect the doors a few years back because of trespassers and fear of liability if someone got hurt. Spelunkers, always on the lookout for a virgin or wild cave, were notorious for ignoring signs.

Once the doors were open and they'd all donned hard

hats with carbide lamps attached and picked up flashlights, they entered the mouth of the cavern. Startled cave swallows that had built nests inside flew out in a cloudy swoop.

They were in the twilight zone, that area at the mouth where sunlight reached. Beyond that was pitch blackness. Any animals they saw beyond this area—fish, lizards, whatever—would be blind and colorless, having adapted thousands of years ago to the environment.

"Man, does this bring back memories!" Mark said. "I could probably make my way in here blindfolded."

"You spent a lot of time in here?" Caleb asked.

"Oh, yeah! Me and my friends used to pretend we were Indians hiding out, or homesteaders hiding from Indians, or explorers searching for lost gold. I loved this place. Kid paradise, for sure."

"Ever find anything?" Caleb moved his flashlight in an arc, not seeing much, since there was a long tunnel before descending into the cavern proper.

"No gold, but lots of Indian artifacts. Arrowheads, mostly. You've seen Gram's collection in cases on the parlor walls, haven't you, Claire?"

"I have." Claire stood at Caleb's side and surprised the hell out of him when she took his hand in hers.

He wondered if she had taken Mark's hand on the other side. He shone his flashlight that way and saw that she hadn't. He found himself pleased by that. Which caused him to not be pleased with himself. Which caused him to wonder why holding hands held such appeal. He'd never been a hand-holding kind of guy. More of a let's-get-to-the-good-stuff kind of guy. Maybe his clock was ticking, too. Scary thought, that.

"That's why I'm here," Claire continued. "I believe there's even more history to this cavern than we know."

The air was cool and so still, it was as if the outside world no longer existed. There was a dim natural light in this section, which was half the size of a tennis court.

"It's logical that the Lenni Lenape would have made use of caves in the region," Claire added. "I get an eerie feeling standing here, as if I can sense the Indians who were here. Their spirits remain, that's for sure."

He and Mark exchanged looks. Cave spirits, that's all they needed.

"They would have used the cavern for hiding purposes, but also for a primitive form of refrigeration," Claire blathered on. "The area abounds with ice caves. I'd like to examine the ground and walls more closely once this project is completed, even do a chemical analysis of the dirt. Exactly where has your family found Indian relics in the cavern?" Claire asked.

"Mostly they were farther in. Not much here at the opening except an assortment of animals. They might have destroyed any evidence. Mice, squirrels, snakes, even wolves or bobcats occasionally. One winter we had a bear, but the animals have probably made themselves scarce if Gram and Peach have been stomping around in here the past day or so."

Yep, stomping is a good thing. "Even Sparky?" He glanced at Claire to see if she was smirking.

She was.

"You've heard about Sparky? He's a sly one. Real slick at hiding unless he wants to make himself known." Mark was smirking, too. "Like now."

Huh?

Mark aimed his flashlight at an area behind and above Caleb's head.

Slowly, Caleb turned, and sure enough, a bigass snake occupied a ten-foot section of a ledge. "Sonofabitch!" Caleb took a step backward, dropping Claire's hand. "That is one huge mother." Caleb could swear the reptile's big beady eyes were staring at him, probably thinking, *Yum, yum!* "You better keep your rat dog out of here. Sparky might just eat Boner for brunch."

"*Boney* is tougher than you think."

"In his own pea-sized brain, maybe."

Trying to alleviate Caleb's fears, Mark assured him, "Sparky is nonpoisonous. He can't hurt you."

"That's what I told him," Claire said.

"Hah! That snake wouldn't have to bite. All it would have to do is fall on me and crush my skull." Caleb wasn't about to let his repugnance transform him into a wuss, though. He walked over near the ledge and snapped on a series of lights, including some of the free-standing lamps he'd brought in yesterday. The corridor was immediately flooded with light. He proceeded to free-climb up the wall, prepared to show the snake who was boss. *I must be friggin' nuts. Next I'll be doing backflips.*

Sparky took one look at this wacko person climbing up his wall and slithered off to wherever he lived.

Dropping back down, Caleb saw Claire and Mark gaping at him.

"Wow!" Mark said.

"That was mature," Claire said.

Is there anything sexier than a sarcastic woman? Not! "At least I got rid of him. He's off to get a little action from Mrs. Sparky, no doubt. Snake sex. Making little Sparkys."

Claire laughed. "Is that how you handle all your fears, head-on? Here snakie, here snakie, I am macho man and I want to wrestle you."

"I am *not* afraid of snakes." He glowered at her and hissed under his breath, "You are gonna pay, lady."

Mark was already leading the way, slowly, down the steep stairs with his one hand on a handmade rail for balance. "Whoa! I've never seen the cavern under this much light. Ah-mazing!"

That was an understatement. The cavern was like a crystal palace. Beautiful and frightening at the same time. The only sounds were the drip-drip-drip of moisture and the occasional flap of bat wings. There were about two gazillion bats hanging from various parts of the ceiling. And cave crickets abounded, too.

Claire moved to descend the steps next, with Caleb behind her. Big mistake, that.

He reached out and pinched her butt. *Payback time!*

"Hey!" she squealed.

"Oops. I was reaching for the rail and must have missed."

"Something wrong?" Mark asked, turning around at the bottom of the steps.

"No," Claire said. "I thought I felt something slimy on me, but it was just a worm."

I'll give you a worm, lady. But he had more important things on his mind as he snapped on more of the lights.

Mark proceeded to give them a mind-blowing tour, complete with family history passed through the generations. What most amazed him—Claire, too—were the speleothems, those stalactite, stalagmite, and helictite formations that looked like crystal shapes hanging from the hundred-foot ceiling, or rising from the floor, or growing every which way in twists and spirals. In some cases the stalactites and stalagmites had grown together, forming columns. Steady drips had formed a flowstone drapery on one wall, resembling a waterfall. In other places, there were those amazing gypsum flowers with feathery "petals," and other formations known as dog-tooth, boxwork, selenite needles, popcorn, and moon milk. Some of the ceiling limestone pieces resembled chandeliers. An amazing collection of nature's own sculpted art.

Into the almost churchlike silence, Claire whispered, "It makes you realize how insignificant each human being is in the grand scheme of things, doesn't it? It took thousands, maybe hundreds of thousands of years, to create these marvels of nature."

"Yep, fly specks on the windshield of life, that's us," Caleb commented.

Claire gave him a dirty look for not taking her words seriously, although he did. Sometimes a human just had to be awed by the incredible things God created. Besides, his own research had revealed that it took about a hundred years just to form one inch of some of these massive formations.

"Seeing and exploring this cavern is a life-changing experience," Claire continued, "or it should be." She glanced at him, no doubt expecting him to make fun of her observation.

He surprised her by saying, "I agree."

He and Claire both turned to Mark.

"Okay, okay, I get the message. Life-changing.

Change my life. I'm not totally brain-dead. We call this the Room of Sorrow," Mark announced. Pointing down at the dirt floor, away from their path, toward the base of some of the stalagmites, he said, "See that darkish rust coloring?"

He and Claire nodded.

"Blood."

"What?" he and Claire exclaimed together.

"There were skeletons here at one time, dozens of them. Most of them minus hair, which would indicate scalping," Mark continued. "We believe they were Lenapes from about two hundred and fifty years ago."

"What makes you think so?" Caleb asked.

Claire answered for Mark. "Most Lenape fell into one of three tribes: the Unami or 'turtle tribe'; the Minsi, whose totem was the wolf; and the Unalachtigo, or 'turkey tribe.' The Minsi were the most warlike and the first to migrate westward from the Delaware River Valley when us white folks moved into this country. The Minsi were known to be responsible for lots of kidnapping and torture and murder of white settlers in the Juniata Valley, but the Iroquois were on the rampage then, too, massacring not just white homesteaders, but Indians, as well. So Minsi or Iroquois would be my guess."

"I gotta give you credit, lady. You do know your Indians." Caleb patted Claire on the shoulder.

She made a tsking noise, thinking he was mocking her, which he wasn't. It was just that she went on and on and on.

"As for skeletons, see," Claire pointed to Caleb, "this is why Park Service oversight is necessary." Then she narrowed her green eyes at Mark. "Where are the skeletons? It's against the law to disturb a historical site or to remove any human remains. Like grave robbing, but worse."

Mark waved his hand dismissively. "They'd have a helluva time prosecuting. The culprits who removed the bones have been dead for more than two hundred years."

"Oh."

Caleb had to admire Claire's succinctness—for once, she didn't blather on endlessly—and the heightened color on her face indicated she knew she had spoken too quickly.

He smirked at her, just to show he had noticed.

She elbowed him.

"What's up with you two?" Mark studied them both. "You already got a love connection or something goin' on?"

"No!" he practically shouted.

"Maybe," she said at the same time.

He glared at her.

"Just kidding. Caleb doesn't have a sense of humor," she told Mark. "Comes from being an Amishman, I suspect, or an I'm-too-sexy-for-the-average-lady Navy SEAL."

"Give me a break." *Hot damn! Did she call me too sexy for the average lady? Hoo-yah!* "You are not like any historical archaeologist I've ever known." *Shit! If the snake doesn't turn me into a wuss, this woman will.*

"Known a lot of historical archaeologists, have you?" Mark asked.

"No, but that's beside the point." *Yep! Wusses "R" Us.*

Mark continued to show them around. There were many other corridors in the maze of underground cavities, ranging for at least a mile, but the openings were too small for any human to get through, and no effort had been made to widen them.

The spot they had targeted was on a wide ledge, at least six feet wide, up about fifty feet, where an enormous rock had been placed many, many years ago. Allegedly, humans had put the rock there to hide a deep, flooded chamber where the cave pearls would be found. *If* the pearls were actually there. The gems hadn't been seen for two hundred years, before the time when the water table rose and filled the cavity.

They were about to return to the outside when someone shouted, "Yo!" The call echoed through the cavern with progressively lower volume. "Yo, yo, yo, yo, yo . . ."

As they moved back toward the entrance, they glanced up the stairway to what had to be Caleb's worst nightmare. There stood LeDeux with a grimace of apology on his face. Next to him was his great-aunt Louise Rivard, better known as Tante Lulu, the world's most interfering, infuriating Cajun combination of Granny Clampett from the *Beverly Hillbillies* and Sophia Petrillo from the *Golden Girls*. Today her eightysomething hair was frizzed up and colored blonde. She wore a safari outfit with pith helmet, right out of Banana Republic. She must have imagined herself a senior-citizen female version of Indiana Jones.

What the hell are you doing here? "How nice to see you again, Tante Lulu." Meanwhile he glared at LeDeux.

The young Cajun rascal just shrugged. "Tante Lulu decided to give me a birthday surprise. My brother

Remy dropped her here in that farm field across the road."

"Dropped?" Mark asked.

"A Piper Cessna."

Mark's face lit up. "Holy crap! Old Man Hollick is gonna shit a brick if his cornfield is disturbed."

"Not to worry, *cher,*" Tante Lulu said. "I already had a talk with George. Didja know he has a cuzzin what lives in Baton Rouge? I promised ta make him some corn bread fritters with some of that damaged corn. What happened ta yer arm? Never mind. You kin tell me later, but we gots ta do somethin' 'bout fattenin' ya up. An' ya needs more sun, yes, ya do. Good ol' sunshine kin be the bes' medicine. I knows 'cause I'm a *traiteur.* Thass a folk healer."

Mark blinked several times. That was the usual reaction on first meeting the first lady of Bayou Black. Then he hurried up the steps as fast as he could while holding on to the rail.

"A healer," Claire murmured, as impressed as if Tante Lulu had said she was a movie star . . . or a Lenni Lenape princess.

Meanwhile, Tante Lulu's rheumy eyes were staring about the cavern with wonder. "Holy smokes! Ain't this sumpin'? Me, I allus wanted ta go cavin'. Whoo-ee!"

If this old bat thinks she's going to climb a rope ladder or dive in a fifty-foot pool, she's got another think coming. "Umm, how long will you be staying?" Caleb asked.

"Remy's already gone ta Vermont; then he'll go back ta Houma. He figgers he won't be comin' back this way fer two weeks."

Oh. My. God!

Just then Tante Lulu noticed Claire coming up the steps behind him. Caleb introduced them, which caused the old lady to beam.

"What?" Claire asked him in an undertone. "Why is she watching me like that?"

"You don't want to know."

"Yes, I—"

"I kin hear the thunderbolts already." Tante Lulu slapped her leg with glee.

Here it comes.

"The thunderbolts of love."

Caleb groaned.

Claire giggled, after her gaping mouth clicked shut.

Then the old lady pulled the zinger on him. "Ya gots yer hope chest yet, boy? No? Well, best ya skedaddle, 'cause the thunderbolt doan wait fer nothin'."

Hail, hail, the gang's all here . . .

Claire looked around the library of the B & B and wondered just what kind of motley crew she would be working with the next few weeks. A low hum of conversation buzzed as individuals, each more unique than the next, talked to each other in low tones.

Abbie and Tante Lulu—already recipe-exchanging best buds—were off in the kitchen, cleaning up from the sumptuous dinner of lemon-fried trout, baked potatoes, salad, fresh corn on the cob, and sweet beignets direct from Louisiana. And planning some mischief, if their sly old eyes were any indication. Actually, they were planning to drive over to one of the farmers' stands near

Tyrone in hopes of finding some fresh okra so that Tante Lulu could make gumbo. She was bound and determined to fatten up Mark, who kept protesting, to no avail, that he wasn't eating that slimy vegetable, no way, no how. Tante Lulu's response had been to whack him on the shoulder with her wooden spoon and say, "Wanna bet?"

Tante Lulu had brought with her a suitcase full of St. Jude statues of various sizes, which she handed out to everyone. St. Jude—her favorite of all the saints, she told them—was the patron saint of hopeless causes. Thinking about the baby she would like to have someday, Claire took two.

The meeting was about to begin.

Veronica Jinkowsky, or Ronnie as she asked to be called, was the owner of Jinx, Inc. Slim, about the same age as Claire, Ronnie stood with her hands in the pockets of her cream-colored, pleated slacks, talking animatedly to Caleb. The slacks, along with a jungle-print silk blouse and low-heeled sandals, were probably designer; Claire wasn't up on that kind of thing.

Her partner, Jake Jensen, an internationally known poker player, wore faded jeans, a T-shirt that said "Ace Kicker!," and a Jinx, Inc., baseball cap over his short black hair. He sat slouched in a chair at the back of the room talking with Mark, who also slouched. Jake's dark complexion was a sharp contrast to Mark's sickbed pallor, but both men were very attractive. Even as he talked to Mark, Jake watched Ronnie like a hawk. Jake was obviously leery of Caleb, though he had no reason to be. The lovebirds—albeit four-times-divorced lovebirds and not married at the present time—had eyes only for each other.

Adam Famosa, the college prof, and John LeDeux, the Cajun rascal, sat at the library table studying maps. Some of the layouts of the cavern were a hundred years old, but some were only a few days old, prepared by Caleb. Adam and John were attractive guys, too, not that Claire was interested, despite the perusals she got from both of them.

Nope, none of them compared to the Amish Navy SEAL treasure hunter, in Claire's opinion. At the ripe old age of thirty-five, she was developing an embarrassing crush on a man who was so much her polar opposite they could be an eskimo and a hula dancer.

Caleb glanced her way, then did a double take on noticing her scrutiny. His eyes quickly took in her sleeveless green shirtwaist dress, a shade darker than her pale green eyes, and upswept hair. The dress was professional and not at all sexy, except in Caleb's eyes, she could tell. He turned back to Ronnie, but a flush crept up the back of his neck and even colored his ears. Claire was enjoying his discomfort. Nice to know she could still rattle a man's chain.

"Hey, everyone," Ronnie said.

The room went silent.

"Jake and I wanted to stop by to launch this project. We'll be on our way tomorrow to another contract in Mexico, where Brenda is already setting up." For Claire's benefit, she explained, "Brenda Caslow is another member of the Jinx team." Then she continued, "If the Pearl Project is completed before we're done, some of you will be joining us there. Or vice versa. Now I'll turn the meeting over to Caleb, your project manager. Good luck!"

Everyone clapped.

Ronnie sat down as Caleb stepped into her place.

"Okay, here's the deal. We start early tomorrow morning. Let's say oh-eight-hundred, I mean, eight A.M. Abbie will serve breakfast from seven to eight."

"Have you talked to any authorities about geological concerns regarding the project?" Claire asked.

She could tell that Caleb didn't appreciate her bringing up that subject before he even started his presentation, but it had to be addressed sometime.

"I have. We won't be doing any major excavating, and certainly no dynamiting. If we do decide to widen any of the known corridors or dig to expose hidden ones, we'll employ only environmentally friendly methods. Anything else, Dr. Cassidy?"

Oooh, aren't we getting formal all of a sudden? "Not for now."

"There was already a minimal amount of lighting in the cavern run by generator," Caleb continued from where she'd interrupted. "I set up a few freestanding lights today, but we're going to need to run more lighting cables before we do anything else."

"LeDeux and I can handle that," Adam said.

"After that, Mark and I will give you all a walk-through. Always have a partner with you. Remember, hard hats, carbide lamps, and flashlights at all times. Wear long pants and boots. No shorts. There could be snakes and other animals." He glanced at Claire to see her reaction, then grinned. "To tell the truth, there is one bigass snake called Sparky. It's nonpoisonous, but it's, well, *big*."

"How big?" Jake yelled.

"Ten, twelve feet. Eight-inch circumference."

Jake laughed. "Hey, Ronnie, just like my—"

Ronnie shook her head at Jake as if he were hopeless, but her eyes told a different story. She adored the guy. "You wish!"

He blew her a kiss.

"Me, I have no problem with snakes," John said. "Now, alligators, thass another story. We got gators the size of Buicks in the bayou. In fact, my brother Remy has a pet alligator called Useless."

"You are so full of it," Adam said, jabbing John with an elbow.

John made two slashes across his chest. "Cross my heart." Then he winked at Claire.

Caleb frowned at John's wink. Or maybe he was just frowning. He did that a lot.

"We won't need the climbing ropes and ladders till the next day. That goes for the diving gear, as well. There's always a risk of carbon monoxide, so watch your meters," Caleb went on. "I'll handle the photography. Dr. Cassidy will record data for us and the Park Service. Be on your toes—the good doctor might be telling your secrets."

She made a tsking sound at his teasing. "The only secrets I'm interested in involve Native Americans who might have occupied the cavern." *And your secrets, too, Mr. Amish Navy SEAL.*

Caleb wrapped up his talk, then invited Claire to step forward. "Dr. Cassidy has a few *rules* to lay down for us." He took several steps to the side and leaned against the wall.

She shot him a glower, then turned back to the group. "Hi! Despite what Caleb says, I am not here with a whip and chain—"

"Now, there's a picture," Caleb murmured for her ears only.

But some of them overheard. John looked at her, then looked at Caleb, and let out a hoot of laughter. "*Mon Dieu!* Looks lak Tante Lulu's thunderbolt has hit a bull's-eye already."

"It has not. The only bull here is coming out of your mouth," Caleb said, and made a motion for John to zip it up.

Which, of course, caused John to blather on. "My aunt has so many thunderbolt victims under her belt, she cain't hardly walk. There were my half brothers Luc and Remy, and my half sister Charmaine, and then Jake and Ronnie here. Sort of lak the scalps yer Indians took, Claire."

Jake and Ronnie grinned at each other, clearly glad to have been "scalped" by Tante Lulu.

"Why not you?" Claire asked John.

He waggled his eyebrows at her. "I'm too young. Oh, not too young fer *that*. It's just not mah time fer marriage."

"Marriage? No way!" Caleb exclaimed, then regretted having voiced his sentiments when everyone stared at him. Red-faced, he folded his arms over his chest and pulled his usual frowny face.

Claire didn't want to be hit by any love bolt, either, but she rather resented Caleb's protests. She favored him one of her "You are such a jerk!" looks and continued with her part of the introductory meeting. "I'm here on behalf of the Park Service, but I'm not here to be a cog in the wheels of this project. You just need to protect any historically significant objects."

"And how do we do that?" Adam asked. At least *he* was being polite.

"Be very, very careful. Don't touch or move anything until we take pictures and record data."

"How will they know what's historically significant?" Ronnie asked. "I mean, isn't that sometimes a subjective call?"

"It could be. But I repeat, I'm not here to . . . ," she gave Caleb another of her looks, "crack any whips. After all, this is private property. All we're asking . . . no, demanding . . . is that if there are historical artifacts, we have the opportunity to examine them first."

"Are there any circumstances under which you would *attempt* to put a halt on this project?" Caleb inquired.

Yes. "Maybe."

A communal groan passed over the room.

"Does the government intend to lay a claim on any treasure found in this cavern?" That was Mark cutting to the chase.

"Not unless the treasure has historical significance."

"Which brings us right back to what is historically significant," Ronnie pointed out, and the others nodded.

"Why look for trouble? Let's assume there will be no glitches. You do your work, I'll do mine." She passed out some sheets to all of them then, outlining Park Service dos and don'ts for historical preservation. After that, they circled the big library table and studied the maps.

"This is where our activity will be directed. At least initially," Caleb said, pointing to a spot on the most recent layout of the cavern. "We'll have to climb roughly fifty feet up to a ledge, bringing with us crowbars and picks. Once on the ledge, we need to remove this enormous boulder that's blocking an opening. On the other side of that opening, it's believed that there's a small, very deep cavern filled with water. It's at the bottom of that pit that a nest of cave pearls is supposed to be located."

"How does anyone know what's on the other side if the cavern opening is inaccessible?" Adam wanted to know.

"It wasn't always that way. Legend says that Indians saw the pearls a couple centuries back. During Hurricane Agnes, in 1972, there was flooding in this area, which caused the already high water table to oversaturate and break through one of the walls."

"Why didn't they take the pearls out when they saw them?" Jake's brow furrowed with puzzlement.

Mark answered for Caleb. "The nest was at the bottom of a steep drop from the top. Without modern equipment like we have today, they wouldn't have taken the risk. No one has touched those pearls for more than two hundred years."

"Who put the boulder there? And why?" Ronnie asked.

"No one knows for sure," Mark said. "Lots of theories, but nothing certain."

"That should make this project even more interesting," Caleb remarked, gazing at Claire as he spoke.

That's what I need. Something more interesting than what's looking me in the face.

Chapter
4

I've got a secret . . .

Ronnie and Jake made their way, arms around each other's waists, up to the third floor of the B & B, where they would spend the night before catching a plane for Mexico. Actually, Jake would be stopping off at Las Vegas for a poker tournament before joining her at the excavation site.

Every few steps, Jake kept stopping and backing her up against the wall to kiss her deeply. Despite their four divorces, the man did love her—that had never been in doubt. And vice versa. For more than two years they had been together again, keeping their fingers crossed that this time they could make it work.

Against her lips, he whispered, "I missed you, honey."

She laughed against his lips. "We haven't been apart for more than an hour the past three months."

He nudged her with his hips, and another body part. "I meant this kind of missing."

"Oh. Well, we made love up here when we first arrived this afternoon."

"That long ago? See. I've been lax in my work."

She moaned when he did something especially nice with his tongue. "You do good work, honey."

"Damn straight!"

On another step, between kisses, he asked, "Are you satisfied with Caleb running this project?"

"Yes. He has everything under control. And did you notice the sparks flying between him and that historical archaeologist?"

Jake grinned and nipped at her bottom lip. "One of Tante Lulu's love thunderbolts, huh?"

"Hey, don't knock it. It worked on us."

Finally, they arrived at their room, which was very small, though decorated with a charming antique canopy bed, which she loved, and a claw-footed tub in the adjoining bathroom, which Jake loved. "I have plans," he had said with a twinkle in his eye on first seeing the tub. Now he went in and turned on the faucets and poured in a huge dollop of bath foam from her cosmetic bag.

Then they undressed each other, slowly. When they were naked and Jake was about to lead her to the tub, she dug in her heels and said, "Wait."

He arched his brows in question.

"I have something to tell you . . . well, show you."

More arching of eyebrows.

"Come here." She took his hand and walked over to a full-length, freestanding oval mirror.

Coming up behind her, he kissed the back of her neck, then stared at the two of them in the mirror. "I better go turn off the water if we're going to have sex here."

She shook her head. "No. This will only take a second."

"Hah! I've never done the deed in one second in my life."

"Tsk-tsk-tsk!" She pulled both of his arms around her waist, then very deliberately placed the palm of one hand on her flat belly.

"Happy birthday, baby."

"Huh? My birthday isn't till next month."

"You can call this an early birthday present."

He still didn't understand, so she placed both of her hands over his one.

Understanding bloomed on his face with a flash. "A baby? We're going to have a baby?"

She nodded.

His breath hitched, and he walked over to a ladder-back chair, where he sat down and put his face in his hands.

Ronnie's heart squeezed with anguish. This wasn't the reaction she'd expected from Jake. She went into the bathroom and turned off the water. Then she walked over and placed a hand on his shoulder. "I thought you'd be happy."

"I am happy," he said, raising his head. There were tears in his blue eyes.

"Oh, sweetheart!"

"Do you think I got you pregnant on purpose to keep you with me?"

"You big lug! It takes two to get pregnant. Maybe you think I'm trying to trap *you*."

He pulled her onto his lap and kissed her mouth and cheeks and forehead and chin. "Are we going to get married . . . again?"

"I don't know. Is that a proposal?"

"Do you want it to be?"

"Do you?"

"This is an insane conversation."

"Isn't it?"

Their eyes clung, her arms around his neck, his looped round her waist, both of them naked and completely oblivious to the fact, except for something hard prodding her bare behind.

"If we get married again . . . *if*, we'll have to think of a new marriage name," she mused. In the past, they'd given names to their four marriages: the Sappy Marriage, the Cowboy Marriage, the Tequila Marriage, and the Insanity Marriage.

"The Baby Marriage," he offered tentatively.

"No. If we get married again, I don't want it to be because of the baby."

He nodded, then his eyes brightened. "I know. The Forever Marriage."

It was her eyes that filled with tears then. "Is it any wonder that I love you?"

"Nope."

And then they christened their unborn baby with, what else? A bubble bath.

Oh, brother! . . .

There were freckles on Claire's shoulders and arms. *Holy freakin' hell!*

How he'd missed them earlier today in that jogging bra was a miracle. There weren't a lot of them. But he was having a hard time wondering if they were all over her body and whether she was up for a game of connect-the-dots.

Not!

Caleb gave himself a mental thwap for such errant thoughts. He had a serious case of lust overload. Something had to be done about it, or the Pearl Project would be down the toilet before it even began.

And he didn't mean jacking off by himself.

"You!" he said, pointing to the object of his half-erection. "Outside. Now."

Everyone was standing around following the meeting, and Claire's head shot up with surprise from where she was leaning down to peer at one of the maps. Luckily, she was the only one who heard him. "What? Me?" She turned to look behind her.

"Yeah, you, Tinkerbell."

"You can't be serious if you think I would obey that kind of order."

He inhaled, then exhaled with a whoosh, trying to tamp down his temper, and other things. "Would you please come outside, Claire? I'd like to talk to you in private."

"No."

"No?" He could feel the vein in his forehead pop out, just like it did whenever he was about to lose control, which he would not allow. He grabbed her hand and pulled her forcibly through the library door, down the corridor leading to the kitchen, then out the back door. She dragged her feet the entire way, which was no problem for him, being bigger and stronger. If he didn't know better, he would think she was stifling a laugh.

They passed LeDeux and Famosa on the way.

"You Yankees, ya got no finesse," he heard LeDeux say to Famosa, and the Cuban responded, "You wouldn't know finesse if it bit you in your redneck butt."

"Let's go into town. See if we can find some action."

"Hell, no! I'm hitting the sack early."

"*Mon Dieu!* It's only nine o'clock! You forget to bring your Viagra with you, old man?"

"Ronnie and Jake are going to bed, too."

"Earth to clueless Yankee. *Bed* is the operative word with them. You need a course in good ol' Cajun sex education."

"You're as funny as jock itch."

"Good one. Ya cain't expect to get rode if ya don't enter the rodeo."

"I swear, you are as subtle as a shovelful of shit, LeDeux."

"Well, you ain't got no couth, and that's the truth. Hey, I made a rhyme."

Once Caleb and Claire were out on the patio, which was dark, except for a small kitchen lamp filtering light through the French doors, he let loose her hand.

"Have you lost your mind?"

"Probably." He ran the fingers of both hands through his hair and would have pulled if it wasn't so short. Then he looked at her, which was a mistake.

She looked unbelievable in that dress that matched her eyes and left bare her arms up to her freckled shoulders and her legs down her freckled calves. The dress shouldn't have been sexy, but to him it shouted, "Peel me like a green banana."

"Listen, I've been around the block so many times it

would make you dizzy. I never was much of a player, and I definitely don't want to play games now."

"Who invited you to play games?"

"You did."

"I beg your pardon."

"You don't call your ticking-clock comment playing games?"

"No."

"And saying you're attracted to me?"

"I am."

"See, that's what I mean."

"You've lost me here. Speak plainly."

I've got a dick that's on cruise control, way over the speed limit. "You want plain, you get plain. I've got a pocketful of condoms. Let's go back to your place and see if this chemistry you've ignited between us sets off any rockets." *Or out-of-control dicks.*

"Talk about overreaction. All I said was that I was attracted to you. Haven't any women ever said that to you before?"

"Sure. Plenty of times. Usually when they were about to shuck their panties."

"Jeesh! I'm thirty-five years old and unattached. I have been considering artificial insemination, but when I first saw you, I thought, why bother with test tubes when this stud is carrying the goodies around in his pants."

Stud? Goodies? "Un-be-friggin'-lievable! Do you realize how insulting that is?" *And tempting.*

"Obviously you're not interested. Subject closed."

More like too *interested.* "Have I mentioned to you how much I like your freckles?" He used a forefinger to trace several from her shoulder to her elbow.

"Huh?" She shivered at the sensation.

"Have I told you I've been fantasizing about connecting the dots? Between all your freckles. Everywhere."

Her jaw literally dropped. After she clicked it shut, she said, "Forget I said anything about ticking clocks or attractions and I'll forget about rockets and, uh, connecting dots." Her voice squeaked at that last. "Ahem! End of story."

"Hah! That egg ain't goin' back in the shell, no way."

She grinned, probably at his egg reference.

He growled.

Luckily, they were interrupted by Tante Lulu coming toward them.

Or not so luckily.

"Yoo-hoo, Caleb. Lookee who I found down at the farmers' market." The old lady was leading a man around the house toward them. Tonight her hair was still curly blonde, but she'd covered it with a straw farmer's hat, and she wore dwarf-size coveralls. This must be her go-to-farmers'-market outfit. "He dint wanna come, but I tol' him St. Jude dint lak it when folks ignore miracles. And this is fer sure a St. Jude kind of miracle."

At first Caleb couldn't see in the dim light.

And then he could.

"Son of a bitch!" he muttered.

The man came right up to Caleb, practically nose to nose. "Our mother is not a bitch, and dontcha be sayin' so."

Here stood a mirror image of himself, except for the Amish clothing. Black broadcloth trousers, suspenders, flat-brimmed hat, beard.

It was his twin brother.

"Jonas?" he said tentatively. He knew it was his

brother, but he hadn't seen him in seventeen years. Maybe his eyes were playing tricks on him.

Instead of answering, his brother shoved him in the chest and gritted out, "Whatcha been doin' all these years, ya *dummkopf?* Where ya been?"

"Since when do you care?" He shoved him back.

Jonas made a disgusted sound. "You shouldna left thataway, Caleb. *Ach,* the damitch ya caused!"

"Oh, I have a pretty fair idea. Dat drummed that into me, literally, before I left. And by the way, it's nice to see you again, Jonas. How's life treating you? You must be in hog heaven, running the farm. It's what you always wanted."

"*Ach!* You are such a lunkhead. *Doppitch, doppitch, doppitch!*"

Dumb, dumb, dumb, huh? I could tell you a thing or two about dumb, brother. He wanted to ask about Dat and Mam but couldn't bring himself to mention such a sore subject. Instead he asked about both sets of their grandparents.

Jonas shook his head sadly. "Grossmanni Effie and Grossmanni Jean, along with Dawdi Etters and Dawdi Peachey, are all gone to Glory more than five years now."

How sad and even obscene that he hadn't been aware that four people who'd been so close to him had died!

"Ya asked if I'm enjoyin' the farm, Caleb. Well, here's news for ya. I don't have the farm."

He arched an eyebrow.

"Dat and Mam had another baby."

"They did?" Now, that was a surprise. His mother had been forty-five when he left, and his father fifty. Who knew the old goat had it in him!

"*Jah.* Joseph."

Understanding slowly crept into his thick skull. "A younger brother. Then that means . . ."

Jonas nodded. "I dint get the farm, either."

"So Dat, by screwing his ol' heart out, screwed both of us." Caleb started to laugh at the absurdity of it all.

Jonas laughed, too, though Caleb could tell that he didn't want to. After a few moments, Jonas turned serious again and said, "Ya shoulda come back."

"How? I'm being shunned."

"So am I," Jonas said, so softly that at first Caleb didn't hear.

His eyes went wide. "Both of us? Under the *Bann?*"

"Both of us."

"But . . ." He stared pointedly at Jonas's Amish clothing and the beard, which was a requirement of married men of the People.

"Mennonite."

Ah, he noticed now. The beard was trimmed, which would not have been allowed in the Amish sect. A sign of vanity.

"This is unbelievable." Caleb didn't even hesitate then. He pulled his brother into a hug, and it was debatable which of them held on tighter.

"There were times I hated ya, Caleb. I wantcha ta know that," Jonas said against his ear, but he hugged tight while he spoke.

Caleb blinked several times, then gazed over Jonas's shoulder, where he saw the most alarming thing. Not only were Tante Lulu and Claire witnessing the spectacle he and Jonas were making, with tears in their eyes, ferchrissake, but Abbie, Mark, LeDeux, and Famosa were all smiling. Like he was the star of some freak reality TV show.

He stepped away from his brother with embarrassment.

Jonas appeared stunned, by him as well as the crowd.

"Ain't this jist wonderful? Me, I gots a good idea. Let's have us a reunion party," Tante Lulu suggested. "A real *fais do-do*. I bought me a boatload of okra. So we kin have gumbo."

"A what dodo?" he asked.

"A party down on the bayou," LeDeux interpreted, grinning.

"There's no bayou here," he argued.

"No bayou? Whaddya call that over yonder?" Tante Lulu pointed to the creek. "Mebbe there's no gators or crawfish or hangin' moss, but where I come from, thass a bayou."

"You tell 'em," Abbie said, speaking for the first time. She was blowing smoke rings while she talked. "We haven't had a party here since Mark went off to war."

A moment of silence followed in which everyone turned with sympathy to a mortified Mark.

"There is *not* going to be a party," Caleb insisted. "We have work to do."

"You know what they say 'bout all work and no play?" Tante Lulu turned to Abbie, and they began discussing a menu.

He put his face in his hands.

"I'll tell you one thing, Tante Lulu. You won't be seeing me at any party," Mark said.

"Is that so?" Tante Lulu put her hands on her tiny

hips. "Someone oughta tol' you a long time ago ta not let the seeds spoil yer melon. Just spit out the buggers."

"What . . . what does that mean?"

"It means it's time ta shake off yer troubles and enjoy life. Ya cain't unscramble yer eggs, boy, but ya kin make a darn fine omelette."

Mark was too flabbergasted at her nerve to respond.

"I'll be in charge of music," LeDeux said. "There's gotta be dancin', or it won't be a party. Maybe Claire knows some hot babes."

"I don't know any hot babes." Claire glanced at Caleb. "Except for me."

"Very funny," he replied. *But true.*

"No problem. If there are hotties within a twenty-mile radius, I'll find 'em." Humility was not one of LeDeux's attributes. "I might even find an overaged one for Mister Fuddy-Duddy Professor here. I get first dibs on the oversexed ones."

Famosa just shook his head, already used to LeDeux's antics.

"Behave yerself, boy," Tante Lulu told her great-nephew.

He just winked at her.

"I dairsent dance," Jonas remarked, still appearing stunned.

"Ah, sweetie," Tante Lulu said, coming up and patting Jonas on the shoulder. She had to reach up to do so, since she was about five foot zero, and Jonas matched Caleb's six foot four. "I'll teach ya."

"I didn't mean . . ." Jonas glanced Caleb's way for help.

Caleb shrugged. There was no stopping the stubborn Cajun lady when she got a bee in her bonnet.

"Are ya married?" Tante Lulu asked Jonas.

"*Jah.*"

Tante Lulu's wrinkly face sagged with disappointment.

"Actually, I'm a widower." Jonas was clearly uncomfortable with the personal question, as evidenced by the flush on his face that soon covered his neck and ears, a trait he shared with Caleb.

The old bat lost a few wrinkles. She was no longer disappointed, if that wily gleam in her eyes was any indication.

Caleb hadn't even been aware that Jonas had married, though the Amish—and Mennonites—married young. Jonas had probably been married for more than ten years. He wondered idly if he had children but had no chance to ask.

"*Mais oui!* Now I understand. Thass too bad." Tante Lulu patted Jonas's shoulder some more, then cackled with glee. "Ya got a hope chest, boy?"

Everyone laughed. Including Caleb.

Until Tante Lulu added, "I never put together hope chests fer twins before."

Jonas's glance to him was a plea for rescue. Like he could do anything to stop the Cajun tornado!

"An' dontcha go slinkin' away, Mister Feel-Sorry-fer-Myself war hero. Me 'n' St. Jude gots plans fer you, too."

A lot of groaning and grinning followed from the victims and bystanders, respectively.

Tante Lulu was oblivious to it all. "Whoo-ee, this oughta be fun!"

❦

It was no joke . . .

Jonas kept glancing over at Caleb, and it saddened him that he did not know this man, his brother.

They were twins, but he could not imagine that he bore any resemblance to this hardened man with the close-cropped hair and English clothing. Practically joined at the hip, Mam usta say about them. How could they have grown so far apart?

"Are ya married, Caleb?"

Caleb never took his eyes off the road. His right hand held the steering wheel of his vehicle, and his left elbow rested on the open window frame. "No."

"Never?"

"Never."

"Why?"

"Never found anyone I wanted to spend more than a weekend with, I guess."

There was such a sadness in Caleb. In his eyes. In the tightness of his mouth that smiled sparingly. There had been a time when the two of them were so close they finished each other's sentences. They'd even felt each other's pain from a distance. Eventually, the shared sensations wore off. But once, five years ago, Jonas had suddenly got a pain in his thigh, so severe his legs had buckled under him and he'd fallen to the ground, and he'd wondered if Caleb might have been injured somewhere.

Everything came back to the shunning and what happened seventeen years ago. When the two of them were seventeen, in the midst of their second year of *Rumspringa,* the sanctioned running-around period for young Amish, Caleb got drunk from beer he'd bought from some Englishers over in Tyrone and raced his buggy. He was struck by a car coming in the other direction when he failed to make a curve in the two-lane road. He was uninjured, but Hannah Yoder, the girl he'd been courting and expected to marry, died in the accident.

"I am so sorry, Caleb. I shoulda said it ta you back then, but I was scared. And I was hurtin'."

"It's too late for apologies, Jonas."

He shook his head fiercely. "It's never too late."

"Okay, answer some questions, then. Did you know Hannah was pregnant? Were you in love with her? Why the hell didn't you tell me?"

"*Jah,* I was in love with her, but she was yers first. And her family wanted her to marry you, since you was gettin' the farm. I had ta step back. And no, I didn't know she was pregnant. I'm not sure she knew."

"But you let everyone assume the baby was mine. You let them shun me for not apologizing for something I never did."

Jonas hung his head in shame. He had been living with the weight of his sin for seventeen years now. Yes, Caleb had been responsible for the accident that led to Hannah's death, but he'd let him take the blame for the pregnancy, too. "I did finally tell everyone what I did, but you were already gone by then, and I couldn't find ya."

"You tried to find me?"

"I did. For weeks and weeks. I even went to Lancaster, thinkin' ya mighta gone to Cousin Moses's place."

Caleb let out a whooshy exhale. "Well, it's all water under the dam now. At least I beat the crap out of you before I left. I always wondered why you just stood there and took it. You were feeling guilty."

He nodded. Their father, Samuel Peachey, a deacon in Sinking Valley's Amish order, had punished Caleb relentlessly at the time. Not just for the drinking and the accident and the sex outside marriage that resulted in a baby—all considered worldly and sinful by their conservative cult—but the violent, one-sided fight that had followed with his brother.

And Caleb, mule-headed as ever, had refused to participate in the kneeling ritual whereby he would confess all his sins to the congregation. Instead, Caleb had adopted the English motto "If you've got the name, you might as well play the game." He became the wild, worldly boy their father had accused him of being. So, at the age of seventeen, he had been exiled from his family and Amish community.

"If you finally confessed that the baby was yours, why did you get shunned?"

"I did a lot of yellin' and demandin' that the *Bann* be taken offa you, and when they wouldn't listen, I started drinkin', too. A lot. They put the *Bann* on me then. Eventually I found my way to a Mennonite church and settled down. We heard the next year that ya entered the Navy. After that I gave up on gettin' yer *Bann* lifted, 'cause there's no way they woulda taken ya back then lessen ya confessed till yer knees was bloody." He looked at Jonas and waited for him to look back at him. "Can ya ever forgive me?"

"Ah, Jonas, of course I can. You're my brother. We both screwed up." Caleb reached over and squeezed his hand.

In the silence that followed, Jonas blinked rapidly to

prevent the tears in his eyes from welling over. Once he'd calmed down and the lump in his throat disappeared, he said, "Ya mentioned ya never got married. Is it because of the *Bann?*"

"Huh? What would the *Bann* have to do with my getting married? It didn't stop you, apparently."

"*Jah,* but it affected me awful much. And it musta been harder on you, goin' away and all."

"To tell you the truth, I don't think about it anymore. Yeah, in the beginning I was so angry and pissed with the world that the least little thing would set me off."

"Is that why ya went into the military? To get back at Dat . . . and the others?"

"Probably, but the Navy was good for me. And I don't apologize to anyone for serving my country."

"Not even the killin'? It wonders me how ya could kill people, Caleb."

Jonas's question cut Caleb to the quick, and he had to restrain himself from saying something really nasty. All the peaceniks in the world thought the terrorists would go away if the USA just played nice-nice. Hah! All these sign-carrying hippies were Pollyannas. Besides, most times they wanted the bad guys gone, but they didn't want to do it themselves or know the details. Let the special forces do the dirty work.

When his temper was tamped down, he replied, "How could I kill? Let me ask you this, big brother, do you have any kids?"

"*Jah.* Twelve-year-old Sarah. Nine-year-old Noah. And eight-year-old Fanny. My wife—do ya remember Annie Stoltzfus?—died seven years ago of the cancer."

"And you've been raising those kids yourself? Shit!

Your little one couldn't have been much more than a toddler. No help from Mam and the family?"

He shook his head. "I tol' ya, I'm under the *Bann*, too. Oh, they talk to the kids, and invite them to weddin's and such, but never me."

Caleb took his eyes off the road and stared at him for a long moment, as if finding it hard to believe his words. Yeah, they shunned him, but Jonas was in their back yard. They had to be freezing him in person. "Back to your question about my not being sorry for killing. Suppose a group of men kidnapped your Sarah, and not just raped and sodomized her repeatedly and forced her to give them blow job after blow job, but then buried her alive. Or suppose someone stuck a bomb inside your Noah's ass and forced him to walk into a busy marketplace to explode himself and everyone around him. What if Fanny were sold as a sex slave to a prostitution ring? And yes, there are grown men who get their jollies from girls that young. If any or all of those things happened to your children, would you sit back and turn the other cheek? Or would you want to wipe such scum off the face of the Earth?"

"Have you truly seen such things?"

"I have, and much worse."

"But to kill—"

"Listen, we're going to have to agree to disagree on the pacifist thing. I did the necessary job other Americans don't want to do."

"Then why did you quit?"

The car stopped in front of Jonas's small farmhouse in Sinking Valley. It was set back a ways from the highway, fronted by a dozen green houses. A corrugated metal building and an ancient pickup truck bore signs that said "Peachey's Landscaping." In the dimness he could see vast numbers of burlap-bundled trees, bushes, and flowers that Jonas must sell here, mainly to Englishers. He'd done well for himself, despite the shunning.

All the lights were on in the house, he noticed, and laughter came through the open window of one of the upstairs bedrooms, even though it was past bedtime. At the sound of popular music, Caleb arched his brows as if scandalized. "Could that possibly be Mariah Carey?"

Jonas cringed. "That would be our sister, Elizabeth. Lizzie is nineteen now, going on thirty. I've told her not to bring her radio over here when she comes to babysit, but she never listens. Dat would have a fit if he knew she even owned a radio, let alone danced and sang worldly songs."

Caleb grinned.

"She's prob'ly teachin' the girls how to 'boogie' again. I told her not ta do that, either. The first time I heard her say 'Let's boogie,' I thought she said *booger*. Noah has been sayin' 'booger, booger, booger' over and over, just to annoy his sisters."

Caleb grinned some more. It felt good to be sitting here next to his brother.

"Back to my question. Why did you leave the military if you consider it noble work?"

"Why did I quit the teams?" Caleb sighed deeply. "My belt fell apart from all the notches on it."

"Aaah, Caleb," Jonas said, squeezing his shoulder. "Sad it is ta see ya so world-weary and unable to smile."

"Who says I can't smile? I smile when I have good reason. You tell me something funny, and I damn sure will smile till my lips get tired."

"How 'bout this? Do ya remember Lizzie at all?"

Caleb frowned. "Yeah, I remember Lizzie, though she was only two when I left."

"Well, Lizzie is nineteen now, and still in *Rumspringa.* Dat threatens to end her running-around days soon if she doesn't take church vows. Either that, or marry up with Abram Zook . . . *jah,* the dog-breath fella who usta eat snot when we was kids. He's almost thirty years old now."

"And Lizzie getting married is a problem, *why?*" Caleb knew that Amish girls mostly married up with men their parents chose, or at least approved of.

"Because Lizzie considers herself an Amish J-Lo—"

Caleb's jaw dropped. "You're joking, right? How the hell would she, or you, even know who J-Lo is?"

"—and she wants to be a contestant on *American Idol.*"

Caleb's jaw dropped even lower, and his eyes widened with shock. Ever so slowly, a smile crept over his lips.

Then, they both burst out laughing.

Chapter
5

Beware of grandmothers with an agenda . . .

Abbie set her burning cigarette on an ashtray and took the fragile documents out of the antique cedar box, laying them on the kitchen table for Mark to examine.

"Be careful," she cautioned in a low tone of voice. Presumably, everyone was asleep, but better safe than sorry. "The paper is brittle."

"Where did you find these?"

"In the attic. Under the rafters on the old side. I had to pull up insulation to set some mousetraps last year. I was being overrun with the pests. Mouse poop everywhere. The book must have fallen from a box and got covered over a long time ago."

With his one hand, Mark lightly touched the two cracked leather covers, front and back, which were no longer bound together. Then he began to peruse the dozens of sepia-toned loose pages, each in clear protective sleeves, which had once been part of a journal.

"Zebadiah Franklin, Spruce Creek, 1784, 1785,

1786, 1787, 1788, 1789," he read aloud. "Good Lord! When you promise a secret, Gram, you sure do deliver."

Abbie smiled. She'd been pleased to see him show some interest today in the Pearl Project. Hopefully, this journal would be the clincher in pulling him out of his self-imposed exile. The boy needed to get a life again.

"You should probably check with a museum or preservationist on how to store these properly. And could you please blow that fucking smoke in the other direction? You oughta quit."

"I'll quit smokin' when you quit swearin'." She blew some more smoke, but in the other direction now. "I already contacted the Palmer Museum. Until I brought them out today, they've been in special acid-proof enclosures I bought from the curator. I keep them in a safety deposit box at my bank. I made copies, but I wanted you to see the originals at least once."

He was already engrossed in the journal's contents.

First, there were several yellowed newspaper clippings, most about the massacre of ninety Christian Delaware Indians—twenty-nine men, twenty-seven women, and thirty-four children—by a Colonel William Crawford, who was later burned at the stake to atone for what came to be called the Gnadenhuetten Massacre. The Indians had been taken into two slaughterhouses, where they were beaten to death with wooden mallets. There were also clippings about county events and local news, such as new laws pertaining to loose pigs and marriage announcements. And there were receipts for farm products purchased and sold.

Next Mark turned to the journal itself. "Look at this for 1784. April 2, James Aaron Franklin born just past dawn. Agnes in labor half a day. Indian midwife, Little

Dove, assures me she is doing well. Little Dove says war drums sound as more Delaware tribes move east, pushed by British.

"May 5, heavy rain, pray for good crop. God willing, we will be eating corn till we grow tassels. Half dozen Delaware passed through and stopped for water. Agnes gave them bread and dried venison. One woman and baby with them.

"May 10, market trip to Huntingdon and baby baptism. Two birds, one stone, baby cried the whole way. Thank God we go only twice a year.

"May 20, Cousin George from Punxsutawney visited with his family. George said they are seeing Indian migration east up his way, too. Some are being pursued by the British and their allies, the Iroquois. Who knew one man could drink so much corn liquor? Who knew five children could make so much noise?"

"Nice to know one of our ancestors had a sense of humor," Abbie interrupted.

"Yeah, but he wasn't laughing here," Mark said, moving ahead several pages. "September 13, Iroquois on war path. Headed this way. We leave for the stockade at Fort Roberdeau."

"That's not all." She pointed to a later entry. "September 25. Returned today. House and crops burned to ground. Total massacre at Lenape village on Little Juniata. Retaliation for living peacefully alongside 'pale faces.' God help us!

"Christmas, living in small cabin, will rebuild house in spring. Money tight. Will survive."

They remained silent for a moment, picturing just how hard that time must have been.

"Then, here. Two years later." Mark skipped ahead

quite a few pages. "Explored the cave with neighbor Frank Willets and his boy Harry. Couldn't go in far, even with torches. Black as pitch. And spooky with all them bats. But found decomposed corpses, almost skeletons, of five males, two females, a boy child and a baby. All minus scalps. Must have been Lenapes hiding during that Iroquois attack two years past. We buried the bones on the hill above the cavern."

"Oh, how sad!" she said.

Mark just shook his head.

There were about twenty entries for each year. Mostly everyday things like harvest totals, three more babies born, family marriages, people who died. But in the last year, 1789, there was startling news. Mark read it aloud. "February 11. Great-Grandpa Franklin died up in Ohio. Left me and cousin Ellie each a thousand dollars. Where the old buzzard got that much money is a puzzle. He for certain never shared it with anyone whilst he was living, not even with Great-Grandma Abigail, who never had no help on that big farm of theirs. Maybe he got it way back when he prospected for gold as a youngun'. Maybe he stole it."

"If you read more, over the next few months you'll see Zeb debating with his wife Agnes whether they should take the money and move to Bellefonte, where they would be safe from Indians. In the end, Zeb convinced her to stay by promising to build her a fine brick house, which he did." Abbie waved a hand, with a smoking cigarette, of course, to indicate the very house they were in.

"And that was their downfall," Mark said. "November 2. Iroquois on war path again. I will not leave my house again, by damn. Three of the neighbors and their families are holed up with us in the house. I dare them savages to burn down my brick house."

"That was the last entry," Abbie pointed out. She pulled out an old history of Huntingdon County, which she had bookmarked to a certain page. "November 10, 1789. Homesteads from Alexandria to Warriors Mark were hit last week by bands of Iroquois moving west." She skimmed over some of the text, till she came to the part most important to them. "Three families in Spruce Creek were among those who died. Zebadiah and Agnes Franklin and their three children; Frank and Esther Willets and their two children; and John and Harriet Jacobs. One of the Franklin children, five-year-old James, survived after hiding in the forest during the raid. The Franklins' fine brick house still stands, but the interior was burned and vandalized by the savages. Governor Curtin promises more troops for the fort."

His grandmother was smiling like a Cheshire cat. There must have been something more, and she was dying to tell him.

"What?"

"Once I found the journal, I did a little more digging up in the attic and found a box of old letters that one of our ancestors, that five-year-old James who survived, wrote when he was about thirty-six years old." She removed several old newspaper clippings first. All of them dealt with a famous highwayman who was born in 1790 and died in a Bellefonte jail in 1820. David Lewis, better known as Robber Lewis or Davie Lewis. His exploits, all over central Pennsylvania, involved robbing from wealthy landowners and merchants to assist poor farmers. The interesting thing, though, was that Lewis died without disclosing exactly where he'd hidden his last treasure in gold.

"Many people believed that the money was stashed in Indian Caverns, but thus far no one ever found it. However, this James Franklin, in letters to a cousin in Ohio, thought the coins might be in the cave right here on the Franklin property. In fact, he mentioned a huge boulder having been pushed over the hole where the gold was hidden. Ironically, it was the same place where there was supposed to be cave pearls, or so the legend went."

"This is unbelievable, Gram. How come we never heard about this before?"

She shrugged. "James and his cousin urged secrecy in their letter."

"That's some secret."

"James Franklin tried to recover the treasure himself, to no avail, a year or so after Lewis died. See here: 'Black as pitch in that hellish hole. I almost killed myself getting up and down from the high ledge. Ladder broke halfway down. There's bat shit a foot deep in there.' Well, if you keep on reading, you'll see that James got very ill soon after from some mysterious illness. He believed the cavern was cursed and boarded it up. His descendants must have felt the same way, and that's why it was never opened up till your grandfather's days."

"He got sick from the bat droppings, I'll bet," Mark said. "Everyone knows today that breathing in guano dust can cause an illness with flulike symptoms that can be fatal if not treated."

"Probably."

"And you used to have me shoveling that shit. Shame on you, Gram."

"How was I to know it was dangerous? I just wanted bigger roses, for heaven's sake."

"So, all these years that people have been trying to find the treasure in Indian Caverns, it might very well have been here instead?"

"Yep."

Mark sat down with a sigh. "You really should do something with these documents, Gram."

"Like what? Give them to a museum or something?"

"Well, yes, but more than that. There's a lot of family and local history in these pages. Maybe you should write a book."

"Me? Cripes! I'm too old for that. Maybe *you* should write a book. And I'll tell you something else," she added before he could protest, "it's about time we did something to open that cavern up to the public. Other folks are makin' money off their caves. Why not us?"

"It would take a helluva lot of money to make Spruce Creek Cavern a tourist enterprise."

"If this Pearl Project is successful, we might just have that money."

Understanding suddenly bloomed in her grandson's eyes as he realized just why she'd shown him the old journal. "Ah, now I see. There's a chance there's a lot more than pearls in that cavern."

"Yep."

His shoulders slumped. "Gram, I'm not physically able to go after that hidden treasure."

"I know that, honey. But you can help."

"Does that mean you're willing to share with the Jinx team?"

"Ain't got no choice, the way I see it. That's where you come in. I want you to negotiate a fair split with

Jinx. I ain't willin' to give them half, but maybe a third. Start with ten percent and work from there."

"Why can't you—" he started to say.

"No! It's past time you started to carry your own weight around here. Besides, I'm going to be busy with other stuff."

Mark's eyes narrowed. "What other stuff?"

"Me and Louise are thinkin' about doin' an intervention."

He frowned. "Louise who?"

"Tante Lulu."

"Oh. What kind of intervention? Holy shit! Not for me, I hope."

"Everything in the world isn't about you, Mister Potty Mouth."

He looked suitably chastised. But then his eyes narrowed again. "Who, then?"

"Lily. We were thinkin' about goin' to The Red Zone and doin' an intervention for Lily. I've never been to one of those places before. Tante Lulu has, though. She's gonna show me the ropes."

Now he looked like he was going to have a heart attack. Either that, or he was about to strangle her. "You are *not* going to a strip joint."

"You're not the boss of me."

"I mean it."

"Will you go?"

"Where?"

"The Red Zone. After all, it's your fault she's turned to a sad life of boob barin' and hiney shakin'."

"Aaarrgh! Lily does not work at The Red Zone. She's a student at Penn State, studying to be an architect."

"Are you sure about that? Maybe she was so devastated by your jiltin' her that she quit school."

"Our breakup was mutually agreeable."

She snorted her opinion. "You know, if you burn your tail, you've just gotta sit on the blister."

"I think Tante Lulu is having a bad influence on you."

"What? I can't get ideas on my own?"

"Here's the deal, Gram. No Red Zone. No matchmaking. You stop bringing up Lily, and I'll help with the project. I'll even think about opening up Spruce Creek Cavern to the public."

She nodded. *I better hurry on over to Lily's apartment in Julian and warn her that Mark thinks she's a stripper. Oooh, boy!*

Up bat-shit creek without a paddle . . .

"Don't you laugh. Don't you dare laugh, or your pretty little ass is going to be sitting right down here in the bat shit with me."

Claire laughed anyway.

And wouldn't allow herself to relish the fact that Caleb thought her ass was pretty. Or little.

Caleb had slipped up to his calves in a pudding-like mixture of mud, bat guano, and slimy critters. His boots made sucking sounds as he lifted himself back onto the hard dirt path.

"It's barely noon, and already everything has gone to hell in a handbasket." Caleb threw his hands up in the air and stomped away, up the steps, through the corridor, flipping the bird to Sparky along the way. Outside, he yanked off his paper mask and waded into the stream, where he jiggled one foot, then the other, to remove the goop from his boots. He was wet to his thighs when he joined her up on the arched bridge overlooking Spruce Creek, about forty feet wide at this point.

Claire had just arrived in the cavern after spending several hours studying the Franklin journal. Even with the temporary lighting strung along the corridor of the cavern and down into the first chamber, there was a sensation of total blackness and silence. Otherworldly. Now, back outside, the sunlight blinded her, and the chatter of birds and the ripple of the stream seemed almost raucous.

"It's not that bad . . . your progress so far," Claire said. "In fact, all things considered, you should be very happy."

"How so?" He glanced at her, then leaned his elbows on the bridge rail. When he did, the muscles on his back bunched.

Good golly! The man was gorgeous. He wore a long-sleeved denim shirt tucked into jeans, which were tucked into heavy boots. His hard hat with carbide light was still on his head, same as hers, and work gloves hung from a back pocket. He hadn't shaved this morning, so there was a slight stubble of beard. All in all, he looked like one of those construction worker calendar models . . . the Diet Pepsi guy, but better.

She shook her head to clear it of her inappropriate thoughts. "That journal that Abbie and Mark showed us this morning ratchets this enterprise up another notch or two, I would think. Not only will you be making history here, but chances are there's more treasure to be found than the pearls. Even with a one-third cut, you could hit the mother lode of treasure hunts."

"Yeah, but this is no longer a simple project. We're going to have to build a walkway from the path through the mud and bat shit, over to the wall. Not an easy job when trying to avoid damage to those crystal stalagmites rising from the floor, or hitting our heads on the stalactites hanging from the ceiling. And snakes . . ." He shivered. "I must have flung a dozen of those buggers out of my way this morning."

"Sparky's kids, no doubt."

He pinched her arm for razzing him. "My luck that Sparky's a superstud. Anyhow, Famosa and Mark went into Tyrone to get some precut planks. We can get to work once they get back."

"Didn't you already know this about the cavern? I saw your maps last night."

"We knew the logistics, except Abbie and Mark have now decided that they might want to develop Spruce Creek Cavern as a tourist attraction, and that means minimal or no damage to the formations. They're demanding extra-special care. That's not the worst thing, though. That boulder has got to be chipped away, bit by bit, and the pieces removed carefully from the cavern. Again, to preserve the natural state. Which I can appreciate. LeDeux is trying to rent some tools from the archaeology department over at Juniata College so we can chip away at the boulder, granule by friggin' granule.

"And we need way more lighting and longer extension cords. And, by the way, you never mentioned that you'd been semi-engaged until recently."

"It appears that Adam has a big mouth," she said. The question was why. Why would Adam consider her personal relationships important enough to mention to Caleb? "When I was studying the maps last night, I pointed out some of the unusual rock formations to Adam. The only reason I know about that kind of technical data is that my friend Del Finley, a geologist from Penns Valley, has studied caverns in the region. We're just friends." Actually, she might have hinted to Adam, when he pressed her for a date, that she had something going with Del. But semi-engaged? She'd never used that term.

Was Adam goading Caleb?

Why would Caleb care?

"Friends with benefits?"

Whoa! "What gives you the right to ask that?"

"When you ask a guy for a sperm donation, that gives him rights. Why didn't you get Del to be your sperm donor?"

"I didn't want his sperm."

"Should I be flattered?"

"I'm thinking seriously about pushing you over this rail and into the creek."

His lips twitched with suppressed laughter. "Hey, I'm sorry. I was being an ass."

"Yes, you were." *The question is why?* "Del is a friend. Adam was yanking your chain."

"Oh, great! That makes me feel better."

"Del's a nice guy, though, and I don't rule out a connection in the future." She had to add that to get the last word in, even though it was a lie.

Unfortunately, the ass wasn't about to let that happen. "Just out of curiosity, how many men have you mentioned that ticking-clock business to?"

Just you. "Dozens."

He scowled at her.

And Claire was oddly pleased.

Caleb glanced around at the serene setting with absolutely no human activity taking place. He exhaled on a loud whoosh. "Holy hell, we're gonna be here a month at this rate."

The conversation they'd been engaged in the last ten minutes contained more words put together at one time by this usually taciturn man than usual, so she just let him keep talking. *Would a month here be so bad?* she wanted to ask, but she knew it would set off alarm bells in Caleb's already red-alert system where she was concerned.

"I heard John on the phone before he left. Sounded to me like he was making a date."

"Hah! No surprise there. LeDeux could work as a garbage collector and manage to attract chicks. In fact, Famosa came crawling into my room about two A.M. last night. Don't think that didn't give me the creeps. But he only wanted to sleep in the other bed. LeDeux brought some babe to the room he was sharing with Famosa. How could the kid have possibly hooked up so soon out here in the boondocks?" He paused. "I talk too much when I'm around you. Dammit."

"Do I fluster you?"

"Fluster? Now, there's a new word. Not my favorite F-word, but it'll do." He winked at her. "Yeah, you fluster me."

That wink went straight to unmentionable places in Claire's body.

She decided to get back to the subject at hand. "I can help with the walkway and with the rock. Mark could help, too, if we manage to get him up to the ledge, which I think would be a good idea, regardless."

"And why is that?"

"He needs to be needed."

"Says the shrink?"

"You don't have to be a psychiatrist to know Mark is hurting. This project could be a jump-start out of his depression. And developing the cavern into a tourist site would be a new career path for him."

"You've thought all this psychobabble through, huh?"

"Don't be sarcastic. Not everyone has to be a gloomy gus all the time."

"Gloomy gus?" He smiled, and Lord, his smile could make a nun melt. Reaching out, he used his fingertips to twine an errant strand of her hair behind her ear. "You shouldn't look at me like that."

She didn't need to ask what he meant, but she did press her lips together just to make sure her tongue wasn't hanging out. "And you shouldn't touch me."

"That was not touching, baby. Believe me, when I touch you, you'll know it."

"What a macho thing to say!"

"Ya think?" Raking the fingers of both hands through his short hair, he stared at her. "You know that we're going to end up in bed together, don't you?"

She shrugged. "Maybe."

He arched his eyebrows in question. When she remained silent, he said, "Please don't tell me you were serious about the baby making."

"I was serious, all right."

"And that would be your condition before letting me in?"

Letting him "in"? Ooooh, boy, I am in over my head. "I didn't say that."

His eyes raked her body. Slowly. And you would have thought she wore a bikini and not a long-sleeved PSU sweatshirt, jeans, and hiking boots. And a stupid hard hat scrooching her hair down. He was probably fixating on her freckles again.

"I'm good," he said.

I don't doubt that for one minute. Navy SEAL. Stamina and all that. But if he thinks he can disconcert me so easily, he's got another think coming. She laughed. "Hey, sailor, I'm pretty good myself."

That got his attention. She could tell by the slight tensing of his jaw and the flare of his nostrils. He was an expert at hiding his emotions, though.

He leaned his head down, inch by inch, giving her every opportunity to pull back. Instead of kissing her, though, he laved her lips with his tongue, then blew against the wetness.

Kiss me.

Still only a hairsbreadth away, he whispered against her mouth, "I want to lick you. All over. Till you beg."

"I don't beg," she rasped out. *Kiss me.*

"You will," he promised, swiping his thumb across her bottom lip.

Kiss me. Dammit!

Never actually touching her with his mouth or his hands, he moved his lips from side to side, over and over, almost but not quite kissing her.

It was the most infuriating, tantalizing thing he could do. And he knew it. *Kiss me, kiss me, kiss me.*

He was running a fingertip, light as a feather, along the curve of exposed skin from her chin to her collarbone, then back up. *Who knew I was so sensitive there?*

Claire couldn't let this man have the upper hand like this. "We'll see who's the one to beg first." With a grunt of disgust, she took him by the ears, tugged him closer, and kissed the bejesus out of him. Then she drew back slightly, nipped his bottom lip with her teeth, and swung around, walking away.

She thought she heard him moan.

Moaning was definitely the first step toward begging.

Unfortunately, his moan made her feel like begging.

Time flies when you're having fun . . .

By the end of day two of the project, they had chipped away fifty gallons of rock flakes and chunks. Speck by speck. Minute by minute. Still, half the boulder remained.

With the improvised pulley system they'd erected, those up on the ledge filled the metal buckets, which went down to those on the path, who carried the debris outside, where it was dumped into a sinkhole to be covered later with topsoil and grass seed. It was a painstaking procedure, but necessary to maintain the integrity of the cavern.

He glanced over at Claire and Mark, who were on the other side of the boulder, talking excitedly about the project as they worked. They'd managed to get Mark up here with their support on the rope ladder. He'd been reluctant at first, but once on the ledge, he was as excited as the rest of them. Claire had been right about involving Mark in the project.

"Pennsylvania Archives." "Oral histories, deed books, microfiche." "Family genealogy papers." "Pennsylvania Indian wars." "Juniata: River of Sorrows." These were snippets of their conversation that Caleb was able to glean. The two chatterboxes weren't even deterred by the paper respiratory masks Caleb had ordered everyone to wear against the bat guano. Nope, the two of them were planning a joint research project, possibly even a book, about the history of the cavern. Caleb had already photographed everything in sight from every possible angle. Claire recorded audio data on each step of their work, which would later be translated by voice transmission onto a laptop. Now all they needed was to find some treasure.

"What do you say we quit for the day?" he yelled down to Famosa and LeDeux, who were as sweaty and dirty as he was after all their carrying and dumping.

"Think we'll break through tomorrow?" LeDeux yelled back.

"We better. Meet us inside in an hour for a planning session."

Famosa and LeDeux headed out, waving up to him. From the distance he heard Famosa holler, "Hey, Peach. Sparky is hanging around here, as if he's just waiting for someone. I think he's got the hots for you."

They all knew by now the aversion he had to snakes, and they bled it for every ounce of humor. Not that he was laughing. *That snake is just achin' to be made into a pair of shoes.*

He stood and arched his back to work out the kinks. To his satisfaction, he noticed Claire noticing him. *Am I pathetic or what?* Well, after the way she'd kissed him yesterday, then tossed out that challenge about who would beg first, he'd been noticing her a lot, too. They were both acting pathetic.

It took Caleb and Claire a good half hour to help Mark down off the ledge and onto his shaky legs on the path. Caleb could have asked Famosa and LeDeux to stay and help, but he figured Mark was embarrassed enough. Caleb followed Claire and Mark along the corridor, turning off lights in their wake.

He took special delight in watching Claire's rear end in front of his face going up the steep steps. Till she glanced back and gave him a glower that pretty much said, "Stop looking at my ass." Which he totally ignored, of course.

When they got to the area of the cave where only sunshine crept inside a short distance, he noticed Sparky drop down off the ledge and stretch himself across the entrance, just daring him to get near.

"Get a life!" he said, jumping over the snake before it could take a bite out of him.

Mark and Claire were grinning at him when he got outside.

"Get a life!" he told them, too.

They were headed across the back lawn toward the house when an Amish horse and buggy pulled into the front parking lot. He didn't think it was Jonas, since he'd seen a pickup truck with a Peachey Landscaping logo on it last night. The Mennonites were more lenient than the Amish when it came to electricity and motor vehicles.

No, it was a young Amish woman alighting. She wore a long blue cape dress with a black apron, her blonde hair parted down the middle and all tucked severely under a mesh prayer cap with ties dangling, the black color denoting her single status. She was pretty in a plain sort of way. Coming closer, she smiled tentatively, as if unsure of her welcome.

"Hullo, Caleb."

He cocked his head to the side, still not able to place the woman, who was probably in her late teens. He kept walking with the curious Claire and Mark in tow.

"Caleb?" the girl said, coming up closer.

He nodded.

"Dontcha recognize me? I'm your sister Elizabeth."

Aaah. Now he saw the Peachey family features. The honey brown eyes, strong chin, straight nose, and unusual height. She must be five-eight, at least. "Lizzie?"

"*Jah!*" Her bottom lip began to quiver then, just like it had when she was two. "Can I come live with you?"

"Huh?" She launched herself at him, almost knocking him over. With her arms around his shoulders and her wet face in his neck, she proceeded to sob loudly and explain something to him. Reluctantly, he placed his arms around her, trying to calm her down.

All he could make out between her sobs was "Dat . . . *Ordnung* . . . *Rumspringa* . . . music . . . idol . . . marriage." *Ordnung* was the unwritten rules of the Amish for holy living. Then she ended with the usual teenage complaint, "My life is over. I gotta come live with you."

Patting her on the back, he closed his eyes and inhaled the scent of Ivory soap. Good Lord! How could he have remembered that scent after all these years? It had been one of Mam's few concessions to store-bought goods.

"Please, Caleb, ya gotta help me."

He was about to tell her that she couldn't move in with him because he didn't have a permanent home, just a one-bedroom apartment in Asbury Park, and besides, what did he know about raising teenage girls? He didn't even know her, ferchrissake. But the sound of a horse clop-clop-clopping on concrete could be heard from the highway.

And he knew . . . he just knew . . . his life was going to get way more screwed up.

Chapter
6

He was a chip off the ol' blockhead . . .

Claire knew she should scoot off and give Caleb some privacy, but she stood frozen, watching the amazing tableau unfold before her. Mark was equally stunned, but in his case, he was gawking at Caleb's sister Lizzie as if she was a *Playboy* centerfold.

The man who unfolded himself from the carriage had to be Caleb's father. He was just as tall, and despite the long gray beard, Amish clothing, and lean frame, there was a strong resemblance. Not surprisingly, they shared a dour expression.

An Amish woman emerged from the other side. Her attire was the same as Lizzie's, except her prayer cap was white. Caleb, who stood with his arm looped over Lizzie's shoulders, observed the woman with his heart in his eyes, and she did the same back at him. It must be his mother. A mother who hadn't seen or spoken to her son in almost twenty years.

"Mam," he said.

The woman glanced at her husband for approval.

He frowned.

So the woman stepped back with tears welling in her eyes.

Claire had never really known her mother and had no idea who her father was. She'd been in and out of foster care till her mother OD'd when she was eight and was placed permanently in foster care from then on. A problem child, she'd been dubbed. In other words, unadoptable. To someone who'd always yearned for a real family, this shunning practice was an abomination. How dare they squander the precious gift they'd been given? Family. The love of a parent for a child and vice versa was inviolate, in her opinion. Not to be tampered with by men or churches or cultural rules. Even the Lenape in their early primitive culture, which went back ten thousand years at least, recognized the value of family. She wanted to rush forward and knock some sense into their heads.

"Get in the buggy, Elizabeth," the elder Peachey ordered.

Lizzie's brown eyes darted to Caleb. "No. I don't wanna."

Mrs. Peachey whimpered.

Mr. Peachey stiffened.

"I sing good, Dat."

He made a clucking sound of disgust. "Such nonsense!"

"Why cantcha understand? I want a career. God wouldn't have given me the talent if he didn't want me ta be a singer."

"*Ach!* God wants ya to take yer vows and marry up

with a goot Amish boy. Ye career is ta have babies and take care of yer husband."

Caleb's gaze connected with Claire's.

Claire rolled her eyes and barely restrained herself from voicing an opinion.

"Get in the buggy, Elizabeth," her father repeated, more sternly this time.

"Hello, Dat." Wasn't that just like Caleb . . . to force the issue?

His father looked directly at him and deliberately looked away. No acknowledgment that Caleb had spoken. Claire noticed something about the old man, though. His face was flushed, even his neck and ears. His hands kept fisting and unfisting. He loved Caleb, and it pained him to treat his son so.

What a mess! Claire couldn't just stand by and do nothing. "Hi, everyone, I'm Doctor Claire Cassidy. I live up the road a ways. I believe I buy vegetables from your roadside stand sometimes. Your rhubarb jelly is out of this world."

Neither Mr. nor Mrs. Peachey acknowledged her introduction or friendly overture. Caleb appeared amused at her effort.

"Lizzie, why don't you come inside with me and have some lemonade? Mrs. Peachey, you come, too. We can talk. They can talk to me, can't they, Mr. Peachey, since I'm not being *shunned?*" She said that last word as if it was distasteful.

Caleb glanced at her with surprise. And relief.

"Mark, would you go see if your mother and Tante Lulu are up for company? As for you two," she said to Caleb and his father. "You two can just stand here and glare at each other till you go cross-eyed, for all I care. Men!"

She could swear she saw grins twitching at Lizzie and Mrs. Peachey's lips.

Caleb and his father interrupted their glaring at each other to glare at her.

Big whoop!

When Amish and Cajun collide . . .

Whoo-ee!

Tante Lulu was in her element. And yes, after all these years, Louise Rivard thought of herself as Tante Lulu.

Crowds of people to feed. Gumbo on the stove. Two of her Peachy Praline Cobbler Cakes in the oven. Lazy bread warming on the counter. Thunderbolts of love snapping all over the place. A war hero to be saved. An Amish family in need of healing. Weddings to plan. Treasure to be found. It was enough to make an old lady's juices come to life.

She wrung her hands with glee, then took the pitcher of lemonade over to the table and refilled the glasses sitting in front of Claire and the two Amish ladies, Rebekah and Lizzie Peachey, who were talking softly. Tante Lulu was fascinated by the peculiar clothing and language. Not that she was being judgmental; after all, she was from a culture that had suffered its share of ridicule over the years.

Mark was in the shower, following Tee-John and Adam, who were outside moving two picnic tables from

the streamside up to the lawn beside the patio, under
Abbie's supervision. Caleb was in the front of the
house, trying to out-glower his father.

Ever since Katrina hit southern Louisiana, Tante
Lulu had been depressed. She kept it from her family,
but sometimes she just needed to get away from all the
devastation.

From the minute that blasted hurricane had hit, she'd
worked dawn till dusk and continued for weeks, using
her *traiteur* skills to heal the injured unable to find hos-
pitals. And poor René! For years her great-nephew had
been one of those government lobbyists, fighting to save
the bayou and wetlands. He'd been predicting this catas-
trophe for years. Now he blamed himself for not having
tried harder.

Her cottage on Bayou Black hadn't suffered that
much, except for some lost shingles and one ancient
tupolo tree that toppled over. All the live-oak trees lost
their hanging moss for a long time. Of course, gators
and snakes by the dozens had to be chased out of her
house as the water level rose, but that was part of living
on the bayou.

The rest of the LeDeuxs had been similarly spared.
But friends and neighbors, especially those toward
Nawleans . . . Ah, it had been more than two years, but
they would never totally recover.

Tante Lulu needed a break, and that's why she'd
come to central Pennsylvania. Plus, that scamp Tee-
John needed some reining in now and then.

Pouring her own glass, she sat down. The three of
them hardly noticed her, so engrossed were they in
outtalking each other.

"It wonders me how ya can break yer Dat's heart like

this," Rebekah told her daughter. "He can't go through the heart pain he did with Caleb and Jonas again."

"It's not fair to play the guilt card, Rebekah," Claire offered.

"*Jah.* Why should I be responsible for what my brothers did? And I'm tellin' ya, Mam, I'm thinkin' Caleb and Jonas had the right idea."

"On the other hand, Lizzie, cutting family ties isn't the answer, either. Don't do anything rash."

Claire was trying to be logical in a situation that was pure emotion, in Tante Lulu's opinion. It was like trying to talk the crawfish into the boil pot by saying he'd enjoy the swim. Tante Lulu figured she would have to step in soon.

Rebekah put a hand to her heart in distress. "Ya gotta come home and stop this foolishness. It ain't right, ya runnin' off like this."

"You and Dat forced me ta take drastic measures," Lizzie said, throwing her hands in the air with exasperation. "Don't blame me."

Rebekah gasped.

"Ya wouldn't listen. I don't wanna take my vows. Not yet. And for sure and for certain, I ain't gonna marry Abram Zook."

"There ain't nothin' wrong with Abram, but if he don't suit ya, there's other fellas."

"It's more than that, Mam. I have an awful hankerin' to sing."

"Ya can sing at Sunday service."

"*Himmel!* Not that kind of music."

Rebekah's thin eyebrows rose as she regarded her daughter. "Ya haven't been listenin' to that devil music, have ya? Oh, ya wicked girl! What have ya done?"

"I like rock 'n' roll. I wanna try out for *American Idol*," Lizzie blurted out.

Tante Lulu choked on her lemonade, and Claire's jaw about dropped onto her chest. Now, this was something to perk up the old blood.

"An Amish girl on *American Idol?* Hmmm." Tante Lulu tapped her fingertips on the table. "That Simon Cowell guy would swallow a cow, thass fer sure. But wait a minute, this could be a great hook . . . an Amish rock star. I never had no family members in show business, though they do a good version of the Village People, and René does play in a zydeco band."

"Your family does a Village People show?" Claire's eyebrows rose with interest.

"*Oui!* Whenever the menfolk in my family finally gets their heads on straight after being thunderstruck with love, they usually need help in winnin' their wimmen."

"Oh, my God!" Claire murmured.

"Get awt!" Rebekah murmured.

"Exceptin' fer Remy. No Village People for him. Instead, he pretended to be Richard Gere from that movie *An Officer and a Gentleman*."

"Oh, my God!" Claire murmured again. Rebekah just looked confused. Lizzie was grinning.

"With my help and Tee-John's and, of course, St. Jude, this girl might just have a chance."

"What's idle American?" Rebekah wanted to know.

"It's a TV show," Claire said.

"No! Lizzie, ya can't be thinkin' of doin' ye singin' in front of Englishers."

"That's exactly what I'm thinkin'."

"Why can't ya be satisfied with the Sunday-night singin's?"

"It's not the same thing, Mam. So there's no sense ya tryin' ta talk me inta comin' home. Besides, I'm still in *Rumspringa.* I'm allowed my running around as long as I need it." The girl thrust her chin out in defiance.

"Your running around has gone on far too many years, daughter. Ya been pushin' it fe a long time."

"Okeydokey! Enough is enough!" Tante Lulu stood and braced her hands on the table. "Here's what we're gonna do. Claire, take Lizzie for a walk down by the bayou. Me and Rebekah need ta talk."

Once those two had left, Tante Lulu gave Rekekah her "look." The one that made her nephews cower. The one that pretty much said, "You are such a dumb cluck."

The woman didn't budge.

"Rebekah, *chère,* do ya love yer son Caleb?"

Rebekah stiffened with affront. "'Course I do."

"Then how in the name of St. Jude kin ya cut the boy off fer almos' twenty years?"

Tears welled in Rebekah's eyes. "Ya just don't understand our way. It was Caleb's choice. And Jonas's, too. They coulda stayed and repented. But they alveese was stubborn boys."

"Rebekah, Rebekah, Rebekah." She took the weeping woman's hands in hers. "I'm Cajun, and I'm Catholic. Thass my blood and allus will be; I wouldn't give up either. But family comes first, and I sure as shootin' would've found a way to get around that shunnin' business."

"You have no right to say that," Rebekah said. Then, "What way? My husband would never break the *Bann.*"

"Women has all the power, honey. We have ways ta

make men do what we want without them ever knowin' it weren't their idea ta begin with. Ya know what they say, ya kin make a gator do the polka iffen ya know how ta teach it the right moves."

"Huh?"

"Never mind. By the way, dontcha get hot wearin' all those clothes? It's only seventy today, but when it goes up to ninety, I imagine you feel like a vampire under a swelterin' Looz-ee-anna sun."

"Vam-vampire?" Rebekah stuttered as if she had invoked the devil. "*Jah,* it gets hot sometimes, but ya get used ta it. Besides, I'm outside most of the time, milkin' the cows, hangin' laundry, workin' in my garden."

Now it was Tante Lulu's turn to go boggle-eyed. "I ain't no wimmen's libber, but, sweetie, you are killin' yerself fer nothin'." She put up a hand to halt Rebekah's protests. "But that's neither here nor there. Far as I kin see, ya got two big problems here: Lizzie, and the shunnin' of yer two sons. Let's take care of Lizzie first. Is there any place she kin go fer a coolin'-off period? If we was back in Loo-zee-anna, I'd move her into my cottage on the bayou, but I'm stayin' here at Abbie's house, and I'm thinkin' ya doan want a young girl in a houseful of horny men."

Rebekah's eyebrows were going to freeze upward if she wasn't careful. "Definitely not. And no, there's no neutral place. Jonas's place is no goot 'cause of the shunnin'."

"Hmmm." Tante Lulu tapped her closed lips thoughtfully. "How 'bout she stays with Claire fer a few days? I could stay there, too, ta keep an eye on things."

"Oh, I don't know. You're makin' me *ferhoodled.*"

"Thass okay, honey. I gets *ferhoodled* myself sometimes." Tante Lulu patted Rebekah's arm. "Claire is some kinda doctor, and she's got a few years on Lizzie here. I'm thinkin' ya kin trust her not ta take yer girl honky-tonkin' or anythin'."

"Honking what?"

Tante Lulu had to smile. At some honky-tonks, there actually was a lot of honking goin' on, if you considered loud noise honking. Like Swampy's Tavern down on the bayou.

"How do ya know Claire would welcome my daughter . . . or you?"

Tante Lulu waved a hand dismissively. "I got St. Jude on my side. Now, about this shunnin' malarkey . . ."

Rebekah looked as if she'd like to put her face in her hands. "Do ya alveese meddle in other people's business?"

Tante Lulu smiled brightly. "*Oui!* It's what I do best."

Then there was light . . .

This was the day.

Caleb had just finished taking the latest set of photographs for the visual record of the project. And Claire had used a pocket tape recorder to note various aspects of the cave that would show up on those pictures.

The two of them leaned against the wall of the five-foot ledge, watching Mark use a claw hammer to make the last couple of hits that would finally open the new cave room, or whatever they would find on the other side. Everyone else stood on the pathway below, waiting with anticipation, including Abbie and Tante Lulu.

"It was nice of you to let Mark be the first one in," she said.

He shrugged. "The cavern belongs to his family. It was only right."

"It was still nice."

"Nice isn't the way I want you thinking of me."

"Oh?" She smiled.

The witch.

"What words would you prefer?"

Sexy.

"Sexy?"

Great! Now she's reading my mind. "That'll do. Hey, it was nice of you, too, to take my sister Lizzie and Tante Lulu into your home."

"Hah! I had no choice. Once that old lady gets an idea in her head, she's like Attila the Caj-Hun."

He smiled.

Her eyes went half-mast.

Uh-oh!

She gave him a sultry look.

Damn! She's up to something.

"Nice isn't how I want you thinking of me, either."

For a second, he couldn't speak over his thumping heart. "You don't like being called nice, huh? How about bad?"

"I can be bad."

Now another body part was thumping. *I stepped into that one. Like an Amishman in a pigpen on a hot summer day.*

"But I'll tell you one thing, I do deserve a medal. Tante Lulu has already taken over my life. One night and she's rearranged my kitchen cabinets '*the right way*,' she promised to take your sister clothes shopping 'at the Gap,' and she's planning my wedding menu 'Cajun style.' She even had the nerve to say I'm almost over the hill and I better get moving while I can still get up the hill. And have I checked lately to see if I have a dimpled butt like a golf ball? Then she gave me a set of St. Jude wind chimes."

Good old Tante Lulu! Doesn't mince words. But then he homed in on something she'd said. "What wedding?"

Claire rolled her eyes.

That was all the answer he needed. "Oh, no! No, no, no! I want to get laid, not laid out. Marriage is not on my radar screen."

Claire bristled. "What a jackass! I never said I wanted a wedding. I was just relating what Tante Lulu said. Jeesh! Talk about overreacting."

"Sorry." He closed his eyes and let out a loud exhale. When he opened his eyes, he put a hand on her arm. "I really am sorry. I was out of line. The problem is . . ." He gulped. "The problem is I have marriage issues."

She nodded, accepting his apology. Then tossed in the zinger. "Like that's a big secret. Honey, you have marriage issues because you have family issues." She went on then about Indians and men and commitment and family. On and on. Yada, yada. He wondered if she ever got bored by her own ramblings. "And that's really why you're scared of marriage," she concluded.

God spare me from opinionated women. Why can't I fall for dumb women who don't need to psychoanalyze me? He was about to argue with her, then stopped himself. "Maybe." He wasn't stupid enough to piss her off now and burn any bridges in the sex department.

"Tante Lulu also wants to teach me some sex exercises . . . stuff that makes grown men grovel."

Guess she was thinking about sex, too. Good sign. "Forget the old biddy. I can teach you sex moves that would make your eyes roll back in your head."

She shook her head at him as if he were hopeless. "How did we get on this subject? You must think I'm easy."

"Hah! I wish you were easy."

She studied him for a long moment. "It's been a long time since I met a guy as hot as you."

Me? Hot? Hot must be in the eye of the beholder. He laughed. "I am going to enjoy fucking you till you scream. And scream. And scream."

Instead of being offended and calling him a jackass again, she leaned closer and whispered, "I love it when you talk dirty to me."

What a woman! She didn't flinch or bend at all. Took it in the face and threw it right back at him. That was proven when she added, "Maybe I'm going to be the one fucking you, big boy. Until you scream. And scream. And scream."

"I can only hope."

"Yo, Peach! You two gonna do the deed right in front of us?" It was LeDeux yelling up at them. "My aunt is about to have a hot flash."

"I am not!" his aunt protested.

He glanced down, and Tante Lulu had binoculars, of all things, aimed at them. Today her hair was perfectly styled and bluish gray, maybe a wig. She had on some kind of spandex jumpsuit thing in an ungodly shade of puke green, with kid-size combat boots on her feet.

"Me, I'm gonna send for popcorn," LeDeux continued. "Ya want I should get you a cigarette, *cher?*"

"Wait till I go get the video camera." Now Famosa joined the peanut gallery.

And yep, his head had been lowered, and he'd been about to kiss Claire.

"Shush yerself, boy." Tante Lulu slapped her nephew on the arm. "Cain't ya see the thunderbolt workin'? Ya should never interfere with the thunderbolt. Or St. Jude."

"Is she for real?" Claire said under her breath. Her cheeks carried a nice blush. Now, that was interesting. They could use blue language with each other, and she wasn't fazed a bit. But spectators embarrassed her.

"I've got it!" Mark shouted. "I've got it! Un-be-freakin'-liev-able!"

Loose pebbles could be heard falling on the other side of the opening. It took a long time, but finally there was a splash.

Amid the cheers and high fives all around, Mark stood clumsily by bracing one hand on the wall. "You got the flashlight, Claire?"

She stepped forward, and the two of them leaned slightly into the opening, which was about five feet wide, four feet high, and three feet deep. Claire had the flashlight in one hand and her other arm around Mark's waist for balance.

"Unbelievable!" Mark said.

"Oh, my God! It's huge," Claire observed.

"That's what a guy likes to hear when he shucks his skivvies for the first time," he remarked in an undertone. Luckily, no one was paying any attention.

Mark picked up a small rock and dropped it into the hole. Caleb counted the seconds on his watch till he heard the splash of water, then did a quick mental calculation. "It's a twenty-foot drop to the water's surface. I wonder how deep the water is. We'll have to use a weighted tape measure."

"I have a good idea for another feature if you open this cavern up to tourists," Claire told Mark. "You know how they call regular pearls 'mermaid tears'? You could call the pearls taken from this cavern 'dragon tears', as in prehistoric cavern, dragon, fantasy world, that kind of thing."

Mark loved the idea.

Caleb did, too, and was only surprised that Claire hadn't pinned some Native American appellation on the pearls. It might still come.

Caleb was next at the opening when Mark stepped to the side, yelling down to those below just what he had seen, or not seen.

The chamber was utter blackness and still as death.

He and Claire lay on their bellies, with their feet still on the ledge. The carbide lamps on their hard hats did little to show what was on the other side of the gaping hole, but the high-powered flashlights let them see in a narrow, headlight sort of way.

Eerie stalactites, like grotesque monster fingers, rimmed the roof of the circular room down to a rough ledge formed of helictite formations. In this light, the pool was black as silk with no ripples.

"I'd say the room is about seventy feet in diameter." He would have a lot of observations to record once he got back to the house.

"Uh-huh. Look over there. Doesn't that look like an opening?"

Caleb was still side by side with Claire, so close he could feel her breath on his face when she spoke. "I'm not sure. It might be just a dark shadow. But right next to it . . . that pile of stuff. Could be bones, or maybe just shattered rock."

She sighed at the possibility. "And beside it. That wall, where it's smooth, it looks like drawings. Be still my heart!"

"Are you sure? Nah, it's too far away to be sure. It might just be discolorations in the rock from centuries of dripping moisture."

"I think it's drawings," she insisted.

Probably wishful thinking, but he kept his opinion to himself. "I figure this chamber must have been dry at one time, thousands of years ago, or at least only shallow water at the bottom."

"It would have had to be in order for the pearls to form. They have a nucleus, usually a grain of sand, same as oyster pearls, but unlike regular pearls, these don't need constant agitation or rotation to form. Just the slow, constant drip of water, which caves have in abundance."

"It's dank in here, but not rank like stagnant water. I'm thinking there might still be an underground stream."

"Maybe we should have a geologist check it out."

"Your semi-fiancé?" he asked, referring to Adam's joking about her once being semi-engaged to Del Finley.

"Get over it!"

He decided to drop that subject.

"This is so exciting. I feel as if I have adrenaline pumping through my veins warp speed. Is that how you feel every time you make a new discovery?"

"Yep." He winked at her. "You ever heard of adrenaline sex?"

"Is that all you ever think of?"

"Around you, yeah."

He could tell that pleased her.

Note to Caleb. Pursue the adrenaline sex later while the adrenaline's still pumping.

"Okay, first things first. We've got to get some light in here. Lots of it. I'm thinking maybe we could run cables all around the edges and loop them over the outcroppings."

"Caleb! How could you possibly manage that? This inner ledge is at most a foot wide in some places and almost nonexistent in others."

"This is what we do best. It'll be like mountain climbing, in a way. Famosa, LeDeux, and I have expertise in that arena. I remember one time when a buddy and I were hanging by a hair from a cliff in Afghanistan while the Taliban were running all over the place hunting for us, guns blazing. Believe me, fear gives a guy the strength to hold on."

Too much information, he realized instantly at the expression of horror on her face.

She shook her head to clear it . . . of the image of his ass being a hanging al-Qaeda target, no doubt. "I've mountain climbed, too, but that doesn't mean I'd dangle myself over a bottomless pool with God only knows what sticking up from the bottom."

He grinned and chucked her under the chin with his flashlight, which, framed by the darkness, illuminated her face and made her look ethereal and beautiful. Which he shouldn't be thinking about now. "Piece a cake!"

Mark and Claire went down below, and Famosa and LeDeux joined him up above with long loops of rappelling rope and lifelines with underwater lights attached at intervals. The three of them cased the situation and came up with a plan.

First they used a weighted measuring tape and determined that it was twenty-two feet to the top of the water, and the pool itself was roughly forty feet deep, not including any mud or silt on the bottom. With double tanks of oxygen, and a pony tank, a diver should be able to stay down there more than an hour. But they had a lot of work to do before they reached that stage of the operation.

Using a grapple gun, Caleb shot rope in one direction, then another, so that two arcs were cut on two sides of the circle, tips meeting in the opening. The ropes were more than secure but were intended to be guidelines with little or no weight on them. Whoever was climbing would have a strong rope attached to a back brace, as well, in case of an accidental fall.

Soon Caleb dangled over the side, arms holding on to the rappelling rope, bracing his taut legs against the walls as he crab-walked sideways slowly. With one hand holding on to the guideline, he used his other hand to hang the light cables off of protruding abutments. He and Famosa and LeDeux took turns over the next three hours setting out the light cables. This kind of prep work would save hours, maybe days of work later if they didn't have the cave illuminated properly.

It was four o'clock before they finished. The three of them were sitting on various narrow ledges around the chamber, lit so far only by their carbide lamps and flashlights. "Time to flick and see if we can rock 'n' roll. Hit the switch!" Caleb yelled to Mark, Claire, and Tante Lulu, who were peering through the hole.

"Turn her on," Mark yelled back to his grandmother, who was presumably back at the mouth of the cave, manning the electrical switch box.

The chamber was suddenly, magically illuminated, like the White House Christmas tree.

"Aaaaaah!" they all said.

It wasn't the best lighting in the world, but they were now able to see the exotic speleothems that lined the ceilings and sides. Like magical icicles, some of them were. Others were shaped like animals, even stars. And they weren't all white or crystal clear. Many of them appeared to be pink, all different shades of pink.

"I guess we know what this chamber will be called," Famosa mused. "The Pink Palace."

"Sounds good to me," Mark said.

Claire was wiggling her way farther through the hole, the Jinx camera in her hands, clicking like crazy.

"Be careful," Caleb warned her.

"Dontcha worry," Tante Lulu told him. "I gots a hold of her belt."

"Oh, that makes me feel better," he muttered.

"Tante Lulu, don't you dare come in here," LeDeux warned his aunt.

"'Course I ain't comin' in there. Do ya think I'm crazy?"

No one responded to that.

"I wonder if this pool could be drained." Mark's head, where it could be seen through the opening, was peering from right to left with excitement. "It would make another great chamber if we decide to make this a tourist attraction."

"Definitely," Famosa said. "We could have Claire's semi-fiancé come check for underground streams, maybe even join the team."

Not in my lifetime. He glanced over at Famosa and saw him grinning. *Am I that transparent?*

"We'll know better once we get down there," LeDeux remarked.

"Right," Caleb agreed. "Is it standing water? Is there an ingress and egress? What's the content of the water we want to pump out, and would it harm the outside environment? That kind of thing. Did you get the water samples, LeDeux?"

"Sure thing, boss."

The wily Cajun no more considered him his boss than he considered God a Yankee.

"When we dive tomorrow for the pearls, we've got to be really careful about stirring up the bottom," Famosa told him and LeDeux. "Visibility will be shit if we run a rake. So we should try to determine the pearl location before we attempt recovery."

They all agreed.

"What say we finish surveying this cavern, get all the measurements down pat, then go back and check on our diving gear?"

"Sounds good to me," Famosa said.

"Me, too," LeDeux said.

"There is one glaring thing we're all dancing around here," Caleb pointed out. "The outlaw's stash mentioned in those letters."

"I didn't want to say anything," Claire said from up above.

"Maybe it never was here, or more likely, it was recovered sometime in that last two hundred years," Famosa speculated.

"I think it's down in the water with the pearls," LeDeux said.

"Huh?" the rest of them said.

"Think about it. If it had been sitting on this inner ledge anywhere over the years, but especially during the Agnes flood, it would have been jarred off its perch. Anyhow, that's my theory, and I'm stickin' to it."

"I like John's theory." Claire and the Cajun exchanged smiles.

"It's a possibility," Caleb conceded. "Especially since I just noticed this." He pointed to a short length of half-rotted rope, attached to the sharp edge of a part of the ledge, two feet away from the hole. The ends of it, extending about three yards down, were frayed, as if it had broken long ago.

"Looks like something could have been hanging from that rope at one time and fell off." LeDeux said what they all were thinking. Maybe there really was a hidden outlaw's treasure.

"Yippee, I allus wanted ta find a pirate's treasure, like Jean Lafitte. This is almos' as good," Tante Lulu said.

"Hey, guys, this calls for a celebration," Mark announced. "The beer's on me at the Trout Tavern. Wednesdays are limbo night."

"Limbo?" he and Famosa and LeDeux exclaimed as one.

"Isn't that a little bit old fogey?" LeDeux wanted to know.

"Hey, you're in Spruce Creek, not Los Angeles." Mark laughed as he began to ease himself out of the hole.

"Besides, we don't have anything to celebrate . . . yet," Caleb told him.

"Hah! I think breaking through that freakin' boulder is enough cause for celebration."

"We haven't found the treasure yet. No cause for a victory celebration," he pointed out.

"A semivictory celebration, then." With those words, Mark's face disappeared.

Tante Lulu squirmed back, too, and the only one left was Claire.

"Are you going? To the tavern?" Caleb called to Claire, who was speaking into a small tape recorder in between taking pictures.

"What? Oh. Maybe. Yeah, I guess."

He smiled then, and he wasn't thinking about limbo music, or a boulder-breaking celebration. He was thinking cold beer.

And hot as hell, screaming, adrenaline sex.

Chapter
7

Line dancing: the ultimate dumb man
joke . . .

A gang of them entered the Trout Tavern later that
night to celebrate their semivictory.

The Pearl Project's routine wrap-up meeting of the
day lasted two hours because of the excitement and not-
so-routine details to be worked out for tomorrow's schedule. It should be a red letter day, if all went as planned.

Because there were eight of them—and possibly
more coming, according to Abbie—the waitress seated
them in a separate room. They could still see the band
and dance floor through the wide archway, but they
were removed enough from the blasting country music
and rowdy barroom conversation to be able to hear each
other talk. The band was playing a medley of Toby
Keith songs, including right now, "I Love This Bar," following on "Get Drunk and Be Somebody" and "How
Do You Like Me Now?" Many of the tavern patrons,
true-blue country fans, sang along with the band.

Lizzie sat on Caleb's right side and Tante Lulu on the other. Next to Tante Lulu was Abbie. Tante Lulu and Abbie had chosen—though only God knew why—to dress in similar outfits, but in different colors. Abbie wore white polyester pants with a red blouse, and Tante Lulu wore red pants with a white blouse.

Claire and LeDeux were opposite him, with Mark and Famosa at the ends.

"Don't you dare order an alcoholic beverage or take a sip from anyone's glass," he warned his sister. "By all rights, you shouldn't even be in an establishment that serves liquor, but Abbie promised the owner you would behave."

Lizzie raised her chin with affront. "Dontcha be givin' me lectures, Caleb. I know how ta behave." The saucy look she gave him implied that he, on the other hand, might not . . . know how to behave, that was.

Lizzie was wearing a little pink T-shirt that missed the waistband of her hip-hugging jeans by about three inches. No prayer cap for Lizzie tonight. Nope, she'd curled her blonde hair into a style that would better suit Jessica Simpson. And she was wearing makeup. Not a lot, but she had enough eyeliner on to make a randy raccoon get a hard-on. His father would have a stroke if he saw her. And blame him.

Oh, well. I'm already in deep shit with the old man. May as well go for broke.

"Thank ya for helpin' me, though. I just couldn't go back home. Not yet." She leaned over and kissed his cheek.

Perfume, too. Lord help me! "You should be with Jonas. His lifestyle is more like the Amish than mine."

"Jonas won't have me."

"Whaaat?"

"Oh, I'm welcome in his house and fer babysittin', but he lives too close to Dat and Mam. They'd be over there pesterin' him all the time ta send me home."

"You don't think they'll be on my tail, too?"

"They might, but I figure we'll be far away soon."

"Whoa, whoa, whoa. I never said you could come live with me. Hell, Lizzie, I don't even have a real home."

"Ya could get one. New York City would be nice. Or Los Angeles. Oooh, oooh, ooh, I know . . . Nashville."

Caleb's eyes about went cross-eyed at that prospect.

Lizzie started talking to LeDeux then. The Cajun was into all kinds of music, and Lizzie seemed to be knowledgeable about the modern artists he mentioned.

Caleb turned to Tante Lulu. "Did you have to buy her such suggestive clothes?"

"Huh? Who? Me? I doan know what yer talkin' 'bout. We dint get a chance ta go to the mall today. Those clothes are her doin'. If I was the one what gussied her up, she'd be wearin' brighter colors. And sequins."

"That's just great."

"I bin workin' on yer hope chest."

"Oh, God!"

She smacked him on the arm. "Dontcha be swearin'. St. Jude doan answer prayers fer swearin' folks."

"I'm not Catholic." *In fact, I'm not anything anymore.*

"Not to worry, hon. St. Jude is one of them ecumenical kinda saints. All ya gotta do is be hopeless."

Hopeless? That's me, all right. "How are you working on a hope chest when you're here helping Abbie at the B & B?"

"I gots a cell phone, boy. I ain't an old fuddy-duddy, ya know. I was a wimmin's libber afore Gloria Stain-ham was a gleam in her daddy's eye. Nope, I called the wood craftsman who makes the hope chests fer me and told him ta send two of 'em up here. One fer you and one fer yer brother. Actually, between you and me, I told him ta make one up fer Mark, too."

Caleb glanced down the table where Mark was nursing a beer, forlorn and miserable. He was the one who'd suggested this outing and seemed now to have regretted outing himself from his self-imposed isolation.

"Pssst. Kin I tell ya a secret?" Tante Lulu pulled him down so she could whisper in his ear. "Me and Abbie has a plan fer Mark. Wait till ya see what's gonna happen. Whoo-ee! I do love a surprise."

They both glanced at Mark then.

Mark noticed their scrutiny and squirmed uncomfortably to be the cause of their attention.

He should be uncomfortable.

Should I warn him?

Nah!

Turning back to Lizzie, he noticed that she was still engrossed in conversation with LeDeux. He flashed LeDeux one of those black looks, the kind that said "Touch my sister and you'll be minus a cock." In the past, he'd been the recipient of that same look whenever introduced to sisters of his fellow SEALs. Who knew he'd be doing it himself one day?

LeDeux noticed his glower and grinned.

Caleb thought about jumping over the table and wiping that grin off his face.

"John says he can help me with my singin'," Lizzie said to him. "He has a brother who plays in a band. Maybe we could move to Louisiana. I wanta be ready to try out fer *American Idol* next time they have auditions. Ain't that wonderful, Caleb?"

Caleb must have looked as poleaxed as he felt, because Claire reached across the table and squeezed his hand. "Don't worry, Caleb. Things have a way of working themselves out."

He didn't think so, but then he forgot about Lizzie. Watching Claire did that to him. She was dressed like a Lenape maiden. She gave new meaning to the term "Native American". Probably the first green-eyed, red-headed Lenape Indian in the world. The only thing missing was a feather sticking up out of a headband. Or a tomahawk. No wonder people called her crazy.

Her hair was pulled back off her face into a single long, thick braid, tied with a leather thong, leaving her neck bare, further exposed by a white blouse edged with some kind of weird embroidery, probably Indian. The blouse had an elastic neck—the kind that could be tugged off the shoulders if one were so inclined.

He was.

The whole business was tucked into a short buckskin skirt, fringed at the hem, that bared about two miles of finely sculpted legs. The skirt was cinched in at the waist with a thick woven belt, also Indian, no doubt. Moccasins adorned her bare feet.

The ensemble was what Frogman, one of his old SEAL buddies, used to eloquently call a "fuck me" outfit, which was not to be confused with hooker or slut clothes. When a dozen or so guys were out on a special op, with only themselves for company for a week and more, they tended to talk about crap like that. Of course, a "fuck me" outfit was in the eye of the beholder. While he considered Claire's attire hot, hot, hot, some other guy might prefer, oh, let's say, Jessica Simpson in a pair of Daisy Dukes.

Frogman also had a theory called the Trifacta Factor, which essentially said that all men had three things they homed in on women, usually tits, ass, and mouth—Froggie's exact words—but there were also men who went for hair or feet, of all things, even belly buttons—innies or outies—eyes, knees, voice, personality. In his taste, it was breasts, legs, and the small of a woman's back. And man oh man, Claire had his Trifacta Factor in spades.

If that wasn't bad enough, a set of bigass feather earrings dangled from her ears. They looked like gobs of fly-fishing lures, except he was the one being lured because of the interesting fantasies he was having about what he'd like to do with those feathers—and it wasn't catch fish.

"Caleb. You're staring," Claire hissed at him.

"You bet your ass I am." He winked at her.

Her face pinkened just a little bit, but he noticed that the flush spread over her neck and down to her chest. The lady was as turned on by him as he was by her.

He had a pretty good idea where this game between the two of them was headed. He wondered if she did, too. Or was it just a game to her? Like that ticking-clock/sperm-donation remark of hers was probably just intended to ward him off. Hah! He wasn't that easily intimidated.

She returned his gaze for a long moment. But then their food orders arrived, and they all dug in. Barbecued ribs. Hot wings. French fries. Coleslaw. Warm French bread.

It was a lesson in erotica just watching Claire eat a rib. First she licked off the sauce, up one side and down the other. Nibbled off the meat. Then sucked on the bone.

He glanced down at his crotch, then over at her.

Claire watched Caleb watching her.

She knew exactly what she was doing, turning him on. A part of her brain had gone on meltdown the first time she'd seen him, and she'd been behaving like a wanton teenager ever since. There was no explanation, other than the fact that he attracted her. A lot. And yeah, she would like to have a baby someday, while she was still able, but this chemistry thing had gone way beyond that. At the moment, she'd take him any way she could get him. Even a one-night stand had growing appeal, and Claire did not do casual sex.

Until now.

No, I wouldn't do that.

Well, maybe.

"You're talkin' to yerself, *chère,*" John said in her ear.

She saw Caleb's nostrils flare at John's close proximity. It was the only betrayal of his emotions before he took another draw on his bottle of beer. So of course, Claire reciprocated by whispering in John's ear, "Be careful. Caleb looks as if he wants to castrate you."

John chuckled and whispered back, "The guy's got the hots fer you."

"Really? You think so?" she whispered back.

They both laughed then.

Adam, on her other side, asked, "What's the joke?"

"No joke. John is just trying to annoy Caleb."

Adam smiled with understanding. "My favorite thing." He put an arm around Claire's shoulder and squeezed. "Save the first slow dance for me, baby," he said, loud enough for Caleb to hear.

Caleb made a low growling sound before standing and stomping off to the men's room.

"Oh, my God! You didn't!" Mark's exclamation surprised everyone. He was standing, his one hand braced on the table as he glared at his grandmother, then pivoted to glare at a young woman approaching their table. She wore a sky blue spaghetti-strap sundress, and her long black hair hung to her butt. About five-three, and thin, she was pretty . . . and staring at Mark with her heart in her sky blue eyes.

"Hi, Mrs. Franklin. Hi, Mark."

"Lily, what the hell are you doing here?" Mark snarled out, leaning forward over the table.

Lily flinched, about to burst into tears.

"Stop being a horse's hind end," Abbie told her grandson and waved for Lily to sit down next to her, across from Mark.

Ah, this must be the ex-girlfriend, the one Mark ditched once he got home from Afghanistan.

Mark sat back down.

Abbie ordered a screwdriver, heavy on the orange juice, for Lily, without asking. Presumably, Lily was older than she looked, of legal age to drink.

Mark gave serious attention to his beer.

"I'm Louise Rivard, but ya can call me Tante Lulu, like ever'one else," the Cajun lady introduced herself. "So, how's the strippin' bizness these days?"

Claire about choked on her own screwdriver.

Lily raised her chin haughtily and said, "Just fine."

"What a crock! You're no more a stripper than I'm a . . . gymnast." Mark gave Lily a condescending once-over, which even Claire found offensive.

"Hey, I used to be a stripper," John said to Lily, speaking around Claire and Famosa. "Maybe we can trade dance moves."

"You was only a stripper fer two weeks, till I dragged ya out of that casino," Tante Lulu reminded him.

"Sure," Lily replied to John. "Can you shimmy?"

"Can I shimmy? Oh, baby!" John said. "They practically named the bump 'n' grind after me."

"Back off, butthead," Mark told John.

"You ever heard of dog in the manger, man? You know, you don't want her, but you don't want anyone else to have her?"

"Shush!" Tante Lulu told her grandson. "Yer messin' things up."

"What things?"

"Shush!"

Claire gaped at John. A stripper? "I thought you were about to be a cop."

"I am."

"Cain't a cop be a former stripper?" Tante Lulu asked, as if Claire were dense.

"You are not a stripper, Lily. No way!" Mark was back to addressing Lily.

"How would you know, Mark? You haven't talked to me in nine months. I could be dead for all you know."

Mark propped his elbow on the table and put his chin in his palm, staring at Lily. Instead of laying into her, he now gazed at her with such sadness. "You know why, Lily."

"No, I don't know why. And if you didn't want me, then why shouldn't I take off my clothes and see if some other man would like me?"

Mark closed his eyes for a second, then said, "I never said I didn't want you."

"Yes. Yes, you did."

"Well, I didn't mean it."

"How was I to know that? And I heard that you think I don't have the body to be a stripper."

Mark turned to his grandmother. "Blabbermouth!"

His grandmother made a face at him.

"Is she really a stripper?" Claire leaned around Adam and asked Abbie in an undertone.

"Pfff! Lily's a college student. This is just a plan me and Tante Lulu dreamed up."

"Well, I can tell you, there are men out there who like me just fine," Lily continued.

"How could you, Lily? Do you like having frat guys jerk off while you show them your ass?"

Tears began to stream down Lily's face.

"Sonofabitch!" Mark stood abruptly and walked around the table. Taking Lily by the arm, he dragged her away from the table and through the archway. At first he seemed to be yelling at her, but suddenly Lily put her arms around his neck. He hesitated, as if shocked, then put his one arm around her waist, drawing her closer. They slow danced, her face pressed against his chest, his mouth against the top of her head as the band wailed out Garth Brooks's "Last Dance." They both kept their eyes closed.

Everyone was all teary-eyed, watching.

Except Caleb, who'd just returned to the table. After hitting the head, he'd tap-danced for a half hour at the bar in an impromptu interview with a reporter for the *Huntingdon News* who'd gotten wind of the treasure hunt. Publicity was the last thing he needed at this stage. People converging on the site would not help matters along at all. So he'd employed an old SEAL tactic, evade and escape.

"What the hell's going on? You all look like you're attending a funeral," he remarked, sitting down next to Claire in LeDeux's empty seat. The Cajun Casanova and his sister were out on the dance floor. LeDeux was an incredible dancer. Caleb had seen him in action before. But Lizzie wasn't shabby, either. Where she'd learned to dance like that, he had no idea. Not at any Amish gathering, that was for sure. "Tears?" He reached out a forefinger and swiped at the wetness on the edge of Claire's eyelashes. Abbie and Tante Lulu were in similar shape.

Claire pointed to Mark, who was slow dancing with a woman. In fact, the two of them were just swaying from side to side, holding on to each other for dear life.

"Lily?"

She nodded.

"Good."

She arched her eyebrows at him.

"He's made the first step to getting his life back by participating in the project. Connecting with his girl can't hurt the recovery."

"You an expert on love as an antidote for depression?" she teased.

He didn't joke about this kind of thing. "I've been around plenty of military men who've come back from war less than they were when they left, physically and emotionally. PTSD is the least of their troubles. It's hard, but they need to regain normalcy."

"You think that's what it is with Mark. Posttraumatic stress disorder?"

He shrugged. "I'm glad he's thinking about making the cavern a business venture."

"Me, too." Claire gave him a flirty sideways glance. Little did she know there was no need for her to flirt with him. He was already hooked and ready for the frying pan. "Do you want to dance?"

He shook his head slowly. "I don't dance." Then he

gave in to the temptation to pull her braid over her shoulder, and he brushed the end strands over his own lips. Like the finest sable artist's brush.

She seemed mesmerized by the movement of her hair over his lips. Not surprisingly, her voice was low and sultry when she asked, "Not ever?"

"Hardly ever."

Concentrating on her lips now, he used her own hair like a lip brush, outlining the edges, filling in the fullness of her top lip, across the parted bottom lip. If her lips were as erotically sensitive as his, she was getting turned on big-time. At least he hoped so.

He tugged her closer by yanking on the braid. Almost against her mouth, he asked, "Are you ready to beg me?"

She laughed and her breath was as erotic as the braid had been. "To dance?"

"Hardly." He nipped her bottom lip with his teeth.

He was about to kiss her when someone tapped on his shoulder. *No, no, no! Not now! Go away!*

The tapping persisted, now accompanied by, "Yoo-hoo!"

He and Claire turned as one to see Tante Lulu watching them closely.

"What?" he snapped.

"Hey, don't get yer jockeys in a twist jist 'cause ya were up to some hanky-panky."

"What?" Claire asked in a gentler voice.

"I was just wonderin' if you two want CC or CP or PC."

"Huh?" they both said.

"The monogram on yer hankies and pillowcases and doilies and such. You know. Claire and Caleb, CC. Cassidy and Peachey, CP. Or Peachey and Cassidy, PC."

"You are not monogramming anything for me, old lady," Caleb insisted, no longer in the mood for kissing. Well, he would still be in the mood, once the dingbat from down South left the scene.

"That is so sweet," Claire said.

He gave her a dirty look.

"But no, thank you," she added.

"Ain't up to you two. It's all in the hands of St. Jude now." With that ominous news she was off to the dance floor, where the band leader had just announced that line dancing was about to begin, starting with "Achy Breaky Heart." They even had an instructor to teach them the dirty slide, honky-tonk stomp, slap leather, tush push, pivot, and electric slide.

"Do you want to line dance?" Claire asked.

"Only when you put my feet to the fire, pull out my nose hairs one at a time, and lasso my balls."

"I take that to be no."

"That would be a 'Hell, no!'"

"Come on, you guys," Famosa said. He had just come from the bar and had his arm around the waist of a really hot twentysomething woman with Angelina Jolie lips and tight jeans. "This should be fun."

Caleb shook his head at the stupidity of what some men would do to impress a woman. Line dancing . . . good God almighty! He would rather do a HALO drop over freakin' Iraq.

"Yeah, it does sound like fun," Claire said, standing.

His eyes went wide at that, and, yeah, he felt a little hurt that she would rather make a fool of herself on the dance floor than stay with him and make sparks off each other.

But then she leaned down and whispered in his ear,

"I need to put some space between us before I go up in flames." With those words, she danced off.

And he thought, *No, no, no, no, no! You should stay. Flames are good.*

To make up or break up, that is the question . . .

Mark inhaled deeply, savoring the scent of Lily's lemon-scented hair and he wished . . . Oh, hell, he wished he could push back the hands of time.

He had one arm—his only arm—around Lily's waist. She had both of her arms looped around his neck. If he closed his eyes, he could pretend it was two years ago, and he had two arms and a life.

"Mark—" she started to say.

"Shhhh. No talk," he said against her ear. He would have to walk away from her in a minute, but not just yet.

The band was playing that Rascal Flatts song "I Melt," and, yep, that was just how he felt. He'd known Lily since they went to junior high together. They'd both been virgins the first time they made love, after the senior prom. He didn't know about her, and he didn't want to know, but she was the only woman he'd ever been with. How pitiful was that? If she was stripping . . . and he could hardly believe that was possible . . . maybe she'd been with lots of other men by now.

But back then, before the disaster that had become his life, she'd dreamed of being an architect. He'd dreamed of being a carpenter/craftsman, after his military stint. They would open their own home renovation business. In fact, there was a place they already had in mind, an abandoned church that would make a unique home. So much for dreams!

He started to push away from her, but she held on tight. For such a skinny little thing, she was strong.

"Don't," she ordered. "Don't even think about walking away from me now."

"It's over, Lily. How many times do I have to tell you that? I'm going home."

With his one hand, he peeled her off him and headed for the door.

She followed after him. "I'll drive you."

He agreed, but only because he wanted to put some closure on Lily's hopes for him. They were never gonna happen.

They were silent on the ride back home, but once they came to a stop, he said, "Good night, Lily. Have a nice life, honey. You deserve it."

"No! I'll tell you what I deserve," she said, pressing the lock button for the doors.

He had to grin. "What? You gonna take me captive?"

"If I have to."

"All right, say what you have to say, then leave me alone. I mean it."

She winced.

"So, are you really stripping at The Red Zone?"

"Not yet."

"What the hell does that mean?"

"It means that I am desperate enough to do anything to get you back."

"Have you lost your mind? Where's the logic in that? Why would your stripping make me do anything?"

"I'm hoping that you still love me and you'll come to

your senses before I offer myself to other men, so to speak."

"There are ways of hooking up with men without flashing your ass."

"But none so dramatic."

"I'm not the person I was two years ago, Lily."

"Neither am I."

"I have no job, no job prospects, no job skills. In other words, no future. I can't go into a renovation business with you now, Lily, but you can do it with someone else. Or by yourself. Don't give up your dreams for me. You don't want to hook up with a loser."

"You're not a loser. In fact, you are the most honest, courageous—"

"Yeah, yeah, yeah, I've heard it all before. 'Stop pitying yourself. Get a prosthesis. Take career training. Go to college. Enter the handicapped olympics, for chrissake!' Like that's going to happen!"

"You lost an arm, Mark. Not two arms. Not a leg. Not your eyesight or your voice. Not your penis."

"Oh, my God! Lily Hudson saying *penis* out loud. Hope the sky doesn't fall down." He was laughing at her, which he could tell she didn't appreciate.

"I'm not wearing any panties," she said.

"Whaaat?"

"Tante Lulu gave me some advice."

"That dingbat told you to go out in public with your bare ass waving in the wind, and you listened to her?"

She didn't answer. Instead, she pressed the button that automatically slid the front seats back. Before he could blink, she swung one leg over both of his and straddled his lap. She bunched her dress up to her waist, and yep, she wasn't wearing any underwear. Then she wiggled herself on his lap and smiled. His eyes about rolled up into his head at the sheer one-hundred-proof pleasure.

"I'd say a part of you likes me just fine."

He gritted his teeth. "Stop it, Lily. This isn't fair."

"Fair has gotten me nowhere during the past year. Time to pull out all the punches, according to Tante Lulu." She held his eyes then as she lowered first one strap, then the other of her sundress, letting it drop and pool at her waist. Then she took his one hand and laid it on her right breast.

She moaned.

He moaned, too. "I surrender," he said as she unzipped his pants and took him into her hand, steering him into her body.

Surrender was never so sweet.

"But it's only for tonight," he told her before drawing her mouth down to his.

"We'll see," she whispered against his mouth. "I was introduced to this guy recently, and . . ."

How could she talk and screw his brains out at the same time? And especially how could she talk about another guy? Through a haze of searing-hot arousal, he asked, "What guy?"

"St. Jude."

Chapter
8

How low can you go? . . .

Claire was having a great time. Between line dancing and oyster shooters—a high-octane bourbon drink that John had introduced to them all on learning that the tavern had a shipment of fresh oysters back in its kitchen—and now a limbo contest, she was flying high.

Caleb sat at the table most of the time, just watching them all. He'd stuck to beer, which meant he was only slightly wasted, compared to the rest of them.

The limbo contest had been going on for a half hour now. In the beginning, almost everyone had participated, including Abbie and Tante Lulu, who was surprisingly limber considering her age. Her explanation: "I does jumping jacks every morning and takes juju tea every night." Which, of course, prompted everyone to grill her on where to get some of that juju tea.

But the field was narrowed down now to only two dancers. John and Denise, the pretty woman who had been dancing with Adam. She was a massage therapist from Tyrone, which of course prompted much rolling of eyes among the men. Amid cheers and laughter and the band playing the "Limbo Rock," made famous by Chubby Checker, two of the waitresses began moving the pole a few inches lower.

"That's two feet, folks. Twenty-four inches. If they make this pass, they tie with the record here at the Trout Tavern," the band leader announced. "Let's give John and Denise a big hand and see if they can set a new record. Winner gets a Trout Tavern T-shirt and a free tab for the rest of the evening."

Denise hit the pole and was eliminated . . . though she'd given quite a show, with her breasts almost popping out of her tank top when she arched her body. About three dozen men lined up to ask her to dance after the contest, or to set up "massage" appointments. Adam seemed particularly pleased with himself for having found her first.

John played the crowd a bit, drumming up bets on whether he would succeed at the next level. Now that the pole was reset, the band encouraged the crowd to chant, "How low can he go? How low can he go? How low can he go?"

He worked his body slowly till it was almost parallel to the floor from knees to head. And he made it. The roof was practically raised with all the cheering when the band leader announced, "Are we about to have a new record holder? Yahoo! Meet John LeDeux, who hails from good ol' Loo-zee-anna. Hey, John, do you suppose you could get me a T-shirt like the one I saw there last year when we participated in a hurricane relief concert? It said, 'Katrina: Best blow job I ever got!'"

The crowd howled with laughter. John raised a thumb and forefinger to form an A-OK circle.

The pole was moved to twenty-three inches, and after another oyster shooter "for stamina," he assumed the position again. This time he hit the pole.

"That's okay, John. Good job! We have a tie for the record now at twenty-four inches. Anyone else want to give it a try at twenty-three inches? Are we gonna let a Southern rebel outdo us Yankees? Come on, you wusses!"

Claire noticed Caleb leaning against the archway between the anteroom and the dance floor, a longneck bottle of beer dangling from one hand. She walked over, unsteadily, and he looped an arm over her shoulder.

"Are you guys done with the silliness?" he asked.

"That's what's known as fun, Mister Stoneface."

"I have a different definition of fun."

She could guess what that would be. "John was close to making it under that last pole. He's really good."

"You think? This isn't horseshoes. Closeies don't count."

"Think you could do any better?"

"Maybe."

"Oh, ho! Easy for you to say when you're standing here as a spectator."

He shrugged.

"Seriously. Do you think you could do better?"

He shrugged again. "With the right incentive."

"And that would be?"

He winked at her.

"Have you ever done the limbo before?"

"Nope."

She decided to call his bluff. "I'll bet you can't do any better."

"And just what do you bet, sweetheart?"

"What would you like?"

He studied her, hotly, especially the edge of her blouse. In fact, he slipped a forefinger into the front, pulled out, then let it snap back. "A kiss."

"A kiss? That's all?" She'd been expecting that he would ask for more. Lots more.

"Honey, there are all kinds of kisses. A kiss can be a nip or a slow exploration. It can spark arousal, be the beginning of foreplay, or be a complete experience in itself."

"Oh. My. God."

He offered her a sudden, arresting smile. "What I would like, if I win, is a really good kiss. Long and wet."

She gulped. How could her mouth be so dry after all she had drunk? "You're on, big boy."

He grinned, as if he'd just suckered her into something.

"Are you sure you've never done the limbo?"

"Never." Taking a long draw on his bottle of beer, he handed it to her and proceeded to walk out onto the dance floor.

"Whoa, whoa, whoa, folks! We have a new contender." The band launched into the "Limbo Rock" again. Meanwhile, John went up and whispered something into the band leader's ears. "Uh-oh! We've got an ex–Navy SEAL here. Caleb Peachey. God bless the USA."

There was much patriotic clapping for that.

Caleb glared at John.

John made a face back at him.

While the crowd began yelling, "Caleb, Caleb, Caleb . . . ," the band sang, a refrain urging Caleb to be nimble and quick, before going under the limbo stick.

When Caleb stood a few feet away from the pole, he glanced over at Claire. Then he studied the pole from several angles, almost like golfers did when setting up a shot. Slowly, he began bending his knees and arching his back, moving his feet at a snail's pace toward the barrier, all in a sort of rhythm to the song. What a body! He was the poster boy for physical fitness.

But, holy moly! It was amazing that any human could contort his body in such a way without falling. Incredible strength, balance, and patience were the key, of course. Still, everyone marveled at the feat Caleb was accomplishing.

And he passed under, clearing the pole, setting a new record at twenty-three inches.

Thundering applause, cheers, and a rebel yell from John followed Caleb as he walked back to Claire. He said nothing but waggled his eyebrows at her, then took the longneck out of her hand, raised it, and drank thirstily, setting down the empty bottle on a nearby table.

Every hair on Claire's body was standing at attention as she watched him.

Then he leaned against the wall next to her, ignoring the crowd, which was shouting for more.

"You're not going to try any lower?"

He shook his head.

"Could you go lower?"

He remained silent.

"Ah, come on, Caleb. You can't really go any lower. Can you?"

He grinned. "Wanna bet?"

"You know, I used to think you were a grim ol' scrooge, but you've been doing a lot more grinning lately."

"That's because I want to get laid."

She should have been insulted at his bluntness, but she just shook her head at him. "What incentive do you need to try again? And getting laid is not on the table."

He pretended to be pondering her question. "The kiss . . . I know, the kiss should take place topless."

Oh, my goodness! "Who would be topless? Me or you?"

Once again, he pretended to ponder her question. "Both."

The picture in her head would probably be cemented there for all time. "And if you lose, what do I get?"

"All your freakin' paperwork completed before noon tomorrow."

She really didn't think he could manage twenty-two inches. She wasn't sure anyone ever had. "Okay."

He sauntered out to the middle of the dance floor. The bar had already been lowered, the band was playing "Limbo Rock," and the crowd was singing, "How low can you go?"

Caleb demonstrated another feat of extreme physical fitness by clearing the pole again. The crowd went wild. Tante Lulu was standing on a table, cheering. The Jinx team members had formed a sort of cheerleading squad, led by John, shouting, "Caleb! Caleb! Caleb!"

A waiter handed Caleb a cold beer as he walked back to her. The man wasn't even breathing hard.

"You lied to me, Caleb. You've done the limbo before, haven't you?"

"No, but we had barbed-wire exercises on the O-course that make limbo dancing kid sport. And believe me, that paperwork of yours was the barbed wire I was imagining on my way under."

While he took a draw on his longneck, he eyed her with amusement, ignoring the crowd's shouts for more.

"You're quitting?"

"Yeah. No reason to make more a fool of myself than

I already have." Another drink of beer. "Unless I had a powerful reason to try once more."

"Like?"

"Hmmmm. Like maybe that topless kiss takes place horizontally."

Claire just knew that if she found herself topless, lying down with this man's lips on hers, more than kissing would take place. Was she ready to commit to that? She shook her head. "I'm folding."

"That's okay, baby. I still consider myself the winner."

Watch out, Carrie Underwood, here comes Lizzie . . .

Everything was going according to Tante Lulu's plan.

Until Lizzie got up on the bandstand, with encouragement from that rascal nephew of hers, and began to belt out the rowdy song "Redneck Woman," with the band accompanying her. That was when all hell broke loose.

Caleb was on the other side of the room, making goo-goo eyes with Claire. So at first, he didn't realize it was his Amish sister singing and gyrating her hips. In fact, Tee-John was up there with her, gyrating his hips, too. Tante Lulu was gonna smack that boy's hiney when she got a hold of him.

When the song ended, the band leader said, "That was just great. Give a big hand to the next American Idol. This little gal will be tryin' out this fall. And now, how about another song? Another Gretchen Wilson song, 'When You Think about Cheatin'.' Good choice, Lizzie."

Caleb drew his head up slowly and pivoted at the

mention of his sister's name. His jaw slackened as he noticed her up on the bandstand. "Noooo!" he roared, rushing toward the stage.

It took Adam, John, and two bouncers to hold him back.

At the same time, the front door of the tavern opened and in walked Caleb's twin brother, Jonas, clearly embarrassed to be inside a saloon. People were gawking at him and at the spectacle Caleb was putting on. Meanwhile, Lizzie continued to sing.

When Jonas realized that it was his sister singing, and that she was dressed in English clothing, not as a Plain person, he roared, "Noooo!" just like his brother and made for the stage.

Two waiters kept Jonas from jumping up on the stage. And wasn't that a sight! Him in his Amish britches and straw hat and short beard!

Tante Lulu exchanged looks with Abbie, and the two of them headed toward all the commotion. Claire was already there, trying to calm Caleb down. Mark and Lily had left a short time earlier. Together. Praise the Lord! And St. Jude! Famosa and the massage lady had left together, too. Tante Lulu could guess what they were doing. Hanky-panky with a twist.

"Are you crazy, Caleb? All she's doing is singing," Claire said.

"All she's doing is singing," he mimicked, "*in a bar,* surrounded by booze, dressed like some kind of mall rat, with horny guys drooling over her. My mother trusted me to take care of her. Dat predicted I would lead her into sinful ways."

"Singing is not sinful," Claire argued.

"It is when it's in an ungodly house of liquor," Jonas

added. "What were ya thinkin', Caleb, ta bring a young girl inta this place of sin? Yer *dummkopf* all right, touched in the head just like Claire said."

"I said that?" Claire frowned with puzzlement.

"This is not a place of sin. What century are you two lunkheads livin' in? Besides, does ya think I'd be here if sinnin' was goin' on?" Tante Lulu asked, full of indignation.

No one answered her.

"And she had all of us as chaperones," Abbie added.

No one answered her, either.

Just then, a tall woman walked up. She must have been close to six feet tall, and all of her curves were poured into a pair of white jeans, a tight red shirt that said 'I'm a nurse, Wanna play doctor?' and red leather cowboy boots. Tante Lulu's kind of girl! "That gal's jeans fit tighter'n a bride's behind," she remarked aloud, cocking her head to the side for a better view.

Abbie looked askance at Tante Lulu. Her new friend wasn't used to her ways yet. Jonas's face was so heated up he might have been havin' a stroke. Caleb just shook his head at Tante Lulu as if she was a hopeless cause, which she wasn't. How could she be with St. Jude on her side?

The blonde bombshell, who resembled her niece Charmaine, was tapping on Jonas's shoulder.

That amazing fact caused all the commotion concerning Lizzie to die down as everyone turned to see what the woman wanted.

Jonas glanced over his shoulder, then did a double take. "Wha-what?"

"Wanna dance, sugar?"

Jonas turned all the way around to see if she was talking to someone behind him.

She wasn't.

Tante Lulu slapped her leg with glee, and Abbie smiled from ear to ear. This was turning into one of the best nights she'd had in years. And Abbie probably didn't get out much, either. Not that Tante Lulu didn't get out. It was just that people—her nephews in particular—treated her like she was fragile glass just because she was eightysomething. That's what the young folks called it today. Twentysomething. Thirtysomething. Eightysomething.

The woman took hold of Jonas's hand and pulled him into the center of the dance floor. Lizzie had left the bandstand and hightailed it for the restroom. Smart girl! The band was now playing a slow dance, that old Elvis ballad "Love Me Tender."

Jonas seemed to be arguing with the woman, who just smiled and put her arms around his neck, yanking him closer. He pulled her arms off his shoulders, but she just moved them to his butt. The expression on Jonas's face was priceless. Like someone had goosed him, when all the woman had done was cup his sweet cheeks. Maybe Amish women didn't pinch their hubbies' hind ends. Too bad!

Meanwhile, the woman was swaying from side to side against him while Jonas stood stock still.

Even Caleb was smiling now.

Two old codgers—seventysomethings, at least, and twins to boot—came up to her and Abbie.

"Hi, I'm Amos," one of them introduced himself.

"And I'm Andy," the other said, "We're farmers from Pine Grove Mills. Do you gals wanna dance?"

Abbie was poleaxed by the prospect.

Tante Lulu jumped at the chance.

While the two pairs were walking to the dance floor, Tante Lulu checked out their butts. They had none to speak of. At first she was disappointed, but then she had to admit she'd lost her own butt about 1982. The men were short, but that didn't matter, and even if these gents' hair was pure white, there was lots of it, sort of like Bill Clinton, who was a hottie, for sure. What was it they said about men with snow on the roof?

Yep, life was looking good. Thunderbolts a-flashing. Family problems to be solved. And boyfriends for her and Abbie.

Whoo-ee!

Paybacks can be hell . . . or heaven . . .

Life was not looking so good for Caleb.

Fifteen minutes ago, he'd been flying high. Well on his way down the fast track to hot, sweaty, screaming sex.

But then he'd noticed his sister on the stage of a barroom belting out some raunchy song about redneck women. His plan was to get Lizzie out of here ASAP before anyone of the Plain persuasion heard about this abomination, and yes, that's what the Amish would consider Lizzie's performance. But Lizzie had disappeared into the ladies' room.

If that wasn't bad enough, his brother had shown up and been hit on by some barroom tart and was now sitting at a table, waiting for Caleb to clean up the mess. The tart hadn't given up. She was sitting at the table with him, enthralled. Jonas didn't have it in him to be impolite to a lady. As a result, Caleb wouldn't be surprised if the babe showed up at Jonas's home one of these days. That should give the neighboring elders something to talk about for the next, oh, let's say decade.

Tante Lulu and Abbie had discovered senior citizen stud muffins and didn't want to go home yet. In fact, Tante Lulu came up to him now and asked, "Ya got any of those little blue pills on ya?"

"Hell, no!"

"No need ta get snippy. Aintcha ever had a noodle instead of a cannoli?"

He put his face in his hands. When he glanced up, Tante Lulu was gone and Claire was in his face. He liked that better.

"Caleb, be gentle with Lizzie. She's afraid to come out of the ladies' room."

"Why? What does she think I'm going to do?"

"Send her back home."

"Oh, well, that's not a bad idea."

"She didn't think she was doing anything wrong."

Claire was talking logically. That meant her alcohol buzz must be wearing off.

Damn!

"It's my fault anyway, *cher*," LeDeux said, plopping down into a chair next to him. "She wouldn't have gone up on that stage if I hadn't encouraged her."

"Can I send *you* home?"

LeDeux ignored his jibe. "Holy crawfish! Is that my aunt dirty dancing with that old fogey? Who knew she had a bootie to shake like that?"

"She and Abbie hooked up with those two farmer

dudes. I think they're planning a double date for next Saturday. Isn't that cool?" Claire remarked.

"Yeah," LeDeux answered.

"No," Caleb said.

"Maybe I should ask what his intentions are." LeDeux flashed a big ol' grin.

"I heard your aunt tell those guys about The Red Zone. Do you think she would actually go to a strip joint?"

LeDeux leaned back in his chair, still grinning. "Did I ever tell you about the time she and Charmaine entered a belly dancing competition? Guess who won?"

I've landed in a zoo.

"Back to Lizzie. She's talented, Caleb. Really talented," Claire told him. "Did you hear her?"

"No, I was too busy trying to keep the flames from shooting out my ears." Actually, he did hear part of that cheatin' song, and while he didn't know jack shit about music, he could tell she was pretty good.

"You should give her a chance," LeDeux said.

"You should mind your own business."

"You know what they say down on the bayou, *mon cher.*"

Oh, God! Another half-assed Cajun saying!

"Crawfish gotta stick together when the fishing nets come."

"What the hell does that mean?"

"Friends stick together. Your business is my business."

"I'm your friend, too." Claire put a hand on his arm.

He looked at her hand, then he looked at her flushed face, and then he looked at that teaser of a blouse. "Friend, my ass!"

Plain speaking . . .

Jonas finally extricated himself from his newfound woman friend. He would have much to confess at the next meeting of the Mennonite deacons.

Laura Jones, a nurse at Huntingdon Hospital, had latched on to him like a bear on a honey pot. She was tall, blonde, and buxom, and, *jah,* he had noticed her body. Even Amishmen, and Mennonites, appreciated a good bosom.

The woman had invited him to have dinner with her on Saturday night. Jonas had been *ferhoodled* at that; Plain women did not make overtures to their men; though, truth to tell, he had been flattered. When he'd politely declined, she'd asked if he was afraid of her. More like she should be afraid of him. Those red boots of hers had planted some mighty indecent ideas in his head. And he had not been with a woman in seven years. *Tsk-tsk-tsk!* He was a grown man with three children. He should not be thinking about red boots and bosoms. Leastways, that's what he told himself.

He made his way toward Caleb and sat down with a sigh of disgust.

Claire and the Cajun fella left to give them some privacy. Caleb watched as they began dancing, bending their bodies sinuously to the rhythm of the music. Indecent, really, though he hated making judgments. Hard to believe, with all that had happened, that the tavern was still crowded, the band playing, everything going on as usual.

"So, how'd you lose your girlfriend?" Caleb asked him.

Girlfriend? Oh. He must be teasing. I hope no one

saw me gawking at her bosom. Suddenly, he recalled a time when he and Caleb were nine years old, and they'd been fascinated by Mrs. Fisher's massive breasts. Especially after they'd come across her in the barn one day after Meeting and saw her husband rubbing his hands over those breasts. Old Mr. Fisher had been grinnin' like crazy.

"I tol' her I left my horse outside, untended," he answered.

"Did you?"

"I don't have a horse, Caleb." *If you'd stuck around all these years, you would know that, brother.*

Caleb laughed.

"It's not funny." *Well,* jah, *it is, but it's best not to encourage you. Ah, Caleb, how did we get so far apart? How could you have left like that? How could we have let you leave?*

"Oh, yes, it is funny, big brother. When was the last time you got some?"

"Some what?" Oh, good Lord! He must mean *that.* "For shame, Caleb!"

"Are you really my brother?"

"*Jah,* I am."

"When was the last time you got laid?"

"Shush! You shouldna talk 'bout things like . . . that."

"Like sex?" Caleb's eyes twinkled with merriment. This was the old Caleb, the one he had missed so awful much. Not the grim, overserious fella he'd witnessed since their reunion.

"This will prob'ly amuse ya, but I have only ever been with one woman, my wife, since I got married."

Caleb's eyes went wide, eyes that he knew mirrored his own. "The wife who died seven years ago?"

He nodded.

Caleb howled with laughter. "You must give new meaning to blue balls."

Jonas was unaccustomed to such coarse talk, but not really offended. This was his brother. They should be able to say anything to each other. "I alveese intended ta remarry."

"And?"

"I never found anyone I liked enough, I guess."

"Same here."

"I saw ya makin' eyes with Claire. 'Pears ta me ya like her well enough."

"Yeah, I'm liking her a little too much."

"And that is a bad thing?"

"Marriage and family and all that . . . I gave up thoughts of that a long time ago. And believe me, Claire isn't into casual sex. We only met two days ago, but already she wants to have my baby, for chrissake!"

Jonas's jaw dropped. "She told you that?"

"Oh, yeah."

"Why aren't marriage and family for you?"

"Because losing family is too hard. I won't risk that. Not again."

Jonas understood. Being cut off from family was a horrible thing. Like cutting off an arm or a leg . . . or cutting out the heart.

"So, what are you doing here?" Caleb asked.

Jonas flinched. He shouldn't need a reason for seeking out his brother. "I came ta warn you."

"About what?"

"The church elders held a council tonight led by Bishop Lapp. About you."

"Me? What did I do? It's too early for them to know

about Lizzie. And son of a gun, that jackass Lapp is still around?"

"Ya shouldn't speak of a church man thataway, Caleb."

"Even a jackass churchman?"

"*Jah*," Jonas said, a smile twitching at his lips. Bishop Lapp was hard to take sometimes. "Anyways, it's not what ya did but what they think you're gonna do."

"Spit it out, Jonas."

"They think you've got the devil in ya and that you've returned here to spread evil among the People. They think the work you're doing with the cavern is Satan's work, that you're engaged in some kinda rituals in there. The teenagers are talkin' 'bout you, in an admiring way, and they fear more of the young ones will leave for the English world."

"Why would they admire me?"

Jonas's heart ached to hear his brother doubt his own worth. "Because ya left and didn't come back with your tail between your legs. Most folks do, ya know. They admire your bravery."

"Bullshit!"

Jonas winced at his language. "I admire you."

Caleb made a pff-ing sound of disbelief.

"I wanted to leave, same as you, when the shunnin' started, but I didn't have the courage like you did. It's hard being raised in such a close-knit community, where family is everything, ta suddenly find yourself alone in a strange world."

"Tell me about it. I lived in a homeless shelter for three weeks." His brow creased. "Where did you go when you first left?"

"I hid in the barn of some English folks over near

Belleville for a week, eatin' berries and nuts. I wanted to find ya, but I had no idea where to start, and ya had already been gone two months by then." Even today, Jonas remembered vividly how lost he'd felt. Alone in the world.

"Ah, Jonas!" His brother squeezed his hand.

"It's hard for the English to understand how good and strong family is in the Amish community, and how bereft one can be without it. All they see is inbreeding, which we never had."

Caleb agreed. "Some people think the Amish are like a cult. That their people have been brainwashed from a young age to accept the beliefs. Mind control."

"Maybe some are, but family ties are one of the goot things about the Amish. I give them that. And stern as he was at times, Dat was a goot father . . . before the shunnings."

They both nodded.

"Remember when Dat usta take us fly fishing?" Jonas asked.

"I do. Those were good days, weren't they?"

"Anyways, you should know, Dat defended you tonight."

"What?"

Jonas could see Caleb reel with shock. He was still reeling himself.

"Dat defied the elders, said the only thing you was guilty of was leavin' the community and even then, you was falsely accused. He said that instead of condemning you, Bishop Lapp should be makin' every effort to bring ya back inta the fold."

"No way!"

"*Jah*. He defended me, too. Said they was too harsh

with both of us." Jonas was thirty-four years old, but he'd had tears in his eyes tonight, just like one of his children when they was over-sad.

"Are you going back?"

"No!" For sure, Dat's defying the elders had touched Jonas. Being touched was one thing. Being touched in the head was quite another. There had been too much water under the dam.

"Who told you all this?"

"Mam." And what a shock and wonder it was to see her walking into his house after all these years.

"She defied the *Ordnung* and talked to you?"

"*Jah.* Amazin', ain't it?" His mother had been bawling as much as talking. He'd felt like bawling himself.

Caleb shook his head with disbelief. "Why did you need to tell me all this tonight?"

"Because Mam fears the rigid ones might do somethin' to harm ya." *Warn Caleb,* Mam had said. *They's mighty angry.*

"Huh? These are nonviolent people."

"In the name of God, people does crazy things. Jist be careful, that's what Mam wanted me ta tell ya."

"What a mess we've made of things! Well, not you. You found a way to stay Plain, and you married and had kids. Me? I'm still screwed up."

"I don't think so. I'm thinkin' ya landed where ya were supposed to."

"That's debatable."

"I been thinkin' on what ya said yesterday, Caleb, about me bein' a pacifist and you servin' in the military. I'm thinkin' maybe it's easier ta be goot and noble when ya never been tested, like us Amish and Mennonites. I'm thinkin' it's wrong ta judge."

"There was a philosopher, John Milton, who talked about something called cloistered virtue. He said it's easy to be good when you're cut off from the world, but the real virtue comes when you live in the world, are tested, and still remain good. Not that I'm claiming to be good."

Jonas grinned. His brother might not realize it, but he was good of heart, and that was the most important thing.

"Enough of that. What're we gonna to do about Lizzie?"

"I think she should come home with me tonight. Just till things settle down. That way, if word gets back to the community that Lizzie was here, I can try to explain."

"Good idea! It's called damage control," Caleb told him.

"*Jah*. I agree." Now if only heartbreak control could be so easy.

Chapter
9

Parting was never such sweet sorrow . . .

After Jonas and Lizzie left, with Caleb promising to meet them both tomorrow to iron things out, Caleb scanned the bar and realized that he, LeDeux, and Claire were the only ones of the gang left. He walked over to where the two of them were dancing. "I'd say it's time we hit the road. What do you say?"

"Yeah," Claire agreed.

"I'm gonna stick around a while longer," LeDeux said, eyeing a pretty brown-haired girl on the other side of the room with a Brass Balls Saloon T-shirt and a come-and-get-me smile.

After paying his tab, he and Claire headed out to the parking lot. He walked Claire to her car.

"It was fun tonight," Claire said. "Thanks."

This must be one of those fun-is-in-the-eyes-of-the-beholder kind of things. To him it had seemed like a goat fuck. Except for Claire's promise of a kiss . . . a topless kiss.

"What are you smiling about?"

"My winnings."

"Oh. The kiss?"

"The *topless* kiss."

"Do you want it now?"

"Here, in a parking lot? Hardly! Nah, I can wait. Too bad Tante Lulu and Lizzie are sleeping at your place . . . well, Tante Lulu tonight."

She didn't disagree with him, which he took for a good sign. Must mean she would have invited him home if she were alone.

"It's gonna be a big day tomorrow." He brushed his lips lightly over hers. No way was he going to do more than that. Otherwise he'd be jumping her in the backseat of her station wagon like an oversexed teenager. As compared to an oversexed adult male.

"Hopefully we'll uncover the pearls by day's end. And maybe even the outlaw's loot, as well." She brushed her lips across his, too.

"See you early, then."

"If I get there by six, can I run with you?"

He grinned. "Think you can keep up with me?"

She grinned back, not missing the innuendo. "Baby, the question is, can you keep up with me?"

Reluctantly, he let her go.

Well, hallelujah . . . finally! . . .

He was back at the B & B. The house was quiet, everyone in bed. In the kitchen, he was pouring himself a glass of ice water when he heard a rustle behind him.

It was Tante Lulu in a flowered muumuu, or whatever the hell you called those loose Hawaiian-style gowns, her hair in pink foam rollers, a bunch of gunk on her face, and Donald Duck slippers on her feet. What a sight!

"Damn! You scared me."

"I forgot ta take my blood-pressure pill," she said, coming up next to him and taking a prescription bottle off the counter. "And I had lots of cause to raise my blood pressure tonight, if ya know what I mean."

He did, and it wasn't something he wanted to discuss.

"Did ya see my friend Amos tonight?"

He nodded.

"I've allus had the hots fer Richard Simmons, and he looks jist like Richard Simmons, dontcha think?"

Huh? In what world? He decided no answer was the best answer, especially when he was trying to avoid thinking of this octogenarian having the hots. Not a pretty picture.

"Yer hope chest should arrive tomorrow, iffen ya was worried about that."

He wasn't, but thank God for the change of subject. "That's great."

"Ya been prayin' to St. Jude?"

"Not lately."

"Ya should, honey. He kin help ya."

He was about to tell her that he didn't need any help. But then he realized that maybe he did. "Thanks."

After the old lady went to bed, he stood in the kitchen, staring out the window. A sudden thought occurred to him. He felt like knocking himself upside the head for his stupidity.

Tante Lulu was here. He didn't know why, but she wasn't sleeping at Claire's tonight. And neither was Lizzie.

Maybe St. Jude was watching out for him, after all.

It was a merry Christmas in July . . .

Nude, except for a pair of silk panties, in her bathroom, and still slightly buzzed, Claire leaned against the sink and loosened her braid, then finger combed her hair, about to tie it into a high ponytail before entering the shower. As tired as she was, she hated to go to bed with the barroom smell that permeated her skin . . . cigarette smoke and stale beer.

But then she heard Boney start barking, the five cats meowing, the caged crow with the broken wing squawking, and the caged porcupine squeaking, followed by a knock on the back door.

She'd never been skittish about living alone, but she knew to be careful, with her home being so close to a public road. Pulling a nightshirt over her head, she picked up a fireplace iron and her cordless phone, preset to 911, as she made her way through the dark living room and kitchen.

It took her only a second to make out the large shape on her deck, framed through her sliding glass door. It was Caleb. She opened the door.

"I thought you went back to Abbie's."

He arched an eyebrow at the poker and the phone. "Which were you planning to hit me with?"

"Both," she said.

He surveyed her disheveled hair and short nightshirt that proclaimed "Make Me Purr" under the picture of a grinning calico cat. She thought she heard him murmur, "Gladly."

Meanwhile, Boney was yipping and nipping at his ankles, and the five cats, including Priscella, who could very well be dropping her kittens tonight, were arching their backs and rubbing against his pants legs. He was standing in a puddle of pets. Luckily, the crow and porcupine had settled down. Without comment, he picked up Boney and walked away. The five cats followed him in a single file. Soon, he had them all locked in her small laundry room, indignantly yipping and meowing with displeasure.

On return, he just leaned against the wall, arms folded, watching her with a slight smile on his lips. No words were necessary. The man had plans.

Flustered, which was a novelty for her, she blurted out, "I was about to take a shower. My clothes and my hair smell like smoke and beer. Why don't you sit down? I think there's still some coffee in the pot."

He sniffed his T-shirt. "Me, too."

"What?"

"I need to take a shower, too."

Okaay. He probably didn't mean that the way it sounded. She pointed to the coffeemaker.

He shook his head. "I don't want any coffee."

No need for her to ask him what he did want. It was clear in his smoldering eyes. In fact, he already had his shirt over his head and tossed it to the floor. Then he toed off his shoes and socks, leaving him in a pair of low-hung jeans, and that was all.

She was about to protest his being barefoot, which

had not been a concession in their agreement, but she knew how silly she would sound and that she would be revealing just how sexy she considered his big, high-arched feet. "Whoa! What's going on here?" *Is that really my voice, sounding so squeaky?*

"I'm here to collect my debt."

I like his short hair. How odd! I never liked short hair before. Especially military short. Must be hormones. Or oyster shooters.

"Did you hear me, Claire?" His lips twitched with amusement. "I'm here to collect my debt."

"What debt? Oh, the kiss." *Holy moly! Look at his body! Is he on steroids, or an exercise fanatic? Maybe it's just good genes. Amish hunk genes? Ha, ha, ha! But wait. He wants to kiss me. Now. With what have to be the most kissable lips I've ever seen.*

He gave said lips a quick lick of his tongue, as if he knew what she'd been thinking.

There was a lurching at the jointure of her thighs. *How embarrassing!*

"The *topless* kiss."

More lurching. "This really isn't a good time." *If you come within a foot of me now, I'll probably knock you down and have my way with you.* "As I said, I'm about to take a shower." *Could I sound any more lame? And good Lord, is that really a bulge in his jeans? Yes, it is. I'm not looking. Whoo-boy, I am not looking.*

"I'm game."

"Huh?"

He grinned.

The lout knew exactly what effect he was having on her. "I'm game for a shower."

"I never said anything about the kiss taking place in

a shower." *That is just great. Plant an idea like that in my hormone-overloaded brain.*

"Agreements can always be amended." He batted his eyelashes at her innocently.

Claire suspected she'd been set up, bigtime. *But frankly, Rhett, I can't seem to give a damn.* "I need a shower . . . a cold shower . . . before the kiss," she muttered and made her way to the bathroom.

"Bad idea," he said, getting to the door ahead of her. Then, in true Rhett Butler style, he picked her up and carried her back to the living room. Easing himself down into a low, armless rocking chair, he arranged her so that she straddled his lap, her bare feet on the floor.

"This feels like Christmas," he said in a low, silky voice.

"How so?" Her voice was low, too, but raspy with a hair-trigger arousal caused by the crotch of her panties being aligned just so with the ridge of his erection. For a second, she saw stars behind her closed lids.

Claire was no kid. She'd been around the block. She knew what was what. But dammit, every second she'd been around Caleb the past two days had felt like foreplay. She was more than ready.

"What does Christmas have to do with this?" She wiggled on his lap, adjusting herself, to show what she referred to. And yeah, to assert a little control of the situation.

His groan was her reward. "The best part is unwrapping a present," he explained, lifting the hem of her T-shirt. He raised it over her head and tossed it to the floor.

He smiled then, showing just how much he liked his "present," and flicked one of her feather earrings.

And that old adage "It is better to give than to receive" was proved true when he began to rock. And rock. And rock.

Without ever actually touching her, he caused her to climax against him, arching her back, spreading her legs wider. Keening, for heaven's sake!

"Oh, baby," he murmured as he pulled her closer.

And the kiss hadn't even begun.

Who knew begging could be so sweet? . . .

Caleb was so hard he could barely breathe, and it felt hot-damn painfully fantastic.

She had come for him. While he watched. Without his ever actually touching her. How amazing was that?

"I'm not embarrassed by what just happened," she said.

Huh? Did I say you were? Why should you be? "Neither am I."

They gazed at each other, waiting. Even the waiting was arousing.

Claire's auburn hair was a wild, wonderful mess, spread down her back and over her creamy-smooth bare shoulders. Her lips were parted with arousal. Glancing lower, he feasted on full, pink-tipped breasts that seemed larger than they were because of her slim frame. Narrow waist, slightly flaring hips, and long, long legs.

"I'm not perfect," she said under his scrutiny.

"Neither am I."

Both of them had a few years on them. Small, not un-attractive, lines bracketed her eyes and lips, mirroring his own. Her breasts were firm, but not as high as they once were, he suspected. Who the hell cared?

"Don't get hung up on age or body issues," he advised. "You make me breathless, and most twenty-year-olds can't do that to me anymore."

He could tell she liked his words.

Still studying her, he noted her freckles. Not too many, but enough that he recalled his earlier fantasy about connecting the dots. He wondered idly if she had any washable markers. No, no, no. A soft artist's brush and melted chocolate would do better.

"Why are you smiling?" she asked.

Because maybe . . . just maybe . . . I'm about to get lucky. "Your freckles."

"You think my freckles are funny?"

"No. I think they're erogenous zones, and I'm smiling because of what I'd like to do with those freckles."

"I have fantasies, too."

Hallelujah! I've landed in hottie heaven! "Oh?"

She pointed at his chain tattoo.

He frowned, unable to imagine what she could do with that tattoo, but then shrugged. He liked surprises as much as the next guy. Sexual surprises, that was.

"We should probably talk."

No, no, no! Talk was a buzzkill to sex, Caleb knew from past experience. A bucket of ice water on a raging erection. Women always wanted to discuss things to death, most of it boiling down to the question "What are you thinking?" And she wouldn't like it one damn bit if he told her that his thinking at the moment was centered not on what her tongue had to say but on what he'd like her tongue to do. "No, Claire, we should definitely not talk."

"I don't want you to think I'm trying to trap you into anything."

"Do I look trapped?"

"No, you look so hot I feel like the luckiest girl alive."

Oh, man! "Right answer, honey."

Before she had a chance to say another word, he tugged her closer and moved his chest from side to side, abrading her breasts. He watched as her nipples grew under his friction. She was watching, too. But then she closed her eyes and made a small whimpering sound of pleasure. And it was now she, with her hands on her knees and her neck arched back, who was caressing him with her breasts.

He might have whimpered, too.

Placing one arm around her waist and a hand behind her nape, under her hair, he slowly, very slowly, savored the thrill of lowering his mouth inch by inch to her mouth. At first he just shaped his mouth to hers. She must have brushed her teeth, because she tasted like mint. And sex.

But then he kissed her with all the pent-up hunger that had been building for what seemed like a lifetime. This woman, this crazy woman, was turning him inside out, and he didn't know why. That didn't mean he wasn't going to savor the gift that was Claire, sitting on his lap, with her tongue in his mouth, making little mewling sounds that about drove *him* crazy.

Then he did the most surprising, and embarrassing, thing. Without warning, he shot his rocks off in his pants. Holy hell! He hadn't done that since he was a teenager, thinking about Mrs. Fisher and her massive breasts that defied gravity.

Claire didn't seem to have noticed, deep kissing him as she was. Even when he arched himself against her and let loose with a long, drawn-out groan against her lips.

Enough! He stood suddenly, taking her with him so that she was forced to wrap her legs around his hips for balance. "Are we really going to stop this thing with a kiss?" he asked in a voice so gravelly he barely recognized himself.

"What thing?" She tilted her head to the side in a teasing way.

If she thought he was going to engage in a flirty conversation now, she really was crazy.

"You know damn well what thing. We connected from the minute we first met. Hooking up, like this, was inevitable."

She hesitated, then nodded. "Does that mean you're ready to beg?"

Okay, so now she was going to tighten the screw. Two could play that game. "I don't know. I was kinda hoping you were ready to beg."

Meanwhile, he had walked them both into her bedroom, kicking the door shut behind him. There was a wide picture window at one end of the small room, providing enough moonlight to see her clearly.

They regarded each other with parted lips, both breathing heavily, both still aroused.

As one, they both said, "Please."

Also as one, they smiled at each other.

Mutual begging. He liked that idea.

And, so, apparently, did she.

✦

Let the games begin . . .

Claire was lying on her bed, naked.

He was standing by her bed, naked.

"First things first. Hand me one of those sex toys, honey."

"Sex toys? What sex toys? Do you mean my vibrator?"

Ooooh, boy! "No, I mean those erotic feathers hanging from your ears." *Note to Caleb: Vibrator. Later.*

He had to give Claire credit. She didn't even blush. "You think these are sexy?" She sat up, removed both of the earrings, and gave them to him.

He handed her a strip of condoms, wanting to get that established up front. No babies. The condoms didn't seem to bother her, which was a relief to him.

He used the feathers then, painting imaginary pictures all over her body. Especially her breasts, which he brushed so long and in ways that were damn creative before he put his mouth to each nipple and suckled hard. Claire was alternately screaming for him to not stop and get on with it. Man oh man, her arousal ratcheted his arousal to the point where they were both hot, hot, hot.

Caleb did what he did best then. Using the stamina of his SEAL training, the experience of some fifteen-plus years of sex, his general love of the female body, and that old Elvis principle "A Little Less Talk, a Lot More Action," he brought Claire to climax more times than he could count over the next few hours. And Claire reciprocated very, very nicely, thank you very much. There was something to be said for two physically fit bodies in the sack.

At some point in the middle of the night, she pulled

the quilt up over them both, threw her arms over her head, and said, "Wow!" before falling into a dead, satisfied sleep.

"Wow, indeed!" he thought, and he was about to follow suit, probably with a dippy grin on his face.

But then Claire did something that scared the spit out of him. She snuggled up to him and murmured against his neck, "I love you."

About last night, baby . . .

It was almost dawn when Claire awakened, stretched out the kinks of the most delicious sex she'd ever had, then noticed that Caleb was missing. His side of the bed was still warm, though.

Immediately, she recalled what she'd told him just before falling asleep. "I love you." Well, she couldn't take it back, and she wouldn't. Above all else, she was an honest woman. And she'd fallen hook, line, and sinker for the guy almost from the moment she'd first laid eyes on his perfect-ten body.

He, on the other hand, was probably repulsed. Or at least scared to death. She would have to reassure him that she didn't expect reciprocation. But first, where was he? Did he go for his morning run without her? The rat! Or did he go back to the B & B without her? The rat!

Her questions were soon answered as she donned her nightshirt and walked into the living room, yawning widely. The dog and cat dishes had been replenished with food and water. The coffeemaker was beginning to perk. Even the bird and porcupine had been cared for. And there was Caleb out on the deck—*Be still my heart!*—wearing only his athletic shoes and a pair of boxers. He was doing push-ups, while lined up watching him, heads tilted to the side, were Boney and her five cats. They regarded him as if he was looney . . . or manna from heaven.

If she didn't already love him, she would now.

She leaned against the kitchen counter for a few moments just watching him. Caleb was a complex man. There was so much she didn't know about him. But she knew without a doubt that he was a good man, whose shunning had affected him tremendously in ways even he didn't recognize. Yeah, he had been military and probably held conservative views that would clash with hers, but she wanted him anyhow.

He noticed her then.

And he didn't smile as he stood and came inside.

Uh-oh! Looks like the I-love-you isn't sitting too well this morning. Talk about morning-after regrets. Isn't that supposed to be the woman's prerogative?

"Hey, babe," she said, walking up, going on tiptoe, and giving him a quick kiss.

He grabbed her and pulled her back. "What kind of good-morning kiss is that?" He kissed her thoroughly then, lifting her off the floor, high in his arms, burying his tongue deep in her mouth, before setting her on her feet. Then he nipped her bottom lip. Her lips burned in the aftermath of that short, fiery possession. "We need to get over to the cavern ASAP, but I was wondering, do you think we have time for a quick shower?"

Caleb's lips looked kind of bruised. *From my kisses?* And an expression of supreme male satisfaction had overtaken his normally rigid facial expression. *From my lovemaking?* Claire knew that men liked putting their marks on women . . . marking the territory, so to speak. She'd never felt that way. Till now.

"I like the *we* part of the shower suggestion," she said, taking him by the hand.

Less than an hour later, they were outside getting into their respective vehicles. Caleb felt as if his life had suddenly gone off balance. Not in a bad way. Just . . . disconcerting.

Claire had thrown the three-word bomb at him last night. "I love you." Shiiiiit! Why did women always have to say that? It wasn't true, of course. It was probably lust speaking. But holy crap, that kind of talk was not welcome at this stage in his life, if ever, because sure as shit, to a woman like Claire, love meant marriage and kids. The whole works. He wasn't about to bring it up, though, knowing Claire would want to discuss the subject to death. If he just ignored the issue, maybe it would go away.

After she stowed some gear in her station wagon, Claire turned to him.

His heart skipped a beat. Yeah, it was a cliché, but she had this odd effect on him. And the fact that the lady looked ridden hard in the best possible sense was a real boost to his ego. He'd sensed that Claire would be a passionate lover, but her lack of inhibitions had been a gift. She'd more than matched him in the stamina department, too, praise God and good genes.

"I need to leave the project around noon to come back here."

He arched his brows.

"Even though I have another month till the closing, my buyer wants another run-through of the property."

"You've sold this?" He waved a hand to encompass her cabin and the river. "Why? It's a great place. Spectacular location."

"It is, and I got a good price for it, but I needed all the cash I could put together for my other property."

Caleb eyed Claire warily. The woman had put him off guard from the first moment he'd met her, and she sure as hell had thrown him for a loop last night when she'd told him she loved him. He sensed that she was about to throw him another zinger.

"Okay, I'll bite. What other property?"

"A small farm over in Alexandria. It borders on the river."

Caleb groaned. The two things he'd been avoiding for half his life . . . family and farming. God must have some sense of humor to have wrapped both of them in a tempting package like Claire.

I hope she isn't seeing me in that farming/family picture?

Of course she isn't. We just met three days ago.

Yeah, but she already said she loves me. Even if she didn't mean it.

Maybe I should ask.

Note to Caleb: Are you nuts?

Caleb was beginning to feel as if he'd landed in a no-win situation. Damned if he did. Damned if he didn't. Hopeless.

Where is St. Jude when a guy needs him?

✦

St. Jude was on vacation . . .

Shock.

They were all in for a major shock. And it wasn't just the sight of the two of them looking like sin on the hoof.

When she and Caleb arrived back at the B & B, unnoticed by the just-arising inhabitants, they walked into the kitchen from two different directions—he from the front door and through the hall, and she around the side and through the kitchen door. It was silly, really, acting like teenagers with something to hide. But neither of them was in the mood for teasing, which would be inevitable with this crew.

They headed for the coffeemaker, which was perking away, obviously on a timer. She'd barely taken her first sip before Tante Lulu walked in wearing a yellow miniskirt to match her blonde curls, with a tight red T-shirt that said "Cajun Goddess" and white sneakers with pink laces and pom-poms and white lace anklets. Good thing Claire didn't have a hangover. She'd be blinded by all those colors.

Noticing Claire's gaze, Tante Lulu said, "Me 'n' Abbie decided to go over to Pine Grove Mills to check out Amos and Andy's farm. Do ya think I look hot enough?"

Oh, good Lord! What did one say to that?

"Hotter than hot," Caleb observed, waggling his eyebrows at Tante Lulu.

Tante Lulu blushed. Who knew the old lady could blush? But then she pulled out her usual zinger. "You two look lak ya been wrestlin' in a briar patch. Know what they call a hickey down in bayou land? A whisker kiss. Ha, ha, ha! Heard any thunderbolts yet?"

With that cue, the two of them turned on their heels and headed out the door toward the cave, especially since the rest of the gang could be heard coming down the hall toward the kitchen. Claire heard Tante Lulu tell someone, "Caleb and Claire been havin' hanky-panky. Someone better fetch the preacher."

"Now, auntie," Tee-John could be heard remarking, "there's hanky-panky, and then there's hanky-panky. Not all hanky-panky warrants a weddin' cake. Is that Cajun coffee I smell? Praise the Lord and pass the beignets!"

"Hah! This hanky-panky has rice, weddin' veils, and 'I do's' all over it. Talk about!"

She and Caleb were both a bit red-faced and quiet as they were about to cross the bridge over the creek. Then they noticed the condition of the cavern door. It had been bashed in, probably with an ax.

"Sonofabitch!" Caleb exclaimed and started to run.

Claire was right behind him.

Grabbing flashlights, the two of them headed inside, only to find worse destruction. The lighting cables had been sliced. Diving equipment bashed in. The actual cavern formations hadn't been harmed, thank God for that, but everything pertaining to the Pearl Project was damaged beyond repair.

She and Caleb stared at each other, stunned.

"Someone doesn't want this project to go on," she remarked.

"And I know exactly who," Caleb said, stone-cold fury in his voice. "You call the police."

"Where are you going?"

"To kick ass and take names."

Chapter
10

It was a sinnin' shame . . .

Jonas was standing outside one of his greenhouses, giving Lizzie directions on watering the azaleas. Lizzie worked for him in the summertime.

His daughter Sarah, at twelve, was in the house doing her cleaning chores, and eight-year-old Fanny was gathering eggs. Noah had begged him to go off with his friends to the farmers' market in Belleville, which was a busy, exciting place for a nine-year-old boy with its auctions and flea markets and food stands every Wednesday, spring through autumn, but Noah would have plenty of digging of mulch to do here when he returned. He expected his children to work, but, unlike the Amish, and even some of the Mennonites, he allowed his children to go to school beyond eighth grade. And they would continue through high school, if they wanted. Maybe even college. He'd heard through the grapevine that Dat thought it was a sin for him to be so lenient.

"I still don't see why I can't go stay with Caleb. Or

with Claire and Tante Lulu. *They* like me." Lizzie was back to wearing her plain clothing, which he'd insisted on if she was to stay with him, even for only one day, but somehow she'd managed a few English touches, like holes in her ears and pink paint on her fingernails. To say she was unhappy about his rules—no music, no dancing, no running around—would be like saying the Amish were a little bit strict. *"That is so uncool," she'd said this morning, stomping off. Since when did Amish girls stomp off?* Lizzie was out of control, and he didn't know if his parents would ever be able to reel her back in.

For now, Lizzie appeared to be paying attention to his outline for her day's work, but he was no fool. His sister was just biding her time.

"I know they like ya, but ya gotta take things slow. Dat ain't gonna let ya take off just like that." He snapped his fingers.

"Slow? How slow can I go? *Ach,* fer two years I been talkin' 'bout singin'. The next *American Idol* auditions are comin' up in two months. I gotta get ready."

Jonas groaned. He was sick of hearing about that ridiculous television program where Simon said this and Paula said that. Where she was watching the show, he had no idea, and he didn't want to know. "Lizziebelle," he began, "ya can't give someone castor oil and expect them to drink the whole bottle. Ya gotta give 'em one sip at a time."

"Oh, so now I'm castor oil? Why dontcha just call me pig poop?"

He had to grin at her choice of words. "I'm willin' ta intercede with Dat for ya. Ask 'im if ya can stay with me for a bit. But there's gotta be rules, and for sure and for certain, ya can't—"

His words were cut off by the roar of an engine and blare of a horn as a dark green Jeep sped by. He and Lizzie stared at the vehicle and then at each other. "Caleb," they said as one. And he was headed in the direction of the old homestead.

"Uh-oh!" he said, sensing trouble.

Lizzie was smiling, relishing the idea of trouble.

Both of them jumped into Jonas's pickup truck and followed after Caleb.

Jonas couldn't help but ruminate on the sad state of his life. Caleb was back but would soon return to a life of sin. Lizzie had been singing last night in a house of sin. A woman in red boots, of all things, had tried to entice him into sin. And he had an awful bad suspicion that there was gonna be some sinnin' in his future.

What else can go wrong?

He could swear he heard laughter in his head.

Can't we all just get along? . . .

Samuel Peachey watched as two vehicles came squealing into his yard, making more noise than pigs being chased by a swarm of honeybees. It was his sons Caleb and Jonas and his daughter Lizzie.

Tears welled in his eyes on seeing these three lost sheep of his, back where they belonged. Home. But no, that was two lost. Lizzie was not yet lost, although she was *ferlunkin* if she thought he would not notice those holes in her ears and the painted nails she tried to hide in her apron when he'd seen her over in Spruce Creek yesterday. Of his nine children, these three were the most willful and wild, and he loved them so much his heart ached.

But he was Amish to the bone. Came from five generations of Anabaptists before him. He was a divided man and had been unable to find a way to reconcile his love of God and love of family for seventeen long years. The shunning practice was evil, to be sure, but a necessary evil. Or so he had always believed.

Rebekah came out on the porch to stand beside him, wringing her apron with dismay. They had been married for forty-three years come November, long enough for him to recognize the silent plea in her eyes: *Don't be so stern, Samuel. Even the strongest tree's gotta bend sometimes.* It was a message she'd delivered repeatedly ever since they'd "lost" their two sons to the *Ordnung.*

He put an arm over her shoulders and squeezed, trying to reassure her, but in truth he had no idea how to proceed with these three errant fruits of his loins.

"Hullo, Caleb."

"What the hell have you done?" Caleb shouted at him.

Samuel flinched. "What?" *Why, when I was in a bending mood, does he throw those bad words at me? Has he no sense at all? Does he want to widen the breach, not close it?*

Caleb looked as if he'd like to strike him.

Jonas tried to pull Caleb back, to no avail. He came up to him, practically nose to nose, his hands fisting.

"Is this what they teach you in the English world . . . in your war-making military? To hit your own father?"

It was Caleb who flinched then.

Rebekah gasped beside him. So much for his not being so stern!

"I have no intention of hitting you. This is nothing to do with the English world or the Navy. It's about the wanton destruction at Spruce Creek Cavern. How could you do such a thing, Dat? It's one thing to hurt me, but lots of other people are affected by your rampage. Innocent people."

He and Rebekah, Jonas, and Lizzie gazed at each other, stunned at the news.

"Explain yourself, boy," he told Caleb, and, *jah,* his voice sounded stern, even to his own ears. "I deserve to know what I'm bein' accused of."

"Like you gave *me* a chance before the shunning?"

Caleb was not going to make this easy. Well, he could be stubborn, too. He raised his chin and squared his jaw.

"Or like the chance you gave me?" Jonas came up to stand beside his brother.

Their standing together did not bother him too much. Brothers, especially twin brothers, should stick together. Even if they didn't look much alike anymore. They were the same height, but their builds were different and their hair, and their clothing, of course. Caleb was a hardened man; there were things in Caleb's brown eyes that spoke of horrors he'd seen, maybe even horrors he'd done himself. Jonas, with his trimmed Mennonite beard, was just mulish.

How did they get to be men? How could the years have flown by with my missing the change from boy to man? One minute they were fly fishin' with me over at Shy Sisters Creek, and the next they were big strappin' men with minds of their own. How could our lives get so nutzed up?

Joseph came out of the barn, where he'd been shoe-

ing one of the plow horses. At sixteen and already be-
trothed, he was a good and honest Amishman. His brow
furrowing with concern . . . at all the shouting, no
doubt . . . he put his anvil down and proceeded to walk
toward them.

Joseph, clean-shaven like all unwed Amishmen, took
off his straw hat and wiped his brow with the sleeve of
his shirt. He nodded at Jonas, who was of course being
shunned and couldn't be spoken to, and he frowned at
Lizzie, knowing full well how wild she had become of
late. Then he gave his attention to Caleb, frowning at
him also.

"Joseph, this is your brother Caleb. Caleb, this is
your youngest brother, Joseph."

Neither of them reached out to shake hands, regarding each other with hostility. Well, at least Joseph was
hostile. Caleb was just silent.

"Dat?" Joseph asked with concern. "What's wrong?"

"Everything, apparently," Samuel replied. "Rebekah,
go into the house and get some eatin's. Lizzie, help yer
mother." For once, Lizzie heeded his orders without
question. But before his wife left, she walked up to first
Caleb and then Jonas and hugged them with sobs she
was unable to hold back. Both sons seemed poleaxed
once she walked away. She deliberately avoided making
eye contact with Samuel as she passed, knowing he
would disapprove. *The Bann, the Bann, the Bann,* he
had to keep reminding himself.

"We need to talk," he told Caleb and Jonas. The fact
that he did not include Joseph didn't go unnoticed.
Color blossomed on his youngest's face, and he spun on
his heel, storming away. He would talk to Joseph later
about his unseemly temper. Joseph always had been in-

secure about his rights to the farm, fearing, he supposed, that his father would break tradition and give it to either Jonas or Caleb, if they would come back like lost lambs with their tails between their legs. But that would never happen, even if they did come back to the flock. Samuel would be handing the farm over to Joseph and his bride when they married in two years. And he and Rebekah would be moving into the Dawdi Haus, an addition on the house intended for grandparents.

Samuel motioned for Caleb and Jonas to join him on the porch, where there were several benches and a swing. He sat on the bench, his two sons on the swing.

"I had nothin' ta do with any damitch at yer cavern."

Caleb appeared about to argue, but Jonas put a hand on his arm and said, "Dat doesn't lie."

With obvious reluctance, Caleb nodded. "How come you're talking to us? Aren't you worried about the *Bann?*" The sneer on his face was unacceptable for a son to his father, and Samuel would have chastised the boy under normal circumstances. But he feared that Caleb would leave abruptly before they'd had a chance to clear the air.

Samuel looked sheepishly at them both and admitted, "I suspect I'm 'bout to be shunned myself. Bishop Lapp ain't too happy with me right now."

"Don't go out on any limbs for me," Caleb lashed out. "It's a little too late for that."

"Shut up!" Jonas told his brother. "Give Dat a chance."

"Shut up, yourself," Caleb retorted.

"Make me."

"Get real!"

Then the two of them grinned at each other. You'd

think they were still twelve years old, arguing over Mrs. Fisher's breasts. And *jah,* he had known back then how all the boys had been fascinated by Grace Fisher's bosom. In truth, lots of men's eyeballs had been glued on them udders of hers, too.

"Tell me what happened at the cavern," he urged Caleb.

"Sometime between last night and early this morning, someone put an ax to the entrance door of the cavern. Then they used wire cutters to sever all the lighting cables leading into the cavern. We had caving and diving equipment stored inside the cave entrance. Wet suits, oxygen tank hoses, helmets, flashlights, digging tools . . . all smashed beyond repair. The cave formations were left untouched, thank God. And Sparky."

He and Jonas tilted their heads in question. "Sparky?"

"A resident snake."

"Ya gives snakes names in the English world?" Dat shook his head with wonder.

"No, we don't name snakes, except big ones. And this one is a really big mother."

"Mother snake?" he inquired. "How do you know it's a mother?"

Caleb smiled, despite his nasty mood.

Samuel had no idea what was funny about his question.

"Ya alveese was afraid of snakes," Jonas remarked.

"I was *not* afraid," Caleb snapped back. "I just don't like them. Why doesn't anyone believe me?"

"Maybe 'cause I remember the time ya almos' wet yer pants when a black snake crawled up the plow handle and stuck its tongue out at ya." Jonas mouthed, "Fraidy cat."

"You are such a kid," Caleb responded.

"I'm thinkin' ya both act like kids," Dat observed. "Now, why would ya think I was responsible fer that damitch, Caleb?"

"Because Jonas told me about the meeting yesterday and what the elders said about me and the cavern."

Dat raised his eyebrows at Jonas. "And who would've told ya 'bout private business of the church?"

Jonas refused to answer, but Samuel suspected it was Rebekah who'd tattled. He'd have a talk with her later. The woman did not know her place sometimes.

"You might not have done the damage yourself," Caleb conceded. "But you know who did, don't you?"

"I 'spect I do," he said with a long sigh.

"Who?"

He remained silent. He needed to pray on this and decide how much he could reveal. "Did ya hear nothin' during the night? Cars comin' inta the yard?" He paused. "Buggies?"

Caleb's face grew pink, even his ears.

Ahhhh! He knew then, without a doubt, that Caleb hadn't been there at the time. "Is it the woman with the wanton red hair who came out practic'ly swingin' her fists at me in yer defense?"

"It's not red. It's auburn."

"When was this?" Jonas wanted to know.

Samuel ignored Jonas's question and wagged a fore-finger at Caleb. He might not have been talkin' to him all these years, but Caleb was still his son. "I think ya need ta think 'bout fornicatin' with a woman outside of marriage, son."

Caleb's eyes went wide at his wagging finger. Then he composed himself. "I don't give a rat's ass what you think."

"Tsk-tsk," was all he said, though he didn't like his language one bit. Or his lack of respect.

"The police will have to be involved," Caleb said.

He put a hand to his heart with alarm. "Can't we handle this private-like?"

"Dat?" Jonas shot to his feet and came over to kneel next to his chair. "Are ya all right? Is it yer heart?"

Jonas's question surprised him, but he was not above using an opportunity when it was thrown in his lap. "Jist a little twinge."

Caleb narrowed his eyes at him, suspicious. "Have you been to a doctor?"

He shook his head. "And don't be tellin' your mother about this. No need to worry her none."

"Back to the cavern . . . and the police. I'm not going to drop this, Dat. Too much damage was done."

"Will ya let me talk to a few folks first? Will ya wait on callin' in the police?"

"The police are probably already there. I told Claire to call them before I left."

He sighed. "Maybe we can still settle this ourselves."

"I doubt it, but I'll give you till tonight."

Samuel bristled. It didn't sit well for him to be given orders by his son . . . any of his sons. "I'll see what I can do."

"Does this mean you've stopped shunnin' me and Caleb?" Jonas asked.

"No. I mean, I don't know." He stroked his long beard between the fingers of one hand. A nervous habit. "I just don't know."

The disappointment on Jonas's face was a stab to his heart. The lack of disappointment on Caleb's face hurt even more.

In truth, he was disappointed in himself.

It was plain crazy . . .

Claire, Tante Lulu, and John were traveling down a narrow two-lane back road in Sinking Valley, searching for Caleb's Jeep.

She was very worried about the man and what he might do, considering the rage he was in when he'd spun gravel leaving the B & B.

After the state police left a half hour ago, promising to come back later in the day, Tante Lulu was the one who'd alerted the rest of them to the fact that Caleb's father and the elders of the Amish church might be responsible for the vandalism. She'd overheard Jonas warning Caleb last night at the tavern.

Adam was back at the B & B with Abbie and Mark. Adam was dealing with Jinx's insurance company, and Abbie, who had rallied herself after the initial shock, was checking out the personal insurance on her property. The adjusters promised to be there this afternoon. Adam and Mark were tabulating all the damage and making lists of items to be replaced before they could restart the project.

Tante Lulu was sitting between her and her nephew on the front bench seat of John's red Chevy Impala convertible. She and Tante Lulu were having a fascinating discussion about her *traiteur* work on the bayou. As ditzy as the old lady was in general, she was clearly an expert when it came to her profession, and that was probably the reason for John's knowing smile—people underestimated his aunt. Many of the herbs she gathered for her healings were the same as those the Lenni Lenape used in their own medicine.

"What I find most interesting is the signature plants the Native Americans used. Plants that resemble the ailments they treat, like those with twisted roots for snake bites or arthritic pain, or milkweed for breast problems."

"*Oui!* I allus tell people that with all the fancy medicines we gots today, most of 'em came from plants what been around fer centuries. I have a big handwritten journal of all my remedies that Tee-John sez he's gonna put in a book someday."

John squeezed his aunt's knee. "For sure, I will, auntie."

"Oh, I would love to see it," Claire said.

"There it is. There it is." Tante Lulu interrupted their conversation and pointed to a white farmhouse in the distance, where Caleb's Jeep was parked in the barnyard on the side. How she could see from this distance, or from her height, was amazing. Her eyes, behind rhinestone-studded cat sunglasses, were about level with the dashboard. The muffler was so loud that cows were doing double takes as they passed. The old lady had had the foresight to put a scarf on her head. Claire's hair was blowing every which way.

As John put on his turn signal and began to make his way down a long dirt road, she couldn't help but notice the neatness of the fields, knee-high corn on one side and oats on the other. Getting closer to the house, she saw an immaculately trimmed lawn and a vegetable garden that would feed an army, including an impressive amount of celery. The Amish planted huge beds of celery, which was a staple of their wedding feasts.

"I gotta pee," Tante Lulu said as they pulled in behind Caleb's Jeep. A truck was there, too, with the logo "Peachey's Landscaping." It must belong to Jonas.

"Auntie! Just ten minutes ago, you had us stop at that general store so you could pee."

"So? I'm old. I gotta pee a lot. 'Sides, I allus wanted ta see the inside of an Amish house."

"Uh, I've got news for you," Claire said, pulling a brush out of her purse to try to untangle her windblown hair. "The Amish don't have indoor plumbing."

When understanding seeped into the tight blonde curls the old lady was fluffing as she stepped out of the vehicle, she brightened. "An outhouse? Well, good golly, I ain't peed in an outhouse since I was a girl. Didja know we had outhouses when I was growin' up?" she asked her nephew.

He patted her on the shoulder. "Yeah, you told us a time or two about the *olden days*. Wasn't that when you and Rhett Butler had a thing goin' on?"

"Wipe that grin off yer face, boy. Jist 'cause I'm old doan mean I'm stoopid. Actually, I'm thinkin' I need a drink a water. Fergit about the outhouse."

The old lady was so transparent, she and Tee-John burst out laughing. But then they rounded the side of the house and saw Caleb and Jonas sitting at a long picnic table in the back yard with their father and mother, Lizzie and a scowling young Amishman.

They stared at them as if they were aliens dropping by. Tante Lulu especially got their attention in her yellow miniskirt and red "Cajun Goddess" T-shirt.

Caleb stood, as shocked as the rest to see them show up uninvited at his family's homestead. And not pleased. Claire also knew he'd been stunned by her telling him last night that she loved him, then telling him this morning she'd bought a farm. It was a whole lot for the poor man to take in all at once. She wanted to help him, to assure him that she, at least, was not going to be a problem.

"What are you doing here?" he asked when he came up to the three of them.

"We was afraid ya was gonna shoot someone," Tante Lulu said before she or John could respond.

"Do I look like I have a weapon on me?" he scoffed.

Nope, nothing could fit inside those tight jeans and T-shirt besides that magnificent body. Ooops! Not a subject she should be thinking about right now.

"I doan know. You Navy SEALs have ways of concealing weapons, I been told." She stared pointedly at his groin. "But hey, I got a pistol in my purse, iffen ya need one."

"I tol' ya ta get rid of that thing, auntie! *Mon dieu!* Ya could shoot yer eye out or somethin'."

"Guns . . . ya brought guns here?" Rebekah sputtered.

"Hey, Rebekah!" Tante Lulu gave a little wave to the Amish woman, who gave her a weak wave in return.

They'd all met Rebekah before, but not all of them knew Mr. Peachey, so Caleb introduced everyone, including the scowling young man, Joseph, his brother, who was barely civil to any of them. In an aside, Caleb whispered to her, "If my father wags his finger at you or mentions fornicating, just tell him to buzz off."

"Forn-forn-icating?" She was the one sputtering now.

"By the way, thanks for last night, babe." He patted her butt. "It seems like a million years ago, doesn't it?"

"I know this isn't the right time, but I don't want you spooked by what I said last night or about the farm I bought or even when I said that stuff about sperm banks. You've got enough problems with the project without me adding to your troubles."

"Do I look like I'm spooked?"

"Yes."

He laughed and pinched her butt this time.

When Caleb glanced away, his father gave her a piercing glower, and she could swear he knew where Caleb's hand had been. Well, at least he didn't wag his forefinger at her.

She turned her attention to Caleb, who was talking to Lizzie. Good thing, because she was alternately flattered and offended at his remark, and who knew what she might have blurted out? *He's thanking me for sex? Like a favor? I wonder how he would react if I thanked him? Hah! Who am I kidding? He'd grin and say, "My pleasure, babe."*

Within minutes the men had brought benches, sawhorses, and long planks from the barn to make tables, which Tante Lulu and Rebekah were covering with plastic tablecloths. Soon both tables were covered with a surprising amount of food, considering none of them had been expected.

"You were really lucky to grow up on a farm like this," she remarked to Caleb.

"Yeah, it was lots of fun getting up before dawn, milking cows, plowing fields, raking hay, building barns, shoveling cow shit—"

"Enough! I concede that it's hard work, but look at

all the instant gratification in seeing the fruit of your labor. And frankly, I don't think there's a better way to raise a family."

He visibly stiffened at her mention of family. "Oh, don't worry. I've given up on the baby stuff with you."

"Why? I mean, I'm glad you don't view me as your personal sperm donor, but why?"

"Just because I like to make love with you doesn't mean I'm going to push any baby talk on you."

"You like making love with me?" He used a finger to twirl a strand of her hair into a tight curl.

"Oh, yeah!"

"Do you know your hair looks like polished mahogany in the sunlight?"

"Is that good?"

He repeated her words then and said, "Oh, yeah!"

They were smiling at each other, which didn't go unnoticed by his frowning father when his mother announced, "Come, dish up."

As they sat down along with all the others, John came up behind Caleb and whispered, loud enough for her to hear, "Just so you know, my aunt and your mother are discussing your hope chest. I didn't know the Amish had hope chests, too. Guess yours will be a Cajun/Amish hope chest, huh?"

Caleb reached behind to swat at John, but he ducked away, laughing. Silence followed as they began to eat.

There was ham sliced off the bone, smoked sausage, potato and macaroni salads, homemade bread, apple butter, chow-chow, pickled beets, eggs, pigs' feet, souse, spaetzle noodles with butter, and various desserts, including cold watermelon slices, huckleberry strudel, shoofly pie, and sinfully sweet whoopie pies, which were like glorified Oreos, except these were the size of small saucers and made of cake, not cookie. For beverages they were served lemonade and ice water "fresh from the spring." A veritable Amish feast.

Which of course called for more people.

"Oh, my God!" Caleb swore, glancing over to the barn parking area. Pulling up were more than a dozen buggies containing men, women, and children. "This is so surreal. I feel as if I've landed in a slow-motion version of hell."

This must be why there had been so much food already prepared. They'd been expecting company.

Caleb's father went over to talk to the newcomers, gesticulating with his hands as he spoke, raising his voice, at one point wagging a forefinger. Claire wondered with hysterical irrelevance if one of them was a fornicator.

"Hardly," Caleb responded.

She hadn't realized that she'd spoken aloud.

Turning to stare at Caleb beside her on a bench, she asked, "Who are they?"

"My brothers and sisters." He shook his head sadly. "Don't expect a warm welcome."

"Why not?"

"Everyone's jockeying for position here, same as any other big family. They're probably afraid Jonas or I will upset the balance somehow. Get something from Dat that they consider their entitlements. Plus, they take the shunning seriously."

"Even if your father tells them it's okay to talk to you?"

"Do you see Joseph giving me any warm hugs, or even a 'How are you, Caleb?'"

He was right. Joseph was being downright rude. To all of them, but especially to Caleb.

The group was heading toward them now, the six men, including Caleb's father in front, like a posse. All of them had long, straggly beards denoting their married state, unlike Jonas's trimmed beard. They were dressed in traditional Amish clothes, wide-brimmed straw hats, homemade dark blue or black shirts with no pockets, and black broadcloth pants with flaps in front. Zippers were considered too modern. Behind came six women in dark blue cape dresses, which were supposed to be eight inches from the ground and covered with black aprons. On their feet were lace-up leather shoes, despite the hot weather. Their hair was parted down the middle and skinned back under prayer caps, which they wore even when sleeping. With the women and following them were several dozen babies and children and teenagers.

"When I left here, I had four brothers and three sisters. Now I have a menagerie," Caleb said with a mixture of wonder and disgust.

So many people from these two people, Samuel and Rebekah. What a family tree!

It was odd, really, the way she and Caleb could look at things and see them in different ways because, while she thought his family made a lovely picture as they approached, Caleb murmured to her, "Jesus, Mary, and Joseph! My brothers and sisters must propagate like jackrabbits. They resemble a bunch of jabbering black crows."

The men glared at Caleb, while the women shrank back with shyness, waiting for their men to give them permission to step forward.

"Caleb, ya remember Levi, dontcha? He was twenty-three when ya left. That's his wife, Sharon. They farm the old Beiler place north of here."

With a sigh of resignation, Caleb stepped forward to stand beside his father. He reached out a hand. At first the stern-faced, forty-year-old Levi just stared at the hand, but then he shook it, though he didn't speak. Nor did the other brothers, Aaron and Ezekiel, or "Zeke," when they were introduced. Caleb's sisters Katherine, Judith, and Miriam, or "Mimi," just nodded quietly. The same for the brothers' wives and children, two of whom were already married and had children of their own. Most of them were farmers or did work related to farming, like blacksmithing or buggy making.

They were an attractive family, all of them, but sort of homogeneous because of their clothing. Which was the point of one style and color of clothing, Claire supposed.

Tante Lulu and John were introduced then. Jonas already knew them all, of course, even though he'd been shunned, like Caleb.

Everyone sat down to eat again, more sawhorses and planks having been brought from the barn and more food spread out from the kitchen and baskets that had been brought by the visitors. The other family members did not sit with Caleb or Jonas, because apparently the shunning forbade eating at the same table. And none of them had spoken to them yet, either. An uncomfortable silence followed as the meal continued.

Till the ice was broken by . . . who else? Tante Lulu. She said, "I ain't seen so much black and blue since Tee-John fell off a tupelo tree and practic'ly broke his tailbone."

Everyone looked at her.

"He was skinny-dippin' from a limb over Bayou Black when it broke and sent him flyin'. 'Member that, Tee-John? Ha, ha, ha! The nurse at the hospital took one gander at yer bruised hiney and said mebbe they oughta put a cast there."

"*Mais, oui!* After that, I started flashin' my ass, I mean, hiney, at the girls in my class at Our Lady of the Bayou School. That black-and-blue butt, she was lak a badge of honor, yes."

"Sister Serenity soon put a stop ta that, though, bless her heart."

"Tell me about it. She gave me a matchin' color on my other cheek with that switch of hers. Talk about!"

Stone-cold silence continued.

"What?" Tante Lulu asked, looking right and left. "Did y'all suck on a bunch a lemons? Did we say sumpin' wrong?"

"Maybe they don't like you mentionin' skinny-dippin'," John said with a grin. It was obvious that the scamp could care less if they'd offended anyone.

"Don't Amish kids go skinny-dippin'?"

"It's the words *butt, hiney*, and *ass* that've thrown them for a loop," Caleb drawled, then made a comical face at Levi's sneering face.

"Well, mercy's sake! Everybody's got one." Tante Lulu threw her hands up in the air with exasperation. "Though I lost mine about nineteen-eighty-two."

A ripple of giggles erupted, then an outright hoot from Caleb's father, followed by a wave of laughter. His mother had a hand over her mouth, hiding her amusement.

"God bless that old woman," Caleb said to Claire.

"You should probably thank St. Jude, too," Tante Lulu called down the table. She must have ears like an elephant.

Finally, it was all too much for Caleb. The poor man put his face in his hands. His shoulders were shaking. Claire feared he would have a breakdown in front of everyone. Did he really want to be seen crying like this?

"Caleb? Honey? Do you need a tissue?"

He raised his head, and she realized he wasn't crying. He was laughing hysterically. Like a screwball.

And people say I'm crazy.

Chapter
11

The homecoming from hell . . .

"Take this church spread wit ya, Caleb. It alveese was yer favorite."

Caleb stared at the plastic container his mother shoved in his hands as he prepared to leave. "Ah, Mam!" It was sad beyond belief that she didn't know the Caleb he was now. He would no more eat that concoction of syrup, marshmallow, and peanut butter on a piece of no-fiber white bread than he would shoot up with sugar.

Still, he took the container from her and leaned down to give her a kiss on the top of her head. "*Denki*," he said.

"You're welcome."

Everyone had left within the past fifteen minutes. All the family had gone in their buggies, including Dat, who was off to Bishop Lapp's home; Jonas, with Lizzie, in his truck back to his business; and the Jinx folk back to the B & B. He was about to follow.

Claire had wanted to stay behind, but he wouldn't let her. Clearly fuming over his shunning, she'd probably be giving Dat and Mam lectures on Indian family practices and how the Amish could learn a thing or two from them. Or else she'd have a slug fest with his father, despite her claims of being a pacifist.

Not one of his brothers and sisters, his nieces and nephews, had dared break the *Bann* today. It was ridiculous the way they'd had to communicate with hand signals for "Pass the bread" and "More lemonade?" and then "Your turn" at the outhouse. Aaron, his second oldest brother at forty-one, who'd always been a pole-up-the-ass jerk even when he was younger, probably broke a few *Ordnung* rules when he'd mouthed at Caleb, "Traitor," but that was okay, because Caleb had mouthed back at him, "Asshole!," causing Aaron's eyes to about pop out of his sanctimonious head.

"What will happen next, Mam? Is this a one-day reprieve, and will we go back to the way things were? Will Jonas and I still be shunned?"

His mother took his hand and walked toward the Jeep with him. Her silence was answer enough.

Son of a bitch! Son of a fucking bitch! he railed inside, but he remained silent, too, just watching this older woman who was his mother, yet was not.

Had she shrunk? He didn't recall her being this short or frail-looking. She was sixty-five, but sixty-five wasn't that old today in the regular world. Yeah, he'd expected the gray hair, which had been mostly blonde the last time he'd seen her, but her back was slightly bowed from all those years of bending . . . over wash-tubs, gardens, quilting, and endless canning. And Dat . . . oh, how he had aged! Pure white hair and beard down to his belly, spindly legs and arms, eyes a bit rheumy, possibly with cataracts from the way he squinted sometimes. They'd all changed so much.

"You look so different now, son," she said, as if reading his mind.

"Better or worse?"

"Different."

That was a nonanswer if he ever heard one.

"You left a boy and returned a man. You left hurt and angry and returned hurt and hardened."

He shrugged, not about to apologize for being hard. That's how he'd survived. "We all change." He forced himself to smile and squeezed her hand. "Even Dat."

Dat had shocked them all today by welcoming him and Jonas to his table, by speaking to them when the *Bann* clearly forbade both. *What does it mean?*

"*Jah,* he shocked me, too." Then she motioned for him to sit on a bench near the chicken coop. She had a tight hold on their linked fingers and wouldn't let go, even as they sank down. "Did ya miss home, Caleb?"

The birds behind them squawked their opinion of these two humans sitting so close without feeding them. God, the place reeked of chicken shit and cow manure. How could he have forgotten how overpowering the outside smells were? And pee-you, but a couple of his brothers and nephews could use a stick of Right Guard. No electricity or plumbing. Stubborn mules for plowing. Putrid pigs to slaughter. No, he hadn't missed this a bit . . . or at least not for more than a dozen years. "I missed *you,*" was all he would say. "And Dat, too, except I was mostly angry at him for not standing up for me. You backed him up, Mam. How could you do that?"

"With a broken heart and a bucket of tears. It is our

way, son. Alveese has been." Unspoken was "always will be."

"What next?"

"Well, Dat is gonna talk ta the bishop and elders. If they did this vile thing, they will pay for it."

That's not what he meant. Oh, well! "In money? That's all?"

"There will be church penalties, too. Maybe they will be barred from service for a time. And forced ta confess their sins before the congregation at Sunday meeting."

"And that's all? I get shunned for life because of an accident, and they get a smack on the hands?"

"The difference is in the confessing. Ya never would do yer kneeling. Ya wouldn't bend ta the elders' will."

That's for damn sure. "Listen, I've got to go. I've been away from the project too long as it is." His cell phone had been ringing constantly the past hour. Ronnie with concerns about their safety and giving him the Jinx policy numbers for the insurance adjusters, which he'd already relayed to Famosa. Abbie with an update on her insurance situation. Mark with a preliminary list of damages.

His mother nodded, tears in her eyes.

"I don't know when I'll see you again . . . *if* I'll see you again." He waited for her to say something like, "Of course we will be together again," but she didn't. She couldn't.

As if sensing his thoughts, she said, "Try to understand, Caleb. I would leave . . . maybe yer Dat would, too. We could go live Mennonite like Jonas. But I couldn't bear the shunnin'. Not bein' able to talk to my children and grandchildren. Not bein' able to eat wit' them at my table."

But what about me? What about Jonas? Are we disposable and the rest of them aren't? How fair is that? He said none of that, even though he felt as if a KA-BAR knife had been stuck in his heart. It was hopeless to expect anything more, he realized, but that's just what he'd done. *Fool, fool, fool!* When Dat and Mam had talked to him today, he'd foolishly hoped that their shunning of him and Jonas was over. Now he just leaned down and kissed his mother's cheek. "Good-bye, Mam," he said, and he meant just that, with finality.

As he backed the Jeep down the drive, he noticed his mother sitting in the same spot, tears streaming down her face.

Hopeless.

Sometimes only a brother's shoulder would do . . .

Despite the need to get back to work, Caleb stopped at Jonas's home first.

Before he'd even turned the ignition off, Jonas was out on the porch. "Welcome, brother, welcome," he said, motioning for him to come up the steps. Then he surprised the hell out of him by pulling him into a big hug and refusing to let go—or maybe it was Caleb who was holding fast.

"What a day! What a day!" Jonas said against his ear.

Caleb couldn't speak over the lump in his throat, knowing that Jonas suffered just as much as he did. He understood, without words. Finally, he drew away and noticed the wetness in Jonas's eyes, probably matching his own. "You know what really sucks, Jonas?"

He had to give Jonas credit for not flinching at the word *suck* or asking what it meant. "What, Caleb? What . . . sucks?"

"They love the others more than they love us."

"*Ach,* Caleb, that's not true."

"Yes, it is. Today they made a choice. Do they continue the *Bann* or shove it down the bishop's throat? They chose the status quo."

"You're bein' too harsh."

"I wish! Mam said as much to me a few minutes ago. She and Dat would ignore the *Bann,* or leave the church, except for the pain of losing their other children and grandchildren."

Jonas flinched.

"I'll go even further than that. You know how some kids who've suffered child abuse from a father or male figure end up hating their mother when they grow up, for not stepping in and ending the cruelty? Well, I'm starting to feel that way about Mam."

"Dat never abused us."

"You don't think the shunning is a form of abuse?"

Jonas looped an arm over his shoulder, squeezing. "Well, at least we have each other now, *jah?*"

"*Jah,* mine *Brudder,*" Caleb said in an exaggerated Pennsylvania Dutch voice that made Jonas's lips turn up with humor.

"Come meet the rest of your family, brother. My children."

Soon Jonas's kids, initially shy of Caleb, were crawling all over him, asking question after question, while Lizzie and Jonas watched, beaming with pleasure.

"Have ya ever been in an airplane?"

"Have ya ever jumped out of an airplane?"

"Do ya know the president of the United States?"

"Can ya go fly fishin' with us?"

"Where's yer gun?"

"Why don't ya have a gun?"

"How come ya don't have kids?"

"Have you ever kill—"

"That will be enough," Jonas said, cutting his son Noah off. "Caleb has ta go back ta work."

"Will ya come back? I kin make ya some tasty gingersnaps." Eight-year-old Fanny sat on his lap, arms wrapped around his neck, and refused to get off till he answered.

"You couldn't keep me away, sweetie, and gingersnaps are my favorite," he said, pushing some blonde hairs that had slipped out of her braids behind her ears. The girl was adorable.

"I have a snakeskin collection," nine-year-old Noah told him.

What a thing to collect? Eew! "Hey, I happen to be personally acquainted with the biggest snake in these parts." He extended his arms wide to illustrate. "His name is Sparky. I'll bet we could find one of his shedded skins around the cavern somewhere."

Noah stared at him as if he was some kind of god, or Santa Claus. "A snake with a name? A big snake?"

"Yep." He ruffled Noah's shaggy hair, which hung down past his ears. It looked as if his hair had been cut with a bowl over his head, bangs and all, like a Dutch boy.

Jonas's kids dressed plain, but not as plain as the Amish. They wore colors and patterns and different styles. Some of the Mennonites also used electricity and drove cars.

"Why dontcha come back fer supper t'night?" Jonas suggested, walking him to the door.

"I don't know if I can. It depends on how things go this afternoon."

"We could eat late . . . at seven?"

Seven is late? "I'll try, but how will I let you know if I can't make it?"

"Ya could call me on the phone." Jonas grinned at him.

"*You* have a phone?"

"*Jah.* I need it fer my business." He handed Caleb a business card.

"Why didn't you tell me before?"

"Ya didn't ask."

He punched his brother in the arm. "You have a beautiful family, Jonas."

"It's yer family, too. Uncle Caleb."

They smiled at each other.

But then a silver Corvette pulled into the lane beside the house, and out crawled the nurse of red-boots fame, except today she wore high-heeled sandals, tight black jeans, and a glittery yellow tank top. "Hi!" She waved. "I brought homemade lasagna. Anyone hungry?"

Jonas's jaw was practically sitting on his chest. "Don't ya dare leave now," he whispered to Caleb.

Caleb figured it was his cue to leave Dodge. "Brotherly love only goes so far. She's all yours."

Welcome to my wigwam, baby . . .

"The tab so far is twenty thousand dollars. Are you sure they'll pay for those kinds of damages?" Famosa was tapping away at a calculator on the library desk.

"They better," Caleb said. "Either that, or charges will be filed. Either way, they pay."

"We don't have any proof," LeDeux pointed out.

"And really, Peach, why would the Amish do something so . . . violent?" Famosa wanted to know.

"They think that I'm a bad influence. A shunned Amishman coming back, flashing a car, English clothing, and all the trappings of a world they consider evil. Temptation on the hoof. Throw into the mix my military background, and they consider me Lucifer in the flesh. Put me in a cavern that's all dark and spooky, and they figure it's the ultimate bad guy's lair where I'll be performing Satanic rituals, all to lure their young people away from the fold."

"If you're Satan, *mon Dieu,* what're we?" LeDeux pointed to himself, Famosa, and Mark, as if they were less devilish than he was.

"My minions."

"Minions! Talk about! No way am I a minion," LeDeux declared. "I've gotta be a fallen angel, at least."

"LeDeux, you are a moron," Famosa said.

"Why, thank you very much," LeDeux replied.

"Are they always like this?" Mark asked him.

"Always," LeDeux and Famosa answered for him.

"Anyhow, stop worrying about the money, you guys. I'll meet with my father and the church leaders tonight. Meantime, we've got to get these items shipped or picked up. Read the list back again, Mark, to see if we've missed anything."

Mark picked up the notebook in which he'd been writing. Luckily, he was right-handed. "Three air tanks, one wet suit, three sets of flippers, two twenty-foot and four thirty-foot lighting cables with bulbs, a caving ladder, six lengths of SRT nylon rope with accelerators and decelerators, two SRT harnesses, six safety helmets, and a bunch of small miscellaneous items. Oh, and I made arrangements for a new door to be built. Ironically, the carpenter is Amish, from over in Belleville. He won't be able to come for three days, though."

"Okay, Famosa, you're making a trip to the Jinx warehouse in Barnegat to pick up the diving equipment, right?"

"Yeah, but some of it needs to be special-ordered and delivered here. No sense having them ship to Jersey."

He groaned. "And how long will that take?"

"Two days with special handling."

"And I've gotta make a trip today to Pittsburgh to a lighting supply manufacturer," LeDeux said. "Some of these cables we need aren't available locally."

"I figure it's going to take us five days to get back to the point where we were yesterday at this time," Mark announced.

The rest of them groaned at the delay. A simple job was evolving into a major project.

"Well, both of you keep in touch in case we discover any other damage or equipment we need," he told Famosa and LeDeux as they prepared to leave the library where they'd all been working. "We can at least start laying the cables tomorrow. And LeDeux, do not take any woman along with you. I need your focus to be on the project."

"Hey, I'm great at multitasking." The Cajun fool actually appeared offended that he would think otherwise. "By the way, is it okay if I leave my aunt here?"

Do you have to? "Yeah, I guess so. Are you sure she isn't going to be bored with you gone?"

"Are you kidding? Tante Lulu finds fun no matter where she is. Besides, today she and Abbie went to Amos and Andy's farm, remember, and after that to a flea market."

They all grinned, not just at the prospect of the two old ladies having gentleman friends, but because a mother would actually name her twin sons Amos and Andy.

After Famosa and LeDeux left, Caleb asked Mark, "Are you okay with your grandmother having a boyfriend? I feel kinda responsible since I allowed Tante Lulu to stay here."

"Hey, anything that keeps my grandmother busy is fine with me. At least she's not bugging me about hooking up with Lily if she's gallivanting around with Tante Lulu."

"I thought you and Lily were back together." After the way he'd seen them dancing at the tavern last night—*Was it really only last night? Seems like a lifetime ago*—he would have bet that the two of them were reconciled, back to being engaged.

Mark's face flushed, and he turned to avoid eye contact with Caleb. "That was last night. Now things are no different than before. Lily and I don't have a future."

"I know it's none of my business, but why the hell not?"

"I'll say it once. Then I'd rather not discuss it again. Lily and I had a dream, for as long as I can remember, of starting a home-renovation business. We would buy these fixer-uppers. She would do design work. I would do the carpentry work and fine wood detailing. We'd both paint the walls and refinish the woodwork. We'd renovate, then resell, then buy another. All Lily's letters to me in Afghanistan were filled with ideas for our business. We even knew which places we wanted to target first. There's an abandoned church over in Franklinville that would make a spectacular home, stained-glass windows and all." He glanced pointedly at the space where his missing limb would be. "Not gonna happen."

"Can't you have more than one dream? Can't you and Lily open some other business? Maybe operate the cavern together?"

He shook his head. "Lily has spent four years of college studying architecture, and has three more to go, just so she can do this. I've got to let her find someone else to do it with. Or else she can do it herself. If I stuck with her, she'd give it up. I just know she would."

"Architecture, huh? When she's not stripping?"

"She is not going to strip."

Caleb noticed that Mark used future tense, not past, but he figured he'd butted in enough. "Let's go see if we can clear some of the debris out of the cavern. And shove the pity-party business. You can carry a rope or a helmet with one arm."

The house was quiet as they passed through, Tante Lulu and Abbie being gone. Lizzie was still at Jonas's place, though he'd promised to pick her up tonight after his meeting with Dat. He would let her stay with him at the B & B for a few days, with Tante Lulu and Abbie as chaperones. He checked his watch. Claire had gone back to her cabin to meet with her buyer at noon. It was two o'clock now. She should be back soon.

But no, his timing was off. Crossing the back yard, he saw that Claire's station wagon had been driven across the grass and parked near the wooden bridge. On top were strapped a dozen or so skins of some kind. And Claire was on the other side of the creek, seated Indian style on the ground in the clearing in front of the cavern, using a small ax to cut the side branches off some long, thin striplings.

Boner was in the creek yipping and yapping at something, probably a trout. Then, giving up, he began a grand pursuit of butterflies . . . running, skidding to a stop, doing a quick about-face on his tiny feet, then running and yipping in the other direction. Dog heaven, he supposed.

It wasn't Boner that got Mark's attention, though. "*What* is she doing?" Mark was practically bug-eyed with disbelief.

"Call me crazy, but I think she's building a wigwam. No, I take that back. Call *her* crazy."

"Hi!" she yelled, standing and waving at them. Her hair, which appeared more red than auburn in the sunlight, was piled on top of her head. Her face had a nice summer-suntanny glow . . . or was it afterglow from their lovemaking? *I can only hope.* She wore another jogger-type bra, this time black, with a pair of black nylon shorts and white athletic shoes. She looked good enough to eat, and he meant that in the best possible way.

"Uh . . . what are you doing?" he asked.

"I figure security will be an issue till a new door is

put on. Actually, even after, probably till the project is completed. So I'm putting up a wigwam. We can take turns sleeping out here, to keep watch."

"Couldn't we have put up a tent?" Mark asked.

She gave him a look that put him in the category of imbeciles and clueless men. "Why would we do that when all the natural resources are right here?" She waved at the forest behind her.

"Oh. Okay. Sure. Thanks," Mark said, but when Claire glanced away, he made a twirling motion near his head for Caleb's benefit.

Caleb moved closer to Claire, so close he could smell the shampoo in her hair . . . the same shampoo he'd used this morning in her shower. Pretending to examine the striplings she was working on, he whispered, "Dare I hope you and I have the first watch tonight?"

She smiled at him. A big ol' come-hither, big-boy, sex-on-the-rocks-comin'-up kind of smile. Words were unnecessary.

For the first time today, since they'd discovered the vandalism, since the pathetic meeting with his mother and father, he was beginning to think his life was not so bad. Sex in a teepee—rather, wigwam—with a crazy woman. "Should I wear my loincloth?" He waggled his eyebrows at her.

"Only if you bring your tomahawk." She was staring at the area where his loincloth might be.

God, he loved a woman who knew her mind. Even if she was a little bit crazy.

His corn was tasty . . .

"You know, Caleb, the Native Americans got it right with their philosophy of life," Claire told him two hours later as they stood on the bridge over the creek.

He barely stifled a moan and put his face in his hands. It had been about ninety degrees out today. He was sweaty and irritable after having spent the afternoon pulling all the debris out of the cave, with Mark's help. He had a headache that felt like a machine gun going off in his skull. *Rat-tat-tat-rat-tat-tat-rat-tat-tat . . .* And now Claire wanted to give him a lecture on Indian philosophy crap.

She was watching him expectantly.

Okay, I can tell her to shove it, that I'm not interested. But do I want to risk not having sex with her at least one more time? No-brainer there! "I give up. What did the Indians do right?"

"They had this philosophy of planting called the Three Sisters. It involved planting squash, corn, and beans on the same hillock. The corn would grow tall and support the tendrils of the beans, and the squash leaves would spread out and help the ground retain moisture to nourish them all."

My brain feels like squash about now. "And this should matter to me, why?"

"Tsk-tsk-tsk. Let me finish. There is great symbolism there. We, all people, cannot stand alone. We supplement and complement one another. We can grow only with the assistance of others."

Uh-oh! "I'm not going to like the point of this story, am I?"

"It occurred to me after being on your parents' farm

yesterday that the Amish in general do a good job of following the Three Sisters philosophy. To me, the corn is like the father and mother, the bean sprouts all the children, and the squash the community."

She's got a death wish. She's got a freakin' death wish, bringing up my family when I'm in this mood. Mark had already escaped to the house. Caleb started to walk away, in the direction of the wigwam she'd put together all by herself. Ducking down, he crawled inside, but not before giving Boner a black look that said, *Come inside and you are hot-dog soup.* It was surprisingly spacious and, more important, cool inside. The air was sweetly scented from a smudge pot next to a large Indian blanket covering the dirt. And it was surprisingly light because of the smoke hole in the ceiling, not that he expected Claire to do any smoking. Except in the sexual sense. *God, what is this? Ghoul humor? No, horny man humor.*

She crawled in after him. "What I was trying to say is that it was downright cruel of your parents and community to toss you out to grow on your own. It's probably why you've been such a loner. It's why you are generally so dour. I saw it the minute I met you, your drive to succeed, despite your loneliness. The Three Sisters have let you down in the past, so you can't trust anyone to do it again."

Dammit! Holy sonofabitch dammit to hell! God spare me from a man-analyzing woman. Why do they have to dissect every little thing? "I've done just fine, Claire."

"I know you have. More the credit to you."

"Where's the 'but' in there?"

"But I believe, to be really complete, you need to reconcile with your family and Amish community."

If a guy said that to me, he'd probably be flattened by now. "My mother already made it clear that the shunning would be resuming. So that horse has already left the barn, Dr. Phil."

He could tell that disturbed her. Hah! It disturbed him, too. He had been in a crouch position, the ceiling of the wigwam not being high enough to accommodate his six-foot-four frame. Now he dropped down to his knees, then rolled over, flat on his back, arms folded under his neck, and stared at the smoke hole. *Could Sparky crawl up the side of the wigwam and drop down on me from that hole?* he wondered.

"You didn't let me finish." She knelt beside him on the blanket. "I was going to say, barring a reconciliation with your family, you should plant new beans and squash to complement you in the future."

This would be laughable if it weren't so intrusive. "Aha! I get it now. We're back to the sperm bank business. If I had a wife and kids and a farm, everything would be just hunky-dory."

"No, that's not true. My mentioning a baby was only a slip of the tongue to begin with."

He raised a brow in disbelief.

"I mean it, the baby business is off the table. Not an issue."

He reached for her wrist and pulled her down beside him, putting an arm around her and resting her head on his chest. He kissed the top of her head, then said, "So where do we go from here?"

"Can we pretend I never said those words?"

If only! "I can't give you the things you want, Claire.

I have no idea what I'm doing today, let alone tomorrow. I'm all screwed up inside. I can't fulfill my own expectations, let alone someone else's. Not yours. Not Lizzie's."

"Now, see, that's where you're wrong. I really don't have expectations of you. Hopes, maybe, but not expectations."

He doubted that.

"Let's just enjoy each other while you're here, and let it go at that. That should work for both of us."

He doubted that even more.

Somehow, in the course of their conversation, Caleb had removed her bra, rearranged her on top of him, and slid his hands under the back of her shorts, cupping her bare ass. It was probably some subconscious effort to put her on top so that if Sparky dropped in, he would hit her first. *Hah! Nice try, cowboy! My putting Claire there in the saddle has nothing to do with snakes. Well, not the reptile kind anyway.* Trying for a change of subject, he asked, "So, I'm a stalk of corn, huh? What does that make you?"

She smiled, though the smile didn't reach her sad eyes. Then she slipped her hand between their bodies, taking his cock in her hand.

He about went cross-eyed at the sheer mind-blowing pleasure. At least his headache was gone.

"Hmmm. I could be the tassel on your stalk." She loosened her hair with her free hand and brushed it across his chest. "Or I could be the bee who comes to prick your corn. Is your corn sweet?"

A choked laugh escaped his lips. "The only one doing any pricking is gonna be me. And I'm damn sweet when I want to be."

"Promises, promises."

When he did in fact "prick her" and was embedded in her tight clasp up to the hilt, he confessed, "For what it's worth, baby, I liked hearing *those* words from you."

Her response was a long, muscle-fisted, spasming orgasm that said without words, from the inside out, clear as a sailor's grody chant, "I love you."

God help me!

Chapter
12

The lady had plans . . . big plans . . .

"We're plannin' a party, a real *fais do-do* here on the Spruce Creek bayou," Tante Lulu told Claire the minute she entered the B & B kitchen.

Claire had gone home to shower and gather her laptop and Park Service files. She and Mark were going to work together for a few hours, piecing together data gathered in the cavern with historical data, including the journal entries. After that, she was going out on a dinner date surprisingly offered by Caleb this afternoon. Caleb was out at his father's place, for a rescheduled meeting with the Amish church leaders. She'd offered to go with him, but he'd declined the offer, telling her Jonas would "cover his six."

At Abbie's motion offering a glass of lemonade, Claire sat down at the table with them. Just for a moment. "A party, huh? What's the occasion? There's not a lot to celebrate."

"Bite yer tongue, girl." Tante Lulu wagged a forefinger at her. Her hair was gray and curly today. And she wore a pretty floral print dress with short sleeves. On her feet were white orthopedic shoes, a concession, Claire supposed, for the trek around the flea market. Abbie also looked good in a black-and-white polka-dot sundress with white sandals. "St. Jude's been workin' overtime on you. You best be grateful."

"Me? I meant the bad luck with the cavern. What makes you think St. Jude's doing something for me?"

"Ya felt any thunderbolts lately?" The Cajun lady narrowed her eyes at Claire, as if she could read her mind. "Ya know what they say down on the bayou. Ya cain't make the gumbo with an instant soup mix."

"Huh?"

"It takes time, sweetie. Give ol' Jude some workin' room."

Claire took a sip from the icy glass. The lemonade was delicious, just the right mix of tart and sweet. "Well, to tell the truth, I do feel a bit like I've been hit with a Mack truck."

"The thunderbolt'll do that to ya."

Abbie just smiled, going with the flow where her new best friend was concerned. Actually, Abbie was so grateful for the change in Mark that nothing else seemed to bother her.

"I have to tell you, though, that the feeling's not mutual," Claire was quick to add. "Not that there's anything wrong with that."

Tante Lulu waved a hand dismissively. "He'll come around. St. Jude never fails. Why ya all dolled up, honey?"

Claire blushed, something she was doing a lot lately.

"Caleb and I are going out to dinner, to Mimi's in Huntingdon."

"Oh, they have wonderful food there," Abbie said.

"And atmosphere?" Tante Lulu asked Abbie.

"I'd describe it as upscale casual. There's a side room with low lighting. And a small band plays some nights."

Tante Lulu clapped her hands together. "St. Jude at work already. I best get ta work on Caleb's hope chest."

Tante Lulu was serious. Claire boggled at the prospect.

"Now, why dontcha help us with the guest list?" Tante Lulu asked. "Read the list back fer us, Abbie."

"The Jinx staff . . . Caleb, Adam, John—"

"And me," Tante Lulu interjected.

Good Lord, she considers herself a member of the Pearl Project team.

"Claire, myself, Mark, Lily, even though Mark will have a fit," Abbie continued. "Lily's parents, Amos and Andy, Jonas and his kids, Mr. and Mrs. Peachey and all their children's families, though I suspect Lizzie is the only one who'll come, except for Jonas."

"Kin ya think of anyone else?" Tante Lulu inquired of Claire. "Oooh, oooh, oooh! I betcha if I invited Luc and Remy and Charmaine and their broods, they might come."

Claire shook her head in wonder. "Tell me again what we're celebrating."

"Oh, lotsa things. Mark bein' a hero and comin' back alive from the war."

Abbie cringed at that topic, knowing Mark would not be pleased.

"If Mark thinks he's got a war injury, wait till he sees

Remy. Whooee, that boy's got more burn marks than a barbecued gator. Not that he ain't still handsome."

Remy was the pilot who'd brought Tante Lulu here, Claire recalled.

"Also, the reunion between Caleb and Jonas," Tante Lulu went on. "Tee-John's birthday. Moving the boulder. Family—we gotta celebrate family in hopes those stiff-necked Amish'll drop that stupid shunning business."

"Amos and Andy's birthdays are coming up next week," Abbie pointed out.

"Right. Thanks fer remindin' me. I think I'll buy me a pair of those underpants with the padding in the rear. I noticed Amos oglin' my behind today. Mebbe I should give him sumpin ta drool over."

Claire and Abbie gawked at Tante Lulu.

"What? A lady's gotta keep herself up, even if she is up in years. I saw a T-shirt at the flea market today that said it all: 'Over the Hill? What Hill?'"

Some music started then, coming from the front of the house. It sounded like someone singing to a karaoke machine. She cocked her head in question.

"Thass Tee-John and Lizzie. He's helpin' her put an act together fer *American Idol*. I wish René would come. He plays in a band sometimes, an' he could give her tips on moves and such."

Claire and Abbie rolled their eyes at each other.

"Maybe we could have some music at this event," Abbie offered, getting into the spirit. "Lizzie could perform."

"An' if my nephews come, they kin do their Village People act. They could teach y'all a bit about *joie de vivre*. That means 'joy of life.' Come ta think on it, they'd prob'ly come if they knew we was celebratin' Tee-John's birthday."

Claire would love to see Tante Lulu's nephews and niece perform that kind of act. If they were anything like John, it would be a great show.

"Back to you and Caleb," Tante Lulu said. "I think ya should get a knock-his-eyeballs-out kinda dress fer the party. Make Caleb so hot he cain't resist ya. Not that I'm recommendin' hanky-panky, but sometimes St. Jude doesn't mind a little help." Then she went off on another tangent, something about the red dress and red high heels that Charmaine wore at her wedding. "Her *last* weddin'. Well, her first and her last, since she hitched up with Raoul twice. Lordy, Lordy, that gal's been married so many times it's a wonder she don't get veil rash."

You had to love the Cajun lady, meddling and all. She had a finger in every pie and a heart as big as . . . well, the bayou. They could all take lessons in her zest for life.

The end of the road . . .

Caleb sat in the front room of Dat and Mam's house, surrounded by his father and five other Amishmen. The meeting had been moved to late this afternoon, rather than the evening, so the farmers could get home to milk their cows.

He felt as if he were twelve years old being called on the carpet for some mischief or other. And he wasn't even the guilty party here.

The room hadn't changed in all that time. In fact, it probably hadn't changed in the fifty years the Peacheys had occupied the property. It was spotlessly clean and contained only essential furniture, with no curtains on the windows or pictures on the walls, in compliance with Old Order Amish rules, as spelled out in the *Ordnung*. How many times had he had those rules recited to him? A lifetime ago.

The Amish church was divided into districts, each of which had a bishop and a set number of deacons and preachers. There were Old Order Amish or Swartzentruber Amish, depending on how strict the rules.

Because Jonas had a last-minute emergency with his business, Caleb sat alone on the stiff-backed sofa with a half circle of men facing him in folding chairs. Dat was closest to him. The elderly Bishop Lapp, better known as asshole—to him, at least—frowned a greeting. Deacon Abram Zook, the guy who wanted to hook up with Lizzie, nodded at him. "Abe," he said. They used to go to Sunday-night singings together, not that their former friendship would count for anything. The other deacon, who introduced himself as Adam Hostetler, was new to this community; he was from "up Ohio way." Preachers Ezra Troyer and Hosiah Knepp, fortysomethings, stern men he vaguely remembered, completed the group.

He noticed that Knepp's right hand was red and swollen.

He narrowed his eyes to see better, and yep, there were two little dots on his hand. Fang marks.

"I see you met Sparky," he said to Knepp, smiling.

"Huh?"

"Sparky is the guard snake at the Spruce Creek Cavern. I'll have to get him a special snakey treat for doing such a good job. Hmmm. I wonder if there's such a thing as snake kibble."

Knepp bared his teeth at him in a sneer.

"Let us pray," Bishop Lapp began, ignoring the exchange between him and Knepp, and he droned on for at least ten minutes in German. Caleb had no idea if anyone understood what he was saying. He certainly didn't.

Bishop Lapp then flipped to a certain page in his dog-eared Bible and turned to him. Quoting from Romans, he said in English, "Be not conformed to this world, but be transformed by the renewing of your mind that ye may prove what is that good and acceptable and perfect will of God."

Caleb was confused. He didn't mind showing deference for the prayer or for the Bible reading, but something else was going on here. He studied his father, who was stony-faced and obviously bowing to the will of the bishop. What else was new?

"Caleb Peachey, we urge you to drop down and make your kneeling confession. It is not too late to repent and come back to the People, despite all your sins."

He glared at his father, then turned back to the bishop. "I came here to discuss the damages at the Spruce Creek Cavern, not to confess or beg for forgiveness. So let's cut to the chase, boys."

They all flinched at use of the term "boys."

So be it! He stood and handed his father a sheet of paper detailing the damages at the cavern.

His father gasped. "So much?" Then he passed the sheet around the half circle, ending with the bishop, who exclaimed, "This is outrageous. There vas not that much damitch done."

Caleb raised his eyebrows at the bishop's inadvertent admission of involvement in the vandalism. "If anything, that's a conservative estimate of damages. The police are aware of the crime, but not the perpetrators. However, in about one hour, they *will* know and you *will* find them on your doorstep, that I guarantee. Unless we come to some agreement, and soon."

"You alveese ver a vild one," Bishop Lapp said. "Alveese grexing 'bout one thing or 'nother. Alveese pushing, pushing, pushing."

"It wonders me how ya could stay away so long, Caleb. Dontcha care 'bout yer heritich?" Abe asked, not unkindly.

He tried to answer as politely as the question was asked. "I cherish memories of many good things about being Amish and being raised on this farm. But I can't forget or accept the harsh manner in which me and Jonas were forced to leave without a dime in our pockets."

Bishop Lapp shook his head vehemently. "Youse were never forced to leave. You and Jonas chose ta go. Ya refused ta kneel before God and confess yer wrongdoings."

Caleb threw his hands up in disgust. "This is a wasted discussion. We're never going to agree. Most of all, Dat, I'm disappointed in you. I came here expecting apologies and reparations. Instead, it's the same old, same old." He stood, about to leave.

"That's not the vay it is, son." His father cast pleading eyes at him, begging for . . . what? "I am too old to change. I hafta follow the *Ordnung*. I hoped . . . I hoped you would find yer vay back."

"Impossible! And I'll tell you something else, old

man. You're about to lose your daughter, too, unless you lighten up."

Any softening on his father's part went out the window then. Dat exchanged a look with the bishop, then stared at him as if he was a stranger. Caleb pitied him. To be so much under the thumb of a misguided man of God . . . well, it was sad, really.

"Ve vill settle," Bishop Lapp said, "but I cannot apologize for what vas done. There is evil there in that cavern and in you, Caleb Peachey. I don't know if you alveese were thataway, but fer sure and fer certain you are now."

His Dat at least had the grace to reproach the bishop for painting his son in such a drastic manner. "Bishop, you go too far. Caleb is not evil, and I cannot allow you ta say so."

"Hmpfh!" the bishop said. "Wait here till I get the money."

While he went out to his buggy, there was an uncomfortable silence in the room. Caleb's heart ached, because truly this had to be good-bye to his father. His father's tear-filled eyes indicated that he knew that, too. The bishop came back with a strongbox and began to count out twenty-two thousand dollars in hundreds, fifties, and twenties. A ridiculous pile of money, but he had expected as much, since most Amish didn't believe in banks.

When he went out to his Jeep, with a paper grocery bag filled with the money, he saw his mother and father standing on the back porch, just watching him. And that was that. So much for Claire's Three Sisters theory. His vine had definitely left the building . . . uh, stalk.

Something amazing occurred to him then. He was

letting these criminals get away with their crime by not having them arrested. In a way, for a man who had adopted punishment and retaliation as a way of life in the military, this amounted to turning the other cheek. The anger that had fueled him for so many years seemed to have disappeared. What would he do now without that splinter up his butt to spur him on? He felt light as a feather and, at the same time, heavy as Atlas carrying the world. In other words, a mess.

The only saving grace for him and his shattered nerves was the fact that he and Claire were going out to dinner tonight. He needed to be with her.

It was a sign of how distressed he really was that, at that moment, he savored the idea that at least one person loved him.

You want to spread my body with . . . what? . . .

Claire loved him more and more by the minute.

It was exhilarating and scary to know that she could care so deeply about a man she barely knew. Never in her twenty years of dating had she experienced such powerful emotions for another person, even those few that she'd immaturely thought she loved.

Caleb would probably say it was just lust, but that's because he feared she would expect something in return. She didn't. Not yet. Maybe never.

They'd just finished a delicious meal. She'd had Veal Oscar with lump crab, hollandaise, and asparagus. He'd had a ravioli sampler that included lobster, gorgonzola, prosciutto, and wild mushrooms covered lightly with tomato-basil sauce. They'd shared a heart-of-palm salad for appetizer and vanilla crème brûlée for dessert. Now they were sipping at the remainder of their wine as they listened to a two-piece band play instrumental eighties music.

"You look really nice tonight," Caleb said against her ear. He'd pulled his chair from opposite her to her side so they could watch the band together. His arm was around the back of her chair.

"You like this?" She glanced down at the green-and-white floral halter sundress she wore.

"I like the whole package, honey. Your hair . . ." He tugged one of the loose strands that framed her face, strands she'd deliberately loosened from the twist on the top of her head and curled into spirals. "Your makeup." He ran a thumb across her closed lips, and she hoped that the new tube of "Coral Madness" she'd bought was as long-lasting and kiss-proof as promised. "And yeah, I really like your dress—and that intriguing knot." He pretended to loosen the knot at her nape. "You smell like . . . um, let me see, lilies of the valley, right?"

She nodded. "Jessica McClintock."

"Who?"

"It's the name of the perfume."

"Ah. Nice."

"I don't think I've ever met a man who recognized the scent of a particular flower."

"My mother planted lilies of the valley in a circle around an oak tree in the front yard. It was her favorite. I could also probably recognize lilacs, roses, marigolds, irises, and a few others she planted, like honeysuckle— I saw it by the river at your house."

She could tell that he immediately regretted mentioning his mother. When Caleb had returned to the B & B this afternoon with twenty-two thousand dollars in loose bills in a grocery bag, of all things, he'd been grim-faced and tight-mouthed. He'd explained to his team members the gist of his deal with the Amish leaders and predicted there would be no more trouble from them, at least of the physical type. She sensed that he'd been deeply hurt by something regarding his family, though, and her heart went out to him.

"What happened today . . . with your family?"

His eyes went suddenly bleak, and he shook his head. "I'd rather talk about you. Tell me about yourself, about your wild days."

"My mother was a drug addict, as I told you before, and I never knew who my father was," she started.

He squeezed her shoulder. "Go on."

"I'd been in the foster care system even before my mother died when I was eight. An overdose."

"That's how old Jonas's Fanny is," Caleb pointed out, and she knew he was trying to picture his sweet niece in a similar situation and could not. "Why weren't you adopted?"

"I couldn't be while my mother was alive. She kept going on and off the wagon, refusing to give up rights. Then afterward, I guess I became a problem child. Unadoptable."

"How much of a problem could an eight-year-old be?"

"You'd be surprised. And I was an even bigger handful once I hit puberty and mistakenly believed I could earn love with sex. Over the course of eight years, till I was sixteen, I was in twelve different foster homes, some horrendous, some not so bad. After I counted thirty, I lost track of the number of boys I was with."

"That's horrible, Claire. More than horrible. It's outrageous that the system in this country allows that."

"Hey, my experience wasn't that bad compared to other kids I met. At least I was never sexually abused by my caregivers."

He shook his head sadly.

"I'm not looking for pity," she said. "I believe everything in life happens for a reason. My mother's death and my foster care made me stronger. And I found help when I was sixteen. So everything turned out all right."

He studied her for several long moments. "Does that mean I can't tease you about your wild days?"

"Tease all you want, but those horny teenage boys didn't know zippo about sex. And know this, I haven't been promiscuous in a long, long time. If you want the truth, one night of making love with you was better than anything I ever had then, or since."

"You sure know how to make a guy feel good, baby."

"It's the truth. Don't go getting all scared, though. I'm not expecting anything in return."

"Why do you always add that disclaimer?"

"Because I know you're skittish about commitment."

He started to argue with her, then stopped himself. "I've had a lot of sex, too, Claire, and last night wasn't the same old, same old for me, either. And yeah, it scares me how special it was."

They were both silent then, mulling the words they'd exchanged, listening to the band.

Claire broke the silence when she said, "I like the way you look tonight, too, Caleb."

"Yeah?" He smiled at her, and the hand resting on the back of her chair caressed her bare shoulder.

He was clean-shaven and must have had a haircut today, though his hair had been short to begin with. There was the faint scent of some woodsy aftershave the barber must have used. Nice, not overpowering. He wore a white golf shirt with the logo "Coronado Country Club," tucked into the narrow waistband of crease-pleated khakis. On his feet were loafers minus socks.

They had both been like teenagers readying themselves for a big date, Claire realized. She liked the fact that he had made an attempt to please her with his appearance, and she suspected he felt the same way about her.

"Maybe we better head back if we're to make the first shift at the cavern," she suggested. "We can stop by my house for a change of clothes."

Caleb shook his head. "Famosa took the first shift, and LeDeux will take over around two o'clock when he gets back from a date. We can take the full shift tomorrow night."

"Does that mean I'm going to get a chance to test this kiss-proof lipstick?"

"Kiss-proof, huh? You should never issue a challenge to a Navy SEAL, baby. Not even a former Navy SEAL. We take our challenges seriously." He grinned at her.

She grinned back at him. "I can only hope."

Later, Claire decided that she should write a letter of complaint to the manufacturer, or maybe not. The lipstick hadn't even lasted the ten-mile drive back to her cabin. But it was hard to think about complaints when an interested man was standing before her, as naked and beautiful as that statue of David, wearing nothing but a barbed-wire tattoo on his upper arm. And did she mention *interested?*

Even later than that, Caleb left the bed and came back with an artist's brush that must have come from her desk, and a plastic Tupperware-style container.

"What is that?"

"Church spread. It's a ungodly mix of syrup, marshmallow, and peanut butter."

"Does it taste good?"

"Heavenly."

"It's awfully thick."

With a wicked gleam in his eyes, he left, and she could hear the microwave turn on and zap the container for a few seconds. When he came back, he said, "Now I get to connect the dots . . . uh, freckles."

"You're going to paint my body with something from church."

"It's from my mother, not the church."

"Oh, that makes it better."

"You'll like it. Believe me. But man oh man, I don't have any freckles, so I guess you won't be able to reciprocate." He batted his eyelashes at her.

"Tsk-tsk-tsk! You should never issue a challenge to . . ." She repeated his words back at him—". . . a redheaded PhD who's a little bit crazy."

He tilted his head to the side in question, more than interested now.

"I could play tic-tac-toe . . . on your belly. Or I could paint barber-pole stripes if I could only find a pole. Or I could . . ."

Chapter
13

We are fam-i-ly . . . sort of . . .

Caleb was standing in Jonas's back yard, Noah riding on his shoulders, Fanny clutching his knees, and Sarah tugging on his hand to come see her pet goat. Meanwhile, his ear was pressed to his cell phone as he tried to carry on a conversation with his boss.

"Are you sure you don't need me to come back there?" Ronnie asked.

"No, you've got plenty to do there, and everything is under control here now. No more vandalism. All the equipment back in place. We expect to dive tomorrow, if all goes well." He made a motion to Sarah to hold on till he was off the phone. And he removed Noah's forefinger from inside one of his nostrils.

"I know you, Caleb. You're probably blaming yourself for the trouble."

"Of course I am. The Amish wouldn't have been drawn into this if it weren't for me. Ouch!"

"What's wrong?"

"My niece is trying to crawl up my leg, and she grabbed the wrong leg for leverage."

Ronnie laughed.

"Did I tell you the area newspapers picked up on the police report and have been hovering here, waiting for some momentous treasure discovery?"

"That's more of a problem than the vandalism, I would think."

"Yep, but I've appeased them by promising an exclusive story if they stay off the property for now."

"And that worked?"

"So far."

"Listen, we've recovered a few of the stolen statues we were searching for. Once we find the rest, I can be back there to help."

"Well, don't rush. Your help is welcome, of course, but I can handle it myself."

"I have every confidence in you, Caleb. Maybe Jake and I will make it back by the time Tante Lulu holds her big party a week from Saturday."

Caleb groaned. "That woman is going to be the death of me yet."

"By the way, Jake and I might have an announcement to make at that party."

"You're getting married again," he guessed.

"Nope. Well, I'm not ruling it out *ever,* but it's something else. Anyhow, I have a call on the other line. Call me tomorrow after the dive."

"Am I the woman who's going to be the death of you?" Claire asked, coming up beside him and peeling Fanny off his thigh. Together the four of them walked toward the shed where the goat was penned.

"No, Tante Lulu."

Claire was in total agreement. Tante Lulu had been bugging her about monograms on pillowcases this morning.

A silver Corvette pulled into the lane beside the house, and all three kids scampered off. It was the nurse, Laura Jones, who always brought something interesting for the kids. Smart lady!

Jonas came out of one of his greenhouses then, walked over to them, and did a double take as he noticed that Laura had arrived.

"*Ach,* what am I going to do with that woman?" he asked Caleb.

"You need to ask?"

Claire laughed and walked away to introduce herself to Laura.

"You know what I mean. Nothing I say discourages her."

"She's got the hots for you, all right."

Jonas put his face in his hands for a second, then confided, "She touched me last night."

"Huh?"

"First she kissed me; then she touched my . . . uh, privates."

Caleb bit his bottom lip to keep from laughing out loud. "Didn't anyone ever touch you there before?"

"Of course Mary did, but we was married."

"So, you don't believe in premarital . . . touching?"

"Stop making fun, Caleb. This is serious. *Jah,* touching would be okay if we was gonna get married."

"And you're not?"

"Caleb! I'm Plain."

"And she's not."

They both glanced toward the house, where Claire

and Laura were talking animatedly as they set a picnic table on the back patio. Laura wore cutoff jeans, a tight blue T-shirt, and sandals. Her hair was pulled up into a high ponytail. Big gold hoops dangled from her ears. Even from this distance he could see her red lipstick. Definitely not Plain.

"Suppose she suddenly showed up here one day dressed Plain. Would you feel differently?"

Jonas's jaw dropped as he imagined that prospect. "Maybe."

"You like her," Caleb accused.

"*Jah,* I do, but I'm not used ta a woman makin' the moves."

"Take a little brotherly advice?" he asked.

Tentatively, Jonas nodded.

"A woman making the moves is not a bad thing. It can be very, very good."

"You're not helping at all." Jonas sighed deeply and began to walk toward the house. You would have thought he was a prisoner going to his execution.

Caleb stood there smiling. Watching Jonas talk to Laura. Watching the kids giggle with Claire, who appeared to be teaching them to dance to music from a tape player that Lizzie had just brought from the house.

Caleb realized in that instant that he was happy. Just to be alive. Just to be here. Just to be with his newfound family.

Just to be with Claire.

It was the pits . . .

Caleb and Famosa dropped down slowly into the still water of the pit. This would be a bounce dive first time out, quick in and out, just to get the measure of things.

"Take it slow," he said into the mike inside his breathing mask. "Whatever we do, we can't stir that silt at the bottom or we'll be here forever."

"Got it. Man, it's dark in here."

Caleb agreed. They both had a lot of experience diving, but mostly in the ocean or clear fresh waters. Here, now that they were beyond the range of the lighting cables at the top, they could see only as far as their headlamps and flashlights shone, which wasn't far. It was an eerie, otherworldly scene. Totally silent. Totally black.

Finally, just before they reached the bottom, he and Famosa grabbed on to the sides, attempting to keep their feet from sinking into the bottom, not just because of the mud they might stir, but because there could be stalagmites sticking up. These could cause physical harm, even sever air hoses. "I'll go left, you go right. Scope things out," he suggested.

"Gotcha."

First, Caleb dropped a weighted measuring string into the silt. *Damn!* There was six feet of mud at the bottom and nothing resembling treasure sticking out that he could see. Unless they got lucky on a first try scouring the bottom, it would be almost impossible to find the pearls, or anything else down there. Even so, he worked himself around the circular walls of the room, soon meeting up with Famosa.

The Cuban motioned for him to follow. He went

about fifteen feet before stopping and making hand signals.

Caleb put his hand where Famosa indicated and felt the current coming through a slight crack. He nodded his understanding, and without further instruction, they both retraced their movements around the circular pit, seeking a place where water might be escaping. Because sure as hell, if water was coming in, it had to be going out. Otherwise, this pit would be overflowing into the room on the other side of the hole. It took them more than a half hour and almost all the air in their tanks before they found what they were searching for. The crack was wider than the other side. Shining a light inside the crack, it opened wider and wider, like a funnel. It was hard to tell for sure—what they needed was a snake light—but there might be another chamber on the other side, which could be really exciting.

They had decisions to make about how to proceed.

He gave the signal, and both he and Famosa began to rise to the top. When they got there, everyone was full of questions, but he waved them off, telling them they would meet in fifteen minutes in the library, where they could use the survey maps to discuss what they'd seen.

While he stood in the twilight zone near the entrance, taking off his diving gear, he kept an eye out for Sparky. If that snake wasn't careful, it was going to be living at the bottom of the black lagoon.

"Hey, Claire," he yelled.

She had been going back to the house with the rest of the gang. Turning, she raised her brows at him.

"C'mere a minute."

Her brows went even higher, this time in a "You've got to be kidding" manner. She probably thought he wanted a quickie, considering the way they'd been going at each other like jackrabbits the past few days. If only! Or her hackles were on red alert because he'd crooked his finger at her, bringing them back to square one of that "beg" challenge he'd issued to her in the beginning. It was amazing the things a guy said that came back to bite him in the butt. Oh, well. "Please."

She waited for him to catch up with her, of course.

"I was wondering," he started, hating what he was about to ask, "could you call that semi-fiancé of yours?"

Saints above! . . .

Tante Lulu sat in a corner chair of the library, sipping a cup of thick Cajun coffee, watching the drama unfold in front of her. Things were going just the way she liked.

"I don't understand exactly how you could pump water from the one pit into another," Claire remarked as she studied the rough sketches Caleb and Adam had made after their dive this morning.

"Chamber, honey. Chamber," Caleb corrected her with a squeeze of her shoulder.

Honey, huh? The two of them probably didn't even realize how they addressed each other. Or how they managed to touch each other in passing. And when they looked at each other, whoo-ee, the thunderbolt was a-sizzlin'. Reminded her of her nephews and her niece when they was just about to wave the white flag of surrender.

Tante Lulu only hoped that they would get together before she had to head back to Louisiana. An old Cajun lady like herself could stay away from the bayou for only so long before the yearnin' came over her for swamp sounds. Besides, her fam'ly needed her. They allus did.

Tee-John glanced her way, saw the direction of her stare, and pumped an arm in the air with a triumphant "Yes!," attributing the progress between Caleb and Claire to her good work. But she knew better. St. Jude did all the hard work.

And by the way, Jude, what's up with Mark and Lily? They's farther apart than ever.

She thought she heard the familiar voice in her head say, *Give me time. I can only handle one hopeless case at a time.*

I'm gettin' old. I don't have that much time.

And the voice replied, *You think you're old! Hah!*

Oh, and don't forget about Jonas. He needs a woman fer those precious chillun of his.

I'm workin' on it, I'm workin' on it. Even God wasn't so impatient when He took one of Adam's ribs.

Just then a new man walked into the library.

"Del!" Claire walked up to the guy, who was about forty and bald, but in a sexy-bald kind of way. He was short but built like a brick outhouse, as they used to say in the old days. "I'm so glad you could come." Then Claire gave Del, who must be the geologist, a big hug.

Del squeezed Claire in return and said, "Hey, babe."

Which caused Caleb's face to slam-dunk into his Navy SEAL special forces I'm-gonna-kill-ya-if-ya-touch-my-woman type of expression. He did everything but growl.

"Everyone, I want you to meet my *good* friend Delbert Finley."

He smiled and said, "Just call me Del."

Claire linked her arm with the newcomer and introduced each of the others in the room, including her.

And yep, that was a growl she heard from Caleb now. He looked as if he'd swallowed a gallon of pea soup.

A sudden thought came to Tante Lulu, and she slapped her leg with glee. "*Jude, ya did it again.*"

And then arrived the green-eyed monster . . .

Caleb took an instant dislike to Delbert "Just call me Del" Finley.

He was short for a man, about five-eight, and probably on steroids, or else he pumped iron for a living. Okay, he probably got a lot of upper-body exercise, working with rocks and stuff, which required mountain climbing, he supposed. He acted as if the rest of them were dimwits as he explained, slow as molasses, the rock formations of the cavern and what they would have to do to pump the mud and silt out of the chamber. Mostly Caleb didn't like the way the jerk watched Claire. *Good friend, my ass!*

Caleb walked around the library table, edged LeDeux aside with his hip, and stood next to Claire, looping an arm over her shoulder. "So, give us the short stack, Finley. Where do we get the pump? How heavy is it? Do we need special equipment to lower the pump to the bottom? Will its operation be affected by a crapload of mud?"

Del stared pointedly at Caleb's arm. Claire stared pointedly at his arm, too, but at least she left it there. It

would have been a bit embarrassing—okay, mortifying—
if she'd removed it with disdain.

"I'll have to go down with you to better assess the
situation," Del said.

"Are you certified for cave diving?" Caleb asked.

"Of course," he replied, as if that went without
saying.

"Do you have a wet suit and breathing gear with
you?"

"Of course," he said again.

Of course, Caleb mimicked in his head. *You pompous
little shit, you! You and Boner oughta get along great.*
He heard a chuckle on his other side.

It was LeDeux. At first he thought he might have spoken aloud, but then, exchanging a glance with LeDeux,
as well as Mark and Famosa, he realized they shared his
view of the little shit new guy.

Two hours later, though, he had to concede that Finley knew what he was doing both above ground and
underwater in a cavern. He dove well, he took all the
safety precautions, he knew precisely where to go to
find the ingress and egress cracks just from having studied their rough sketches, and he pointed out several
places where the tips of stalagmites could be seen sticking out of the mud, something he and Famosa had
missed first time around.

Caleb still didn't like him, though.

They were both breathing hard when they stood in
the relatively bright twilight zone of the cavern entrance
a short time later, removing their gear.

"Thanks, Baldy," he said.

"No problem, Rambo," Finley replied.

"I appreciate your help, but stay away from Claire."
Where did that brain blip come from?

"I beg your pardon. I didn't see your name tattooed on her forehead."

"It's on her butt." *Could I be any more crude—or delusional?*

"Are you engaged?"

"Hell, no!" *Well, I asked for that.*

"Then back off, bozo. The field is wide open."

Caleb had no chance to challenge that statement, because the rest of the gang came up and surrounded them. He did wonder at his pathetic possessiveness over a woman he barely knew and would probably/hopefully soon forget.

"I can rent a pump for you today, delivered tomorrow," Finley said, thankfully recognizing the need for a change of subject in front of Claire and the rest of the team. "We'll need to rig a harness and use a winch to lower it slowly to the bottom. Then we'll thread tubing through that crack to the other chamber."

"There's definitely another chamber?" Famosa asked.

Finley nodded.

"We snaked a light through the crack and could see a large opening on the other side," Caleb explained. "The light wasn't powerful enough for us to gauge size or anything."

"Wouldn't it be easier to just blow that wall out?" LeDeux wanted to know.

Caleb and Finley both laughed.

"Easier maybe, but not the best thing if Mark and Abbie are going to open the cavern up to tourist trade," Caleb said.

"That's not to say that you won't want to blow that crack into an actual corridor, even if only big enough to crawl through," Finley elaborated, "but you really should try draining first. You'll have a better picture of what to do then."

"How long will the drainage take?" Mark wanted to know.

He and Finley both shrugged.

"As little as a day, or as much as three days, would be my guess," Caleb said.

"Right," Finley agreed. "It will depend on pumping pressure, elevation of the tubing, thickness of the water once it gets down to the mud and silt base, size of the chamber on the other side. Actually, a slow drainage will be best all around."

"Man, this project was supposed to be a quickie," LeDeux remarked. "And now it's turned into a real mother—" He glanced toward the three women, then self-corrected midsentence, "—a real complex project."

"You can say that again," Caleb agreed.

"Okay, everyone, we have a late lunch spread out for you on the patio," Abbie announced.

It was only then that Caleb realized that Claire was nowhere to be seen. Had she gone home for more meetings related to the sale of her cabin? Or in to State College to meet with some of her colleagues about the latest developments with the cavern? But wasn't it odd that she hadn't informed him, especially since her "semi-fiancé" was here working with them?

Caleb got that prickly sensation in the back of his neck then. The one that had warned him of an impending attack in Kabul. The one he'd always relied on to choose the right path in a black op through enemy territory. The one that had caused him to reconfigure a HALO drop over an al-Qaeda hideout in Bora-Bora. The one he'd experienced just before Hurricane Katrina. The one that detoured him away from a St. Louis babe, who later filed a false paternity suit against a buddy of his.

Something bad was about to happen, unless he was careful.

That was just peachy . . .

Claire, Abbie, Tante Lulu, and Lizzie were sitting on the patio, sipping cold drinks and chatting as they waited for Caleb and Del and the rest of the crew to come back with the latest report on the cavern.

"*Jah,* sad it is the way they treat him. An' he jist keeps takin' it and takin' it."

Claire's mind had been wandering when she caught the tail end of Lizzie's remarks. "Are you talking about Jonas?" It had to be Jonas, a pacifist, if they were referring to someone "taking it and taking it" in a turn-the-cheek manner.

"No, Caleb," Lizzie replied, "though Jonas is the same way."

"She was answering my question," Abbie elaborated. "I wanted to know what happened at the meetings between Caleb and his family yesterday morning and then with his father at the church meeting in the afternoon. Caleb gave us the gist of the meetings, but just bare bones. I sense that something bad happened, personally."

"Hah! How much worse could it be than a mommy and daddy refusin' ta talk ta a child fer seventeen years? Didja know they cain't even eat at the same table with those boys, like they's lepers or somethin'?"

"I think . . . ," Lizzie said, then stopped herself.

All eyes turned to her.

"I think deep down, he'd never admit it, but Caleb expected Mam and Dat to be sorry for what they done and welcome him home. Jonas wouldn't expect anythin' 'cause he's been livin' with it here at home all these years."

"And they're not sorry?" Abbie asked.

Lizzie shook her head. "They can't be sorry unless they denounce the *Ordnung* and all the Amish beliefs."

"So? Why don't they do that?" Good ol' Tante Lulu, blunt as usual.

"Because they'd be shunned themselves and banned from talkin' to all my brothers and sisters and nephews and nieces who're still in the church," Lizzie explained. "I'm not defendin' them, but it is our way." She hesitated, then added, "I saw Jonas and Caleb out on the porch huggin' each other yesterday after Caleb stayed to talk with Mam. They both had tears in their eyes, and I ain't never seen a grown man weep."

Claire's heart about broke at that news.

They all remained silent for a long moment, pondering what Lizzie had said.

"In other words, they choose to shun Caleb and Jonas, rather than the dozens of others," Claire concluded.

Lizzie nodded. "That, and them bein' set in their ways."

"How about you, Lizzie? Aren't you breaking the *Bann?*" Abbie wanted to know.

"*Jah,* I am, but as long as I claim *Rumspringa* rights, I can get away with it."

"Not for much longer, though, I suspect," Claire said. Lizzie nodded again.

"What will you do then?" Claire asked, though she already knew the answer.

"I'm gone," Lizzie said emphatically. "Not just because of my music, either. I ain't gonna shun Caleb and Jonas anymore. It ain't right."

"Too bad we cain't convince yer mommy and daddy of the same thing." Tante Lulu glanced over at Claire meaningfully as she spoke.

"What?" Claire wondered. "Oh, no. You shouldn't interfere. It's none of our business, really. Why are you staring at me like that? Oh, good Lord, you think *I* should do it?"

"Ya got a better way with words," Tante Lulu said. "Besides, they think I'm a kook."

Which you are.

"They're not gonna listen to you," Lizzie told her, as if she really expected that Claire would engage in such a foolhardy an̶t̶i̶...

"They will iffen ̶...̶ what I mean. Doan go ca̶u̶t̶omatic-like, iffen ya know fer behavin' like . . . well, lunk̶h̶...̶heads or nothin', gonna be a fraidy cat, I'll go with ya̶...̶ds or nothin', one of those Peachy Praline Cobbler Cakes ̶...̶ yer break the ice. Nothin' like food to soften a body. Hey, I made a joke. Peachy cake fer the Peachey family. ̶...̶ ha."

Ha̶...̶t funny.

"You'll be sorry if ya go today," Lizzie warned. "It's cannin' day. Mam'll be choppin' cabbage and onions and cucumbers fer chow-chow. I try to stay away on cannin' day."

"I love cannin'," Tante Lulu said.

"Nobody *loves* canning," Claire declared. "It's work."

"I likes work," the old lady insisted, rubbing her hands together with glee. "Mebbe I'll bring some of my Cajun spices. Ain't nothin' like Loo-zee-anna chow-chow with a dash of Cajun lightning. Thass Tabasco sauce."

Abbie giggled. "God, I love having you all here. I haven't had so much fun since my husband Stanley died."

"Hah! Wait till tonight." Tante Lulu winked at Abbie. Abbie blushed.

Those two were up to something. And it wasn't a peace mission to an Amish community.

She was the weirdest mediator they'd ever met . . .

. . . . sky.

Tante Lulu loved bei . . . er. From the time she was
It wasn't an nose to her. It probably started when meddled in the affairs of her
a young . . . e married that horrid Valcour LeDeux, fa-
. . . er great-nephews Luc, Remy, René, and Tee-
. . . f and her great-niece Charmaine, and a sle . . .
other, illegitimate, kids. She'd been the anchor . . .

lives, and her meddling had saved them at times from their alcoholic father. Now it was a habit.

"Best ya hurry up. I gots to pee," she told Claire, who was driving them both into Sinking Valley.

"We already stopped twice. Hold it, or else pee your pants."

"Ya doan have to snap."

"Sorry. It's just that I'm more and more convinced this is a bad idea. It's meddling."

"Ya say that like meddlin's a bad thing. I brought a present fer Rebekah. It's black. So I think it'll be all right."

"What is it?" Claire asked, then noted the imprint on the box she pulled out of her handbag. "Oh, no! Victoria's Secret?"

"Oh, yes."

"When did you go to Victoria's Secret?"

"I didn't. It was a gift from Amos, but it's not my size."

Claire looked at her with shock.

"What? Ya doan think older folks has sexual urges?"

Claire groaned. She did that a lot.

"Anyways. It's a black lace bra and panties. Remember how I tol' Rebekah she needs ta work on her husband usin' her female charms? This should do the trick. And it's black, Amish-like. Okay not Amish-like, but the color is. And besides, no one's gonna see what she has under that plain dress of hers, lessen she hangs 'em on the line."

"Here we are," Claire said, turning onto the farm lane. She seemed glad to change the subject.

Mebbe I should buy some lingerie for Claire, too, iffen she's gonna be so uptight. A thong would be good.

That would loosen her up fer sure. Might jump-start Caleb, too. I should call Charmaine. She knows about slutty . . . uh, sexy undies, bein' a bimbo like she is.

"Luckily, there are no vehicles or buggies, which must mean there's no company. Or, if we're lucky, no one is at home."

Yep, Claire was definitely changing the subject. And definitely uptight.

"By the way, Caleb's hope chest was delivered this mornin'. I'm not sure I can get a bride quilt made in time fer the weddin'. Oooh, oooh, I know what. Mebbe I kin get one from Mrs. Peachey. Yep, I bet she'd like ta give her son a weddin' quilt. We could call it a guilt quilt. Ha, ha, ha."

"You have got to stop this wedding business. I know you mean well, but Caleb and I are just . . . friends."

"Is that what they call it now? You got more hickeys than an albino with a heat rash."

That turned her face about purple and shut her up good.

"Listen, honey, even with all the problems they been havin', this project is gonna be over soon. A week or two at the mos'. Ya doan have all the time in the world before Caleb skedaddles off ta his next treasure hunt. Hitch that boy ta the halter, girl, afore he runs off ta greener pastures."

"If it was meant to be, it will be."

"Are ya looney, girl? This ain't no Doris Day movie. *Que Sera, Sera,* my hiney! Since when does love sit around on its behind waitin' fer fate ta take care of business? Sometimes ya just gotta give the love bug a push."

"Caleb is not in love. There is not going to be a wedding. And that's that."

"Who ya tryin' ta convince? Me or you?"

"You're hopeless!" Claire threw her hands up with frustration.

People did that a lot around her. She wagged a forefinger at Claire. "Nothin' in life is hopeless, girl, and doan ya fergit it. Remember St. Jude."

A short time later they were sitting at the Peachey kitchen table chopping vegetables, much to Rebekah's dismay. It wasn't that she didn't welcome them, sort of, in a suspicious way, but their offer to help with her domestic chores threw her off balance. That and the black panty and bra set.

The pristine kitchen smelled of raw vegetables boiling in a pungent broth of vinegar, sugar, celery salt, and turmeric. On another burner was a smaller pot, to which Cajun spices and Tabasco sauce had been added, though Rebekah was skeptical of the results. It was about a hundred and twenty-five degrees in the room, owing to the summer heat and the hot stove. They were all sweating like pigs, but that didn't bother her. She was used to hot temperatures.

"You and yer mister are invited ta the party," Tante Lulu said. "Actually, the rest of yer family is invited, too, but I figger you and yer hubby will be the only ones interested, fer now."

"What party?"

"A week from Saturday. At the B & B. We's havin' a combination birthday party fer my nephew Tee-John. He's gonna be twenty-four, bless his rascal heart. And a reunion celebration fer Caleb and Jonas. Plus, we wants ta honor Mark Franklin fer his service ta his country. He lost his arm in Af-ganny-stan, dontcha know?"

"You should come," Claire spoke up, and it was

about time. Claire had lost her voice after Tante Lulu made that innocent little remark about her hickeys.

Golly gee, wouldn't I love to have a hickey or two at my age? Wonder if Amos could pucker up enough ta give me one. Lordy, wouldn't the gals back at Our Lady of the Bayou Church swallow their false teeth iffen they saw that.

"Your sons have missed you," Claire continued. "Your appearance would mean so much to them."

"We couldn't!" Rebekah put both hands to her face. "Samuel would never approve. The church frowns on English parties, especially if shunned folks are gonna be there."

"Those shunned folks are your sons, Rebekah, and it's about time you realized that." Claire stood angrily, confronting Rebekah.

Uh-oh! Now the you-know-what is gonna hit the fan. Tante Lulu sat back and waited with anticipation for what would surely come next.

Rebekah began to cry.

But Claire was on a rip now. "That's great. Go ahead and cry. But have you considered how often your sons have cried over this? Have you ever, ever considered their feelings? What kind of mother are you?"

"What's goin' on here?" Samuel Peachey stepped into the kitchen. By the looks and smell of his clothes, he'd been out mucking the horse stalls. Tante Lulu was old enough to recall the smell of animal poop from the days when horsepower meant more than the size of a car's engine.

"It's nothin', Samuel." Rebekah was wiping her eyes with the edge of her apron. "Tante Lulu and Claire jist came ta visit." Her eyes pleaded with them not to rile her husband.

Well, phooey to that! "We came ta invite ya ta the party."

Samuel ignored the invitation and glared at her and Claire. "You made my wife cry. I think ya should leave."

"Dontcha even wanna know why we're here?"

"No."

Claire stood and took her elbow, trying to get her to stand, too. "Let's go," she murmured.

"Chicken," she murmured back. "We's here ta be mediators."

Claire groaned and sat back down.

"We don't need no mediators," Samuel said, holding the screen door open for them.

Hah! He could glare all he wanted. She'd been glared at by meaner cusses than him. "Yesiree, ya do. Come on in and sit a spell."

"Leave!" he said coldly.

Through the doorway, Tante Lulu saw a bunch of chickens scoot by, including one strange one that was bobbing its head and bouncing up and down like it was having a fit. Or maybe it was mad chicken disease. "Uh, I think yer chickens are flyin' the coop," she pointed out.

He turned and threw his arms out with dismay. "*Himmel!* I musta left it unlatched when I came runnin' here."

Rebekah, equally distressed, ran around the table and out the door to help her husband round up the chickens.

Tante Lulu stood and yelled out the door, "Doan fergit. Next Saturday. Seven o'clock. At the B & B. Dress casual." She turned to Claire, then laughed. "How does an Amish person know casual from formal? Ha, ha, ha."

Soon the only thing that could be heard was chickens squawking, and Samuel and Rebekah begging, "Here, chickee. Here, chickee." As if any right-minded chicken would fall for that!

"Well, that went well, dontcha think?" she remarked to Claire then. "I gotta go pee before we leave."

Chapter
14

Kissing a frog was never so much fun . . .

They were finishing up a late lunch when Caleb noticed Claire coming around the corner.

He didn't know who looked stranger. Tante Lulu with pink hair topped with a blue-and-white polka-dotted bow, blue jeans, and a T-shirt that said, "I Love Richard Simmons." Or Claire, who was wearing a red wet suit.

"New fashion statement?" he asked Claire when she got closer.

"Can I go down with you?"

"You want to go down on me?" He smirked. "Do you need to ask?"

She smacked him on the arm. "C'mon. I'm an experienced diver. I know I'm not certified for cave diving, but you would be there to help, and we wouldn't be going into any tight passages. Besides, there's not much that can be done in the cavern till you start pumping, so I wouldn't be interfering with work. Take me down with you. Please."

He nodded.

"Can I go down, too?" Tante Lulu came up behind them.

"No!" he said.

"Ya doan hafta yell."

"Sorry. The idea of you cave diving just scared the snot out of me."

"I doan see why. If Claire is gonna do it, why cain't I?"

"Maybe because you've got about fifty years on her."

"I do not! I'm only . . . sixty-five."

"Tante Lulu!" her nephew said, having overheard the conversation. "That is a big fib."

"Well, ya shouldn't be commentin' on a woman's age iffen ya doan want her ta lie." With that, she flounced away toward the house, her brain already jumping to another subject, as evidenced by her asking Abbie, "Hey, Abbie, is there any of that gumbo left from yesterday? I didn't eat anythin' since breakfast. Not even chow-chow."

"What does she mean about chow-chow?" he asked Claire.

Claire's face turned as red as her wet suit. "I have no idea."

"Why are you grinning?" he asked LeDeux. "Is there something I should know?"

"I have no idea," LeDeux repeated Claire's words.

They both looked like they shared some secret.

"Will you spot us if I take Claire down for a quick look-see?" he asked the still-grinning Cajun.

"Sure. Let me go see if my aunt is okay. She forgets ta take her blood pressure pills. And by the way, ya better lock up the diving equipment tonight, or you might find a surprise down in the cavern tomorrow morning. And I don't mean vandalism."

"She wouldn't!" Caleb exclaimed.

"Did I tell ya 'bout the time she went skydiving ta celebrate her eightieth birthday? She said if George Bush Sr. could do it, so could she. She about gave the Blue Angels instructor a heart attack when she showed up for his class."

Caleb and Claire were both gaping at LeDeux.

He waved and started to walk away.

"And stay away from Lizzie," Caleb yelled to his back.

"*Mais oui*," LeDeux said. "Whatever you say." And immediately took a detour toward Lizzie, who was arranging some bedding plants that Jonas had sent over from his nursery as a sort of thank-you. Lizzie was alternately staying with Jonas at his house and with him at the B & B, neither of which pleased their father. Big deal! In his present frame of mind, he was more inclined to do things that displeased his father. In fact, he might even help Lizzie get an audition for *American Idol*, just to piss off Dat. But not by getting LeDeux to help her. That boy was like Godivas to teenage girl chocoholics. Older girls, too, for that matter.

Soon he and Claire were geared up and standing on the ledge before the opening, waiting for LeDeux. She looked mighty fine in her red wet suit, which nicely molded the curves he had come to know and love intimately.

"What's with you and Finley?" He could have bitten his tongue for blurting that out.

She smiled, and man oh man, he loved her smile. "Nothing. We date occasionally, but nothing serious."

He wanted desperately to ask if they'd been lovers. After all, Famosa had first referred to Finley as Claire's semi-fiancé, whatever that meant. Luckily, he managed to maintain a little bit of decorum. Instead he said something equally stupid: "I never kissed a female frogman before."

She winked at him. And man oh man, he loved her winks, too.

"I've kissed a lot of frogs, but no frogmen of any kind."

"Is Finley a frog?"

She tilted her face to the side. "Are you jealous of Del?"

"No! Maybe. Oh, hell! Damn straight I am."

She cupped the side of his face and pulled him toward her. Something intense flared inside him just at being this close to Claire.

"Caleb." She said his name against his mouth as if he were someone special. He liked it.

He made a rough sound in response, then angled his lips against her. As kisses went, it wasn't anything unique, and yet its very gentleness marked something significant between them.

Claire took control of the kiss. Her lips moved against his in changing patterns till he was pliant and at her mercy. As if he weren't already. His heart and another body part lurched. She put a hand on him *there* and smiled against his mouth at how aroused he was from a mere kiss.

He put a hand to her breast and moved his palm in a circular fashion till he imagined that he felt the nipple pearl, even through the neoprene, which was probably impossible. Caleb was the one to smile-kiss then.

"Holy sac-à-lait! You two're gonna need a dunk in that cold water if ya keep it up," LeDeux said behind them, causing them to jerk apart like teenagers caught necking on the front porch.

He and Claire had been so engrossed in each other that they hadn't even realized LeDeux had come back to the cavern, let alone been climbing the ladder.

"Do you always have to sneak up, LeDeux?" he snapped.

"Oh, yeah. Ya see and hear the bes' things that way. By the way, did I ever tell ya 'bout the time I had sex inside a coffin?"

What sex in a coffin had to do with near-sex on a ledge he had no idea. "Alone or with a partner?"

"Both."

"Was she dead or alive?"

"Definitely alive. She was an undertaker from Biloxi. Nothin' like satin on bare skin! We even did it on the hood of her hearse one time. Ya wouldn't believe the things ya kin do with a hood ornament. Whoo-ee!"

He and Claire both laughed then.

"You are so full of it," he said.

LeDeux leaned over their shoulders and glanced down. "At least I talked down your hard-on, buddy."

Swimming with sharks . . . uh, SEALs . . . uh, one ex-SEAL . . .

Claire was an experienced scuba diver, but she'd never cave dived before. It was a remarkable experience, totally different than she'd expected.

First of all was the blackness of the water. The absence of light was blinding to the extreme. You couldn't even see a finger in front of your face unless you shone a light on it.

It was cold in here, too. Colder than the main cavern, and that was colder than the outside temperature of eighty today. The water felt like ice, and divers had to regulate how much time they spent here or suffer hypothermia.

And then there was the depth. She'd scuba dived in the United States, the Bahamas, and the Mediterranean, but she'd never gone this deep before. The lower they went, the less they could see of the floodlights shining on the water's surface. Then finally, the light disappeared totally.

She wasn't frightened, though. A ten-foot safety line connected her to Caleb, and he stayed close, giving her constant hand signals and pats of encouragement from the minute they began rappelling down twenty feet to the water's surface, bracing their legs against the sides for braking. They would abseil up the belaying rope in a little while with John's help.

A white fish swam by, skimming her arm. She jumped, which caused her safety line to tug at Caleb.

"They're blind," Caleb said into the mouthpiece in his face mask, which had two-way communication with hers. "Every animal form in caverns is blind and colorless, adapted to the surroundings."

Studying the surrounding walls as best she could, she tried to imagine what the drained chamber would look like with its thousands of years of limestone formations, each a creative work of art in itself. And if this chamber had been dry at one time as they suspected, there might very well be evidence of human habitation, even prehistoric . . . early Lenape from thousands of years ago, or older than that.

"Is that where you hope to pump?" she asked when Caleb stopped just a foot or so from the mud bottom.

"Yes." He placed her hand over the crack. There was definite movement of the water.

"It's not very wide. Are you sure you can run tubing through there?"

"Positive."

"And you think there might be a chamber on the other side?"

"Could be. This little crack here seems to open in a funnel shape to another chamber."

"It's exciting, isn't it? Not knowing what's on the other side? Or even what's at the bottom here?" She watched him and learned as he led her around, never quite touching the bottom.

At certain points, he took out a gauge to measure the cracks, the diameter of the pit, the location of certain protruding stalagmites from the sides. He also remeasured the depth of the muddy silt bottom in various spots. All of the numbers were relayed up above to John, who would be transferring the data to a tape recorder.

There were several limestone columns formed by stalactites and stalagmites meeting. They had to be careful to swim around them, not wanting to break the delicate formations. "Another indication that the chamber was dry at one time," he noted, taking measurements of each of them.

It wasn't that measurements hadn't been taken before, but each time a diver went down, he noticed different things and refined the data previously noted.

A short time later, they were talking excitedly in the entrance area. Mostly, Claire was doing the talking. He was searching for Sparky to give him a high five for biting Knepp, but the snake was nowhere to be seen.

"And I remember the time we went diving in the Bahamas. The water was so clear that day. You could see forever. But that was nowhere near as exciting as going to my first Lenape powwow in Delaware, where . . . what?"

"You're nervous," he said, leaning down and giving her a quick kiss. "You're talking a mile a minute, even more than you usually do." He dodged a slap from her for that comment. "What's up, honey?"

She gave him a skittish glance, then walked outside. He followed after her.

"Claire?"

"You're going to be really mad at me."

Uh-oh! "Why?"

"I went to see your parents today."

He stopped and stared at her with disbelief.

"With Tante Lulu."

Oh, that makes it better! Not! "Why?" He would have said more, but he was barely restraining his anger.

"We . . . I thought it was unfair, the way they were treating you. Tante Lulu agreed. And we decided to go over to the farm and confront them about it. Except I lost my cool and made your mother cry. And your dad kicked us out. But then the chickens escaped and there was this psycho chicken. And we helped make chow-chow, even Cajun chow-chow, but we never got to eat any. Tante Lulu gave your mother lingerie from Victoria's Secret; can you believe that? And then there was the bride quilt. Oh, God, I think I made things worse."

Chow-chow? Psycho chicken? Victoria's Secret? Bride quilt? "Who's the bride?"

When she didn't answer, he stood stock still. The anger inside him that he'd thought melted away was back in spades. "What the hell were you thinking?"

"Tante Lulu talked me into it."

"Oh, great! Blame a dingbat as old as time. Next you'll be telling me that meddling is contagious."

She raised her chin haughtily . . . at his tone of voice, no doubt. "I was trying to help."

"I don't need your help."

"My intentions were good."

"I don't give a rat's ass what your intentions were. I don't need help, especially from some crazy do-gooder Indian-loving fanatic."

"Everyone needs help sometimes, even stubborn pain-in-the-ass militants who build glass walls around themselves and pretend to be macho when they're really marshmallow inside."

"I am not a marshmallow."

"Marshmallow, marshmallow, marshmallow!"

"Are you deliberately trying to annoy me?"

"Tante Lulu and I were just trying to be mediators."

"If I want mediation, I'll call on the United Nations, not two crazies."

"Oh, this is immature, exchanging insults."

"You started it." He gritted his teeth and counted to five . . . ten would take too long. "You had no right to interfere in my life. You're not my wife. Even if you were, I'd be just as friggin' angry."

She gasped as if he'd hit her. "Just let me explain."

"No! I should have known better. Let a woman get close and she takes over your life. Why is it that women always think men need to be fixed? Why do they think it's necessary to pussy whip a guy till he becomes their puppet?"

"Now you've gone too far. I never asked to take over your life or be your wife. All I did was care about you."

"Care? You said you loved me."

"Oh, you heard that, did you? And you didn't high-tail it out of Dodge? Lucky me!"

"I heard, all right."

"And you thought if you didn't mention it, it would just go away, right?"

She was right about that. His tight jaw twitched, negating any possibility of a denial.

"I know that it's hokey to talk about love at first sight, but I think that's what happened to me . . . from the first moment I saw you. I'm not a kid, and I'm intelligent, a PhD for heaven's sake, so I know how foolish I sound. But there it is."

"Claire—"

"Wait. One more thing. I expect absolutely nothing in return. Not words. And definitely not actions. It was just a statement of fact. No response necessary."

"See, that's where you're wrong, Claire. Once you say those three words, it changes things. That bell can't be unrung. And you're wrong about no response being necessary, because even silence is a response."

She paused, then said in a small voice, "I know."

"Do you want to take them back?"

"No, but it might have been better, for you, if I'd kept it to myself."

This conversation had gone way off track. "Hey,

we're talking about what *you* did today. Stop trying to turn the tables."

"Get over yourself. I went to your parents' house. Big deal! Maybe they won't talk to you anymore. Oh, I forgot. They don't talk to you anyway."

"Enough!" he said. "I've had it. I need a cooling-off period. We both do."

She had tears in her eyes when she spun on her heels and walked away. He didn't follow her. But he wanted to.

What a hell of a mess!

As he worked to tamp down his temper, he tried to imagine Claire telling his *Dat* off. Or Tante Lulu offering his mother sexy underwear.

Laughter bubbled up in him then. He was still angry, but the situation was so ludicrous he'd be a fool not to see the humor.

They both needed some space to sort things out. Maybe tomorrow they could talk more calmly. If he apologized, things could go back to the way they were before.

Yeah, right! he thought he heard a voice in his head say.

They were headed for The Red Zone, and they weren't even football players . . .

Caleb did not come to her house that evening.

He had every right to be angry with her, but the way he had treated her . . . Well, she was angry now, too. Besides, everything was happening at warp speed with them, and he had to be in full-tilt-boogie male panic mode, needing to slow down the train. Her going to his parents' house just gave him an excuse to end it earlier than she'd expected. He would be leaving. This wild party was going to end sometime soon. Maybe it was for the best to end it now. Still, it cut deep.

So what was she doing, driving into the B & B parking lot at 8 P.M.?

Caleb glanced up with surprise when she walked into the library, where he was working at a laptop. He took off a pair of wireless reading glasses.

She blushed at the lack of welcome.

"Claire, what are you—"

She put up a hand to halt his words. "I'm not here to see you. Where's Mark?"

Now the blush on Caleb's face matched her own. "Mark?"

"Yeah, I have a message for him."

He waited for her to elaborate, but she didn't.

"He's got first watch at the cavern tonight."

"Well, somebody else better cover for him." She spun on her heels and left the room.

Caleb caught up with her even before she reached the kitchen.

"What's up?"

"It's personal."

"Between you and Mark?"

"Whatever is or isn't between me and Mark or me and Del or me and any other guy in the blinkin' world is none of your damn business."

"What's got you so pissed off? I mean, I know, but don't you think you're overreacting?"

"Overreacting?" The shrillness of her voice startled them both.

"You're looking at me the same way a Taliban fighter did one time. The guy was trying to lop off my head."

That got her attention. *Somebody tried to chop off his head? Oh, my God! And he says it so casually.*

"You're practically breathing smoke, sweetie. Aren't you even going to give me a chance to apologize?"

"Sweetie?" Her voice got shriller, but then she closed her eyes and counted to ten, restraining herself from clobbering the dope. When she was calm, she said, "Go back to your work, Caleb. Go hide your head in the sand and pretend that everything is hunky-dory. Go pretend that you don't care about anyone in the world."

"Hunky-dory? What the hell is hunky-dory? You've been hanging around Tante Lulu too much." He grinned at her.

"Don't you dare laugh."

"Is this because you miss me?"

She made a hissing sound and shoved him aside.

He eyed her as if she'd suddenly sprung three heads. Typical man that he was, he probably attributed her mood to PMS.

When she got to the wigwam, she saw not just Mark, but John, as well. Good. He needed to hear this, too. The two of them were sitting outside talking, bottles of beer in their hands. She noticed that Caleb had followed her, though at a distance.

"Mark, there was a message on my answering machine from your grandmother when I got back from my run tonight. She and Tante Lulu went to The Red Zone. Apparently Lily is scheduled to dance at nine."

"What? No! That's impossible." Mark stood, letting

his bottle roll over in the grass. "LeDeux, this is your wacky aunt's fault."

"I hope ya mean wacky as a compliment." John stood and faced off with Mark. "Don't attack the people who try to help ya. And say one more bad thing 'bout my aunt and ya might be minus two arms."

"Whoa, whoa, whoa," Caleb said, stepping between the two of them.

John seemed to notice something then, staring off toward the house. "*Mon Dieu!* They took my car."

Everyone turned to look at the parking lot.

"Why is that such a bad thing?" Claire asked.

"Because my aunt drives like a bat outta hell. Because she's had enough tickets to paper a wall. Because she's been known to give the finger to state troopers who get in her way."

"Uh-oh," Claire said.

Everyone turned away from staring at the parking lot to staring at her.

"Uh-oh what?" Caleb asked.

"I think they might have gone to pick up Amos and Andy, too. They mentioned a double date. That must be what Tante Lulu meant when she talked about tonight revving up all their rusted-out engines."

Mark groaned and put his face in his one hand.

John grinned and said, "That's my girl."

"I'll go get them," Caleb offered.

"I'm coming, too," Claire said.

"I can handle it myself."

"I'm coming, too," Mark insisted.

"I wouldn't miss this fer nothin'." John was already walking over the bridge, followed by Claire and Mark.

"Besides, I was a stripper fer two weeks one time. I kin give Lily pointers."

"Fuck you!" Mark said.

"Bite me!" John countered.

"Who'll watch the cavern?" Caleb called after them.

"Call Adam," she suggested. "I think he went to the tavern. I passed him on the way here. Or else watch it yourself. Who needs you?"

As he walked, Caleb flipped open his cell phone and punched a few numbers. "Famosa? Peachey here. Where are you?" He paused for a moment, then continued, "When you finish dinner, can you head back to the B & B and take a shift over at the cavern, just for a few hours? No, Mark or LeDeux can't do it. They're coming with me." Another pause while he listened. "We're going to The Red Zone to get Tante Lulu and Abbie." He glanced over at Mark. "And maybe Lily, too." He held the phone away from his ear then, and they all could hear the shouting. When it went silent, he put the phone to his ear again. "Yeah, yeah, same to you. Thanks."

When they got to the parking lot and had to wait for Caleb to catch up and unlock his vehicle, Claire said, "I'll sit in back with John."

Caleb's upper lip curled back in what could only be described as a sneer. "You'll sit in the front seat. Next to me. And get out of that piss-ant mood you're in, baby, unless you want to be spanked." He picked her up then and shoved her into the front passenger seat, slamming the door after her.

Spanked? She was too shocked to react at first. That was outrageous, even for Caleb. And truth to tell, even though she wasn't into pain or S & M in the least, the image playing through her mind was hot and taboo and very, very tempting.

Mark and John were suspiciously quiet in the backseat, probably waiting for the next scene in this soap opera between her and Caleb.

Caleb slid into the seat next to her, gave her a sideways glance that told her loud and clear that the same image was playing through his head, then pulled out of the parking lot, tires squealing in the gravel.

"Did I ever tell ya 'bout the time I met this dominatrix on Bourbon Street?" John said into the silence.

"Shut up, LeDeux," Caleb said.

John replied in French with what Claire was pretty sure translated to "Up yours, sailor!"

Then slowly, one by one, they began to chuckle, then laugh out loud hysterically. And the fun had just begun.

Chapter
15

Hail, hail, the gang's all here . . .

Caleb had been in worse joints around the world . . . worse meaning sordid . . . but still, The Red Zone was pretty bad. It didn't help that it was Bikers' Night at the stripper club, and the Harley lovers were a rowdy crowd. In fact, there was enough leather in this place to make a horse run for cover.

After paying an exorbitant cover charge just to gawk at some naked bodies, when the same or better could be had by renting an X-rated movie, they entered a large room where a circular stage was surrounded by a bar and seats holding mostly horny college students and overaged bikers. There were also side stages where the women moved once done with their main events, bringing with them their "fans" for special performances. Lap dances and God only knew what else could be had upstairs. There were also adult toys for sale and special viewing booths.

Mostly, there was a lot of gawking going on.

Claire was among those gawking, especially at the young overendowed woman, totally nude, who was dancing on the stage and picking up twenty-dollar bills with her breasts from the mouths of the males at the bar. Only a half-dozen women were in the room, not including the dancers and waitresses.

LeDeux was grinning like a fool, exactly what would be expected of the testosterone-oozing young man. Nothing seemed to shock or faze the boy.

Mark was red-faced, but not with embarrassment. He was probably picturing his ex-girlfriend Lily doing what this woman was doing, except that Lily didn't have much cleavage, as Caleb recalled. She would have to pick up the bills with her teeth, he imagined. Yeech!

"There they are," LeDeux said, pointing to his aunt, Abbie, and their two gentlemen friends. They were seated at a table, not the stage bar, thank God, but all their eyes were riveted on the dancers. This was a bring-your-own-beer-type establishment, and an unopened six-pack sat on their table.

The two gents were wearing cowboy shirts with string ties. Abbie was demure in a short-sleeved floral dress. On the other hand, Tante Lulu, with spiked black hair tonight—she must have used a gallon of mousse—was totally in tune with the theme, wearing a low-cut leather bustier top that revealed a good portion of her chest. And an impressive cleavage.

"Good Lord, she's wearing a push-up bra," Claire remarked.

"I didn't know she had anythin' ta push up," LeDeux replied. "Wait till I tell my brothers about this. Charmaine probably overnighted it ta her."

"Tee-John!" Tante Lulu said when she noticed them approaching. "What're y'all doin' here?"

Like she didn't know! The message on Claire's answering machine had to have been a ploy to get them all there. Especially Mark.

"Come ta take ya home, auntie." LeDeux sat down in an empty chair next to his aunt and gave her a hug.

"I hope you don't think this was my idea," one of the men said. Amos, he was pretty sure.

"They made us bring them," the other man added. Andy.

Neither of them was making any great effort to leave, he noticed.

Abbie squirmed, shame-faced under her grandson's glare, but then she lit up a cigarette, blew smoke, and glared back at him. "Don't scowl at me like you're my boss. It's your fault we're all here."

"Not friggin' likely," he shot back. "Where's Lily?"

Abbie motioned with her head toward the back of the room, where a line of young women was queued up for their turns to dance. There was a nurse, a cowgirl, a French maid, and then Lily . . . a cheerleader. A cheerleader with the shortest miniskirt in the history of cheerleaderdom, topped by a tight sweater with the logo "FU University." She probably didn't have undies on underneath, or else she wore nothing but a G-string.

By the gurgling sound Mark made, Caleb guessed he'd come to the same conclusion.

It was hard to hear over the loud music, catcalls, conversation, and laughter. This was a dry-docked sailor's fantasy, a mother's nightmare. Still, they were able to hear Mark say, "Son of a bitch!" before he stormed toward Lily.

He and Claire and LeDeux pulled up chairs to sit with the old folks, who were transfixed by what the new dancer was doing on the stage. It involved bending over and touching her toes, then smiling at the crowd upside down between her spread legs, her size double D's dangling like twin pendulums. The only thing she wore was red stiletto heels.

"Oh. My. God!" That was a red-faced Claire speaking. Served her right for insisting on coming.

LeDeux, on his other side, said, "I had sex with a woman in that position one time. Let me tell you—"

"Please don't," he urged.

"Ya know, Tee-John, if I've told ya once I've told ya a thousand times 'bout yer braggin'. Remember, a fella what toots his own horn never gets tooted."

Everyone laughed except LeDeux, who pretended affront and said, "I get tooted plenty."

A waitress soon pressured them to order sodas, "if they were going to take up space." At ten dollars a pop.

"I usta be able ta touch my toes," Tante Lulu said.

Everyone looked at her.

"But I never woulda been able to pick up a bill with my boobies. Even when I was twenty, I wasn't that big." She looked at Claire. "How 'bout you?"

"Whaaat?" She frowned at the old lady for drawing her into such a conversation.

He put an arm around the back of her chair and squeezed her shoulder.

She slapped his hand away. Apparently she was still a little miffed with him. *Okay, sweetie, let's see how you like this.* "You know, Claire, you could probably get a job here doing an Indian maiden dance."

She turned slowly, inch by inch, to glower at him. "Do you have a death wish?"

"Come on, honey. Lighten up."

"Lighten up? What happened to the angry man in a snit who pretty much told me earlier today that it was over?"

"The angry man never said it was over. He merely said we need to step back for a bit."

She cocked her head at him.

"I stepped back. My snit ended. How about you?"

"What changed your mind?"

"Do you have any idea what a turn-on it is for a man to meet a woman who gives as good as she gets? You let me get angry, apologized, then told me in no uncertain terms what a dickhead I was. You were smoking hot, baby."

"Am I supposed to be flattered by that?"

"It was a compliment, believe me."

"So now you think we should just pretend that nothing happened?"

"Well, yeah."

"Clueless. You are one hundred and fifty percent clueless."

"Oh, look," Abbie said, pointing to the far side of the room. "Our plan is working."

Or not, Caleb thought as he studied the unfolding scene.

True, Mark and Lily were arguing, and he was attempting to pull her away and toward the door. But Caleb saw something they didn't. Two bouncers the size of Buicks were headed in that direction. He and LeDeux exchanged looks and stood. Amos and Andy, bless their souls, stood, too.

"Ladies, you best go out to the car," Amos said, flexing his fingers.

"I haven't kicked ass since the time Leroy Watkins made that smart remark to Sis at the 4-H barn dance in 1982," Amos said, a smile of anticipation on his face.

Amos's response was a loud, "Yee-haw!"

Caleb thought, *I've fallen down the hole in Alice in Wonderland's garden.*

Claire came up beside Caleb. "I have some killer karate moves."

Abbie said, "I'll go outside and bring the getaway car up to the door."

Or is this "One Flew Over the Cuckoo's Nest*?"*

"I have a gun." Tante Lulu was rummaging through a straw purse so big it would dwarf a sailor's duffel bag.

Everyone said as one, "No!"

Maybe if I pinch myself, I'll wake up from this nightmare.

"Okay, I'll drive the other getaway car. By the way, Tee-John, didja know yer car could go a hundred and ten? And I dint even get a ticket. That police officer was real nice, wasn't he, Amos? He dint even get mad when I tol' him he needed ta get some help with that sputterin' problem of his."

When she started to walk away, LeDeux muttered, "*Mon Dieu!*"

Caleb looked to see what had drawn that reaction from the Cajun. And he seconded the "My God!" Tante Lulu had curvy buttocks in her spandex pseudo-leather pants. She must have bought a pair of those padded panties that were advertised in the back of magazines. Or the infamous Charmaine had sent them along with the push-up bra. *Unbelievable!*

Thus it was that a posse of five headed toward what was sure to be the bar fight to beat all bar fights, with two senior-citizen getaway drivers outside.

From another quarter he saw some bikers rising from their seats. He had no idea whose side they would be on. But then he noticed that one of them wore a Green Beret hat and another wore cammies, and both were eyeing the U.S. Navy SEAL logo on his T-shirt. Lots of men, unbelievably, pretended to be ex-SEALs for prestige or to get chicks, but they must have accepted him for what he was, because they both nodded at him, and he knew they had friends in this place who would cover their sixes.

Two hours later, they were all sitting in the local magistrate's office waiting for their citations. He, LeDeux, Amos, Andy, and six bikers with bloody noses and bruised knuckles; the two bouncers, one with a blackening eye and the other limping because of Claire's karate kick; Claire, with wild hair and wilder eyes, still wearing her jogging outfit; a still-furious Mark with a golf shirt half torn off; an oddly exultant Lily, with her "FU University" sweater; Abbie, also exultant, with an unlit cigarette dangling from her mouth and smudged eye makeup; Tante Lulu in her outrageous leather, her mouth going a mile a minute as she tried to tell a female officer how to make gumbo; and three dancers who'd gotten into the action and were now covered with knee-length, men's yellow prison shirts that had been handed to them by some grinning officers. In fact, the mini-courtroom in the back of the police station was lined with officers, both on and off duty, waiting for the show to begin.

The magistrate finished two DUI cases and a disorderly conduct, then turned to them. With ever-widening eyes, the world-weary judge propped his chin on his hands, elbows braced on his desk, and sighed. "This oughta be good."

Give us an *L*, give us an *O*, give us a *V* . . .

"Ouch, ouch, ouch! What's in that stuff? Acid?"

Lily was dabbing antiseptic ointment on a cut above his right eye. She was probably getting some perverse enjoyment out of his pain.

He was sitting on the closed toilet seat in the bathroom of her Julian apartment, after having removed his tattered shirt. Lily still had on her cheerleading outfit.

"Stop being a baby."

No sympathy there. "Would you really have gone onto the stage?"

"Maybe."

"Why?"

"Because I love you."

"What does love have to do with baring your butt for a thousand guys?"

"I told you before, Mark. If you don't want me, I'll find some guy who does."

"Does it have to be a thousand guys at once?"

"Why not?"

"Why not? I'll tell you why not. You're better than that. You could have any guy you want. And you don't have to strip to get a man."

"I don't want any other man."

He groaned with frustration. "This is all my grandmother's fault, isn't it? And that dingbat from down South?"

"That's just like you. Blame everyone but yourself."

At least she isn't pitying me anymore. "Listen, Lily, I'm starting to get my act together. I'll probably open the cavern to the public. But that doesn't mean I'm whole again. I'm not. I never will be."

"You are a world-class moron if you think being whole has anything to do with body parts."

He let out a whooshy exhale. "You're wearing me out, Lily."

"That's the point."

"What do you want from me?"

"Just your love, honey."

"You've always had that."

"How would I know that, the way you've been treating me?"

"I'm sorry. I honestly didn't . . . don't . . . want to hurt you."

"Then stop being an ass, accept me back, and let's plan a life *together*."

"Could it be as simple as that?"

"Suppose I got cancer and all my hair fell out. Would you love me less?"

"Of course not."

"How would you feel if I shoved you out of my life because I had no hair?"

"This is a ridiculous conversation."

"No more ridiculous than you thinking I can stop loving you just because you lost an arm."

"What about your dreams? What about the renovation business?"

"My dream was to do something with you. It doesn't

have to be renovating or architecture. Frankly, I would love to learn more about caves and how to make yours marketable."

He stared at her skeptically. "You're just saying that."

She put her first-aid supplies aside and sat down on his lap, almost knocking him over, his balance still not quite right. Then she put her arms around his neck and kissed him. "I'm not going anywhere, Mark. There's only one thing that could make me leave."

"And that is?"

"That you no longer love me. Can you say those words? I. Don't. Love. You."

He didn't even try, because he knew the words would never come from his lips.

"I give up," he said finally.

There were tears in her eyes now. "Those aren't the three words I want to hear."

"You want blood, don't you? White flags fluttering, a choir singing 'Hallelujah,' the works?" he asked. "I love you. I love you, I love you, I love you. Are you satisfied now?"

"I will never be satisfied," she said on a sob. "I think you're going to have to repeat those words at least once a day for the rest of our lives *together*."

"Done." He sealed his promise with a kiss. Then he chuckled against her neck.

"What?"

"There is one thing I'd like from you to seal our reunion."

"Reunion sex?" She swiped at the tears rimming her eyes.

"Well, yes, that. But something else." He used his one arm to shove her off his lap, then took her hand and led her into the small living room. Sinking down on the sofa, he glanced up at her and winked. "How about a personal performance of your cheerleader striptease?"

Diamonds . . . uh, pearls . . . are a girl's best friend . . .

Two days later, the cave chamber was drained, additional lighting set up, and they were about to make their first thorough exploration of the bottom.

Unfortunately, that exploration was going to have to involve wading around in three-foot-high "pudding," working the suction tubes. It would have been nice if it was only silt they had to deal with, but after all these years in damp conditions, the bottom was pretty much slushy mud.

If it weren't for the stalagmites rising from the bottom or the fact that Mark and Abbie, and now Lily, too, wanted to preserve the chamber, they could have run rough rakes to gather the pearls, outlaw's booty, and anything else solid hiding down there. He would bet his Budweiser they were also going to find some animal and human bones. Claire was hoping for Indian artifacts, of course.

Claire. He couldn't think about her now. They'd been playing hide-and-seek with each other since The Red Zone incident. He had tried to hook up with her again, halfheartedly—a guy could apologize only so many times—but she wanted nothing to do with him now. He'd have tried harder to convince her that he was worth another shot, but he couldn't do that till he was sure he wanted more than, well, a shot. What a mess!

There were four of them down there right now.

He was walking carefully across the crisscross gird they'd prepared, feeling by hand and foot for any protruding stalagmites. When he found one, he tagged the site with a weighted flag. He had to be careful not to step on the pearls.

LeDeux was following in his path, taking photographs of everything in sight. And making ridiculous, lewd remarks into his earphones about what he ought to do to "light Claire's flame."

Del was using a small pickax to break open the egress crack enough to insert the wider tubing.

Famosa was further refining measurements of the chamber and making notes of formations they'd missed before the brighter lights. Claire would be ecstatic to find out there were some primitive carvings on one of the walls, lower down. Maybe when he told her, she'd jump in his arms and all would be right in their world. No questions asked. No commitments. Just hot sex, then sayonara. *Yeah, right.* He wasn't sure he wanted that anyhow . . . the sayonara bit. Yes, he did. Just not quite yet.

Just then, Caleb felt something beneath his feet. Reaching down through the mud, his fingertips touched a round and smooth object. No, many objects. Could it be the nest of pearls? He grabbed onto one of them and lifted it to the top, rubbing it on his wet suit. "Paydirt!" he yelled. It was a pearl the size of a golf ball. "Whoo-hoo! Look at this beauty, boys!"

LeDeux inched his way over with the camera and a net bag, and patted him on the shoulder. "Guess the drinks are on you tonight, big boy." It was a tradition among treasure hunters that the first person to make a find treated all the others on the project to free drinks. Carefully, the two of them reached down over and over, their arms from fingertips to shoulders covered with muddy slime, and came up with three dozen of the cave pearls. There were more, lots more, but they were smaller. They'd be able to recover them when more of the mud was sucked out.

He and LeDeux gave each other high fives after sending the net up to the top. He could hear Mark, Lily, Abbie, Claire, and Tante Lulu screaming and shouting with excitement. Down below, all of them were still smiling.

Then Famosa, who was working the area directly below the rotted rope hanging from the top, said he felt something odd. What he pulled up was pieces of broken wood, one of which appeared to have a hinge on it.

"A box," they all declared.

"The outlaw's loot?" Famosa asked into his mike.

"Could we be so lucky?" LeDeux asked.

God, he hoped so. They wouldn't know till tomorrow when the bottom was dry. They'd already been down here a total of five hours today.

Maybe this project was going to be worthwhile, after all.

Maybe his team would come out on the top with a double winner . . . pearls and money.

Maybe Claire would make some historical discovery related to her precious Lenape Indians.

Maybe Claire would jump his bones and reward him with celebration sex.

Maybe you are hopeless, a voice in his head said.

Gold and pearls . . . a winning combination . . .

Five days later, they gathered around the large kitchen table, covered with a black velvet cloth, waiting to view the cave pearls and gold coins they'd recovered so far. Claire had never been involved in a treasure hunt before, but she figured this one had to far surpass all their expectations.

"First the cave pearls," Caleb said, coming into the kitchen from a pantry storage area. He carried a farmer's egg basket overflowing with a nest of five dozen cave pearls, ranging from golf ball to teardrop size. Remarkable creations of nature!

"Are you sure these are pearls?" Abbie asked. "They don't look shiny like any pearls I've seen."

"Mebbe they's jist rocks," Tante Lulu offered.

"They're pearls, all right, and don't worry about the sheen. Once we use that fusion process on them, the luster will be as good as any oyster pearl," Adam assured them.

All of them picked up one or two of the pearls and weighed them in their hands, trying to picture them in some jewelry setting.

"Wouldn't this look great hanging from a gold chain," Claire said, admiring a marble-sized stone of perfect symmetry.

She had been speaking to Abbie, but it was Caleb who spoke near her ear, close enough so only she could hear. "Take it," he said.

Turning, her lips almost brushed his. She wouldn't give him the satisfaction. Stepping back, she said, "I couldn't. I don't share in this project's rewards."

"Consider it a gift. From me."

She arched her brows at him, then shook her head. "Too expensive a gift . . . for friends."

Her words clearly offended him.

But what did he expect? They hadn't talked or done anything else since The Red Zone incident. It was partly her fault, but still, her stubborn female pride insisted that he should have made more of an effort.

He mouthed the word, "Later."

Later what? she wondered. *Later he would give her the pearl? Later they would talk? Later they would have wild monkey sex?*

And since when did he get to set the terms of when or if they met again, privately?

"Screw you!" she mouthed back.

"Okay." The lout had the nerve to grin.

Their whispered banter was interrupted then when Adam and LeDeux carried in a commercial-size baking pan in which the gold coins had been soaking in water to remove the centuries-old guck. They wouldn't do anything more serious to polish the coins, not wanting to affect their antique patina. Mark held a cloth sack containing the remnants of the outlaw's bank bag and wooden chest.

"Good ol' Davie Lewis came through fer us bigtime," John said. "Remember that clipping where it said that on his deathbed in a Bellefonte jail in 1820, he claimed to have hidden $20,000 in gold? What do y'all suppose it's worth now?"

"Several hundred thousand, I would guess, but none

of us are experts on old or collectible coins. Ronnie and Jake will take them to a numismatist in Manhattan for an appraisal," Caleb explained. "There's value in the gold alone, of course, but their worth will really be in their rarity."

Everyone nodded.

"Will I . . . me and Mark . . . be able to keep any of the coins?" Abbie asked.

"Possibly. You might want to weigh whether you need the cash or want coins for display when you open the cavern to the public," Caleb told her.

"I would imagine Sotheby's or Christie's would jump at the chance to auction these off," Adam mused.

"In a heartbeat," Caleb agreed.

"Keep in mind that the state and federal government might have something to say about the outcome because of the history," Claire said and immediately put up a halting hand when everyone began to groan and complain. "But I don't think that will be the case, since the money belonged to a private individual, albeit a criminal one."

"Ill-gotten gains, fer sure, but who knows after all these years the identity of the robber's victims?" John said what they were all thinking.

Claire passed around photographs of the pictographs they'd found in the chamber. "You all might be excited about the pearls and gold, but to me this is the real treasure. Just imagine, Native Americans two or three hundred years ago made these drawings. Experts will study them for years to come."

Everyone oohed and aahed, except Caleb, who whispered into her ear, "Baby, you look practically orgasmic when you talk about those pictures."

She gave him a dirty look and barely restrained a shiver at the feel of his breath on the whorls of her ear. "Only you would think of something like that."

He shrugged. "At least someone is getting their rocks off."

She gave him another dirty look.

"What'll we do with the six skeletons down there?" Mark asked.

"I have some members of the Lenape nation coming in tomorrow to view the remains," she said.

"Are ya sure they's Injuns?" Tante Lulu wanted to know. "I mean, a skeleton's a skeleton, ain't it?"

"My opinion is that they're probably Native Americans, as indicated by the location of hairs still remaining on the heads. Male Lenape warriors often plucked out all the hair on both sides of the head, leaving a three-inch 'scalp lock' down the middle, what people today called a Mohawk. There were no weapons or tools of any kind, but there were some ear ornaments. Lenape men and women sometimes sliced along the outer edges of the ears and wrapped those strips of flesh in wire, from which would hang wampum, feathers, or beads."

"Our very own Lenape font of wisdom," Caleb murmured.

She was about to say something foul to him but decided to ignore his sarcasm. "I'm assuming that these Lenape were captured by another tribe, who threw them down in the pit while it was still dry, as a punishment. The pictographs were probably made with broken chunks of stalagmites."

"Sounds logical," Caleb said.

She still ignored him. It was going to take a lot more than that for a peace offering.

"Can I talk to you later?" he asked when their meeting broke up and people stood around chatting.

"Sure. What do you want?"

"Not here. How about your place?"

She just laughed.

Luckily, there were other people around, because she was pretty sure he might have tossed her over his shoulder and taken matters into his own hands. But she'd escaped. Alone.

It was for the best.

Me John Smith, you Pocahontas . . .

The next day, everyone pitched in to tie up all the loose ends of the Pearl Project. And Caleb was so miserable he could puke.

The bottom of the chamber was now relatively dry, after having been drained, then rinsed, over and over a half dozen times. Some of the limestone formations had been damaged in the process, but mostly they were intact. A sturdy rope ladder hung down the side to the bottom. At some point, Mark and Abbie would have to build steps if they were to open the cavern to the public.

I'll be long gone by then. That thought didn't make him happy, for some reason.

Wasn't there an old country music song, "I'm so lonesome I could die"? It shoulda been "I'm so lonesome I could puke."

It was a hugely successful job completed here, but you would have thought someone shot his dog. If he had a dog.

It was Claire, of course, who was causing his angst. After the fiasco at The Red Zone—although it had resulted in Mark and Lily getting back together—Claire had decided that it would be a perfect time to end their relationship, since he would be leaving soon anyway. *What relationship?* he'd wanted to ask. Luckily, he hadn't said that aloud. And how come he had no say in when this breakup would take place? If there was anything a guy hated, it was a preemptive breakup, Seinfeld-style.

"We can still be friends," she'd concluded last night when he'd invited himself to her house and she'd declined.

"Bullshit!" had been his response.

Which hadn't gained him any bootie points. Hell, he wasn't getting any bootie anyhow. So big deal!

Today they were playing the politeness game. Thank you. Please. I would appreciate it. *Did I mention puking?*

The gang was getting a kick out of their "friendliness." Tante Lulu was praying to St. Jude on his behalf when she wasn't crocheting doilies for him. LeDeux was giving him charm lessons. Famosa was probably hitting on Claire behind his back.

But really, it was his fault for having blown up over her going to visit his parents, which when he had time to think about it was really a nice thing for her to do. Meddlesome, but nice.

And then he'd made the mistake of saying that he needed some space. He'd meant for one night, not forever. And now the parting had gone on too long for either of them to take a first step without giving the impression that they really did have a relationship. A royal FUBAR. And he was the one fucked up beyond all recognition.

So now he was expected to stand here with a straight face at the bottom of the pit and watch Claire and her two Lenni Lenape pals from Oklahoma do Indian burial rites over the skeletons that still lay where they'd been found. The bones would be buried tomorrow in Huntingdon, near Standing Stone, an Indian landmark.

It wasn't that he thought the burial rites were funny. But Claire, Little Wolf, and Big Bear—the latter two in traditional Indian garb of feather headdresses, leather loincloths, and knee-high laced moccasins—drew the attention of everyone. Big Bear, carrying a bow and quiver of arrows, weighed about three hundred pounds, most of which was hanging over his loincloth, and the last time he'd gone on a hunt had been when he'd bought steaks on sale at the Shop 'n' Save. Little Wolf, also with an appropriate name, was no taller than Tante Lulu, who was about five-foot-zero. He carried a fierce-looking tomahawk, and his face was adorned with scary paint, but he was a dentist back on the rez. Instead of bringing their own drums, they carried tape players they'd picked up at Wal-Mart on their way here from the airport.

"We're about ready to start," Claire said, wending her way toward him through the stalagmites. "Is anyone else coming?"

"I don't think so," he said. *Those of us here are a captive audience. We couldn't escape in time.* "You can start."

He glanced over at LeDeux and Famosa, who'd stopped working to watch the proceedings, along with Del and his two geologist friends, who paused in their chipping away at the fissure that led to the other chamber, much larger than this one. They might eventually have to dynamite in spots. And of course they would have to find an ecologically acceptable method of draining the chamber now that they'd dumped all the water and mud there.

All eyes were on Claire in her Indian outfit. A knee-length leather dress with fringes, belted at the waist. Moccasins on her feet. And her dark red hair plaited into two braids with a headband wrapped around her forehead, holding a single feather. An Irish Pocahontas.

"Do you want to participate?"

"Huh? What? Me?" *Is she crazy?*

She smiled at his discomfort.

So, of course, he tugged on one of her braids and remarked, "I was kinda hopin' you'd be wearing that Victoria's Secret Indian maiden outfit like in the picture back at your cabin."

"I told you that wasn't authentic Lenni Lenape clothing." She shook her head at his hopelessness. "Victoria's Secret?"

"Well, Hiawatha's Secret."

"You're an idiot." She turned and walked away from him.

When they were done with their "Hi-ah, Hi-ah, Hi-ah" chanting crap, and dancing crap, and incense crap, the bones were raised carefully in special canvas bags, which had been blessed. A hearse was waiting outside.

An hour later, everyone had gone up the ladder, including Big Bear, who put the tensile strength of the rope to the test. They had two more days before the big event they had planned for Saturday. A news conference. Exhibits.

Some special invited guests. Music and refreshments. Then the party on Saturday night.

Jake and Ronnie and Brenda would be back here by then, their project in Mexico having been completed, not as successfully as they'd hoped, but the Pearl Project proceeds would make up for that. Then Caleb was out of here, on to the next treasure hunt, wherever that might be.

Everything would be fine then. Back to the way they were before. Just peachy! Just freakin' peachy!

Staring around him at the huge chamber, rather churchlike with its high dome ceiling and columns, Caleb felt a strange sort of peace. Inside his head, a voice seemed to say, *Everything will be all right.* It was probably just wishful thinking.

Chapter
16

A three-ring Cajun circus . . .

John and his great-aunt were sitting on a back-yard swing having a three-way conversation, via cell phone conference calling, with his brother Luc back in Louisiana.

"Do ya promise that y'all will be here fer the party Saturday night?" Tante Lulu urged.

"I promise, I promise, for the tenth time," Luc said with a laugh. "But I still don't see why we couldn't have the party here. At last count, I figure there must be fifteen of us, including the kids. Besides, Charmaine would love to show off her latest addition to the spa out at the ranch. A vibrating couples' massage table."

"Ooooh, I like the sound of that," John said. "Maybe we should reconsider, Auntie."

His aunt slapped his arm. "Behave yerself. We kin allus go ta the ranch. Besides, this isn't jist a birthday party fer Tee-John. It's also a reunion celebration fer Caleb and his twin brother. They grew up Amish. Kin ya believe that? I was hopin' Caleb and Claire would get together by now, and we could have another surprise weddin' . . ."

Tante Lulu had put together an unbelievable surprise wedding for his brother René and Valerie Breaux two years ago. It was still the talk of the bayou.

". . . but Caleb and Claire gots some kinks ta work out first."

"I like kinky," John interjected.

Without skipping a beat, his aunt gave him a disapproving glare and blathered on, "Claire is nuts about Injuns, bless her heart. Did I tell ya that, Luc? Not that Caleb is an Injun, bless his heart. Nope, he's an ex-Amish Navy SEAL. I ain't never met an Amishman before I came here, but whoo-boy, the place is jumpin' with 'em, buggies an' all. Also, we wanna honor Mark Franklin at this *fais do-do*. He lost an arm in Af-ganny-stan."

Luc groaned at his end of the line. Their aunt had a tendency to go off on several tangents at a time. Amazingly, they had all learned to follow her trains of thought. Once Tante Lulu was on a tear, there was no stopping her.

"Oh, and wouldja tell Sylvie ta pick up a perscription fer me at Boudreaux's drug store. Doc Pitrey called it in."

"For what?" Luc asked. "Blood pressure?"

"No. Sumpin' else."

John narrowed his eyes at his aunt.

"Oh, fer goodness sake! It's jist digitalis."

John's skin turned clammy. Luc swore and was asking Sylvie in the background if she knew about this.

"Digitalis is fer heart problems," John told his aunt.

"So?"

"So, since when do you have a heart problem?"

"It's jist a twinge now and then. Doan go worryin' 'bout me. I'll be there dancin' at yer weddin', boy, lessen ya decide ta become a forty-year-old bachelor. And that ain't gonna happen if I kin help it. I got an in with the thunderbolt guy. And by the way, does ya want blue or yellow embroidery on yer pillowcases?"

Luc was laughing now. Everyone in the family got Tante Lulu's love thunderbolt business at one time or another. Usually just before they met the love of their lives and got married.

John shivered at the thought. "I got a lot of wild oats to sow yet, so doan be bakin' any weddin' cake yet," he told her.

"Yer wild oats is gonna turn inta oatmeal pretty soon iffen ya doan shape up."

"Listen, darlin', I'm like a guy livin' in the middle of the produce section of the French Quarter Market. Why would I eat just one cherry when there are all those peaches, apples, pears, melons, strawberries, bananas, and grapes just begging to be tasted?"

"Hah! Too much fruit gives a man diarrhea."

How did one respond to a statement like that? With silence, he decided.

She'd managed to change the subject with her usual expertise, but she didn't fool him. He was going to investigate his aunt's little heart problem. She was eighty-eight years old, after all, though you'd never know it by all her energy and enthusiasm for life. Hurricane Katrina had had an effect on her. Even though her cottage had been pretty much spared, many of her friends had lost everything. They would never recover, and neither would she.

Meanwhile, his aunt was giving Luc a list of things she wanted him and his brothers to bring.

"Make sure René brings his accordion. We's gonna have music and dancin'. And tell Charmaine we gots this Amish girl what wants ta be on *American Idol.* Ask Charmaine if she has any clothes that might strike the judges' fancy. Not slutty clothes. Simon Cowell would make mincemeat outta her in those. Jist colorful, kinda like what Paula Abdul wears. Ya wouldn't believe how much black and blue these folks wear, and—"

"Oh, good God!" Luc interrupted. Sylvie must have asked what was wrong, and he told her, "Tante Lulu is invading the Amish now."

"Tsk-tsk-tsk!" Tante Lulu said. "And stop by my cottage and get me some more of that juju tea. I was tellin' Amos 'bout it las' night."

"Who's Amos?"

"You don't wanna know," John said quickly, but not quick enough.

"My boyfriend. Me and Abbie're datin' these twin brothers. Amos and Andy. Amos wants me ta move in with him, but I tol' him I cain't live outside the bayou fer long without gettin' a hankerin' fer crawfish. Besides, I doan go fer that hanky-panky outside marriage. Then he asked me ta marry him. Do ya know where he kin buy some Viagra?"

"Oh, good God!" Luc said again. "I thought you were watchin' over her, Tee-John."

"I am."

"Who sez I need a chaperon? Did I tell ya 'bout the strip joint we went to this week, Luc?" She proceeded to tell him how the strippers picked up twenty-dollar bills with their "boobies."

Luc was silent on the other end, either horrified or laughing. Probably both.

"Oh, before I forget. Tell Charmaine to pick me up a bushel of crawfish. They ain't got any crawfish worth eatin' here."

"Tante Lulu! Charmaine and Rusty are coming on a commercial airline. They won't allow food products like that to be carried. Plus, they'll probably be considered terrorists or something."

"Terrorists?" Tee-John hooted with laughter. "What? Terrorists now carry bombs in food products?"

"You try carrying a bushel of crawfish on a plane, then, smartass," Luc replied.

"Jist put 'em inside that hope chest that Remy is bringin' fer Mark," Tante Lulu suggested.

"You've already got that thing filled with doilies and pot holders and monogrammed sheets and stuff," Luc reminded her. "Did you really make up his-and-her St. Jude nightshirts?"

"Jist bring the blasted crawfish," his aunt said, throwing a hand up with disgust. "Y'all kin stick 'em in yer britches fer all I care. Jist bring 'em."

"Oh, I have some gossip, Tee-John." Luc's voice was suspiciously serious all of a sudden. "Looks like we might have two more brothers we never heard of. Twins."

"Huh?" he and Tante Lulu said as one.

"These two guys approached Remy recently when he was making a delivery to a customer up in Alaska. They claim to be sons of Valcour LeDeux."

"I fer one ain't surprised. I wouldn't trust that Valcour any farther than I could sling an alligator," Tante Lulu said.

"How old are they?" he asked.

"Are they Eskimos?" Tante Lulu asked.

He could hear Luc laughing on the other end of the line. "No, they're not Eskimos. They're into ranching or logging or something. Remy wasn't clear. And besides, they weren't overly friendly. They're twenty-eight."

"Hmmm. While he was with my mom but not married to her yet," Tee-John calculated.

"Suppose that means I'll hafta make more hope chests."

"Don't jump the gun," Luc cautioned. "They might not really be our half brothers."

"Hah! Would anyone in their right mind wanna claim Valcour LeDeux as a daddy iffen they dint hafta?" was Tante Lulu's opinion.

Once the phone call ended, he and his aunt sat swinging slowly. She was quiet for once, probably contemplating okra.

Then, out of the blue, she asked, "How long do ya think it might be till yer ready ta settle down and get married?"

Huh? How about never? He shrugged, then lied, "Four or five years, maybe."

She remained quiet for a few long moments, then said, "I suppose I kin hold out that long."

And John felt as if a vice were squeezing his heart.

✦

Plain thinking . . .

Samuel Peachey threw his work gloves down with disgust and quit his morning chores halfway through. It was an unprecedented act for him in all his sixty-seven years.

He walked into the house and found Rebekah sitting at the kitchen table, both hands wrapped around a cup of tea, which she was staring at. Meanwhile, there was wet laundry to be hung on the line and tomato sauce bubbling on the stove, waiting to be canned. Rebekah being idle was unprecedented, too.

"Rebekah?" he said, sitting down next to her. "Does something ail ya? Do ya have the stomachache again?"

She shook her head. There were tears in her pale blue eyes.

Truth to tell, he felt like cryin' himself.

"The boys?"

She nodded, knowing perfectly well what boys he referred to. Caleb and Jonas. Though they were grown men now. It was a subject that they'd avoided talking about for ever so long, and yet it was like a big wall between them.

He braced both elbows on the table and put his fists under his chin. After several long moments, he asked, "Could we have been wrong all these years?"

"I don't know, Samuel, but it feels wrong."

"If we break the *Bann,* we'll be shunned ourselves, Rebekah. Do ya think ya could stand that?"

"I don't know. I jist know this ain't right."

"I have an idea."

"What?"

"I think it's time ta go fly fishin'."

She slapped his arm as she dabbed at her wet eyes with the hem of her apron. "It's not the time fer joshin'."

"I'm serious. I do my best thinkin' when I fly fish."

"Ya goin' alone? Or are ya invitin' Caleb and Jonas?"

"None of those." He smiled, happy that he was finally about to do something.

"I'm goin' ta Claire's place over on the Little Juniata ta get me some advice. She noticed my fly rod when she was here the other day and invited me ta fly fish on her property."

"Yer gonna take advice from an Englisher? Yer gone ferhoodled, fer sure and fer certain."

"*Jah.* An Englisher who loves Caleb, I'm guessin'."

"Ah!" Now she understood. "Well, as long as yer not consultin' with that crazy Cajun woman."

"*Ach,* but she gave ya some pretty underthings. Dint know I still had it in me." He waggled his eyebrows at her.

Rebekah blushed. "Should I plan on trout fer supper tonight, Samuel?"

"No, but I do expect I'll smell like fish."

They smiled at each other then. Maybe there was hope.

Ann Landers of the Little Juniata . . .

Claire awakened just past dawn, as usual. No alarm necessary. Still, she lay in bed for another half hour, just thinking.

Then, with a wide yawn, she padded out to her kitchen and turned on the coffeemaker. She reached down and patted Boney on his head, which he was rubbing against her bare leg below her nightshirt while he yipped loudly. It didn't take much to get Boney barking. The cats, being more refined, all meowed good morning to her.

It looked as if it would be another sunny day, she thought as she yawned again and glanced out her back window. Then did a double take.

There was an Amishman standing in the middle of the river, wearing hip boots and a flat-brimmed straw hat. She didn't own the river, so of course anyone could be seen fishing there on occasion. But an Amishman? That was a first for her.

Especially since it was Caleb's father, she realized, peering closer.

Should she call Caleb and alert him to his father's presence? No. First of all, she was a little peeved with the guy for not making more of an effort to see her again before he left town. Yeah, she'd agreed to cutting things off. But that didn't mean she wouldn't welcome a little coaxing on his part.

When her coffee was ready, she went out on the deck with a mug, being careful to close the door on Boney, who would disturb the fisherman. She watched for about fifteen minutes. Mr. Peachey was clearly an experienced fly fisherman. Not just in his technique, but the way he studied the hatches flying above him. At one point, he reached upward and caught one in his fist . . . probably a green drake, it being too late for mayflies. He studied it in his palm, then took a new fly from his vest and put it on his line. Soon after, he had a twenty-inch rainbow on his line, which he immediately released, in tune with the catch-and-release pattern followed by most people in the area.

Which would be really unusual for an Amishman, she realized. Their culture was pretty much based on work and day-to-day survival. Fly fishing for the fun of it just didn't seem to jive.

But actually, the man was relaxed as he cast, drawing his line back slowly, taking in his surroundings, which indicated to her that he was using the exercise for thinking. In fact, many books had been written about the philosophy of fly fishing, even one called *All I Need to Know about Ministry I Learned from Fly Fishing*.

Eventually Mr. Peachey noticed her and gave a wave, after which he pulled in his line and waded toward shore.

"Don't stop on my account," she yelled down to him.

He shook his head. "I've had enough fer today."

When he walked up the steps to the deck, she pointed to the extra mug of coffee she'd brought out for him.

"*Denki,*" he said, sinking down to the chair beside her with a long sigh, but not before going wide-eyed at the yip-yip-yipping dog and five meowing cats lined up at the kitchen sliding door, begging to come out. "I ain't been fly fishin' fer years. Guess I'm a bit rusty."

"You looked pretty good to me."

He fidgeted. Clearly, he had something else on his mind. "I come ta talk ta ya 'bout Caleb."

Ooookay. "Are you sure that's a good idea? I mean, he might not appreciate us talking behind his back."

"We need advice. Rebekah and me."

And you've come to me? Oh, boy! This is a disaster in the making. "What can I do for you?"

"I want ta know 'bout Caleb."

She frowned, not sure what he meant.

"He seems so sad."

"Of course he is. Were you hoping he would be happy about his parents cutting him off for seventeen years?"

He flinched.

She couldn't be sorry. They were harsh words, but true.

"We cannot approve of his life in the military, or a life spent huntin' fer treasures, but we thought he at least was content. We missed him awful much, but until he came back, we thought he'd settled in his new life."

"He had, pretty much. I'm a bit of a pacifist myself, Mr. Peachey, but I have to say that Caleb's career in the military has been an admirable one. You should be proud of him. As for the treasure hunting, there's nothing wrong with that, but I suspect Caleb is still trying to find himself. And even if he were set up with the perfect career, that would never make up for the hole in his heart."

"Hole in the heart?"

"His estranged family."

Mr. Peachey's throat worked for several seconds, as if he was unable to speak over some strong emotion. "*Ach,* there is a hole in our hearts, too." He put up a hand to halt her from speaking. "It may not seem that way ta you, but we are in pain, too."

"Then why don't you do something about it?" Her tone of voice was more exasperated than she would like, but really, these people were all hurting each other unnecessarily.

"That's why I'm here." He took a long sip of his coffee and set the mug down. "I usta think all this was

Caleb and Jonas's fault 'cause of the choices they made. Not the buggy accident or Hannah bein' pregnant with Jonas's baby, but the choices they made not to apologize ta the church."

What buggy accident? What pregnancy? Caleb had never really explained the details of his and Jonas's shunning.

"It was such a little thing ta do, the kneeling confession, but they refused."

She wanted to ask about *his* choice . . . his and Rebekah's . . . to shun their own sons. Where was the fairness in that? Instead, she asked, "And now?"

"Now I'm not so sure. The only thing I'm sure about is we have a broken family that needs fixin'."

"And you think I can help, how?"

"Do ya love Caleb?"

She didn't even hesitate. "I do, but that doesn't mean we have a future together. My dreams are a big road-block to him."

His brow furrowed with puzzlement.

"A farm. Babies. If not marriage, at least long-term commitment. Most of all, love."

He waved a hand as if all that were irrelevant, which it was not. "Knowing Caleb . . . and lovin' him like ya do . . . surely ya have some suggestion on how we can fix this mess."

Caleb is going to kill me for interfering. Hah! He'll be gone soon anyhow. "Well, actually, I do, Mr. Peachey." And she told him. In no uncertain terms.

It was the craziest thing, but for a blip of a second she felt as if someone was doing a high five Snoopy dance in her head. *I've been hanging around Tante Lulu too much.*

Welcome to the fair . . .

The grounds of the Butterfly B & B resembled a fair-grounds Saturday morning as Veronica and Jake, arms looped around each others' waists, walked over the lawns on the side and back of the historic brick house.

It would be another half hour before it was opened to the public. The public being the news media—TV, radio, newspapers, and cavern and history magazines. Also, tourism boards, historical societies, and museum reps, a few Lenape Indians still residing in the area, the Nittany Grotto Club and other caving enthusiasts, township and county officials who could be helpful to Mark and Abbie once they needed permits to open the cavern, and a few friends and family.

An exclusive interview had been given to an area newspaper, which had held off printing any info on the treasure hunt till now. But that wouldn't run till this evening.

"Caleb did a wonderful job with the Pearl Project, his first as manager, didn't he, honey?" Veronica remarked.

"Yep. Far better than we did in Mexico searching for those friggin' lost Aztec relics. I never saw so many scorpions in all my life."

Veronica laughed. "I think you're as afraid of spiders as Caleb is of snakes."

"That is one big mother of a snake. If a guy's gonna be afraid of snakes, that would be the one."

"Did you see the snakeskin collection his nephew Noah has over on that table near the refreshment table?"

He nodded. "Mark added a couple of Sparky's, too. Cute kid."

They looked at each other then. Her pregnancy remained new to them and a marvel. Every time they saw a baby or child, they shared the same thought. *We're going to have one of those? Amazing!* It was still their secret. Maybe they'd share it at the party tonight.

"You know, this project will not only give Jinx, Inc., some great profits, but I have to give Caleb credit for coming up with this idea for an invited-guest-only extravaganza this morning," Veronica remarked.

"I agree. Proactive rather than defensive way of presenting our story to the media. Goodwill with the community and publicity for Jinx, Inc."

Caleb must have overheard them as he approached. "I wouldn't have been able to put this together so soon or so professionally if I didn't have help from Ross Bennett Consulting in Reedsville. You'll be getting the bill."

"Money well spent," Veronica said.

"Bennett is a computer genius. He designed and produced all the brochures and graphics displays, even those for Jinx, Inc. Check out that high-definition large-screen TV that has a running video of the recovery operation, not to mention other Jinx projects. And those smaller DVD players have PowerPoint presentations on everything from history of the region to the mechanics of cave diving. We all had fun with the animated video he did of Robber Davie Lewis and his exploits. Very funny!"

"I love the treasure chest logo he used on the Jinx pamphlets," Veronica said. "I assume we can use it in the future."

"I love the way he described me as 'Cool Hand Jake,

the coolest professional poker player on the circuit today.'" He winked at her. "Not to mention the handsomest, sexiest, and wittiest—"

Veronica smacked his arm. "The brochure does not say that."

"It hinted," he amended, smiling at her.

God, she loved the rogue. More and more every day. "Well, the teamwork has been phenomenal." Veronica waved an arm to indicate the various tents filling the area, all manned by project members, as well as Abbie, Mark, Mark's fiancée Lily, the Park Service rep Dr. Claire Cassidy, Tante Lulu, Caleb's Amish sister Lizzie, and Del Finley, a geologist. She and Jake would be handling the Jinx, Inc., table to promote the company. You never knew where the next job would come from.

Adam had brought in the inventor of the device that hopefully added luster to cave pearls. They were setting up a demonstration under one of the tents, where the cave pearls were exhibited nicely in a big silk-lined basket. Beside Adam, under the same tent, John was guarding an exhibit of Robber Lewis's hidden treasure, along with historical data and pieces of the broken chest, not to mention the animated video on a laptop. As they passed by, she noticed that Adam and John were exchanging insults, as usual, this time about which one of them knew more about a woman's G-spot. The inventor guy was gaping at their exchange.

"Hey, I could tell you about tantric sex," Jake called out to them.

They all stared at Jake with interest, even Caleb.

She dropped her arm from around Jake's waist and jabbed him with an elbow. "Behave."

Rubbing his elbow, he pretended to be hurt. "Maybe not."

In another tent, Mark, Lily, and Del had laid out numerous diagrams and photographs of the cavern and the project as it had played out. Actual tours of the cavern would not be permitted today for liability reasons.

Brenda, who'd returned with them from Mexico, was helping Lizzie over at the music tent. There had been some arguments about what to play while the visitors strolled the grounds. Jake had wanted Sting and Police songs, his favorite. John had wanted Cajun music. Lizzie had wanted country. Famosa pitched Cuban. In the end, soft Mozart played in the background coming from several strategically placed speakers. The rental company who'd supplied the tents, tables, and chairs had also provided a mini stage and dance floor for the party tonight. Mozart would not be played then, that was for sure.

Tante Lulu was handling the refreshments, with Brenda's help, now that the music situation had been ironed out. They'd had to curb her enthusiasm. If she'd had her way, they would have been providing a feast for their guests. In the end, they'd settled for cheese trays, small sandwiches, and wine or soda. The old lady had been promised she could go whole hog for the feast this evening, and she'd taken them literally. A hog was roasting in one of those rental pig thingees on the other side of the house.

Veronica was glad to see Brenda keeping herself busy. She'd been unusually quiet and rather depressed on this trip. It might have something to do with a *People* magazine article on her ex-husband Lance Caslow, a Nascar driver, although Brenda claimed to have no feelings for the renowned womanizer anymore. In the magazine, he'd been shown kissing some young starlet who had a thing for race car drivers. Rumors abounded about an upcoming marriage. The only remark Brenda had made about the photo, which Jake had shown her with typical male cluelessness, was, "You could fit two of her in my jeans." Brenda had weight issues.

When Veronica had called Jake on his insensitivity in showing Brenda that picture, he'd said, "But she says she's over the guy."

Her response had been, "Sometimes men have the brains of a gnat. Just because a woman says she doesn't care doesn't mean that she doesn't care."

"Huh?" he'd responded.

They came to the next tent, where Abbie was showing off some copies of the Franklin journal she'd found in her attic. She'd decided to give the public only a peek at some pages, wanting to save the rest for a book Mark and Lily might want to write.

Sharing the tent with Abbie was Claire, who was talking to Del. She wore full Lenni Lenape Indian clothing, from moccasins to feather in the headband. Before her she displayed Abbie's collection of Native American artifacts taken from the cavern in the past, along with her own regional collection. Arrowheads, tomahawks, fetishes, and various histories of the Lenape in this area over the years, plus two large foam boards on easels showing Indian trails and Indian villages in Pennsylvania during the 1700s and 1800s.

Veronica was about to join Claire and Del when she noticed the expression on Caleb's face. He was watching Claire with what could only be described as hunger. At one time, before she and Jake had reconciled, Caleb had hit on her. It had been only a halfhearted attempt, she realized now. If he'd looked at her like that, who knew what she might have done? Well, actually, she did know. She wouldn't have succumbed, because of Jake. Still . . .

Jake was talking to Abbie, leaving her and Caleb alone for a minute. "So, do you and Claire have a thing going on?"

Instead of denying it, as she'd expected, he said, "Not anymore."

She arched her eyebrows at him.

"She wants to have my baby."

She put a hand over her mouth to stifle a laugh. "Is that all?"

"No. She wants to live on a farm."

"Okaaay. A farm and babies. That doesn't sound unreasonable."

"To me it is."

"Not if you love her."

His head swiveled so fast it was a wonder he didn't get whiplash. "Who said anything about love?"

"I don't know, Caleb, but take it from someone who's been married and divorced four times. Love is everything."

He glared at her and walked away.

Yep, he was in love, all right.

Chapter
17

Caught ya! . . .

Claire had either been busy all morning or she was avoiding him like the plague. Probably both.

The guests had left after a successful press conference introducing the Pearl Project and the cavern to the public. Abbie and Tante Lulu were cooking up a storm in the kitchen for tonight. Lizzie and Brenda were sorting through some CDs, preparing for the entertainment.

LeDeux, Famosa, and Del had gone in to State College to pick up the Lousiana family members at University Park Airport. Yes, so many were coming that three vehicles were required. Plus, Del had a truck, which was needed for another of Tante Lulu's hope chests and a bushel of crawfish.

Ronnie and Jake were on the other side of the house, tending the roast pig. Its succulent scent, along with delicious odors coming from the kitchen, made his stomach growl with hunger. He couldn't recall having eaten today. Too much to do.

The caterers were removing some tents, tables, and chairs and replacing them with others. Apparently there was going to be a bayou theme to tonight's combination birthday party, reunion celebration, and military honors. At least, he thought that was fake moss they were hanging from some of the trees. Little American flags were tucked in the table centerpieces. And oh, good Lord, there were tiny twin Amish dolls, portraying him and Jonas, he assumed, in the centerpieces. Jonas would have a fit . . . if he even showed up. Amish, and Mennonites, for that matter, didn't like images made of themselves, whether they be photographs or dolls.

Finally, finally, finally, he saw that Claire was alone. On the other side of the stream, by the cavern, dismantling her wigwam.

He walked over as quietly as he could, a skill learned as part of special-forces training. He didn't want to give her another opportunity to run off.

"Hey, Claire," he said.

She jumped, almost dropping the limbs she was bundling together. "Caleb," she acknowledged. "I didn't hear you coming."

Silent, he began to help her, picking up the thin striplings, then rolling up some of the skins, which she'd brought with her from her home.

"You should be proud, Caleb. The project was a huge success. You and Ronnie were great during the press conference."

He nodded. "I've missed you."

She closed her eyes for a second. Apparently, this was not a subject she wanted to pursue.

Well, screw that! "Have you missed me?" *Pathetic, pathetic, pathetic.*

"You know I have."

"Then why can't we be together?"

"For how long?"

His face heated up. "I'll be here another two days. Gotta tie up some loose ends. And make some plans for Lizzie."

"Oh? And am I a loose end?"

"Absolutely."

She shook her head as if he were clueless, which he was. "I care about you, Caleb, but two days of wild monkey sex and poof! doesn't work for me."

Wild monkey sex? Oh, man, she had to mention that! "You care about me? You said you loved me."

She put both hands on her hips. "You say that as if you like the fact that I love you."

He shrugged. "I'm flattered."

"You are such a . . . man. Go away, Caleb. Good-bye. Nice to have known you and all that." She turned her face away from him. He suspected she had tears in her eyes she didn't want him to see.

"I can't."

She faced him then, and yep, her eyes were glassy with tears. "Can't what?"

"Go away."

"Ever?"

Heated face again. "No. Just not yet."

She said a foul word under her breath, then tossed the roll of skins to the ground and stomped off toward the bridge.

"Where are you going?" he asked, following after her.

"Home? I need to take a nap before tonight's party."

"A nap sounds good to me."

"Give it up, Caleb. Not gonna happen."

Midway across the bridge, he grabbed hold of her upper arm, pulling her to a halt. "I don't want to give it up, Claire." He gulped, then added, "I don't want to give you up."

She tilted her head in question. "What does that mean?"

"I don't know. I'm just so freakin' mixed up." He pulled her into his arms and held her tight in his embrace so she couldn't escape. Kissing the top of her hair, he whispered, "Don't let me go." *Yet.*

She put her arms around his waist and kissed the side of his neck. "Oh, Caleb." He had no idea what she would have said or done next, because two people were crossing the yard, coming toward them. Amish people. People he didn't recognize. No, wait a minute, they weren't Amish. They must be Mennonite. Maybe friends of Jonas.

Actually, there came Jonas, truck tires squealing, into the parking lot with his three kids. And there came Lizzie, running from the other direction, as if alarmed about something.

The man, who was older, in his fifties or sixties, wore typical black broadcloth pants with suspenders over a lavender shirt. His white hair and beard were neatly trimmed. Beside him was a short woman, also older, whose white hair was pulled off her face into a white prayer cap. She wore a calf-length dress with short sleeves of a pale blue material with pink flowers.

"Caleb!" the man and woman called out to him, alternately.

Slowly, he eased himself away from Claire and began to move toward the couple. It was like a slow-motion vignette. Them moving toward each other. The buzzing in his ears. Then slow recognition.

It was his father and mother.

"Dat? Mam? What does this mean?"

"Me and Mam have decided to go Mennonite."

"What?" *WHAT?*

"We decided ta come tell ya now 'cause we can't come to yer party later. The music and dancing and whatnot, dontcha know?" His father put an arm over his mother's shoulder and squeezed. They both smiled at him, expectantly.

"Is this a joke?" *No. Amish didn't joke like that.*

"A wonderful-goot adventure fer old folks like us, ain't so, Caleb?"

Jonas ran up, out of breath, and stood beside him and Claire. "I tried to warn you, but your cell phone wouldn't answer," Jonas whispered to him.

"What do you mean? You've been Amish all your lives. You can't just change now. Can you?"

"No one's stoppin' us. Oh, they'll try, but me and Mam, we decided jist what we're gonna say."

"And that would be?"

"Shun my boys, and ya shun us." His father's lips went rigid, but there was a sort of pleading expression in his eyes. His mother's, too.

"Dat . . . Mam . . . you don't have to do this."

"*Jah*, we do," his mother said, reaching out for him and Jonas both with a sob.

His father put an arm around them, too. A friggin' group hug!

At first there was just the scent of his mother's Ivory soap and his father's tobacco, and the sounds of gentle sobbing. Then, with a laugh, not even caring that his eyes were wet with tears, he pulled away and asked, "What brought this on?"

"Well, yer Claire, of course," Dat said. "When I was fly fishin' over at her place, she set me straight, fer sure and fer certain, she did."

My Claire? Dat fly fishing at Claire's? When was this? He turned to the woman who apparently had meddled in his life once again. Not that he could blame her when the results were this good.

But Claire was gone.

The old lady could still shock them . . .

John leaned back against the kitchen sliding glass door, watching his family as they surrounded Tante Lulu, everyone talking at once. There were sixteen of them, including the kids who were running around the yard.

Two of the older kids had already been warned not to go into that cavern and try to catch the big snake. They were LeDeux kids. They probably wouldn't listen. John was betting on a visit to the emergency room before morning.

A couple of the kids were being helpful, though. Setting the tables for Abbie and Lizzie, who was wearing her Amish attire today, which fascinated Luc's three little girls. "Can you twirl?" he heard one of them ask.

"Huh?" Lizzie bent down to hear what the little girl asked.

And Jeannette, Luc's youngest, spun around, making the hem of her skirt twirl.

Lizzie laughed and tried, but her skirt had no twirl at all. The three little girls frowned with disappointment. Apparently twirling was a requisite for a cool girl's clothing.

"I've got some news for everybody." This was Charmaine speaking from her perch on her husband Rusty's lap. She was all dolled up in her usual big black Texas hair, a red skirt so short she about gave Caleb's father a heart attack when they'd arrived, a tank top that spelled out in sequins, "Hair Today, Gone Tomorrow," in line with her hair salons, and red high-heeled stiletto sandals. Bimbo to the max and proud of it, that was their Charmaine. Not that her husband minded. Even after three years of marriage, Rusty was crazy in love with his ditzy wife.

"Is it 'bout those couples' massage tables?" Tante Lulu asked, sipping at a glass of sweet tea.

"Oh, you heard about that? Tee-John, you have a big mouth."

"Hey, who said it was me?"

"I told her," Luc admitted.

"Anyhow, back to my news," Charmaine said. "Me and Rusty are gonna have a baby."

The women—Sylvie, Rachel, and Val—all screamed with glee and rushed over to hug Charmaine, practically knocking her off Rusty's lap. The men all offered congratulations to the proud, red-faced papa-to-be. Tante Lulu grinned smugly as if she already knew.

It was good news. He knew for a fact that Charmaine and Rusty had been trying for more than a year. God bless the fun of trying, had been his opinion.

"I brought your heart medicine," Luc said then,

which immediately quieted the whole patio. "And I had a long talk with Doc Pitrey."

Tante Lulu glared at Luc. "The doc ain't 'lowed ta talk 'bout me. I know all 'bout the privacy laws."

"Well, apparently those laws haven't made it down to Loo-zee-anna yet." Luc was a lawyer. He ought to know. "Doc Pitrey said you don't have a heart problem, that the pills are for indigestion."

"Heart, gas, whass the difference?"

"Big difference, auntie," John chimed in. "You scared the bejesus out of me and Luc when ya said ya needed heart medicine. Could it be ya were tryin' to trick us inta somethin'?"

"Who? Me?" His aunt actually had the nerve to appear affronted at the suggestion. Then she jumped to another subject. "Did anyone check on my garden this week?"

"I did." Rachel, who was married to his half brother Remy, waved her hand. "You have an awful lot of ripe tomatoes. I put most of them in the fridge. And okra. Lordy, Lordy!" She rolled her eyes.

"Thass good. I already put half of that basket ya brought into the gumbo fer t'night." For emphasis, she walked over and gave the giant kettle a few stirs before replacing the lid. It smelled like home. Well, Tante Lulu's home. His home with his notorious father smelled more like booze. Not that he was living at home these days.

It would be good to go back to the bayou. He'd found over the years that he could stand only so much of the North before he missed the Southern dialect, Southern food, and yep, Southern belles. He would miss Jinx, though, once he started police work. A new phase of his life.

Just then Ronnie and Jake came up, holding hands. They'd gone for a walk to work off the heavy lunch they'd had after the big to-do this morning. Following them were Peach and Famosa.

"You wanted to talk to us about a business proposition?" Ronnie said to Tante Lulu.

All eyes turned on their unpredictable aunt.

This was a surprise. What was she up to now? As one, he and his half brothers, half sister, and the in-laws said, "Uh-oh!"

"Shush!" Tante Lulu said to them. "Sit down, sit down. Have some tea."

When they were all settled, she said to Ronnie and Jake, "I wanta hire ya fer a treasure hunt down in Loo-zee-anna."

"Whaaat?" some of them, himself included, exclaimed. The others just dropped their jaws with surprise.

Except for Caleb. "What kind of treasure hunt?"

Was he taking his ditzy aunt seriously? *Mon Dieu!*

"Jean Lafitte's buried treasure." Tante Lulu folded her arms over her chest and smiled as if she'd just announced she'd found the pirate's treasure in her own back yard.

She hadn't. Had she? "Where is it? How do ya know where it is?" John asked.

"I gots this friend, Lefty Delacroix . . ."

He groaned mentally. Crazy Lefty from Lafayette, who claimed to have been a pirate himself at one time. He and Tante Lulu would make quite a pair. The Fruitcake Duo.

"Lefty knows someone who knows someone who has this treasure map."

"Auntie, hundreds of people have searched for that treasure over the past two hundred years, to no avail." Luc was speaking in his cool, calm lawyer voice.

"I know that. But, jumpin' Jehoshaphat, no one has tried since Hurricane Katrina. And, besides, everyone's been searchin' in the wrong place." She beamed.

Luc and René put their faces on the table, their shoulders shaking. He didn't know if they were laughing or crying.

After she explained in more detail, Ronnie said, "I don't know. It sounds kind of risky. And expensive."

"I gots the money. How much wouldja need fer my share?"

They all cringed. His aunt had no clue how much money was involved in these projects.

Jake shrugged. He was the one handling finances for Jinx, Inc., these days. "Two hundred thousand, maybe."

"I got that," Tante Lulu said with a whoop.

Another shocker from their aunt. Who knew she had that kind of money? Even Ronnie and Jake were taken by surprise. Jake had probably thrown that figure out hoping to discourage her.

"I'm not sure we could move to that project right away," Caleb cautioned. "We have some other jobs we need to complete first, don't we, Ronnie?"

She nodded, dumbfounded.

"Thass no problem. I got cannin' ta do, and healin' my patients and such. Mebbe next spring? Or the next year might be even better. Doan wait too long, though. I might be dead."

Jake and Ronnie nodded hesitantly. They were probably hoping she would forget about it by then.

Hah! Little did they know his aunt.

There was something different about Ronnie. Jake studied her, then Charmaine, then her again. Grinning, he whispered in her ear, "Congratulations, darlin'."

She blushed and whispered back, "How did you know?"

"Ya have that look, sweetie. Jist like Charmaine."

Peach and Famosa overheard, and they both shook Jake's hand.

Meanwhile, his aunt was still blathering on. "I cain't wait ta call Mary LeBlanc and tell her and the ladies at Our Lady of the Bayou Church. Do ya think there's any chance we might get Richard Simmons ta come on down and help with the project? Ya know, 'Sweatin' to the Oldies' could be our mornin' exercise, 'stead of joggin'. Betcha we could get some TV crews down there what with that ol' Jean Lafitte legend and Richard Simmons. An' Richard could stay at my cottage. He is so cute."

What could one say to that?

"Does anyone know where they hide the bourbon? I'm in the mood for an oyster shooter, or five."

It's not a party without you, baby . . .

"Where's Claire?"

"I don't know. It's hard to see anyone in this crowd," Caleb told his brother at the party that night. Actually, he'd been searching for Claire the past half hour, to no avail.

But then, Caleb's eyes went wide at Jonas's companion of the evening, who stepped up beside him.

"You remember Laura, dontcha?" Jonas said, his face, neck, and ears pink with embarrassment.

Caleb nodded a greeting. It was the nurse, Laura Jones, but instead of her usual attire, tonight she wore an ankle-length dress with short sleeves and a demure neckline. It was rose-colored with tiny yellow flowers. Her blonde hair was pulled into a knot at the back of her neck. If it wasn't for the gauzy material of Laura's dress or the long curly strands that had come loose from the bun and framed her face, he would almost have thought she was Mennonite.

Ah! Now he understood Jonas's discomfort. Laura was out for the kill, showing that she would even change her appearance to nab his brother. That speculation was further proven when he noticed her lacing her fingers with Jonas's and tugging him closer to her side. Jonas made no attempt to pull away.

"Jonas and I would like you and Claire to come for dinner on Wednesday," Laura said. "I'm teaching his girls how to make a seafood lasagna. Dat and Mam will be there."

If his eyes had gone wide at her appearance, they went even wider at her use of his parents' names. "I'd love to, but I'm not sure I'll still be here then."

"Caleb! Will ya not even consider my offer? It would be wonderful-goot to have ya be a partner in my landscaping business. Peachey Brothers. We could expand and—"

Caleb put up a halting hand and shook his head. "I

appreciate the offer, Jonas, but it's your business. Not mine."

Jonas seemed about to argue, then gave up. Squeezing his shoulder, he said in a choked voice, "Ya wouldn't leave without sayin' good-bye, wouldja?"

"I'll probably leave on Monday. Gotta get back to Jinx headquarters in New Jersey. But no, I wouldn't leave without seeing you first. And Dat and Mam. For one thing, we need to discuss this whole Mennonite conversion thing. Is it for real?"

"Seems so. Dat talked Zeke, Levi, Katie, and Mimi into converting, 'long with their families. But Aaron, Joseph, and Judith's husband, Isaac Glick, are balkin'. *Ach,* but it's a wonder so many of our family are goin' along with this, and, tell the truth, it's no loss with those three stayin' behind. Aaron alveese was too big fer his britches. Joseph's attitude can be blamed on his age, I suppose, and he might come 'round later, 'specially if he thinks he might lose the farm fer being muleheaded. And ya wouldn't wanna be around Isaac Glick fer long anyhow; he's got more opinions than God has little green apples. Plus he's got a gas problem like ya wouldn't believe."

"Jonas!" Laura chastised.

"Well, it's the truth. He breaks wind everywheres. Even durin' church."

Caleb had to smile at his brother's bluntness. He wouldn't bring it up now, but he could recall a time when an eight-year-old Jonas had deliberately farted in the middle of a three-hour church service, clearing the room like a tornado. He'd been eating baked beans the night before. A lot of baked beans.

Jonas's eyes, gleaming with humor, connected with

his, and he realized that his brother was remembering, too.

"Will Dat and the others continue to live in the same houses?" he asked.

"I 'spect so. The shunnin' will be harder, but no harder than it's been fer me. Easier, actually, if all or most of them stick together."

"Who ever would have thought Dat would bend like this?"

"It's a wonder, all right."

"Well, I think it's great that your family will finally be united again," Laura said. "A blessing, really."

They couldn't argue with that.

"Then there's Lizzie." Caleb sighed. "She's bound and determined to pursue a music career."

"It's foolishness, pure and simple, if ya ask me," Jonas remarked.

"You two do know that Lizzie is a very talented singer, don't you? She sounds a lot like Carrie Underwood," Laura said. "Do you really have the right to deny her a chance to pursue her dreams?"

That was the problem. What did you do with an Amish girl with a talent for country music? Should Caleb take her out into the English world and see if she had enough talent and stamina to compete? Should Jonas take her into his Mennonite home, where there were many restrictions but some forms of music were permitted?

The three of them turned toward the small stage where music was being played on a CD and amp system by Lizzie, Brenda, and LeDeux, whoever was in the vicinity at various times. Lizzie's blonde hair was held off her face by two barrettes and hung down to her waist in back. She wore low-riding jeans and a tiny pink knit top that left about six inches of skin exposed.

"What is that shiny thing on Lizzie's belly?" Jonas cocked his head to the side, trying to figure it out.

Laura giggled at Jonas's naivete.

"It's a belly-button ring," Caleb said.

"How does it stay on?"

Laura giggled again.

"Her belly button is pierced," Caleb explained.

"Oh, good Lord! Why would anyone wanna put a hole in their belly button?"

Laura said, "Uh-oh!"

He and Jonas stared at her, Jonas more surprised than him.

"I have a belly button ring," she disclosed in a small voice.

Caleb had to laugh at the shocked expression on Jonas's face. That pretty much said how intimate, or not, she and Jonas had been so far.

"But I could let it grow over. The hole, I mean."

Jonas was still blinking with shock, trying his best not to gape at her belly.

"Hey, at least Laura doesn't have her tongue pierced," Caleb teased. Then quickly added, "Do you?"

She shook her head.

"Why would that be better or worse?" Jonas grumbled.

Caleb leaned over and whispered the benefits of a tongue piercing to his innocent brother.

"Oh, you!" Jonas said, not believing what he'd told him.

"Listen, brother, you would be surprised at what

some people pierce." He glanced pointedly at his and then Jonas's crotch.

"No way!" Jonas declared.

Their conversation was interrupted then by LeDeux's brother René, who began tuning up an accordion, of all things, preparing to accompany Lizzie on some song. LeDeux had a washboard, which Caleb assumed he was going to play like a Cajun frottoir. Del had a trumpet.

"Ladies and gents," Tante Lulu said, stepping up to the mike, which squealed loudly before René adjusted it for her. Her hair was curly red tonight, which went just super with her purple spandex dress and matching high heels. Actually, a number of the LeDeux women were wearing the same spandex dress in different colors. They planned to put on some kind of a show.

"We're here t'night ta celebrate lots of things," Tante Lulu said, "and helpin' us is Miss Elizabeth Peachey, the next American Idol."

The crowd, at least a hundred of them—where did all these people come from?—clapped and hooted their approval.

"First off, we wanna recognize all our soldiers fightin' in different parts of the world, but 'specially Mark Franklin, who was wounded in Af-ganny-stan." She pointed to Mark, who was trying to slip inside the house, but the sliding door had been locked by his grandmother. Giving in, he gave a little wave, but he was obviously mortified.

"Lizzie is gonna sing that Lee Greenwood song 'God Bless the USA.' Us folks down South know Lee's songs well. We think Lizzie'll do him and Mark proud."

Tante Lulu stepped back and Lizzie stepped forward. These weren't the usual instruments accompanying this song, but Lizzie's voice was powerful and poignant in relaying the lyrics about being proud to be an American and not forgetting those who had died for freedom. Every time she came to the stanza, 'God Bless the USA', the crowd clapped and sang along with her.

She got a standing ovation at the end. There were more than a few teary eyes, especially Abbie and Lily. He and Jonas just gaped at each other. Their sister really was talented.

Tante Lulu was at the mike now. "We're also here ta celebrate the reunion of two brothers."

Oh, great! He'd forgotten about that. Too late to escape.

Jonas stared ahead like a deer caught in the headlights as everyone turned to look at the two of them.

Lizzie took the mike and said, "This is an old song called 'Brotherly Love' that was sung by Keith Whitley before he died way too young. It was a duet, with the other part sung by Earl Thomas Conley. Tonight by René LeDeux." Then she and René proceeded to sing a song whose lyrics hit way too close to home. About a love between two brothers that "time and miles" can't separate. There were parts of the song that were funny, but mostly sad, concluding that there was something special about brotherly love.

He and Jonas were speechless amid the applause. He reached over and squeezed Jonas's hand, a silent promise that they would never be apart for long in the future.

Lizzie stepped off the little stage then, and Tante Lulu chuckled into the microphone. "We gots us a special guest tonight ta celebrate Tee-John's birthday. She come all the way from Hollywood." They dimmed the lights on the little stage, and for a few moments there were sounds of rustling and stumbling and swearing. Finally, when the lights came back on, LeDeux was sitting on a chair raised high like a throne, and there was a huge cake sitting on the stage in front of them. Del blew out an introductory riff, the top of the cake popped open, and out shot . . . Holy crap! Marilyn Monroe. Well, a really good Marilyn Monroe impersonator. Charmaine LeDeux Lanier, in a red spandex dress and red high heels, a blonde Marilyn Monroe wig, and red lipstick began to sing her classic, breathy version of "Happy Birthday." The crowd howled with laughter and appreciation, then joined in singing to the grinning Cajun birthday boy.

After that, the music changed back to CDs as the LeDeuxes prepared for some Village People/Motown floor show that they put on periodically. They'd invited Caleb to be the shirtless military guy in their revue, to which he'd replied, "Not in this lifetime!" People went back to eating and drinking and socializing, and Caleb moved through the crowd.

In the end he came to an alarming conclusion. Claire was not here tonight and never had been.

The chicken!

Well, he was in the mood for a little taste of chicken, thank you very much, he decided. It was well past time he stopped being miserable and pathetic and started being happy and pathetic.

He searched in his pocket for his keys and came up with the St. Jude key chain Tante Lulu had given him earlier. He could swear the old guy winked at him and said, "About time!"

Chapter
18

How do I love thee? Let me count the
orgasms . . .

By the time Caleb arrived at Claire's, he was pissed,
hurt, scared, and horny.

He was pissed because Claire had never come to the
party or bothered to tell him she wasn't coming. He was
hurt for the same reason. The horniness needed no
explanation.

And the fear? Shiiit! He could face off with a half-
dozen tangos in the middle of a freakin' Iraq desert
without hesitation, but the feelings he was finally beginning to recognize for Claire had him shaking in his
shoes. How could he have come to care so much in such
a short time? These were life-changing emotions, and
he knew for damn sure that he wasn't going to be able
to ride off into the sunset this time with no regrets,
which had always been his way.

He opened Claire's front door, without knocking, and
it slammed back against the wall with a thud.

The force of his action surprised him, and it sure as hell surprised Claire, who was sitting, peaceful as could be, in an upholstered chair with a cup of tea on one arm and an opened book on the other. Obviously she wasn't pissed, hurt, scared, or horny. Carefully, he closed the door, then walked over to the kitchen counter, where he placed a bag of food Tante Lulu had pushed on him.

"Caleb? What are you doing here?"

"The question is, what are *you* doing here?"

"I took a nap and overslept."

"Liar."

"Okay, I decided it would be better to stay home."

"Better for whom?"

"For both of us."

"Bullshit."

"Nice talk! Is that food I smell? Yum. I'm hungry."

"Later," he grunted out as he toed off first one loafer, then the other.

"Making yourself at home, are you, big boy? Would you like a cup of tea?"

"No, I don't want any fucking tea, *little girl*."

"Okaaaay. So, are you still leaving on Monday, Mr. Grumpy?"

Mr. Grumpy? You have no idea. "Later," he repeated. "We'll discuss it later."

"Who named you God to make all the rules?"

Sticks and stones, baby. Sticks and stones. But then he noticed more boxes lining the room, and his heart rate accelerated like a motorcycle. *Brmmmm, brmmmm, brmmmm!* "When are you moving?"

"Later," she said with a grin.

Don't lose your cool, Peachey. Don't say what you're really thinking. You gotta ease into a thing like this. Undoing his belt, he tugged his polo shirt out of his pants and yanked it over his head, tossing it behind him.

"What . . . What are you doing?" she said, standing. Unfortunately, or fortunately, the irritation in her voice was overruled by her eyes, which appeared fascinated by the movement of his hands undoing his zipper.

He slowed down, just so she could enjoy the show. Then he shrugged off his khakis and briefs all in one swoop. "What am I doing? I'm doing what I should have done days ago. Knocking down that friggin' wall you've put up."

She made a little squeaking sound as she backed away from him.

"Claire, you have no reason to be afraid of me. I'll leave if you want me to, but I've gotta tell you, my brain is really screwed up right now." *And my heart.* "I need you."

She didn't speak, and he realized that she'd squeaked not out of fear but for another reason. Her eyes were glued to a part of his anatomy that was standing out like a flagpole. He glanced down, did a double take, and might have made a squeaking sound himself. *Oh, good Lord! I look like a male porno star. I don't think I've ever been this big. It's almost embarrassing. Almost.*

He advanced on her. For every step backward she took, he took two forward. Soon she was trapped between the door and his world-class blue steeler.

She was wearing a Garfield nightshirt and nothing else. But not for long. Once she was as naked as he was, he said, "About that wall."

"I'm probably going to regret this later, but damn the wall." She leaped upward, latching her arms around his shoulders and her legs around his waist, her face buried in his neck.

His eyes probably rolled back in his head. Blue was practically doing the rumba. And then, before he had a chance to say Holy crap! or unroll his eyes or tell Blue to behave, Claire wiggled her ass lower and somehow managed to ease herself down to just the right spot. Then, oh, God, *bam,* she moved herself onto him. All. The. Way.

His knees turned to rubber, but he immediately caught himself by putting his hands under her buns and bracing her back against the door. "Cute trick, honey, but this is my show."

"Oh, yeah?" She did some incredibly talented thing with the inner muscles of her body.

And his knees did in fact buckle. He sank to the floor, taking her with him, but somehow she managed to be on top. Was she punishing him, or rewarding him? There was a fine line here that he wasn't about to question.

She rode him like a regular cowgirl then. Totally uninhibited. *God bless Dale Evans and Annie Oakley and rodeos and whatever or whoever taught women how to do this.* Even when she came around him several times, she didn't stop.

She was killing him. She was killing herself. Enough!

Rolling them both over, he held her in place with his cock imbedded in her, unmoving, and his arms braced on either side of her head. He leaned down and brushed his lips across hers. "Does this mean you missed me?"

Her eyelashes fluttered—she was still in a haze of arousal, which was very, very flattering to his ego. "Yes, I missed you. Dammit."

He smiled.

"Did you miss me?"

How could she ask? "Baby, did you happen to notice the hard-on I carted in here? Did you notice I'm still inside you doing the happy dance? Damn straight I missed you."

Then he showed her with the stamina of a Navy SEAL—he knew all those years of PT would pay off someday—and the patience of an Amishman—*Patience makes perfect, Dat used to say*—and a skill perfected over the years—*with way too many women*—just how much he missed her. He was pretty sure he succeeded, if her screaming out his name at the end was any indication. And him? He was cooler. He just murmured her name. Over and over and over.

But she didn't say she loved him. And surprisingly, Caleb was disappointed. How pitiful was that?

He was not James Brown, he was better . . .

Caleb was an amazing sex machine.

Claire would have been impressed if it weren't apparent that he acted out of desperation of some kind.

He'd fucked her against the wall. He'd fucked her down by the river, where they'd been bitten by a thousand mosquitoes. He'd fucked her in her bathtub under scented bubbles followed by their slathering calamine over each other to control the itching. He'd fucked her again when he awakened her in the middle of the night. And yes, *fuck* was precisely the word he would use, crude and to the point, avoiding at all costs the word *love*.

He'd probably do it again as morning light peeped through her shades if she wasn't pretending to be asleep. Really, what was he trying to prove?

"What? What did you say?" he said, pausing as he zipped up his khakis and walked over to the bed, bare-footed and bare-chested. The poster boy for sex on the hoof.

She hadn't meant to speak her thoughts, but what the hell? She sat up in bed against the pillows, pulling the sheet up to cover her. She winced slightly at the delicious ache between her legs and noted the bruise marks on her body and his, as well. In fact, she was pretty sure those were her teeth marks on his shoulder. "What's going on, Caleb? What are you trying to prove?"

He sat down on the edge of the bed and reached for the sheet that covered her. "I thought you liked what we did."

She slapped his hand away. "You know I did."

Cocking his head to the side, he asked, "What's the problem?"

"That's what I'm asking you. What are you trying to prove? If you fuck me enough times, do you figure I won't ask you any questions about when you're leaving or when you'll come back, if ever? If you fuck me well enough, do you figure that will be enough to satisfy me, that I won't want, God forbid, commitment from you? If you fuck me—"

"Stop using that word." He pressed his fingertips against her mouth, then replaced them with his lips in a soft kiss. "Yeah, I know I use that word. Too often. But *you* demean what I did . . . what we did . . . by saying it that way. We made love. Whatever else you believe, whatever memories we created here last night, please think of it as making love."

Memories? That means he's leaving. I knew he was leaving. Why am I acting like such a fool? Oh, God! She blinked rapidly to prevent tears from welling in her eyes. They were the exact words she wanted to hear, about making love, not lust, except for the memories part, and, well, today was Sunday, and he would be leaving tomorrow. *Don't push him, Claire. Don't tell him you love him. Don't ask him if he loves you.*

"Hurry up and get dressed. I'll make coffee and warm up those beignets Tante Lulu packed up for us. Do you have a thermos and a basket so we can take them with us? I'd like to go for a run first, maybe along that bike trail that abuts the Juniata over by the flea market. If you don't mind. We could eat after that, sort of a picnic along the river, then head out. What do you think?"

She thought something was really out of whack in this picture. The usually quiet—you could say taciturn—Caleb was rambling on like . . . like Tante Lulu. She tried to register all that he'd said. Okay, he'd wanted to make love to her all night, and now he wanted her dressed and out of bed. To run, eat, "head out." What was up? "Where are we going?"

"Not camping in a wigwam, that's for damn sure. I've had enough mosquitos to last me a lifetime."

Now he teased? *But he's not smiling.*

And neither was she. "Caleb?" she insisted, getting out of bed with the sheet wrapped around her toga-style. With hysterical irrelevance, she mused over how amazing it was that even the most sophisticated women were afflicted with morning-after modesty. Not so men. Not

so Caleb, who looked sexy and buff with his khakis un-
buttoned and riding low on his hips.

He leaned against the door frame, arms folded. The
pose was casual, but his jaw was tight and his body
tense. He appeared to be bracing himself for something,
like a soldier about to face gunfire. Then he shot the
salvo heard 'round the world. Her world anyway.

"It's about time I saw your bloody farm, baby."

*I love you, baby, but I still don't want no
stinkin' cows . . .*

Two hours later, Caleb had no choice. He'd procras-
tinated with a long run, a long breakfast, and a short
nooner, except it wasn't yet noon. Claire was beginning
to stare at him as if he had a few screws loose . . . which
he did. Now it was time to face the firing squad . . . uh,
the farm.

He hung a left in Alexandria at the newly painted
sign "Hope Farm" and drove white-knuckled up the
lane. Ahead was her farmhouse. "Who owns the crops?"
he asked, pointing to the neat rows of corn on the left
and oats on the right.

"The farmer on the adjacent property. Harald
Gorbitz."

"So you don't plan to farm?"

"Not at first."

*That doesn't sound good. I hear an "eventually" in
there.* "Eventually?"

"It depends. I couldn't do it on my own."

Definitely not good.

"I do want a big garden, though. Tomatoes, snow peas, string beans, onions, beets, turnips, peppers, watermelons, pumpkins . . . everything. And a huge flower garden, of course."

Is that all? The expression on her face was practically beatific, while his heart dropped with each plant she mentioned.

"And I'll want a small orchard, and berry patches, too. In the summer I was thinking about running day camps for kids to teach them about the Lenni Lenape Indians. Maybe later I might get into herb gardening. Maybe go commercial at some point."

It's a farm. F. A. R. M. You can talk day camp and herbs all you want, but it's still gonna be a farm. "How big did you say this place was?"

"Only thirty acres, but that's big enough for me."

I would hope so.

He stopped the car next to a stone farmhouse. It matched the stone bank barn built against a low hill. Behind the house he could see the Frankstown branch of the Juniata flowing through her property. On the banks were a half-dozen cows slurping up the water. *Cows!*

"They're not my cows."

But you'll probably get some. Is that a rash on my arm? Betcha I'm allergic to farms.

They both got out of the car, and she showed him around. Okay, he had to admit it was a nice place. The quaint house, more like an English cottage, had a modern kitchen and bathrooms. There was even a sound system built into the living room walls and a large stone fireplace. The barn was clean and sturdy. The place didn't smell too bad. It didn't feel exactly like his Amish home, which had plagued his nightmares for years.

Standing in the middle of the living room, he had a sudden vision of himself here. A roaring fire, Claire on her computer or in the kitchen stirring up something delicious-smelling, and him lying on the floor playing with two kids, a boy and a girl. Outside the sounds of a chicken cock-a-doodling, a cow lowing. He closed his eyes on the pain in his heart. It was a scenario he'd avoided his whole life. And yet . . . and yet . . .

"What do you think?" Claire asked, breaking into his reverie.

He gulped several times before he could speak. "I'm never going to be a farmer, Claire."

That took her by surprise and raised her hackles about a foot. "Who asked you to? Good grief, Caleb, you look like you're having heart palpitations just being here on a farm."

I'm having palpitations, all right, but not because of the farm. He decided to ignore her sarcasm. "But I think I might be able to live here. Have it be my home base. That third bedroom upstairs would make a good office for me. I assume you'd want to use the downstairs bedroom for your office."

They had been walking back toward the kitchen, but she stopped abruptly and turned to stare at him.

At least she didn't say, "Who asked you to?" again.

"What are you trying to say, Caleb? And take a deep breath, for heaven's sake. Your face is so red, I'm afraid you'll have a stroke."

Whatever it is I'm trying to say, I'm obviously not doing a good job. He stuck his hand in the back pocket of his pants and pulled out an audio tape. "Maybe this will say it better. Tante Lulu told me to use it as a last resort."

"A last resort for what?" Then, "You're taking Tante Lulu's advice?"

"Yeah, crazy, isn't it?"

Just then she noticed the tape case he laid on the mantel. "David Cassidy? Are you kidding me? Is this typical Navy SEAL musical fare?"

Go ahead, make fun of me. The song started to play, and she stood with her head cocked to the side, listening. Slowly, very slowly, she started to understand, especially when Cassidy belted out those cornball lyrics that could be heard at every wedding and special event ad infinitum, "I Think I Love You."

The only problem was, Claire was crying. Big fat tears rolling down her cheeks. Little sobs.

Son of a bitch! Can't I do anything right? "Blame Tante Lulu. I should've known this wouldn't work."

She pulled him back when he was about to eject the tape.

"Caleb, say it," she demanded.

Okay, ground zero. Time to plant my boots on the ground, or run. Which will it be? "I think I love you," he murmured.

"What? I can't hear you."

"I love you. Dammit. And I can't leave here without telling you that, but you never said it again, so it's probably a wasted effort." He stopped himself, realizing he was babbling. "I love you."

She made a flying leap for him, practically strangling him with her arms around his neck, kissing his hair and ears and face. Big slurpy, noisy kisses. They were kinda nice. "I love you, too."

"Well, about time! One lousy time you said it to me, and that was sixteen days ago. All last night, I kept making love to you, hoping you would say it again, but you didn't, and I figured I'd lost my shot."

"You kept track of how many days since I told you that I love you."

"What's your point?"

"So that's why we were engaged in that sex marathon all last night? You thought you'd screw the words out of me?"

"Well, yeah."

"Caleb, you turned purple the first time I said it. I figured you didn't want to hear it again."

"I do. A lot."

"I love you, I love you, I love you."

His heart was so full, he thought it would burst. But he pulled away from her and set her at arm's length. "Listen, I'm an old-fashioned guy at heart. I've got Amish in my blood. I can't be like Jake and Ronnie, having a baby and not being married. I can't be like them getting married and divorced four times, either. So . . ." He got down on one knee, took her hand in his, and said, "Will you marry me?"

She dropped down to her knees in front of him and took his face in her hands. She'd started weeping again. "You don't have to do this."

"Yes, I do. Will you marry me?"

"In a heartbeat, sweetheart."

He kissed her and sat down, pulling her onto his lap. "There are some conditions, though."

"Conditions now?" She'd arched her brows, but frankly she'd probably agree to anything right now.

"I'm going to continue working for Jinx, but this would be my home . . . our home. I'll pay for half of it."

She nodded.

"Only two kids."

"I can live with that." She looked as if he'd handed her a rainbow. "But I'll tell you this, Caleb, if you don't want any children, I could live with that, too. That's how much I love you."

That was a lot, for her. And he felt immensely blessed by that kind of love. "I want to see you grow big with my baby. Honest, I do." He cleared the lump in his throat, then continued, "One cow max, and I'm not milkin' it. Ever."

"As long as I can raise chickens."

"A deal, but only if they're not too close to the house." *Like on the other side of the river.* "But no pigs, goats, or peacocks. And I will never ever push a plow again in this lifetime. Or mend a fence. Or shovel manure."

"Oooh, I like peacocks."

"No peacocks. They're mean and loud and smelly."

"Okay. Can I have a horse?"

"Horses make manure."

"Well, how about bees?"

Bees? BEES? She really is a little bit crazy. "People eat bee shit. Isn't that what's in those honeycombs? Nothing to shovel there, so I'm okay with bees."

"Good. I love honey. I know of at least twelve varieties I'd like to try."

Twelve? That means thousands of bees. Don't say anything, Caleb. Keep your mouth shut.

"I have conditions, too," she said.

"You want me to perform every night of our marriage like I did last night," he teased.

"Definitely," she teased back.

He pretended to wince. Hell, if he could have her as incentive, he'd try his damnedest.

"I really, really yearn for a normal family life, Caleb. And I don't just mean the family you and I create together. Can you promise to work with your family members to bring us closer together?"

He tugged on her ponytail. "As long as I don't have to have Sunday dinner with them every week. Jonas or Lizzie, anytime. Mam and Dat, sometimes. The rest of my siblings, please, only on rare occasions."

"We'll see," she said.

And he knew they would be having the whole kit and caboodle over first chance she got.

"I've never made love with an engaged woman before," he said.

"Funny you should say that. Neither have I. An engaged man, that is."

She came easy into his arms, putting a gentle hand on his face. "I love you, Caleb. I feel as if I've been waiting for you all my life."

He was choked up for a second. "I feel the same way. At first I thought this sensation of coming home was related to my family, but it's you. Wherever you are is going to be home to me."

"Sounds boring to me." She pretended to pout.

"Ya think?" He grinned down at her. "Maybe you could do something exciting to rev up your image."

And she did. Man oh man, did she ever! A half hour later they were both panting for breath. He probably had splinters in his butt, and she for sure had whisker burns on her thighs. But they'd christened their new house in the best way possible.

"Wouldn't it be nice if we just made a baby?" she murmured against his bare chest.

Biting his bottom lip, he stifled a whimper. For the first time in forever, he hadn't used a condom. How could he have forgotten? Maybe there *was* some celestial plan in effect here. Destiny or some other woo-woo thunderbolt crap.

He gave a mental shrug. It was out of his hands now.

They lay there, silent for several moments, just relishing this newfound joy.

She chuckled then. "I know what would look great under that window over there."

He was suspicious, considering the chuckle.

"Your hope chest."

He laughed. "And the St. Jude statue on the mantel."

"Do you believe that old lady—or St. Jude—actually had anything to do with our getting together?"

Or my not using a condom?

Both of them thought they heard a voice in their heads then that said, "You'd better believe."

Epilogue

They were married under a balmy afternoon sun in October at Hope Farm.

Ironically, for Caleb at least, the wedding took place in a barn. Yeah, it had been scrubbed and decorated, but it was still a barn. What was that Jewish expression? *Oy vey!* Yep, that's what Caleb thought, but he wasn't about to complain out loud. He was marrying the woman he loved. Sometimes his heart swelled and swelled, just looking at her.

Tante Lulu, that crazy Cajun dingbat, would probably say it was St. Jude at work. Her nephew, on the other hand, would probably say it was something else entirely at work, located about two feet below his heart.

What had started out as a small private wedding had somehow turned into an outdoor extravaganza with music and two hundred guests. It was a more traditional ceremony than he'd ever envisioned for himself, not that he had ever envisioned tying the knot at all. Till he met Claire.

He was wearing a tux for the first time in his life, as were Jensen, Famosa, Franklin, and LeDeux, his groomsmen. Jonas, his best man, wore a dark Mennonite suit. He'd agreed to participate in an English wedding, even stay for the reception; that was compromise enough in his Plain book.

Claire had Tante Lulu, of all people, as her maid of honor, with Ronnie, Lizzie, Laura, and Lily serving as bridesmaids. Jonas and Laura were openly dating these days; as a result, Jonas had joined him in being labeled "That wild Peachey boy!" among the Amish in Sinking Valley. Jonas's Sarah and Fanny were flower girls.

Boner and the four cats, not to mention a pigload of Priscella's kittens, wore lavender bows around their necks to match the bridesmaids' gowns. He'd told Claire that lavender was a gay color for a boy dog to wear, but she'd answered that rumor said that Napoleon had a few questionable tendencies himself.

Ronnie's pregnancy was beginning to show with a little rounded belly. The way she and Jake stared at each other, well, he could only hope he and Claire would be as happy. He wouldn't be surprised to see these two next down the aisle. Then again, maybe not. They claimed to be happier than they'd ever been during their previous four marriages.

To everyone's amazement, his father gave Claire away. Dat was bending in ways Caleb never would have expected. Oh, he maintained his Amish ways, albeit as a Mennonite now, but he'd opened up his heart and his mind to new ways. Mam had electricity and a brand-new washing machine now; you'd have thought it was a pot of gold. Dat tried not to be too prideful driving his new, shiny red John Deere tractor. Dat had even taken Caleb and his brothers fly fishing last week, while the women worked with Claire, completing her bride quilt. That and all the crap Tante Lulu had sent was causing his hope chest to overflow. Bottom line: Claire was getting the family she'd always wanted, in spades.

He should have felt claustrophobic, having been a loner for so long. But he didn't, as long as he maintained his distance. Unlike Claire, he could take his family only in small doses.

He stood now, leaning back against a tree, a longneck dangling from one hand, on a small rise overlooking the farmyard festivities. Claire came huffing up the hill after him, her gown bunched in both hands up to her knees to avoid it dragging in the dirt.

When he held an arm out for her, she dropped her gown and snuggled up against him, smelling like the sweet outdoors. Fresh. Flowery. Sexy as hell.

She'd gone traditional for her wedding attire, as well. He'd half expected her to show up in some Indian maiden outfit, but instead she wore this frothy white concoction that made her appear good enough to eat. Literally.

"Are you having second thoughts?" she asked in a small voice against his chest.

"Never." He kissed the top of her head. "I just needed a breather."

"How about that poker-playing friend of Jake's, Angel Sabato, showing up here? In a skull and crossbones T-shirt. With all those tattoos. On a Harley. Whoo-ee! I thought your Dat would have a heart attack."

"Save your whoo-ee's for me, sweetheart."

She smiled. "Jealous?"

"Hell, yes."

"I heard him ask Jake if he could give him a job with Jinx, that he was ready to ditch the poker circuit. Do you have any objection to that?"

He shrugged. "It's not my call."

"Is it true that he posed for *Playgirl* magazine one time . . . in the nude?"

He just laughed. "You want nude, I'll give you all the nude you want."

"I'm going to hold you to that promise."

They both remained silent after that, just savoring being alone for the first time that day.

"I know you didn't want all this," she said, waving a hand to indicate all the activity below. "Somehow it got out of hand."

There was sort of an invisible dividing line down below between those open to music, dancing, and booze, and those who shunned the entertainments as worldly. Actually, there were quite a few English on that side, too, which surprised Caleb.

"That's okay, babe. There's still the honeymoon to look forward to."

"Which one?" She laughed and reached up to give him a quick kiss.

He grabbed hold of her on the rebound and pulled her in for a real kiss. Only then did he say, "The second one. In Barbados."

He, Claire, and a whole contingent of family and friends were headed for Philadelphia tomorrow morning to give moral support to Lizzie, who had made it through to the top twenty-four of auditions for *American Idol.* He and Claire laughingly referred to it as their first honeymoon. It would be memorable, that was for sure.

Lizzie—who billed herself as J-Lo meets an Amish Faith Hill—would be performing her first solo as a finalist.

Tante Lulu was going to be her chaperone. How that came about was a story in itself. Wait till Simon Cowell collided with the Cajun bulldozer. *American Idol* would never be the same. René LeDeux had been coaching Lizzie musically. In fact, his band, the Swamp Rats, was performing right now.

Lizzie would be singing the Rascal Flatts hit "I Melt" for her introduction to the public. To his embarrassment, Mam had asked him last week, "What does that mean, Caleb? She melts. How? Like an ice cube?" Dat had whispered in Mam's ear then, and she'd swatted his arm, saying, "Oh, you! Nobody would sing about *that.*"

"I do have a surprise for you, honey," Claire said, raising her face to look at him.

Uh-oh! "I like surprises." *Not!*

"We're going to have our own special wedding night."

Special *being the key word. I hope.* "With all these people around?"

"I found a private place."

Better and better. "Dare I hope it's a Marriott with a heart-shaped jacuzzi and complimentary champagne?"

"Well, there will be champagne, and candles, and fur rugs."

Hoo-yah! "Sounds good to me."

"I built us a wigwam up on the ridge."

About the Author

Sandra Hill is the best-selling author of more than twenty novels and the recipient of numerous awards.

Readers love the trademark humor in her books, whether the heroes are Vikings, Cajuns, Navy SEALs, or treasure hunters, and they tell her so often, sometimes with letters that are laugh-out-loud funny. In addition, her fans feel as if they know the characters in her books on a personal basis, especially the outrageous Tante Lulu.

At home in central Pennsylvania with her husband, four sons, and a dog the size of a horse, Sandra is always looking for new sources of humor. It's not hard to find.

Two of her sons have Domino's Pizza franchises, and one of the two plays in poker competitions. They swear they are going to write a humor book entitled *The Pizza Guys' Guide to Poker.*

Her husband, a stockbroker, is very supportive of her work. In fact, he tells everyone he is a cover model. In fact, he made that claim one time when she did a radio interview and swears the traffic around their home was heavy for awhile as people tried to get a gander at the handsome model. Then there was the time he made a blow-up of one of her early clinch covers with a hunk and a half-naked woman and hung it in his office. He put a placard under it saying, "She lost her shirt in the stock market . . . but does she look like she cares?"

So be careful if you run into Sandra. What you say or do may end up in a book. If you want to take the chance, you can contact her through her Web site at www.sandrahill.net.

The love and laughter
continue in
Sandra Hill's
next Jinx adventure!
Turn the page for
a preview of

Wild Jinx

AVAILABLE IN MASS MARKET SPRING 2008.

Chapter
1

Home, home on the . . . bayou . . .

It was dawn on Bayou Black, and its inhabitants were about to launch their daily musical extravaganza, a beautiful performance as ancient as time.

The various sounds melded: a dozen different frogs, the splash of a sac-a-lait or bream rising for a tasty insect, the whisper of a humid breeze among the moss-draped oaks, the flap of an egret's wings as it soared out from a bald cypress branch. Even the silence had a sound. The only thing not making any noise was the lone human inhabitant, John LeDeux.

But not for long.

"Yoo-hoo!"

About five hundred birds took flight at that shrill greeting, not to mention every snake, rabbit, raccoon, or gator within a one-mile radius.

John jackknifed up in bed and quickly pulled the sheet up to the waist of his naked body. He was in the single bedroom of his fishing camp, another name for a cabin on stilts over the bayou. He knew exactly who was yoo-hooing him. His ninety-two-year-old great-aunt, Louise Rivard, better known as Tante Lulu. *Who else in the world says "Yoo-hoo"?*

He should have known better than to buy a place within a "hoot 'n' a holler" of his aunt's little cottage. She took neighborliness to new heights. *And "hoot 'n' a holler"? Mon Dieu! I'm turning into Tante Lulu.*

By the time the wooden screen door slammed, putting an exclamation mark on his aunt's entry, he'd already pulled on a pair of running shorts. He yawned widely as he walked into the living room, where she was carrying two shopping bags of what appeared to be food. Not a good sign.

But this was his beloved aunt, the only one who'd been there for him and his brothers during some hard times. He'd never say or do anything to hurt her feelings. "What're you doing here, *chère*?" he said. "It's only six-thirty, and I don't have to report for work till ten." John was a detective with the Baton Rouge police department. It was a two-hour drive to town, and most nights he stayed in an efficiency apartment he rented there, but some nights, like last night, he just wanted to be home.

"You gots bags under yer eyes, Tee-John," his aunt said, totally ignoring his question. Tee-John—Little John—was a nickname that he'd been given as a kid, way before he hit his six-foot-two.

She went into the small kitchen and unloaded her goodies. French bread, boudin sausage, eggs, beignets, red and green tomatoes, garlic, okra, butter, Tabasco sauce, and the holy trinity of Southern cooking, celery, onions, and bell peppers. That was just from one bag. His small fridge would never hold all this crap.

"Yeah, I've got bags. I didn't get to bed till three."

"Tsk—tsk—tsk! Thass one of the reasons I'm here."

"Huh?" He sank down into one of the two chairs, breathing deeply in the smell of the strong chicory coffee she'd already set to brewing.

Now she was whipping up what appeared to be an omelet, with sides of sausage and fried green tomatoes. It would do no good to argue that he rarely ate before noon.

"I may be old, sonny, but I ain't dumb. Even here in the bayou, we hear 'bout all yer hanky-panky."

He grinned. "Do you see any hot babes here?"

"Hah! Thass jist 'cause I walked in on you las' month with that Morrison tart, buck naked and her squealin' like a pig. Ya prob'ly do yer hanky-panky elswheres now."

"You got that right," he murmured.

"Why cain't ya find yerself a nice Cajun girl, Tee-John?"

"'Cause I'm not lookin', that's why. Besides, Jenny Morrison is not a tart."

His aunt put her hands on her tiny hips . . . She was only five-foot-zero and ninety pounds sopping wet. "Does she have yer ring on her finger?"

His eyes went wide. "Are you kidding? Hell, no!"

"Ya gonna marry up with the girl?"

"Hell, no!" he repeated.

She shrugged. "Well, then, yer a hound dog and she's a tart. Hanky-panky is only fer people in love who's gonna get married someday."

That was the Bible, according to Tante Lulu.

"Best I bring ya some more St. Jude statues."

"No!"

She raised his eyebrows at his sharp tone.

"Sorry, but come on, auntie. I've got St. Jude statues in my bedroom, bathroom, kitchen, porch, car, and office. There's St. Jude napkins and salt and pepper shakers here on the table, St. Jude pot holders by the stove, a St. Jude wind chime outside, a St. Jude birdbath, and God only knows what else."

"A person cain't have too many St. Judes."

St. Jude was the patron saint of hopeless causes and his aunt's favorite.

"I'm not that hopeless."

She patted his shoulder as she put a steaming mug of coffee in front of him on the table. "I know that, sweetie. Thass one of the reasons I'm here. I had a vision las' night."

He rolled his eyes. *Here it comes.*

"It mighta been a dream, but it felt like a vision. Charmaine says I should go to one of those psychos." Charmaine was his half sister and as psycho as they came.

"Psychics," he corrected.

"Thass what I said. Anyways, back ta my vision. Guess who's gettin' married this year?"

"Who?" He asked the question before he had a chance to bite his tongue.

"You." She beamed.

He choked on his coffee and sprayed droplets all over the table.

She mopped it up with a St. Jude napkin.

"Any clue who the lucky lady will be?" he asked, deciding to go along with the nonsense. He wasn't even dating anyone steadily, and he for damn sure didn't know one single woman he wanted to spend the rest of his life with.

She shook her head. "That wasn't clear, but it's gonna happen. The thunderbolt, she's a-comin'. Best ya be prepared." The thunderbolt she referred to was some screwball thunderbolt of love that she claimed hit the LeDeux men just before they met the loves of their lives.

"No way! And just to make sure, I'm buyin' a lightning rod before I go in to work today. Speaking of which, I've got to take a shower. Can you put a hold on that breakfast for about fifteen minutes?"

"*Oui*, but first I gots to tell you my news."

"Oh?" The hairs stood out on the back of his neck. The last time she had news to announce, she'd popped a surprise wedding on his brother René. Or maybe it was the time she and Charmaine had entered a belly dancing contest. "I thought the vision was your news," he teased.

She smacked his arm with a wooden spoon. "Stop yer sass, boy. My news is that I hired Jinx, Inc., ta come ta Loo-zee-anna."

"The treasure-hunting company? They're coming here?" John had worked one summer for the New Jersey operation that hired out to find lost treasures— sunken shipwrecks, cave pearls, buried gold, just about anything.

She nodded. "We's gonna hunt fer pirate treasure out Grande Terre way. Too bad ya gots to work. It should be fun."

"You're talking about Jean Lafitte, I suppose. Don't you know that treasure legend is just that—a legend?"

"We'll see. I gots clues what no one else has."

That is just great! Probably another vision. "How are you involved?"

"I put up two hundred thousand dollars fer half the profits."

He inhaled sharply. "That's a lot of money."

His alarm must have shown in his voice because she shot back, "It's *my* money to spend anyways I want."

He put up his hands in surrender. "Absolutely. When is this venture going to start?"

"Next month."

"Okay. That's great, really. I wish you all the luck." That's what he said, but what he thought, standing under the shower a short time later, was, *The bayou is never going to be the same again, guaranteed! And treasure hunting is never going to be the same after being hit by Tante Lulu. Talk about!*

The menu at this nightclub was edible . . . uh, incredible . . .

Celine Arseneaux took a deep breath, then started across the crowded parking lot of The Playpen in suburban Baton Rouge, trying to ignore the fact that she was all tarted up like a high-class call girl.

The getup had been the bright idea of Bruce Cavanaugh, her editor at the *New Orleans Times-Picayune*, designed so that Celine would meld in the crowd at this upscale club, which provided sexual favors to both men and women, all run by the Dixie Mafia. Thus the black stiletto sling-backs, the sheer black silk hose, and the black slip dress with red lace edging the bodice and hem, not to mention flame red lipstick. Her shoulder-length boring brown hair had been blown and twisted into a wild curly mane. Normally, her idea of dressing up was new jeans, lip gloss, and a ponytail.

No way would she ever be confused for the award-winning journalist she was. Nor would she be taken for the mother of a five-year-old child. Nope. She was a woman on the make for a little action . . . illegal, paid-for action.

"I look like a Bourbon Street hooker," she'd complained to her fellow reporter Jade Lewis just a half hour ago as she'd helped plant the tape recorder inside her push-up bra and adjusted the tiny camera into the rose-shaped gold-and-rhinestone brooch at the deep V of her front. "I didn't even know I could have cleavage."

Jade had laughed. "Not a hooker. You look too high class for that. With the diamond post earrings and that brooch, you look like a bored upper-class gal with a wad of dough looking for Mister Studmuffin."

"A desperate housewife?"

"Something like that."

So now Celine walked up to the doorman, who resembled a pro wrestler in a tux, and flashed the small card she'd been given for admission. Apparently, no one could enter the private premises unless they were with a member or had obtained one of the cards, cards that were impossible to obtain without being carefully vetted. How Bruce had gotten hers she didn't want to know.

The big bruiser studied the card, then stepped aside and held the door open for her. She could hear soft music up ahead—no sordid bump-and-grind business here. A hostess, who could have passed for a runway model in a trendy culotte, inquired, "Black, white, or blue?"

"Huh?"

A light smile tugged at the hostess's lips. "First time here?"

Celine nodded.

"The black room is for men wanting to hook up with a woman. The white room is for women wanting to hook up with a man. And the blue room is for men and women, together, wanting to hook up with . . . whatever."

At Celine's confused look, she elaborated, "*Ménage à trois*, honey."

Oh, good Lord! Celine hoped she wasn't blushing. "White, please."

She wondered, with a suppressed giggle, how another reporter, Dane Jessup, was going to handle this situation when he did his part of the story tomorrow night. The male angle. If Celine was a geek, Dane was dweeb to the max.

Soon she was seated at a small round table in the back of the room with an empty chair across from her. An in-house phone sat in the center. The room had subtle lighting and the atmosphere of an upscale bar; that image was heightened by the soft rock being played by a two-piece band. No Chippendale-style dancers here or bare-chested waiters. A waitress in a perfectly respectable black uniform asked if she wanted a beverage. They cost ten dollars a pop . . . and that included pop.

The ratio of men to women in the room was about five to one, with about two dozen women sitting at the various tables. Several of them were dancing on the small dance floor with attractive men. Most of the men wore suits, sport coats over khakis, or golf shirts tucked into pleated slacks. No cowboys or construction workers. Subtly again. Those men not partnered on the dance floor leaned against the two bars, nursing drinks. Or leaned against a far wall. A few glanced her way with interest.

It looked like a singles club. Maybe this wouldn't be so bad.

But then she opened the "menu" in front of her . . . and felt like crawling under the table.

Welcome to The Playpen. We are here for your enjoyment. Please study the menu below. Then look around the room. If you see anyone you like, pick up the phone and indicate your choice. Only then will you be approached. If after talking to one of our men, you change your mind, you can make another choice. Accommodations are upstairs, or off-site arrangements can be made. Good luck!

This was followed by a menu of available services . . . very detailed descriptions . . . with prices. She wasn't sure she even knew what some of these things were, and for sure there were some she'd never done or had any desire to do. Eeew!

After the waitress plopped her whiskey sour down on the table, Celine took a big gulp and she braced herself. It was only pretend. It was just a story. She'd done worse things to get a scoop. Well, no, she hadn't, but it was important that these outrageous activities be exposed.

Morphing into professional mode, she made mental

notes of what she'd seen so far and decided she would "interview" three different men before making her escape following a trip to the ladies' room. Pressing one of the roses in her brooch to launch the zoom lenses, she began a slow scan of the men from right to left.

Some of the prostitutes looked downright dangerous. Way too blatantly sexual for her tastes.

Okay, the young blond man would be her first. Extralong hair in a ponytail. Clean-cut. Wearing a button-down blue shirt, tucked into dark blue chinos. He looked like a college student.

Then maybe the older gentleman with salt-and-pepper hair. Fiftyish. Well built. Designer suit.

Third . . . hmmm, she couldn't decide. She should probably invite the guy who looked like Tony from *The Sopranos*, if she had the nerve. Or the scowling man who was both homely and tempting as hell—rough sex, for sure.

She had her hand on the phone, about to request her first "date", when she noticed two men walk into the room laughing at some private joke. Her survey started to swing back, then doubled back.

Oh. My. God!

Could it be . . . ? No, it's impossible.

The tall man with dark hair, late twenties, wearing a black suit over a tight white silk T-shirt, stopped dead and was staring at her, too. Her camera took him in, and she intended to erase his picture the moment she got home.

This was an absolute nightmare. The worst possible thing that could have happened.

It was that oversexed, slimebucket, full-of-himself Cajun jerk. John LeDeux.

The father of her five-year-old son, Etienne.

Who didn't know he had a son.

Whom she had successfully avoided for five long years. What irony, to finally run into him in a . . . a sex club.

If some higher power would just let a crack open in the floor, she would gladly jump in, assignment be damned.

**It's a celebration
for all seasons with**

Sandra Hill's

JINX XMAS!

❧

As a special thank-you for your support
over the years, Sandra Hill has written
this novella for you. It's available exclusively
on her Web site, www.sandrahill.net,
where you can download it for free.

JOIN THE JINX GANG AND THE LEDEUX CLAN
FOR A CAJUN GOOD TIME!